Lilah

Lilah

By Karrie Pope

Lilah   *K. Pope*

This story is dedicated to everyone amazing in my life.

-J.A.V.

-K.A.P.

-M.C.W.

-K.E.B.

-R.W.M.

-C.T.S.

-P.J.M.

-Wattpad readers & fans

You all have believed in me since day one, thank you.

Butterflies

❀Azalea❀

Home used to be a place I loved. Coming home would be the highlight of my day. The sounds of family laughter and the smell of a good, home-cooked meal were the best parts. Never would I have ever thought the sound of shouting and glass shattering would become the new normal.

I hold my pillow tighter against my ears as the sound of our once loved fine China gets thrown against the walls of the home I used to adore. No matter how much it happens, I still can't help but cry. Especially knowing that it's *all my fault*. Knowing how much everything has changed over the past two years, it hurts my heart.

The sound of footsteps coming up the stairs shocks me into reality. I wipe my face clean of the salty tears and blink my eyes at a rapid pace to alleviate their redness. My door opens and my mother comes stumbling in. I rush out of bed and come to her aide. My room is my only escape. I don't want it to become a place for her to take out her frustration like the kitchen. I've been able to keep everything in my room unbroken and I would truly love for it to stay that way. I've even gone as far as keeping my own plates and cups in one of my dresser drawers. All glassware gets broken if left in the kitchen.

"Mom," I try my hardest to hold up her drunken form. She grabs ahold of my light blonde hair to help keep herself from falling and I bite my lip, holding back a yelp. *She didn't mean to.*

"Azzy," she slurs, "we ran out of liquor." My heart falls and I mentally scold myself for thinking that she may actually want to converse with me about other things.

"I'm sorry," I whisper, sitting her on the edge of my bed, unable to hold up her form that is slightly larger than mine.

"Go get me and your father some more whiskey," she mumbles, a sloppy smile on her face. I push my hair behind my ears and straighten out the cloth shorts on my legs. If there's one thing I hate about living in the part of Tennessee I do, it's the easy access to moonshine; my parents' first choice of beverage.

"Mom, you know I can't do that," I wipe her chin-length, dark brown hair away from her dull blue eyes. *I remember when those eyes used to be bright.*

"Why the hell not?" My father's deep voice calls out from my doorway causing me to jump in fright at his sudden appearance.

"I-I'm 19, remember?" I remind them, nervously fiddling with my fingers.

"Donny doesn't care," he slurs, "go to his shop and get it." I look between the both of them, my heart beating wildly.

"I don't know where Donny's shop is," I mumble quietly, and my father slams his hand against my doorway causing me to jump once more. He's not violent, when sober. When drunk he can tend to be a little bit mean to me.

"It's beside Irene's Bait Shop," he slightly glares at me, "you know where that is. Go get it." I remain seated next to mom as I look over at him pleadingly. All I want is for him to have at least a little bit of soberness in him to realize I really don't want to go.

Lilah   *K. Pope*

"Go before I get my belt," he warns, and I rise up from my seat, dreadful memories of him hitting me with his belt in my mind. *But it's only when he's drunk.* I pull a navy sweatshirt over my head and slip on a pair of shoes. My father hands me a crisp twenty-dollar bill and I take it reluctantly.

"Be careful, doll," my mother calls out as I leave my room. I pull out my phone from my sweatshirt pocket and check the time. *10:38 p.m.*

I make my way down the stairs, and I carefully step over the broken glass when walking through the kitchen. I'll clean that up when I get back. I grab the keys to my beloved older model Toyota Forerunner before leaving out the front door. I enter the driver's side and take deep breaths, my routine every time I have to drive myself somewhere. Although driving nearly sends me into having a full-blown heart attack, it's not nearly as bad as riding in the passenger side. Terrible memories come with riding on the passenger side.

"Azzy, you want ice cream?" Jake rolls his head over to me, his right arm extended and gripping loosely onto the wheel. I grin cheekily at him. He knows how much I love my ice cream.

"What a silly question!" I shake my head at him, the cheeky grin still present. He lets his Ray-Bans fall down on his nose and his brown eyes peek at me over the top of them.

"You're crazy, Az."

I blink my blurred eyes and shake my head, clearing the memory.

~~~

I park a little way out of the town square. Maybe it wasn't the best decision though. During the daytime, the town square is wonderful. It's filled with happy people walking, smiling, laughing, shopping, and having a good time. At night, the lights turn off, except for a few distant light poles, and everything is just a tad dark. I've never really been a fan of the dark. I climb out of my car and land on the sidewalk to which I parked parallel. I wrap my arms around myself, in an attempt to make me feel a little less scared. Loud laughter creeps up the long street from a little way behind me and my heart falls to my feet.

When the boutiques and stores close, Red street's bars open.

Due to my slower pace of walking, a trait I've had since I was able to walk, the group of people soon catch up to me. My heart returns almost back to normal as they stumble past me without sparing a glance my way.

Thank you for that one, God.

I watch the group of five, two girls and three boys, as they continue along their journey in front of me to goodness knows where. They seem like they all are close friends. Or maybe they're just drunk. I like to think they're friends. I imagine them having known each other since they were young kids in school. They stayed friends throughout middle school and even high school. Now, as they look as if they're around their late college years, I infer that the five of them had lost a little bit of contact, and tonight, they're meeting up again for old time's sake.

I hope they remain friends.

I let a sad smile reach my lips as I think over my friend group. The pillows on my bed, my feather-filled comforter, my bookcase filled with books I've read over and over, and lastly, Mr. Terrip from my one and only favorite bookstore. Mr. Terrip is a kind-hearted man in his late seventies and he's still going strong. I've known him for many, many years and he's been a guardian figure for me for as long as I can remember.

Even before mom and dad turned to alcohol to escape what I had caused.

Of course, I would love to have friends other than inanimate objects and a grandfatherly bookstore owner. I've tried making friends. In high school, I just never really fit in. It seems like in the adult world, I don't fit in either. I don't know where I belong. It's like I'm so close to finding where it is but as soon as I reach for it, I get pulled back. Most likely by my chatter. A trait I've had ever since I could talk coherent words. Mr. Terrip doesn't mind it much. He's also deaf in one ear, the one he turns toward me when I babble but it's okay.

The sudden sound of a can rattling against the hard sidewalk sends me back into reality. I peer up and over at the same group of five people as they stand over something I can't quite make out considering they're all so far ahead of me now. One of them throws the drink onto the object, spilling liquid all over it. Another one kicks it and I feel my heart clench. I don't know what they're kicking but I'm sure it doesn't deserve it. Just as soon as they start, the group finishes, and they walk away from the object laughing and talking like nothing happened.

I speed up my pace to see what they were doing that to and a quiet gasp escapes my lips as I realize what they were doing. An old and frail homeless man lays on the curb, picking up a few strewn-out belongings. As he notices me stopping in front of him, he backs up with fear pooling his eyes.

"Miss, please," he raises his skinny arms, "I don't mean any trouble."

"No, no!" I say softly, "you're doing nothing wrong."

His eyes remain fear-stricken and my heart hurts for the poor man. Who would just walk up to someone as unfortunate as him and just start beating him up for no reason? And to think I wanted that group of friends to stay friends forever. They don't deserve cowpie now.

"I'm not going to do what those people did, I promise," I raise my hands to show him I mean absolutely no harm. I bend down slowly and help him gather his few items.

"Are you okay?" I question him, my tone worried.

"I'm okay," he gives me a little grateful smile showing off his slightly rotting teeth but I'm never one to judge. Only the good Lord knows what this poor soul has been through.

"Would...Would you like some money for food or maybe a new coat?" I question him, gripping the twenty dollars in my sweatshirt pocket. He needs it so, so much more than my parents. Even if it means getting hit with the belt a few times.

"Really?" he questions in astonishment, his eyes widening, "you don't have to." I hand him over the twenty dollars, silently scolding myself for not bringing my wallet with me as well.

"Take it, please," he takes it gently from my hands, "I hope that helps you a little."

"Oh yes! It will," he smiles, "thank you, ma'am."

"You're welcome," I begin walking away from him and still down toward Donny's shop. I look around for any stores I can go into that a) aren't bars, b) aren't closed, and c) look safe enough for a small teenage girl. I pride myself on being tough. Just not physically, I'm a little vertically challenged at five-foot-two. I cry but never in front of anyone else. Why cry and possibly make someone around you upset when you can smile and maybe make someone around you happy?

I pass through the main part of the town square, where the tall marble fountain runs, and after passing it I begin to slowly walk down the scariest part of the town square. The part where the bars are. Red Street. There's no real reason for me to be frightened of Red Street, it just makes me nervous. But there's no other way to get to the other side of the town square.

I put on my big girl britches and continue on my path.

That is until I spot someone sitting on one of the benches far enough away from the bars that it makes me feel comfortable enough to approach them. Maybe it's another sweet homeless person? A friend is a friend, whether they have a roof over their head or not. I approach the bench and the closer I get, the more I want to turn back and walk away from the bench. More often than not, I'm not a good guesser. But I guess that this man is not homeless.

As I get closer and closer, I see the defined shape of his jaw and his wonderfully sculpted arms that are shaped from a distant light off the front of a bar. Just as I'm about to say forget it to my 'let me go see if this man is homeless too' idea, his head snaps to mine. The darkness surrounding us prevents me from seeing exactly what he looks like but I can feel his gaze on me.

It makes butterflies flutter in my tummy a little bit. Butterflies? What am I even thinking?

"Just so I feel better, you aren't going to punch me right now are you?" I mutter before closing my mouth tightly. That was probably on the top five list of worst things to say to a stranger who's sitting on a bench at night. He doesn't say anything and I'm quite thankful for that. I wouldn't want to embarrass myself further.

"Don't answer that question," I decide to continue after a few more moments of silence, although I don't think he was going to in the first place. It's very possible he's figuring out how to kidnap me right now. Very possible. Instead of responding, he just leans back against the bench. Maybe he doesn't talk. He could be deaf. Or, maybe *he's* scared of *me*. I don't want to scare him.

"I'll be on my way..." I give a small smile in his direction, although he can't see it in this darkness. *He can't see me, and I can't see him.* I could break out in a dance, and he'd only see my shadow. Taking a step forward, my foot catches right onto his.

You know what, this *would* happen to me.

I stick out my arms, preparing for their impact against the ground but it never comes. Instead, the stranger, and my potential kidnapper, catches my body on his arm. *I've got a strong man here.*

"Wow, that's my bad!" I laugh it off as I stand back up straight. I'm not clumsy. Usually, I'm very steady on my feet.

"It's dark, y'know," I explain, for some reason feeling like I need to do so, "I hope your arm's okay! You're foot too. I'm wearing flip-flops so my toe is basically broken in half right now."

He clears his throat and I tuck a piece of my hair behind my ear. I'm really talking this guy's ear off right now. He could literally have a knife in his back pocket and I'm telling him how my toe is broken.

"I mean, I don't know you but the way I picture you in my mind, you don't seem like the type to wear flip flops. I don't know where that sentence came from, it was supposed to stay in my head, that's my bad right there."

9

"Are you done?" The low rumble of his voice shocks me at first. I mean, I wasn't expecting his voice to sound so...manly and just *wonderful. Now I really want to see his face.*

"Yes! I'm done," I nearly faint and he stands from his seat on the bench. The man towers over me. He begins to walk away.

"Goodbye," I call out softly and he stops in his tracks as he passes just in front of me. I watch the outline of his tall and muscular figure as he turns to face me. *Maybe he can be my new friend?*

"Would you maybe like to go get some milkshakes or someth-" I stop talking when his footsteps begin to retreat. What's wrong with me? It's like it's impossible for me to make a friend. I'm not that odd, am I? I like to think I'm not. I keep telling myself I'll stop trying but every time I see someone new, there's just this need. I want to be liked so badly and I don't know how to ensure that. I let out a quiet sigh and just continue down Red Street.

~ ~ ~

By eleven-fifteen, I've found a small coffee shop all the way at the end of town square. I sit down in one of the booths and reflect on my life choices. The horrible and unexplainable life choices that come to me in the blink of an eye. Tonight, I chatted off a poor man's ears. A poor, seemingly attractive, tall man who was probably thinking I was a psycho person. Especially considering I was walking around town square in the dark with a pair of flip flops on. I massage my forehead and let out a quiet groan. *Oh, how I wish we could all just have do-overs in life.*

"What can I get you?" an older, very tired appearing waitress mosies up to my table.

"Oh, I don't have any money," I laugh sheepishly, "I'm not going to order anyth-"

Before I can finish, she walks away leaving me feeling down and terrible about myself for the second time tonight. *Man, I'm just on a roll.* It's times like these where I wish I could just have Mr. Terrip by my

Lilah   *K. Pope*

side. He's really great to confide in. He actually makes it seem like he's listening.

    The lady from before returns to me a few minutes later telling me that the shop is closing and that I need to leave. So here I am, walking *back* down Red Street thinking about how I'm going to break it to my father that I don't have his moonshine or his money. My eyes drift back to the bench where I met that man who didn't want to have a milkshake with me. It's truly a shame on him, I would be a great milkshake-drinking buddy, at least in my opinion.

    I still kind of want to meet him here again though. Of course, I do. I'm all about second chances. First impressions tend to make or break any type of relationship. That's my issue, I need to work on my first impressions on people. *I probably won't ever see him again.* Technically, I didn't *see* him. I saw the outline of his body and the sound of his voice. His *great* voice. I need to stop. He literally said three words that were slight insults. *Get ready for a lot of talking tomorrow, Mr. Terrip.*

CIA Spy

🌸Azalea🌸

I pull into my driveway and dread fills my thoughts. The lights in the house are still on. I turn my car off and hop out. Maybe, just maybe, they won't be mad. Maybe they just forgot to turn the lights off before going to bed. I find myself wishing to be talking to the mysterious guy from earlier and not walking into my house. I carefully and slowly open up the front door and walk in as quietly as I can. From my side, I hear a clearing throat. Both my mother and my father stand in the kitchen, beer cans in their hands and empty ones strewn over the counters.

"Took you a while," my father chides and my heart picks up in pace.

"Where's the moonshine?" my mother's slurred voice bounces off our high ceilings, causing a slight echo effect in my ears.

"I don't have it," I keep my eyes focused on the floor as I tell the truth.

"Why the hell not?"

"I-I," I hesitate, not wanting to lie and not wanting to tell the truth. I hear the sound of my father undoing his belt and I close my eyes tightly in an attempt to keep them from watering. I'm terrified of my father when he's drunk. His dragging footsteps begin toward me, and I gather the courage to run away from him. I don't want this, any of it. I just want my normal parents back. I want my brother back.

Running didn't work. He just whipped the belt at my back from a longer distance. The stinging pain enters at an extreme level, and I fall down on my knee with a quiet cry. His large hand grabs my upper arm, and he yanks me back up. The smell of beer and other strong alcohol envelops my nose, and he folds the belt a single time as I squirm in his hold.

"Daddy, please," I whimper but I get ignored. He brings his arm back before crashing the belt against my back once more. I feel my back welt up and he brings it down another time in a matter of seconds. My eyes find my mother's and she looks concerned. *Concerned, but not making a move to stop him.* He lets go of me and I drop to the floor, holding my back straight to keep the pain from intensifying.

"When we tell you to do something," he grips my chin, making sure I'm looking right at him, "you do it." He pushes my face away harshly before raising his arm and giving me one more whip to the back, one the most painful of all.

"Jack," my mother begins, her voice a little less slurred, "she's learned her lesson, she's done for the night.

I keep my head down low as I let out silent sobs. It's not even the pain of the belt that hurts the worst. It's the fact that this is what everything has come to since Jake went to Heaven. I understand why they drink. I understand why my father does what he does. They both hurt and they take out their frustration on breakable kitchenware and my father takes it out on me at times. I'm the cause of all of this and that alone overpowers the excruciating pain radiating off of my back.

"You don't get the drink and you don't have the money," my father shouts angrily as my entire back pounds and feels as hot as fire.

"I-I'm sorry," I whisper through my tears, looking up at my father who stands above me. I catch a flash of remorse in his eyes but instead of speaking over his actions, he throws the belt on the ground next to me before

Lilah   *K. Pope*

turning and walking out of the kitchen.

"Clean this up," my mother nearly trips over herself as she follows him. I look around and all the glass from before still sits on the ground. I stand from my sitting position on the ground, moving slowly so that my back won't stretch too much which will only make the pain ten times worse. I then begin cleaning everything up. I often tell myself that what he does is just a parent's form of punishment. I tell myself that a lot. '

~~~

"Oh, Mr. Terrip?" I call out, knowing he's most likely hiding from my presence. I turn a corner and run right into his tall and lean figure.

"I didn't hear you come in, Azalea," he gives me his signature 'I'm lying to your face' smile.

"I'm sure you didn't Mr. Terrip," I offer him a smile back.

"It's the hearing, I'm telling you," he informs me and I just nod. I'm *totally* sure that's it.

"Mr. Terrip," I say as I begin helping him put books in their correct places. I 'work' here, although it's unofficial. He won't hire me because he likes to say he's an independent man, but I know he likes to have my help.

"Yes, Azalea?"

"I met a stranger yesterday," I tell him and he shakes his head.

"Honey, you meet strangers often," he raises his long arm, putting a book on one of the top shelves. Shelves cover most of the store. Considering he's not the youngest man ever, most of the store looks quite old. That doesn't keep me from loving it any less. I think it looks quite aesthetic.

"You are correct, Mr. Terrip," I nod, "but, this time, I don't know. He was just mysterious, y'know?"

"Not necessarily," he shakes his head and I giggle. I raise my arm to put a book on a high shelf and when I do, my back stretches painfully. I let out a quiet hiss and unfortunately, Mr. Terrip hears it. *Mhm, but he didn't hear me come in apparently.*

"What'd you do to yourself?" the southern drawl to his words make me think back to my father's voice. When he's not drunk of course.

"I fell off my bed last night," I thankfully recover my mistake, "can you believe me, Mr. Terrip?"

"Crazy girl," he shakes his head and I begin on a nonstop ramble about how bed frames that are shorter should be made more stylish so that I could get one I like. I didn't even fall off my bed, I don't know why I began talking about wanting a shorter bed frame.

"You appear a little low on energy today, Azalea," Mr. Terrip frowns, looking down at me. Unfortunately, I was up all night tossing and turning. When your back hurts as bad as mine does, it's hard to find a comfortable sleeping position.

"You're right, Mr. Terrip," I nod, "I'm going to take a quick trip to the town square for some coffee, would you like some?"

"I'm alright, kid," he shakes his head, "go ahead and get you some go-go juice."

I giggle at his name for coffee and bid goodbye. A short five minutes later, I pull up to the sidewalk leading to the town square. I hop out of my 4Runner and begin walking amongst the many people. I enter the first coffee shop I see and hop right in line. Once it's my turn, I step up and smile at the cashier.

"Hello!" I greet, "I usually get the same thing when I come to coffee shops and don't worry it's not that complicated. Thank goodness I'm not lactose intolerant or something of that nature. I would just like a small caramel iced coffee."

The man looks at me with slightly widened eyes and I feel like slapping my own forehead for going off on a slight ramble.

"Please," I add with a sheepish smile and he just nods, putting in my order on the touchscreen computer thingy in front of him. After getting my coffee, I make my way out of the small coffee shop. I don't drink just straight coffee. I like to add a little kazam! to my coffee. Caramel, chocolate, anything of that nature really. I walk along the street of town square quietly humming Malibu by Miley Cyrus to myself. I end up in the middle of Red Street. I guess I just want to see if that guy is still here. I don't know why he would be considering it's been a whole day, but my eyes still fall on the same bench where I first walked up to him last night.

Now, an older man sits at the bench. Is that him? I mean, it can't be. This guy isn't *that* old, but he isn't really young. He's got graying hair on the sides of his head and slight wrinkles on his forehead. My famous guesstimation: 54 years old. He seems nice though. I imagine him to have two fully grown kids and a loving wife. His oldest child just had a baby and now he's a happy grandfather. He's just got one of those grandfatherly looks.

Realizing I'm looking at this man a little too much, I look away. If he would've caught me, he would most likely think I'm an undercover spy. Or maybe just a weird person with a staring problem. The sound of a door to one of the restaurants by day, bar by night opens sending me out of my mind-ramble and back into reality. If the sound of the door opening right beside me didn't send me enough into the real world, then my body clashing with someone else's does.

I basically ricochet off the person's body but I'm able to keep myself standing by using my special CIA balance technique I learned from watching a CIA training documentary. I'm basically qualified to be an undercover CIA spy. My coffee flops and splashes to the ground though. Apparently, I'm not trained quite enough to be carrying a coffee. Or to deal with the pain of the slashes from the belt on my back because it's returned to stinging right now.

"Fucking watch yourself," the person grumbles angrily as I continue to wobble on my own feet. *I know that voice.* That voice has been stuck inside my head since last night.

"I know you!" I turn my attention to the guy at my side. My eyes widen slightly as I take in his appearance in the light of day. He *is* tall and he *is* muscular. He *is* gorgeous. He's also not that older guy sitting on the bench.

His dark, deadly eyes bore into mine as I stare up at him. His eyes are black. They appear so...empty and scary. *I'd love to know why.* His dark brown hair lays floppily on his head and his long eyelashes cast a shadow over his cheekbones. His nose is only slightly crooked, most likely a sign that it has been broken before. His light pink, plump lips catch my attention next. The corner of his upper lip sits in a small sneer as he glares down at me, his strong jaw clenched tightly. Standing right here in front of him, the top of my head just barely reaches hardly anything past his shoulders.

His voice sounds the same as it does last night. Wonderfully wonderful. His eyebrows pull down and although I'm not the greatest at reading people's expressions, I can tell he has no clue who I am.

"I asked you if you wanted a milkshake late last night," I purse my lips, still smiling a little although I'm trying to keep it off my face. He lets out a deep, quiet scoff bringing his eyes to mine. I try not to nervously fidget as his eyes run up and down my body as he now realizes I'm the odd girl who asked a stranger to get milkshakes.

He licks the corner of his mouth before meeting my eyes once more. Why was I looking at his mouth? Because I'm odd. He doesn't say anything, he just walks past me, slightly hitting his shoulder against my temple, nearly knocking me out for a second. *Hey, watch it. Not everyone here is as tall as you mister.*

"A little bit of an 'excuse me while I pass you so that I don't knock my shoulder into your temple possibly causing you to be knocked out for point three seconds' would be a little bit more appreciated next time," I poke my temple, making sure it's not more indented than it should be. I watch his strong, muscular back as he stops in his tracks, his black shirt nearly matching the intricate tattoo sleeve on his arm.

That's super cool. He turns back around, and I make a 'yikes' face as he steps in front of me, looking directly down at me. His lips part the slightest bit as he glares down at me, his eyes seemingly traveling all over my face, looking for what? I have no clue. Maybe I've got coffee on my face. It did splash quite a bit when it fell.

"You're lucky," his deep voice rumbles quietly. Lucky for what? The last time I checked, my caramel iced coffee was spilled all over the ground. Actually, he's right. I'm lucky to be conscious and not knocked out.

"Your eyelashes are too long for your own good," I reply back at him, not necessarily meaning to let my thoughts run out of my mouth. His glare only deepens. What a crappy way to take a compliment. Well, it was kind of a compliment, I guess. I sort of insinuated he didn't deserve those eyelashes.

"Not that you don't deserve them," I attempt to save myself. I don't think CIA training videos can save me from him if he really wanted to hurt me. I can't even successfully run away from my drunken father.

"Did those hurt?" I point at his tattooed arm, changing the subject to lessen the chance of me further embarrassing myself. He walks away once more. Maybe he's shy. I quickly pick up my coffee and catch up with him.

"I'm sorry for bumping into you. Or not watching where I was going. Or for not seeing you open the door, and for kind of insulting you," I apologize, keeping up with his long strides to the best of my ability. He's not getting away from me without an apology. He only stays silent either ignoring me or...well, he's most likely ignoring me. I don't let that affect me anymore, I've gotten used to it by now.

"Most of the time, when someone apologizes, the person they're apologizing to usually says something like 'it's okay!'" I guide him and he turns his glare back to me. I nearly shrink down at the deadly looks he keeps giving me.

"Why do you keep talking?" he growls out. One simple reason. There's no one else to talk to. It's now that I realize I don't know his name. He also doesn't know mine.

"What's your name?" I question, tilting my head up to see the side of his face as I trail after him. He remains quiet. Or he's ignoring my presence. He might've not heard me but for some reason, I think he heard me just fine.

"It's nice to meet you Silence, I'm Azalea," I smile, slightly giggling at my own joke. I think he thinks my joke is funny because he glances down at me. He doesn't laugh but that's okay. Mr. Terrip would be proud of me for making such a dad joke. Maybe his mother told him to not talk to strangers. I should probably take that advice, actually. I continue to follow his long strides but now, I'm beginning to rethink my decision. He could be leading me to an alley to chop my esophagus out.

"Where are you headed?" I ask in my most casual of voice.

"Away from you," he replies rudely, and I push aside the flicker of pain in my heart.

"Would me buying you a milkshake change your mind?" I offer

before realizing it sounds like I'm trying to pick him up. *I'm not a pimp, I swear.* He's silent once again. But he takes a turn, and we arrive in front of the greatest milkshake place in all of Tennessee; Momma's Milkshakes. Just because the name is less than great, doesn't mean the milkshakes are bad. I crack my knuckles in excitement and I grab the handle to the door.

"Thank you for coming here with me," I tell him as I walk through it, holding it open for him to come in as well. I turn around to catch his reaction but he's nowhere to be found. *Ouch.*

I reopen the door and catch back up with his retreating figure. He could've just told me he didn't want to have a milkshake with me.

"Your manners aren't very good," I place myself in front of his large frame, keeping him from walking any further. Unlike most people on earth, he doesn't stop walking when I stand in front of him. He's like a bulldozer. He walks right into me and to keep my balance, I grab the front of his shirt. His strong, tattooed arm wraps around my waist, keeping me up and pressed against him. Goodness me.

"How old are you?" his eyes fall to mine and although I've seen their darkness before, it still shocks me. *Old enough to know better than to follow mysterious strangers.*

"Nineteen," I mumble, and his eyes fall below my neckline.

"If I get a milkshake with you, will you fuck off?" he questions lowly. *Probably not.*

"I will," I nod.

Sugar

❀Azalea❀

"Why didn't you get anything?" I question the no-name who sits on the other side of the booth. I got my all-time favorite: cookies and cream, aka Oreo. They're basically the same thing. He crosses his arms and leans them against the table. I can't help but watch the way they flex and his beautiful tattoos.

"What's your name?" I question somewhat nervously; afraid he'll ignore me once again.

"Grey." I nearly shiver at his voice. It's just so wonderful. I let a smile appear on my face.

"Azalea Delilah Carson," I tell him fully just in case he didn't hear me outside. *Now he knows my government name, that wasn't my best decision.*

"Is your name short for anything, like Greyson?" I question, trying to get any kind of words out of him.

"No," he slightly glares. Woah, he must not like Greysons. Poor Greysons of the world.

"Where are you from?" I take a sip of my milkshake slightly getting an Oreo chunk stuck in my throat. I hold back from coughing it out, just taking another sip. That'd be the worst way to die. To choke on an Oreo chunk in front of the most attractive man I've ever seen. He clenches his strong jaw and I wince internally. He just doesn't seem to like me at all really.

"Knoxville," he grumbles, and I smile.

"Why are you asking so many questions?" His face turns back into a dark glare.

"Well," I fiddle with my straw, "I just like making new friends." New friends? More like, I like trying to get even one friend.

"What makes you think I want to be your friend," his dark eyes search my face. I think the opposite, quite honestly. I'm just surprised he's stayed here in front of me for this long.

"Everybody needs a friend," I smile, averting my bright green eyes from his. *I* need a friend. That's true for some. Sometimes, people don't want friends and they like to be alone. That's not me. With all the thoughts that run through my head daily, I need someone to talk to or I may end up in a mental facility.

"Th-"

Before I can even finish adding onto my 'everyone needs a friend' argument, he turns his head away from me looking at a man who has just walked into the shop. He pulls his phone out and types on it quickly. I sense some drama. I let a giggle escape my lips and he sends me an evil glare. Now is where he robs me of my remaining two dollars and kicks me in the throat.

"Is everything okay?" I mumble as he looks back down at his phone. He rises from his seat and pulls me with him. My eyes widen as I try and keep up.

"Um, Grey?" I question softly as we finally come to a stop after entering through an "employees only" door. I look around to see a lot of milk and lots of fruit.

"Did you want some fruit, or...?" I face him again. He looks out the small window of the door and my eyebrows furrow. Oh no. My keys. And more importantly, my milkshake.

"Grey, my keys are out there," I say only to get ignored.

"What if they get stol-" he cuts me off by pushing away from the door and coming to stand directly in front of me.

"Do you ever shut your mouth?" he asks pretty angrily. I didn't know I had to. Pardon me for speaking my mind and trying to save my milkshake from its potential hungry kidnapper.

"Are those the only words you can say?" I question, referring to the multiple times he's already asked me that. That question doesn't appear to make him happy. Not much seems to make him happy. Not even milkshakes. It makes me wonder if dogs make him happy. Dogs make everyone happy but honestly, he doesn't seem like everyone.

He leans closer as his eyes fall over every part of me, "You couldn't handle everything I've got to say."

I'll have him know that I was told not-so-nice things to my face in high school quite often, I can handle whatever he's got to say. Plus, I'm not too bad at hiding how I really feel. I've got a mean pair of big girl britches that are ready to be put on at any time.

"I can handle insults pretty well," I keep my chin up, trying to hide how doubtful I truly am. A sinister smirk takes place on his lips, and I keep myself from looking away from his handsome face. *Why does he have to be so attractive?*

"I'm not talking about insults," my back hits the wall behind me, pain travels along the surface of my skin, and I nearly knock over a container of strawberries when he traps me with his strong arms. Does this milkshake place literally have no workers in the back? What the heck? Why am I feeling so nervous? Maybe because he smells like what I envision heaven to smell like and his tattoo sleeve is oddly mesmerizing.

"What are you talking about?" I swallow nervously, having no idea what is going on in his unreadable mind. His eyes narrow down at me slightly and he pulls away. My eyebrows furrow in confusion as his jaw clenches. He looks back out the window before turning back to me.

"Is there someone out there you don't like?" I recover, straightening my shirt that has fallen down onto my shoulder.

"They don't need to see you," he glances over at me, and I bite my lip from the sting his words left. I mean, I get I'm not the coolest person in the world but to not even want to be seen with me hurts a bit.

~~~

It's been twenty minutes. I feel slightly as if he's holding me hostage.

"Would it be stealing if I ate a couple of strawberries?" I question suddenly, eyeing the strawberries that sit right next to me. *I can smell them.*

"Keep your mouth closed."

"I would if you told me why we're back here. I'm left sitting here thinking of my own reasons, and my mind can surely wander off sometimes," I warn him, and his eyes come to rest on mine. *Good Lord, why are his eyes so enthralling?* He basically renders me speechless whenever he looks at me. Or he makes me talk extra, I'm not too sure yet, he's caused both things to happen.

"You get on my fucking nerves," he keeps his eyes on mine although his face isn't set in a *completely* deadly glare.

"And you have me in a supply room, how do you think I feel?" I speak my thoughts. This isn't exactly the ideal place to bring a friend, especially a new one.

"I could have you somewhere else," his eyes gleam a certain way and my head tilts in confusion.

"Well let's go there then, there's nothing to do here," I motion toward the door. He just looks at me with this unreadable look.

"You're oblivious," the tone of his voice turns dark once more. I swear this guy can't decide on being a little, tiny bit normal or mean.

"Grey."

"Lilah."

Lilah?

"It's *De*-lilah and that's my middle name. You're not the greatest listener in the world," I tell him, holding back a small smile.

"Lilah," he decides in a final warning tone. To be completely honest, it kind of tickles my pickle. Did he give me a nickname? Is that what this is?

"Can I call you what I want?" I bite my lip to hold back the biggest smile in the world. Oh, this is just too good.

"No," his eyes fall to my lips, but I ignore that, now unhappy at the fact that I can't call him what I want to.

"I was going to call you Sugar." There's a perfectly amazing reason behind the name Sugar. And it's not because Sugar is a cool stripper name. 'Sugar' fits him spectacularly because behind all that saltiness, I know he's got a least a little bit of sugar in him. It may take some digging but I'm sure it's there. I didn't notice the harshest glare that I think I've ever seen being sent my way. He shoves past me harshly, knocking me back into a metal rack. Pain explodes where every lash my father sent me is located and I look up to the ceiling trying not to have a heart attack.

"What's wrong with you?" he pulls me off and away from the rack, glaring down at me. Well excuse me, you're the one who knocked me into it. He's like a bull in a China closet and I need to get out of here. I can only take but so many of his hateful glares. My big girl britches are slowly falling off.

"Is the person out there gone?" I recover from the pain, but he still looks at me, a deep frown on his face.

"Yeah," he mumbles, and I walk toward the door to leave. I feel his presence behind me as I look out the window to make sure no one will see us exiting the "employees only" door. A second later, I feel his hand touch the small of my back. I would blush but his hand on my back causes another wave of pain. I jump forward.

"Lilah-" I ignore him and just walk out the door, with him following close behind. My heart does take a small skip at what he's decided on calling me. I grab my keys from the table, which thankfully, were not stolen.

Thank you, Jesus. Even better than that, my milkshake is still here. I bet it's melted into a more creamy milkshake but at least it's still here.

"Don't fucking walk away from me," Grey grumbles, following me as I walk out of Momma's Milkshakes.

"What happened to you?" he questions, his dark eyebrows pull into a deep frown as he steps in front of me. I consider doing what he did to me and bulldozing right through him. It wouldn't work out well for me, I'd ricochet off of him.

"What do you mean?" I question him, admittedly playing dumb but not making it obvious.

"Don't be stupid," he glares. I remain silent, just looking down at my feet.

"I fell off my bed," I smile up at him, using the same reason as I told Mr. Terrip. He continues his glare and I shrug it off, it seems like his glares are just normal.

"I've got to get going," I tuck my light blonde hair behind my ear, "Mr. Terrip is probably getting worried. He owns Terrip's Bookstore right down the road." Grey remains silent, his dark eyes boring into mine, making me slightly nervous for the seven hundredth time today.

"You should come and check it out, if you want," I fiddle with the ends of my mid-back length hair, "I spend a lot of my day there, helping out and whatnot. Mr. Terrip is really nice, he's wise too."

"I feel like that went right over your head," I speak on the fact that he doesn't really appear to be listening to my words.

"I'm going to enjoy never hearing your voice again," his dark eyes bore into mine, proving my thoughts, as his face remains completely emotionless. My big girl britches fall to the floor and disintegrate. I clear my throat and peer down and at my tan flats. *Some people just don't get that words can hurt too.*

"Have a nice day," I mumble before turning away, walking away from him, and not looking back.

~ ~ ~

"I wasn't expecting you to be gone that long, Azalea," Mr. Terrip raises his eyebrow at me as I walk in the front door of the store.

"I had to stop on the side of the road to use the bathroom," I give him a smile and he shakes his head at me, obviously knowing I'm kidding.

"How was your coffee?" he questions, leading me to another cart of books that need to be put away.

"The half of my coffee I was able to drink was just wonderful, the other half was enjoyed by the sidewalk," I picture Grey and I running into each other.

"That's a shame," he chides, although I see right through him.

"It's not funny, I was heartbroken Mr. Terrip," I pat my heart as I step up onto my step stool placing a book on one of the top shelves.

"You should be more careful, Azalea," he shrugs and I turn around on my step stool, looking straight at his seasoned face.

"Well, it actually wasn't completely my fault," he hands me another book, and I put it in its place.

"I have trouble believin' that."

"I feel like you're coming at my throat here, Mr. Terrip," I send him narrowed eyes to which he just smiles at.

"You know that stranger I was telling you about earlier? The one I met late last night?" I question him, taking ahold of his slim hand as he helps me off my stool. Always the gentleman, Mr. Terrip is.

"Not really," he doesn't even act as if he does.

"I'm going to pretend you do," I decide, "anyway, I ran into him after getting my coffee."

"Him?" he peers over his reading glasses at me.

"I thought you knew he was a guy?" I raise my eyebrows and he takes a seat at the front desk, removing his glasses.

"I don't even remember what I did ten minutes ago, you expect me to remember everything that comes out of your mouth?" he says and I can't help but admire the way he always speaks the truth. He once told me that the older you get, the less and less you care about what people think about you.

"It would make things easier," I sing, and he huffs.

"Fine, fine. I'll make sure to pay attention," he sits his chin on his hand, acting like he's paying attention but he's probably not. This isn't the first time he's done this.

"We had milkshakes," I mumble, and he looks like he's about to fall asleep. Well, *I* had a milkshake.

"He's a horrible friend," I wince, thinking about all the things he said to me.

"Better luck next time kid, the boy must not be a friendly person. You have to remember that not everyone is nice anymore," his voice turns fatherly.

"He's no boy," I sigh, picturing his manly structure and dark eyes.

"I don't want to be a part of this conversation anymore," he places his glasses back on his nose and I giggle.

"Don't be like that, Mr. Terrip."

"You're too young for boys," he points at me and I internally roll my eyes. He's been telling me this ever since I met him when I was old enough to walk from my house to his shop.

"*Men.* Plus, I'm an adult...for the most part," I correct, and he makes a dismissive noise. The bell at the front of the store chimes and I look to see Aaron walking in as cockily as ever. I internally sigh knowing I can't get out of this interaction he and I are about to have, unfortunately, he's already set his eyes on me. He's attractive, I'll give him that. He always has been. He's also always been a completely arrogant buttface. It just so happens that he was my brother's best friend.

"*Azzy,*" his pearly whites appear as he smiles, showing his dimples.

"Hello, A-a-ron," I nearly laugh at my own joke. He runs his hand through his light brown, wavy hair as his dark blue eyes focus on me. From the corner of my eye, I see Mr. Terrip keeping a close eye on him.

"Got to love that beautiful smile," he flirts.

"Still not going to work," I remind him, and he lets out a little sigh. I wouldn't necessarily consider him a friend. He comes around sporadically, most of the time just to check on me, although I assure him, I don't need checkups. What I do like is that he gives me money. I'm sure I could be his pimp if I really put my mind to it. Being two years older than me, he's in his late college years and he doesn't hesitate to tell me about his often 'hookups'. The perfect hooker for my pimp scheme. Not many people get on my nerves. He does slightly.

"Let's go talk Azzy," he places his admittedly nicely built arm over my shoulder. Yeah, so what, he's got nice arms. He leads me to the reading space around the corner and I just notice Mr. Terrip rolling his chair over to where he can see us. He makes me laugh. He takes a seat on the newer couch Mr. Terrip recently bought and I sit beside him, careful not to hit my back against the couch.

"Relax, Azzy," he smirks, "why so stiff?"

"I'm relaxed, I'm chillaxed, did you see what I did there?" I laugh, "y'know, combining 'relaxed' and 'chill.'" "Genius," he gives me a dimpled smile, "beautiful and a genius."

"Aaron," I warn, and he raises his hands in surrender. I ease back into the couch and return my gaze to his.

"How are you, Azzy?" he questions softly, a concerned glint in his eyes. I look down at my lap and close my eyes for a quick second in an attempt to clear my mind from the picture of when the crash happened.

"I'm doing okay," I plaster a small smile on my face.

"You can talk to me, okay? I know that it's hard for you, Azalea. You were the only one there; you were with hi-"

"Aaron," I stop him, feeling myself get shaky, "I'll talk to you if I need to. I'm fine, really."

No one knows what I saw. Doctors tried to get it out of me. Aaron tried to get it out of me. Mr. Terrip even attempted. I don't want anyone to know how bad it was. I want their mental picture of Jake to stay the way it was. *No one deserves to see what I saw, besides me.* His eyes flicker between mine before he lets out a sigh.

"Are *you* okay, Aaron?" I question. I'm not the only one that was heavily impacted by Jake's passing. Aaron and Jake were inseparable all throughout their lives. They were best friends and had been for many, many years. They were in their last year of high school and Jake's death shocked the entire school. He was loved by everyone, especially me.

He wasn't just my brother. He was my *best friend*. He would always look after me, even in school. When the kids would pick on me, he'd use what he and I would like to call the 'bark'. He would 'bark' strong words at the kids and him being him, they would run off with their tails between their legs. He would have to hold me back from attacking them as they walk away.

Lilah

K. Pope

"Jake, I'm telling you," I start and he smirks down at me as I take a wider stance, "if you would've waited two seconds longer, I would've had all of them on the ground."

"You're wearing crocs, Azzy," he smiles, and I look down at my admittedly cute periwinkle crocs. How dare he insult me like this. I bend down and move the strap from the front of my shoe to the back.

"Now I'm ready, I'm in survival mode," I giggle but instead of laughing as he should, he frowns at my shirt.

"Did they do that?" he looks down at the purple stain on my previously white shirt. Joke's on them, they missed out on some delicious purple Gatorade.

"Well," I hesitate, "I guess they did, I didn't notice."

He gives me a pitiful look and I sigh. He leads me down the hall and into the senior hall. I keep my head down as I walk, not wanting to see the looks on people's faces as they see me. I stand beside him fiddling with my fingers as he opens his locker. I look down at my crocs. They're underrated. I've even got little matching flower charms on them. Plus, gosh darn it if they aren't comfortable and they just slip on easily. It's also not like I wear them every day. I have other shoes, they just caught me on a lazy day. He closes his locker, and we begin to walk again.

"Keep your head up, Azzy," he nudges me, and I lift my head. We stop at the bathroom and the bell rings. He tells me to ignore the bell and I sigh.

"God, could you get any uglier?" one had said.

"She just looks worthless, doesn't she?" another followed. Before I can stop them, tears roll down my cheeks as what they had said to me finally registers. I keep my head down and grab the shirt from Jake before turning to walk into the bathroom. His strong hand grabs my forearm, and he pulls me back around, facing him.

"Azalea Delilah Carson," he says lowly, and I slowly raise my head, looking up at him. I pull my shirt up and cover my face so he doesn't see how their words really affected me.

"I don't even know why I'm crying," I pull my shirt back down, "their insults were childish."

"They weren't even good insults," I try to humor up the situation, but it doesn't really work.

"What'd they tell you, Azzy?" he questions quietly but I remain silent.

"Azzy?" he repeats.

"*Azalea,*" he deadpans.

"*They just said I was ugly, stupid, whatever,*" I wipe my face.

"*Listen to me,*" he says sternly and I look up into his eyes. *The same colored green eyes as mine.*

"*You're beautiful. Don't let anyone tell you any different,*" he tells me sternly.

"*Put on that shirt while I go have a talk with those fuckers.*"

I shake the memory from my head and pay attention to Aaron in front of me.

"I'm doing okay," he smiles.

"How're your parents?" he questions, and I tense up. I've thought about telling him before. About their drinking and maybe even about the lashes I receive from time to time. On the downside, Aaron's rich. If I tell him, his family will just blow it out of proportion. Maybe even send my father or even my mother to jail. It's only discipline, right?

"They're doing pretty good."

Sober

❀Azalea❀

"Do you think I'll ever see him again, Mr. Terrip?" I question which honestly makes me want to throw myself off a bridge. It's been a week and a half. A week and a half of me wondering about him. A week and a half of me trying to tell me to stop thinking about him and to forget about his terrible manners and rude attitude.

"Who?" Mr. Terrip asks, and I feel like throwing a book at his head.

"Albuquerque the turkey, " I deadpan and he laughs.

"Forget I said anything, I think I'm going crazy," I shake my head.

"I think you've been crazy for a while," Mr. Terrip teases and I point a threatening finger at his face.

"On that note, I'm leaving," I pick up my book for the night.

"I'll see you tomorrow, Azalea," he tells me goodbye as we walk out. I stay beside him as he locks up and once he's done, we go our separate ways.

"Where's your car?" he calls out and I wince.

"I walked," I smile.

"I told you not to do that," he scolds, and I sigh.

"Goodbye!" I call over my shoulder and I can just see him shaking his head in disappointment. I swear, he acts like I live an hour away or something. This morning I just woke up with a little extra energy, so I walked. I've grown to like walking better than driving anyway. Although, I haven't walked to the bookstore since before the accident. Maybe that's why my knee is slightly pounding. I make it home and take notice that both parents are home. *God, please give me a good day here.*

I open the front door and keep my head down as I walk through the living room. I catch sight of a couple of Jack Daniels bottles on the coffee table and I close my eyes in an attempt to picture the table the way it used to be before the wreck. *Fresh flowers in a clear vase. Maybe even a couple of 'Good Living' magazines.*

I should've stopped walking when I closed my eyes. But I didn't. For a kid, a father's arms should feel like the safest place in the world. Not the scariest. The smell of alcohol on him was what hit my senses first, then I felt the tight grip of his hand on the back of my shirt. He pulls me away from him like I'm on fire and the neckline of my shirt tightens until it is choking me.

"I-I'm sorry," I struggle, trying to swallow. He lets go of my shirt, shoving me away from him. My knee gives out and I fall, landing on the coffee table. I just catch sight of the Jack Daniels bottle right before it rolls off the table and falls to the ground, breaking on impact with the floor. Fear encases me and my heart sinks to my feet as the dark liquid flows on the hardwood floor. The sound of his belt unbuckling causes my eyes to well up with tears.

"Look at me," the sound of his belt stops. I hesitantly raise my eyes to his. He hooks his belt back and I silently thank God.

"You took him away from us," he slurs, and I bite my lip to hold back a gut-wrenching sob that is begging to be let out.

"I know," I cry out softly, "I know I did." Does he think I don't already know that?

"You were the last face he ever saw," he continues, and I cry harder, "the person who did this to him was the last thing he ever saw." The dark and empty void in my chest only grows as my father tells me things I already tell myself.

"Go upstairs," his voice turns dark. He grasps my arm in a tight hold and he drags me to the stairs. Panic fills my chest as he drags me past my room. He stops in front of Jake's door.

"Please daddy," I sob, "Please don't." He opens the door to the room I haven't been in since the crash. I don't hold back the cries that escape my lips as he forces me into the room.

"You're the reason he's not in here," he slurs angrily in my ear.

"Please, take me out," I sob, trying to escape his hold. *It hurts so bad.*

"Think about what you did," he roughly shoves my arm away from him, and I nearly nosedive to the floor.

"You ruined this family, I hope you know that," he closes the door behind him. I hear the sound of a click and I panic again. I shoot up from my position on the floor and grab the door handle. I wiggle it and try to open it but something on the other side is keeping it closed. The guilt from everything overwhelms me and I fall to the floor in a heap, crying every tear in my ducts. This is worse than any kind of physical harm my father could have done to me, so much worse. I lean my back against the door and for the first time, I peek out from behind my hair at the room. It's the same as the day I last saw it. Except for the silence in it now. A silence so painful sticks to the room and it rings in my ears. The trophies, sports awards, and jerseys stare back at me, only reminding me of how talented and gifted my brother was.

And I took him away from the world.

He flourished in all he did. He was loved by everyone. He was going to college; he had a scholarship to play the sport he loved and I took it all away. *God, it should have been me. Why didn't you take me instead?*

~ ~ ~

The sound of the door jiggling wakes me up in the morning. I gasp and sit up, scared to death that my father is going to come back in here and maybe find something that was worse than spending the night in my brother's room to do to me. The door opens and my mother steps into the room, her work clothes on her body. *She's sober.* A breath of relief leaves my lips as tears cloud my eyes.

"Azalea, oh honey," her eyes fill with concern, and I silently thank God that she's sober and not my father. She falls to the floor beside me and pulls me into her arms. I cry into her shoulder and her hand rubs my back soothingly.

"What happened?" she questions softly, pulling away and wiping my blonde hair from my damp face.

"He locked me in here," I put my face back into her shoulder.

"What the hell are you two doing in here? I thought we all agreed to not go in here," my father's sober voice fills the doorway, and my heart pounds with fear.

I haven't heard him sober in quite a while. Usually, before I get to see them in the morning, I'm already out and at the bookstore. Surprisingly enough, they haven't lost their jobs. I know they have to be hungover, but I guess all the bottles of medicine in the cabinets downstairs help them with that.

"Jack, what the hell?" my mother curses him, surprising me. I've always been too scared to see them sober, afraid that the reality will be that they're the same person sober as they are when drunk. Maybe, at least my mother isn't.

"What?" he questions, and my mother pulls away from me, turning to him. His eyes focus on me, I can feel his gaze on me but I keep my eyes on the floor.

"You put her in here," she scolds harshly and he remains quiet.

"I don't remember doing that," is the only thing that he can say.

"Maybe because you were drunk," I surprise myself by getting a small amount of courage after all this time.

"Excuse me?" he narrows his eyes at me, still slightly scaring me.

"You dragged me up here, you put me in here," a tear rolls down my cheek, "you left me in here."

"Azalea, you're delusional, I didn't do that," he says and I stay quiet. There's no sympathy for spending the night in my dead brother's room.

Lilah   *K. Pope*

There's nothing in his eyes. I'm *delusional.*

    "Okay, Azalea, I think Jake's passing is really just getting to you right now," my mother runs her hand up and down my back. I look between the both of them. I can almost feel my broken heart chipping away and falling into a bottomless pit. I push past both and walk straight into my room. I take a shower and think about everything that just happened. If I could cry more, I would. My head just hurts too bad from doing it so much already. I look at myself in my full-length mirror in my room. The scar above my eyebrow. The huge scar along my shin. The scars on my knee. The terrible scar on my rib.

    Half of me is made of metal now. Three of the four ribs I broke had to be fixed with metal plates. A tube had to be inserted into my chest cavity to reinflate my lung after it collapsed when the ribs broke and poked my lung. My knee basically had to be reconstructed after I shattered the entire patella, not to mention the ACL tear which caused a whole other surgery on its own. My shin bone, both my tibia and fibula had to have metal plates and screws inserted.

    My shoulder and head were the only other things that were completely screwed up, literally. My shoulder was dislocated and scarred all up and I got a grade three concussion. I lost memory of the accident until about two weeks after it happened. The day I woke up and finally remembered what happened, it was the worst day of my life, and it always will be.

    No one knows exactly what happened. Mr. Terrip knows the just of it; My brother and I were in a wreck almost two years ago. He passed away, I didn't.

    I pull on a flowy pale-yellow sundress. I decide against a sweater to go over the top of it but I'll probably regret it, but Mr. Terrip always keeps the store at 58 degrees Fahrenheit. He gets hot easily and it blows my mind. To be frank, I think he keeps it cold on purpose to get on my nerves because he knows I get cold easily.

<p style="text-align:center">~~~</p>

"You're quite late today, Azalea," Mr. Terrip chides without realizing I've been in the store for over thirty minutes.

"I'm flattered that you've noticed my missing presence," I smile at him softly.

"I've been over here figuring you out," he narrows his eyes at my form.

"Figuring me out, huh?" I giggle, shaking my head at him.

"You don't seem normal," he observes and I snort.

"I don't think I *am* normal Mr. Terrip," I give him a smile before continuing while I have his attention.

"You see, I have this problem, bear with me here Mr. Terrip, and this problem is truly unfixable if you ask me," I peek down at him to see that he's already not listening with his nose buried in his newspaper. I give myself a mental high five for dodging Mr. Terrip's questions about why I don't seem *normal* today. I walk away from his desk, a satisfied smile on my lips. I have a seat on my designated little comfy chair, and I pull out my book. I put one earbud in my ear and my thoughts drift away as I listen to music and read words simultaneously. Mr. Terrip constantly nags me on how I should focus on only one, not both at the same time. He says it'll give me more brain farts than I already have. He just doesn't understand that I'm a national champion multi-tasker, a pimp, and a CIA agent; he's got nothing on me. Is a female pimp a pimptress? A pimpa? Pimpina?

"What do you call a female pimp?" I question aloud to Mr. Terrip.

"Azalea, read your book," he sighs disappointedly, and I bite my lip to hold back a giggle. After an hour of reading, I'm ready for adventure.

"Is there anything you would like me to do?" I lean up against Mr. Terrip's desk. He shoos me away with his hand and I hold back the urge to stick my tongue out at him. I just decide to enjoy the fact that my music playlist is completely and utterly psychotic. It's a wide range of music genres. Like unnaturally wide.

Stevie Nicks: *Edge of Seventeen,* Børn: *Electric Love,* Queen: *Too Much Love Will Kill You,* Greta Van Fleet: *Edge of Darkness,* Kacey Musgraves: *Butterflies.*

Heck, I've got any song ranging from the Beach Boys in the 50s to Blackstreet in the late 90s, until now. But the well-known basics don't tickle

36

my pickle. For example, the band Toto's most famous for its song *Africa*. It's a great song, no doubt. It just doesn't butter my biscuit the way *Hold the Line* does, which is by the same group. Dolly Parton's *9 to 5* is great. *Love Is Like a Butterfly* truly does it for me. The basics are great but that shouldn't be what all great artists are known for.

    With me slightly bored out of my mind, I decide to fulfill a dream. I crank up *Old Time Rock N Roll* and head to the back of the store. Although I'm wearing a knee-length sundress and not boxers and a button-up shirt, I do the Risky Business dance. Tom Cruise would be proud. Of course, I can't slide with shoes on but the open space in the back of the store is perfect for any dance routine. And boy do I enjoy making up dances.

    I ignore the pain in my knee as I run down the tall row of books, not so successfully attempting one of those ballerina jumps. I land back on my feet, just barely, and when I look up, *dark* black eyes are staring right back at me. Well, darn if he didn't just see the next star in Swan Lake. I forget for a quick second that he hates every fiber in me. I remove my earbuds from my ears, and I look down at my flats feeling my cheeks heat up just a tad. For a minute, I think I'm hallucinating and that he's not actually here. So, I peer up through my blonde locks and there he stands, tall, strong, and undeniably gorgeous.

    His eyes travel down my attire. They stop on my leg, my fudged up leg. I move my leg from his view, placing it behind my other one in an admittedly odd stance but hey, he already hates me. Why don't I just make him think I'm weird too?

    "Hi Grey," I murmur quietly and his eyes dart back up to mine. Good Lord, every time he looks at me, I feel like he knows everything bad I've ever done in my life.

    "What are you doing here?" I question him, worried he'll snap and tell me off. But I'm prepared. I have a whole list of comebacks. Comeback 1) 'Your mom'.

    "What's on your arm," he says lowly, his deep voice rumbling through his chest and making me turn shy. He's such a *man*.

    "My arm?" I question. The last time I checked the only thing on my arm was pure muscle. I wish. He grasps my forearm and I nearly faint when his skin touches mine. Why am I like this? Am I having a midlife crisis? He lifts my arm ever so slightly and I look down at it. A light bruise sure enough sits on my arm just above my elbow. Where my father was holding me when he dragged me up the stairs. I guess I didn't see it in the lighting of my room but here in the store, you can see it.

"Well, I hit it on my bed frame," I sigh dramatically. He releases my arm and stares down at me coldly.

"Doing what?" he grumbles out and I find myself wishing to see a smile from him. I can't imagine out gorgeous a smile would look on his already breathtaking face.

"Sex," I spit out accidentally. Oh Jesus, forgive me. I'm literally a virgin, I don't have any type of clue where that came from. Why am I thinking about sex? A nicely sculpted, dark eyebrow lifts slightly on his face. His eyes fall to my collarbone, and I find myself wanting to melt into the ground.

"Sex, hm?" he speaks, and just by him saying that word, I'm feeling unnaturally hot. Am I okay?

"What are you doing here, Grey?" I question again, trying my best to change the subject from the sexy time that never happened.

"I need a book," he leans up against the wall, still staring at me like I'm a nicely cooked steak dinner. I thought he hated my guts. Why does he keep looking at my goodies? Or it could be something on my dress. I did have chocolate for breakfast today, it's possible there's chocolate on me. I can't just assume he's looking at my goodies. What goodies? I don't even know. He doesn't even look the book-reading type. He appears to be more like the 'I burn books for fun' type. But who am I to judge?

"What book would you like?" I turn and begin walking, hoping he'll just follow me. He does thankfully. He doesn't say anything for a while. I begin to think he didn't even hear me.

"What book ar-" he cuts me off with his own harsh and deep voice. "I heard you the first time." Excuse me, sir, if you heard me, you should've answered.

"Oh, I've got the perfect book for you," I spot the book. I lift it from its place and turn, showing it off to him. *Being a Nice Human Being - For Dummies.*

"You think you're funny, don't you?" his beautiful eyes narrow into slits as he sneers at me. I don't let him affect me; I knew that was coming. I've been told on many occasions that I'm funny. Correction: I've told *myself* on many occasions that I'm funny.

"I'm funnier than you think I am," I avert my eyes from him, putting the book back in its place. I guess that one just didn't interest him. I feel like he's the type of guy that just doesn't appreciate my humor.

"Plus, you're just too serious," I curse my motor-mouth, turning away from his glaring gaze completely. I make it to the nonfiction corner, and I begin looking at books for him. I'm assuming he wouldn't like to read fairy tales. *Tsunamis; a Natural Disaster.* Nope *Inside the Life of Lady Gaga.* Seems *perfect* for him. *Monster Trucks!* What is he? Eight?

A scent envelops my nose and I nearly close my eyes to enjoy it as much as it deserves to be enjoyed. How can someone smell so good? It's not even a strong cologne smell, it's just naturally *him.* From the corner of my eye, he stops right up beside me. His arm touches mine. Although I feel like a borderline child standing next to his tall frame, I can't help but want to lean into him. *And feel those tattoos of his.*

I take a step back to peer up at the books above my head but instead of looking at those books, my eyes can't seem to stray away from his back. I've never wanted to rub someone's back so bad before. I have to be going crazy. His tense back muscles are just begging me to touch. I'll be darned if his butt isn't too bad to look at too. What am I? A thirsty teenager? In the famous words of Edna Mode: "Get yourself together!" I move down the row, trying to get my mind away from his figure. I focus on the books in front of me and nearly chuckle when I see one. *The Art of Paper Mache*

It would be a trip to see him read this. I pick the book up, feeling quite proud of my find and I turn to show it to him. I come face to face with a chest. His chest. His chest that's pretty close to me. Why is my throat closing?

Kumbaya my Lord, Kumbaya.

I hold the book in front of me, not really knowing what to do with myself. I'm not really a nervous person, only around him. His gorgeous, tattooed arm sneaks around me and he places it on the bookshelf behind me. I gulp, watching his strong arm that looks like it could squeeze me like an anaconda. He takes the book from my hands, leaving me wondering what I'm supposed to do now. He places the book somewhere behind me and I gather my courage and look up at him. I smooth out the skirt of my dress and watch as his eyes follow my movement. As soon as my hands let go of my dress, his eyes fall on mine.

"Fuck," he curses quietly, dropping his head. For some reason, as he looks away from me, I'm left feeling a certain type of way. Like I *want* him to keep those eyes of his on me.

"Are you okay?" I question in my softest of voices, worried that if I speak too loudly, he'll be unhappy.

"I think you're lying," he lifts his head back up, his dark eyes connecting back with mine causing a warm feeling to explode in my stomach. Lying?

"Lying about what?" I let my head fall but he doesn't let it stay down. The hand that was resting on the shelf behind me grips the ends of my hair in the lightest touch possible. My throat goes dry at the way his touch gives me tingles. Goodness, what is going on with my hormones? His other hand comes up to my arm. He lifts it, looking down at the bruise. Is he saying I'm not capable of doing sex? Or *having* it, whatever it's supposed to be.

"You couldn't keep a guy around long enough to fuck you with that pretty little mouth of yours always running."

He thinks my mouth is pretty?

Hold up, excuse me? My mouth gapes as I peer up at him. I'm speechless. For once I don't have a comeback against that because if I'm being honest with myself, he's probably right. Plus, on top of that, he's so *vulgar*. His manners are basically nonexistent.

"You're quite rude you know," a dark glare settles onto his handsome face. He pulls away from me, a small sneer on his face. So he can say rude things to me but when I only tell him he's mean, he gets grumpy? No one leaves my presence unhappy.

Lilah

"But not always," I speak up, "I know you've got some sugar, Sugar."

I consider running away at the deadly glare he gives me. But I won't.

"You don't know shit," his deep voice grumbles. I try my hardest to not admire his features as much as I want to.

I *will* know shiznit, I *will*.

Chapter Five

Nineteen

❀Azalea❀

    I stumble up onto the sidewalk of the town square. I'm back where I started; on my way to get my parents alcohol. A twenty-dollar bill rests firmly in my hand and I don't think I could give it away to the nice homeless man even if I wanted to. The threat my father sent me was enough to make me do anything. *I wish I would just kick him in his nuts.*
    They wouldn't even let me drive here. I had to walk a full thirty-five minutes from my house to the town square. After the crash, every ounce of activeness I had went out the window. Now, I can't even get out of bed without being out of breath.
    After walking for what feels like another three years, I make it to the front of Danny/Donny's shop, whatever his name is. All the lights in the shop are off. Gathering my last little bit of hope, I take a closer look at the door.
Hours:
Wed-Fri 12pm-10pm
Sat-Sun 2pm-10pm

I back away from the door and try not to lose my cool. I have been set up for failure. It's actually not like he knew the hours, he's too drunk to remember. Tears of frustration build in my eyes, but I don't let them fall. I take deep breaths and close my eyes envisioning a big red velvet cupcake. I'm *not* fixing to go home without anything. The last time I did that, I could hardly move my back for a week.

I decide on Red Street. There are bars all over Red Street so unfortunately, that's my best bet. I tug on the bottoms of my admittedly kind of short shorts and hug my torso. Clouds circle over my head and my mostly bare arms begin to get chilly. I should've worn a jacket over my t-shirt. Why is it that none of these little trips ever work out? The first bar I see, I decide it's good enough. That is until I open the door and see a couple of women on poles. I jump out of that place very quickly. *God forgive me of my sins.*

This is going to be harder than I thought. I walk a little further down the street and finally I come to a place that actually doesn't look bad. Or like there are strippers inside. I open the door and faint music and loud talking reach my ears. There are a lot out on the floor with drinks in their hands and the rest are piled up around the actual drink bar, or whatever it's called. It reminds me of the movie *Coyote Ugly* to be honest. Except without the women dancing on the bar and all.

The closer I look around, the more I see the drunken people. One guy is tripping over himself, and another is leaned up against the wall with his friend holding him up. I don't even have an ID and I'm not twenty-one, what am I trying to get away with here? I look seven years old. Maybe they'll see the desperation in my eyes and think 'wow she must be having a hard day, let me give her some moonshine, preferably the closest thing to cherry pie or heck, even peach.' I feel eyes on me and notice and guy staring directly at me. He's obviously drunk. He sits at the bar, a drink in his hand that is currently being poured out because he's too drunk to keep it up straight.

It doesn't help that he looks at least thirty-five. I ignore his gaze and just walk up to the closest empty spot on the bar. I feel my heart pound as I stop at the bar. I've never even been in a bar and now I'm going to order things. How? What do I do? 'Hello, I'd like some cherry pie moonshine!'

'Hey bartender guy, give me some peach moonshine!"
I'm screwed.

Knowing my luck, they wouldn't even have peach or cherry pie. They'll have something like White Lightning and from what my parents said, that's the nastiest kind.

"Shout 'em out!" A loud voice shouts over everyone and voices flow into the bar. My eyes fall upon the bartender who works at a nearly impossible speed, all while a smile stays on his face. His light hair flops over his forehead as he bends under the bar, retrieving a brand-new bottle of goodness knows what type of alcohol. Just as quickly as people call out drinks, he's serving them. Just looking at him makes my head hurt.

"You haven't said a word pretty girl; what'd you like?" he speaks loudly, his eyes darting up to mine for a split second. My heart beats even louder as I look around me at any other person, but I don't think there are any other girls in my general area.

"Peach moonshine," I speak quickly, getting it over with as fast as I can. The craze around the bar simmers down and now he's only making drinks every ten or so seconds. When I finally raise my eyes from my hands, he's looking right at me, a slightly confuzzled look on his face.

"Strong drink for such a small person," he chides and I hold back from jumping over the counter and showing him just how a 'small person' like me can break out CIA/karate moves on him.

"Cherry pie could work too," I bite my lip. I don't think cherry pie is any less strong than peach but hey, maybe it is? I don't know, I'm not a scientist.

"You have an ID?" a small smirk now rests on his face, and I swear if it weren't for this tall counter, he'd wish he wasn't smirking. Like really? Who makes a counter this tall? It's up to my chest. I look down at my feet and notice a step right underneath the counter. *Ohhh*. Duh. I step up and now it's not *as* tall anymore.

"My ID is in my wig that I left a home," I blurt out and internally remind myself to punch *myself* in the face later.

"No ID?" he chuckles. He's pretty darn good. If he can see past my trained lying, he must've done bartending for a while now. Or he works for the CIA too.

"How old do I look?" I narrow my eyes and his face lights up with a smile. Aw, he's cute. What an anus cake.

"I'll be nice and give you eighteen," he tilts his head and I flick him off under the counter.

"Newsflash, I'm thirty-one," I deadpan.

"Damn, at first I was going to say thirty, but I decided against it," he slaps the table, and I bite the inside of my lip to keep from smiling.

"I guess I can give you something as long as you don't tell other people about my mistake," he shakes his head like he's embarrassed.

"I won't tell anyone," I nod and he shakes his head as he bends, grabbing something from under the counter. He pulls out a cup filled with peach-colored moonshine. I stare at it for a couple of seconds.

"Can I get a top for it," I question, and he laughs.

"What, you want to drink moonshine from a sippy cup now?" he replies. One more comment from him and I swear. How am I going to walk all the way home with an open cup? I know for a fact that I'll forget it's in my hand and it'll tip over.

"Fine," I give him the twenty dollars, not even knowing how much it is, and begin to get up. I'm probably still going to get punished for only bringing a cup home but whatever, it's better than nothing.

"I don't think so," the recognizable voice that I haven't heard in a couple of days says. I look up and see Grey in all his gorgeous glory. He lifts the drink away from me and he pours it in the sink.

"Grey," I grumble, and he turns to me.

"What are you doing Lilah? You're nineteen," his dark eyebrows furrow angrily, and I sigh.

"I was close," the bartender guy murmurs, and I hold myself back from attacking him.

"I'm not nineteen," I mumble stubbornly even though I am and he raises an eyebrow at me, placing his arms on the counter in front of me. Does he work here?

"Not what you told me," he says lowly.

"Can I get a scotch?" A guy slurs from behind me. His hand curls around my back and I flinch forward in shock, a slight gasp leaving my lips. Grey throws his forearm forward, slamming it into the guy's chest. My eyes go wide.

"You wanna get handsy, go get a fuckin' hooker," he sneers, and the guy's eyes widen in fear. I'm pretty sure mine do too. Without getting his drink, the guy makes his way back out into the large crowd.

"This is why you don't come to places like this," Grey growls out and I bite the inside of my cheek. *He doesn't understand.*

"I need moonshine," I tell him strongly. I decide against crossing my arms, figuring it'd make me look less like a cool person.

"You're not getting any," he seemingly grows more frustrated.

"I will climb over this counter and get it myself if you don't give me it," I warn and the closest thing to a smirk takes over his face. He leans forward and I nearly swoon, but I hold myself back.

"Try me."

I'll pull out my CIA moves so quick, he won't know what hit him. Instead, I lay my head on my arms and hide my face from him, trying to think of an adequate plan. A slight push on my back gets my attention and I raise my head from my arms. I turn around to see who did it only to be met with a big man's elbow right in the face as he gets into a bar fight with another guy. My head flies back so fast I could've gotten whiplash if I wasn't so CIA trained. *Good God almighty, that hurts like a mother trucker.*

Large hands grab under my arms and lift me back. I feel my butt slide across the counter until I'm on the other side. What a strong guy. The taste of blood seeps into my mouth and I cringe. My nose and top lip feel numb at the moment, but I know that in the morning, I'll definitely be feeling the pain. Unfortunately, I can't even smell Grey due to the blood filling my nose. What a shame. He turns me toward him, and I blink rapidly keeping my eyes from watering up. I can't even think clearly right now. Is he being nice or am I hallucinating?

"Lilah-" the bartender from before starts but Grey cuts him off with a glare. And he's back.

"Her name's Azalea."

"*Azalea*, are you okay?" he winces, handing me a stack of napkins. I shove them on my nose and give him a little nod. Grey stands in between my legs and I'm glad I have napkins over my face because I'm blushing like crazy right now. I pull the napkins away and look up at him.

"This is what you get for not giving me moonshine. A bloody counter," I narrow my eyes. He rolls his dark eyes and grabs my hand, putting it back up to my nose. He lifts me down from the counter and I look down at all the drink selections under the counter. I spot the moonshine. I go for it. I grab the one labeled 'Peach'. Then I put it back realizing that it's missing some because of the glass I was given. I grab the one beside it, thankfully, it's peach too. Before I can put it under my shirt or even make a run for it, Grey's pressed up against my back. His arms come around my frame and he takes it from my hands.

"I told you no," he says lowly down at me. He sits it on the counter and begins leading me into the back of the place where no one can see.

He pushes me lightly into the bathroom, following behind me and shutting the door. I'm not even worried anymore, if he wanted to kill me, he would've already done it. Plus, I could take him in a fight. I remove the napkin from my face and look in the mirror, having to slightly stand on my tippy toes to see myself. Who even makes these tall mirrors? I cringe at myself. Good heavens, I look like I've been brutally beaten with a baseball bat. Or just elbowed in the face, the same thing.

The pain sets in, and I sigh. I turn on the water, putting my hair up to not get it wet. I already look beaten up; I don't want to look like a wet dog on top of that. Grey just stands there silently, with his eyes on me. What a great help he is.

"Exactly why you should just stay where you belong," he grumbles, and I pull away from the water. I belong wherever I want to belong. CIA headquarters? Dang right. Pimp central? Yep. A bar? Sure, why not?

"How many times are you going to tell me that I shouldn't come here?"

"As many times as it takes to get it through your thick fucking skull," he sneers and I hold back my fists that want to go swinging.

"As many times as it takes," I mimic him, only feeling his glare on the side of my head.

"Go ahead, glare at me all you want. Glare at the girl with a busted lip and broken-in-half-nose," I jump at him to scare him, but he doesn't move.

"I will if she's being an immature little shit," he glares harder, stepping up to me, admittedly making me feel smaller. *Big girl britches; activated.*

"Well guess what? You're a *big* crap," bam, suck on that. He grabs another napkin off the sink, and he places it on my nose. I take hold of it and sigh. I thought it had stopped but I guess not.

"Thank you," I say softly.

"So, do you work here?" I question, just to get a conversation going while I try to fix my nose.

"I own it." Woah, what a big boy he is.

"You didn't seem like the bartender type," I ramble, "I figured you were like security or something because hello, your arms are as big as me. Then I was like, well, maybe he's not. Maybe he's a janitor. But you didn't seem like a janitor either. Do bars have janitors?"

"Close your mouth," he grumbles, and I give him a pretty darn good glare.

"How old are you anyway? Please don't tell me you're fifty. You look young to be fifty but nowadays, who knows. Wait, don't say it," I hold my hand up.

"Let me guess," I look up at him as he stares down at me. I let my eyes fall over all of his features. No gray hairs, that's a good sign. No wrinkles, that's also a good sign. Strong build, that's a wonderful sign.

"Seventy-four."

"Nope, just kidding. I'm going to say," I pull on my lip, fully noticing how his eyes fall to my mouth, "twenty-three."

"Twenty-four," he clears his throat. He's in his prime of many years to come, I can see it right in front of me. Hot dang.

"Let me have the moonshine," I stress, "please, it's all I want. I'll give you whatever you want." He glances at me, his eyes swirling in mischievousness.

"I have this blanket at home, it's really, really soft. It's gray, it reminds me of you. I'll give it to you if you give me the jar of peach moonshine," I admit. He doesn't look as open to the idea of the blanket as I am.

"What about...oh! What about I give you a free book at Mr. Terrip's store? You forgot to get a book when you went there," I smile brightly up at him. *I'll give you a free lap dance.* Where the *heck* did that come from?! I sigh and lean back up against the sink. Grey's wonderful scent envelops my nose but that hardly does anything at the moment. I keep my eyes locked on his tattooed arm, not looking anywhere else.

Up close, the tattoos are absolutely amazing. His entire arm, as far as I can see, is covered with ink. Just under the bottom of his shirt sleeve, scary, dark figures sit. Grim reaper-like figures are the closest thing I can think of. They're just dark and deadly. It gives me the shivers. In the background, it's covered with shading and dark colors that accentuate the figures. Did Da Vinci do these tattoos? Goodness. That tattoo artist should win awards or something.

There's smoke that travels from one of the figures and it wraps all throughout the rest of the tattoos on his arm. A tree goes up and dead branches spread out along his arm, and the back of it, although I can't see it, I wish I could. Around the tree, crows fly in the air. The bottom of the tree stops at his wrist where there are roots sticking up and no greenery or bushes at all. Everything's *dead*. In the background of the tree, words fill up the rest of his skin. Except for the symbol-like tattoo beside the tree. I try to read what it says but his arm moves behind me before I can. That brings me back to reality. With both his arms on either side of me, my heart speeds up.

"Tell me why you want it," he says lowly, and I gulp as he stands so close to me. Why is it now that my brain can't think of anything? Any other time I'd come up with at least something. His hand moves to rest on my side. It explodes with tingles. Not actually, because that would be impossible unless I'm allergic to him or something but, it makes butterflies go off in my stomach.

"I want to get away from everything," I whisper. Never would I ever become like my parents. I would never take a sip of alcohol after seeing what it does to them. I want to get away from *them*. I want to get away from the constant reminder of being the cause of Jake's passing, but I would never actually do that by drinking.

"I want to escape for a minute," I add, not going far into an explanation. *I don't want to go home.* I peek up at him only to see his head cast down at the ground, looking at the floor. His head only stays down for a few seconds before he looks back directly at me. His dark eyes craze the butterflies further.

"You shouldn't be drinking that shit," he grumbles, his eyebrows furrowed into a small glare.

"I know," I reply softly. His thumb rubs a single circle on my waist before he pulls away.

"What's your last name?" I question, swinging my feet back and forth while sitting on the counter he oh-so-graciously planted me on. I hardly know anything about him, and I think it's time I do.

"Kingston," his dark voice travels to me as he looks through the stock of their alcohol for my cherry pie moonshine.

"Mine's Carson," I inform him and he stops, turning back toward me.

"You've told me, Lilah." A noise reaches my ears and I freeze.

"I think there's a ghost, Grey," I whisper. My training didn't teach me how to defeat ghosts. And Ghostbusters only goes so far.

"How long have you lived here?" I change the subject although still keeping a close watch to my surroundings.

"Why?" his voice turns deeper and I look up to see him glaring darkly at me.

"I just want to know," I shrug, "I want to know more about you."

"You think I care about what you want?" he sneers and I hold back the world's loudest groan. Why does he change so quickly? He was just being nice.

"You think I care about what you think?" I shoot back, frustration building up in me.

"And you wonder why I want to drink," I grumble, adding to my imaginary list of reasons why I want to drink.

"*Fuck you,*" his voice turns deadly, and I regret my last words. No one's told me that before and I don't really like it.

"Is that all you've got?" I grit out. If he thinks he's going to get to me by just that, he's got a whole storm coming. He takes long strides toward me, and I stare up at him as he does. He grasps my chin in a firm but not painful grip, lifting my head so that I'm looking straight at him.

"Why do you do that?" he clenches his jaw.

"Do what?" I question softly.

"Get me all riled up," his grip softens and so do his features.

"You're the one who started it," I give him a little shrug, biting my lip to keep a smile off my lips. His eyes dart down to them.

"Don't do that," he glares at my lips.

"Why," I crinkle my nose up at him.

"It turns me the fuck on, now quit it," he clenches his jaw and I release my lip as I feel my cheeks heat up. Well, at least we have something in common. He turns me on with one look. Turn on? Goodness, I need a vacation. He picks up the cherry moonshine and the peach one, handing them both to me.

"Leave," he grumbles, lifting me off the counter and setting me down on my feet. Strong man, I like that. I peek out the little window only to see it raining cats and dogs outside. That was the ghost I thought I heard, duh. What a great time to not have my car, how fun is that?

"Um," I start, not knowing where to go from there.

"So, like, you're just going to love this, I don't have my car. Do you have a jacket or something I could borrow maybe?" I question. He sends me a glare.

"No," he gives me a slight push out of the room and I'm back in the main part of the bar. I let out a big sigh and head toward the door. This sucks major nuts. I hold the cherry pie and peach moonshine close to me as I finally exit the bar. The freezing rain hits my skin and I nearly go into shock. I'm actually going to get hypothermia. Then, I'm going to blame it on Grey. And the next time he sees me, he'll hear *all* about it. *If* I make it out alive.

I begin my trek walking down Redstreet. I make it about five stores down from Grey's bar when I feel someone grab onto my shoulders. I thought I was seriously being kidnapped for point three seconds, but it's all good. He puts a sweatshirt over my head that smells exactly like him and I swoon into it. He lifts the hood over my head and pulls the bottom of it down as far as it will go to cover my bare legs. I look up beside me and there is the one and only Grey Kingston. Darn if that rain doesn't make him look real nice.

"What are yo-"

"Just shut up," he grunts out and I do. He leads me out to the parking lot and to the passenger side of a really nice tall, shiny, black Jeep Wrangler. He opens the door for me, and I climb inside with the help of a little push from him. After closing my door, he goes around to his side. The time it takes him to do so, I take in the smell of him, which is the greatest thing ever, and the overall cleanliness of the car. He opens his side, and my eyes catch sight of the shirt that oh-so-heavenly clings to his torso. Good Lord Jesus. That's very nice. That's just, wow.

"Grey," I say quietly, and he looks over at me, water dripping off his gorgeous entire being.

"Thank you," I give him a little smile. He doesn't say anything, which is to be expected. He starts the car and I begin panicking. I close my eyes to calm myself as I feel the car beginning to move. I try to keep the memories of the events before the crash out of my head but some surface through.

"Lilah." His voice brings me back to reality and my eyes snap back open, darting over to him. He looks at me almost worriedly. Worriedly? No, I must be dreaming.

"Huh?"

"What's wrong with you?" he questions, his eyebrows furrowing. I just shake my head.

"What? Oh, nothing," I blow it off with a wave of my hand although I'm still completely freaking out.

"Tell me where to go," he urges, and I follow his orders as best as I can with a calm voice.

Chapter Six

Dangerous

❀Azalea❀

    I stare at my ugly busted bottom lip in the mirror. I guess I was dumb to think he wouldn't actually go as far as elbowing me. Although he tried his best to convince me it was an accident, I knew deep in my heart that an elbow doesn't just fly up at someone by chance. I got his alcohol. Apparently, it was too late for him though. My mother didn't stop it. She sat on the couch and watched as his elbow hit me across my face. It's not like I can hide it with makeup either.

    Not only does my top lip have a small cut on it from last night at the bar, but the bottom lip does too. Although it's quite a bit worse. I let out a quiet sigh. I grab my phone and my car keys that my father kindly threw at me after busting my bottom lip. I turn my light off and open my bedroom door. I close it behind me and stop when I hear someone to the left of me. I turn my head and there stands my father, still in his clothes from last night. I gulp and send a quick prayer up to God.

I guess he's too hungover to go to work today. He can't still be drunk right? I hope to God he's not.

"Why so frightened?" his worn-out voice reaches my ears and I still can't tell if he's drunk or not. *Why such a piece of donkey crap?* I ignore him, wanting to get out of this place as soon as possible. I dart down the stairs and don't stop. Once I've finally made it outside, I lean up against my car, bending down to rub my slightly throbbing knee. I suck it up and make my way to the bookstore. Only two hours later than usual.

"Are you under the weather, Azalea?" Mr. Terrip asks first thing as soon as I enter.

"No," I reply, "Why? Do I look it? You can just tell me if I look ugly or not, you don't have to be nice."

"If you were ugly, I wouldn't allow you to spend all your time in this store," he places his skinny hand on my forehead, "you would scare away all my customers."

"How darling of you to say," I wrap my arms around his frame, relishing in the feeling of his grandfatherly warmth. We pull away and he picks up his glasses from his desk, sitting them on the end of his nose. He squints his eyes before grabbing my face ever so gently and tilting it up so that he can see it through his bifocals.

"What on *earth*?" he sees my busted lips. My exotic dancing training isn't going well. I hit my mouth on my pole. If I would say that to him, he'd surely have a heart attack. Who would I talk to then?

"Here's the deal," I start, "I was lying in bed, my alarm woke me up. It scared me, right? So, I hit my knee on my mouth."

"You need to get out more," he removes his glasses, and my mouth drops open.

"I thought you enjoyed my company!" I gasp and he nods after a second of deciding whether to ignore me or answer me.

"Of course, I do. I'm just figurin' that maybe you could use a relaxing day at home," he shrugs and just the thought of me spending the day at home makes me uneasy.

"No thanks," I say quietly, making my way to my designated chair. I

Lilah

K. Pope

plop down in my seat and lean my head up against the chair. The bell above the door jingles and I shoot up. From my position, I see it's a girl maybe around my age. I let her walk around and look for a while until I'm able to gather up my courage.

"Do you need help finding anything?" I question softly, not wanting to be one of those people who walk up to you and basically corners you into buying something. If I'm lucky, maybe she and I could be friends. She looks over at me and she shakes her head. She's super pretty. I give the back of her head an unfortunately saddened smile and walk over to Mr. Terrip's desk.

"Be honest with me," I say as I approach him. He looks up at me.

"Do I look nice? Approachable even?" I take a seat on the end of his desk.

"Of course you do," he replies but it's kind of that thing where he has to say yes because he knows me. He's biased. The girl approaches us with two books in her hands. Mr. Terrip stands and rings up her books. I keep my eyes downcasted on my black button-down skirt. The bell to the door sounds once more. I look up to see Grey walking in, gorgeous as always. My palms get sweaty seeing him. A single lock of hair falls onto his forehead, and I've never wanted to run my hands through anyone's hair as much before.

"Have a good day," Mr. Terrip tells the girl as she grabs her bag, walking away from the checkout counter. I offer the girl a smile, she doesn't see it. My smile falters as she walks past Grey, obviously checking him out. *He doesn't glare at her like he does to me.* At that, I just look back down at my skirt. My blonde hair falls around my face, blocking the view of Grey. I feel his presence in front of me and I turn to Mr. Terrip.

"Mr. Terrip, this is Grey. Grey this is Mr. Terrip," I mutter softly.

"This is who you've been tal-"

"Mr. Terrip!" I cut him off, "shouldn't you be finishing your crossword puzzles?"

"I mean, I guess-"

"Okay," I pick up his crossword book and hand it to him. He gives me a sly little smile before taking his book and sitting at his desk. At least now I know he actually listens sometimes.

"Are you here for the book you forgot to get?" I question, looking up only to find him glaring at me. I just let out a little sigh. I carefully climb off the counter and walk away from him, toward the back of the store. There's no reason to glare at me especially when he's not glaring at that other girl. What am I? Jealous? She was really pretty though. Maybe he liked her. That's probably what it was. I know I annoy him. He reminds me of that quite often. Maybe I should just stop talking altogether. Walking to a row of books that need to be put away, I pick up one. Grey's hand grasps the back of my shirt, turning me around to face him. His hand comes up and he rests it right at the top of my throat. He lifts my head up and glares. It's hot in here.

"That wasn't there last night," he growls out, looking at my bottom lip.

"Yeah, it was," I reply, "it was dark Grey, you just didn't see it." I raise my head and gently take hold of the hand he has under my jaw. Good lord this man has some nice hands. I lower both of our hands keeping my eyes away from his.

"Your book?" I question nervously.

"I don't want a damn book," he grounds out, agitated. He needs a book on how to communicate properly. I can't read minds here. I look up at him. I wait for him to say something but of course he doesn't. If he doesn't want a book, then what's the point of being here? Does he enjoy making me feel terrible about myself? I get enough of that everywhere else I go. This is the only place where I can be free without having to care whether or not anyone is judging me. Mr. Terrip is the closest thing to family and a friend I've got and even though I know he judges me, he is still always there for me.

"Then why are you here?"

"I wanted to see you hungover."

"Well, I'm not," I fumble with the book in my hands.

"I can see that," his deep voice grows a tad deeper. I search my brain for anything else to say which is unusual.

"I'm sorry you had to drive me home last night," I apologize.

"I don't have your sweatshirt with me, but I can bring it to you tomorrow," I add. *Or maybe I could keep it considering it smells delicious like you and* it's more comfortable than anything else ever.

"Next time drive yourself. That was out of my way," he grumbles, his eyebrows pulling together in a small glare.

"Well, you didn't have to do it. If I knew you were going to act like this then I would've refused to let you drive me home," I turn away from him, finding the book in my hand's correct placement.

"I didn't want to hear your bitchin' about it later," he says from behind and I close my eyes, refusing to let his words do anything to me.

"That's all I hear from you," I fire back at him. With my back facing him, my face morphs into one of a little regret. He may be awfully rude but I'm sure not. I can't help but feel bad. I don't know what goes on with him at home. Maybe he's been through some things. *Maybe he should take my advice.* I decide on turning around to gauge his reaction to my words. Maybe he's laughing. He definitely won't be laughing but maybe, just maybe, he's not that mad. I've 'known' this man for weeks, when is he ever not mad at *anything* I say? I turn and come face to chest. I feel like giving up and just leaning my forehead against his chest and falling asleep.

I'm exhausted. I need a coffee. Then, a nap. Heck, even a spa treatment after my nap.

"Nothing else to say?" he pushes away from me.

"That's all you got?" he repeats the question that I've asked him on a few occasions.

"Grey, stop," I whisper, realizing that I never put on my big girl britches today. I think they flew out the window actually.

"Not so tough now, huh?" he leans into me, so close I can see the faint scar on his jaw. His tattooed hand comes up and he tucks a strand of loose hair behind my ear. My heart speeds up as his hand lingers on my skin, trailing down to under my chin. Wait. He's mean to me. He's a full-fledged jerk. And he's gorgeous. But dangerous. Dangerously gorgeous, there it is. What am I even doing? I hardly know him and I'm letting him this close? There must be something in my water. Why am I not pushing him away? Why do I keep asking myself questions? I wonder how that nice homeless man is doing? Why do I want to kiss him? Grey, not the homeless man...I think? No, no, it's definitely Grey.

With Grey so close in front of me, his hand tilting my chin up, I get the perfect view of his perfect lips. I need help. I need a friend to help me because I have no idea what I'm doing or what to do. I've seen those movies where the friends help each other with basically everything. I feel like Mr. Terrip would ban me from the store if I asked him everything I want to.

Is he going to kiss me? Are we going to kiss? He despises me. I've never been more confused in my entire life.

"Grey," a whisper leaves my lips as I raise my hand to his chest in a pitiful attempt to confusedly push him away. Or to just touch him, I'm not sure. He doesn't like me. I *know* he doesn't. If there's one thing I'm sure about in my life, it's that Grey Kingston does not like me in any type of way. I pull away. He lets me so, I think I was right. It's now that I don't have the courage to look up at him. I'm terrified to see his beautiful black eyes glaring at me again.

I take a step backward and my foot catches a heavy wooden chair. I'm going down, I'm yelling timber. I land on my butt and a terrible feeling breaks out in my knee. Here we go with this stupid thing again. It gets sharper and it intensifies when I try to move it.

"You're pitiful, you know that?" Grey's deep voice travels down to me. I bite my lip harshly. Looks like this doctor trip is going to have to happen sooner than I planned. I finally raise my head. I can tell the pain on my face is clearly visible. Especially considering how he takes a step toward me. He holds out his hand for me to grab all while looking at me with a bored expression. *That's the nicest thing he's ever done for me.* I take hold of his large hand but as I start to move, I have to stop, and a whimper leaves my lips as my knee feels like it's going to fall off. Well, this isn't good.

"Lilah, c'mon," he urges, giving my hand a light squeeze.

"I can't, Grey," I take a deep breath. If I'm passing out, I better do it soon, this hurts like a mother trucker. He bends, his hand trailing up from my hand to my arm. My biceps, oh yeah, I bet he's never felt anything as strong as those boys.

"What is it?" he questions, looking over me for visible injuries.

"My knee," I whisper, and he looks down at the scarred one automatically. He raises his hand over it.

"If you touch it, I'm going to cut your fingers off and cook them into a stew." His eyes dart up to mine. A smirk reaches his lips and I almost gasp. Wowzer, he's attractive.

~~~

"This isn't the orthopedist," I observe as Grey turns onto the driveway of a pretty colonial-style house. I hate to think he's going to kidnap me, because how cliche is that? But it's not looking too good.

"Grey," he ignores me.

"Grey-y-y," I drag out his name.

"Sugar?" he looks over at me and I smile internally. His hand on the wheel jerks to the left a bit and he purposely runs over a pothole. My knee moves and I wince in pain. Apparently, he doesn't understand that my knee could actually fall off.

"Your pain tolerance is shit," he grumbles, and I mock him silently. He has no idea. He parks near the entrance of the house, and I look up at it in awe.

"Is this yours?" I question.

"A friend of mine's," he actually answers.

"You have friends?" I question and he glares at me harshly before getting out and starting to walk to my side. He opens my door and I unbuckle my seatbelt. Just like at the store, he lifts me with no problem. Beginning to go up the porch steps, my leg wiggles a bit and I grip the back of this shirt tightly.

"Where are we?"

"Dr. Wernier is a friend of mine who does favors for my guys sometimes," he explains, and I listen intently.

"Who are your guys?" I ask and he stays quiet for a while.

"Friends," he replies. I wish I had that. He presses the doorbell and steps back to wait.

"Sorry if I'm heavy-"

"Shut up," he cuts me off.

"You didn't have to do this," I start.

"I know how expensive medical bills are," he replies, and my mind goes off into a wondrous state. I know how expensive they are too. The door opens.

"Bos-"

"Karter," Grey cuts him off and Karter looks at me, confusion on his face.

"I really like your house, it's nice. You must have a lot of money. You're Dr. Weiner, right?" I smile and I can feel Grey's eyes on me. Karter shakes out of it and smiles. He can't be any older than thirty.

"Dr. *Wernier*," He corrects, "and yes ma'am."

"She's got a hurt knee," Grey informs him, walking inside when Karter holds the door open. I look around the gorgeous house until I'm carried into the living room and sat on the dark leather couch. I nearly punch Grey in the throat when he doesn't even consider my knee's injury while bumping into it to sit beside me. I look down at my slightly risen skirt from me sitting down. Next thing I know, a dark red couch pillow is shoved onto my bare legs. I look up at Grey only to see his eyes focused on the stone fireplace, his jaw clenched.

"How'd you hurt it?" Karter sits down in a kitchen chair that he brought into the living room, right in front of me.

"She fell over a damn chair," Grey answers for me and I giggle at how much of a mountain-man he sounded like. He always sounds like that when he grumbles.

"Have you injured this knee before?" he questions, and I sigh. He bends his back slightly, picking up my leg ever so gently. I keep it straight and he sets my foot on his lap. He winces at how swollen it is already.

"...Yes," I leave it at that.

"Tell me how..."

"Azalea," Grey inputs for Karter.

"My patella was shattered, and I tore my ACL too," I finish and they don't say anything.

"How long ago was it that you had your knee injuries?" Karter asks.

"A year and a half," I reply quickly.

"Well, you got fucked up, didn't you?" Karter speaks and that wasn't what I was expecting him to say at all.

"Sort of," I agree. He doesn't even know half of the injuries I had.

"It's common to reinjure your ACL within two years after the repair," he explains, and I hold back a groan. I don't want to go through that physical therapy again.

"I can tell that that's news you don't want to hear," he smirks.

"You're darn right," I grumble, now noticing how Grey is fiddling with the hair tie on my wrist.

"It's possible you tore it again," he rips it off like a Band-Aid, "especially with a quick movement like falling over a chair, unfortunately." Like heck it's torn. Not again, I won't allow it. He moves his hand forward to touch my knee.

"Touch it, I dare you," I narrow my eyes at him, feeling Grey's eyes on me once again. Karter looks between me and Grey.

"What a match," he mumbles under his breath.

"Just let me sit for a bit and I'll be better in no time," I say unconvincingly.

"Lilah-"

"Lilah? Oh," Karter raises from his chair giving Grey a little look. Grey glares harshly and Karter just walks through the doorway and into the kitchen.

"You can't wait out an ACL tear-"

"I can, and I will," I cut him off, crossing my arms stubbornly.

"Don't cut me off," he grumbles, narrowing his dark eyes.

"Now is not the time Sugar, I'm already fired up," I narrow my eyes right back knowing darn well he hates that name.

"Fuck off."

"I can't, I'm crippled you freak," I fire back and Karter laughs loudly from the kitchen.

~~~

I open my eyes with a struggle. I remove my head from Grey's shoulder and hold back from wincing.

"You sleep like a fuckin' rock," he grumbles.

"How long was I asleep?" I question.

"An hour and a half," he replies unhappily. I'm actually surprised he let me lay on him for that long. I look down and see a blanket draped over my lower half.

"Your ass was out," he clenches his jaw and I blow my cheeks out to keep them from blushing.

"It was a good sight, wasn't it?" my eyes widen slightly at what just flew out of my mouth. From the corner of my eye, I see him turn to me. I turn to him and he's giving me a look.

"I'll tell you if you take the blanket off again," his face stays emotionless, but his voice gets a tad deeper. My mouth goes dry and my heart speeds up. God, he confuses me. I debate removing the blanket. I'm going wild. I stick my hands down the blanket and fix my risen skirt before removing the blanket. Karter enters the room. The blanket is thrown back over my legs. I turn to see Grey glaring unhappily at him.

"Who fucked your shit up?" Karter motions to my busted lips. Those must be his favorite words.

"Someone bumped into me last night," I answer, and Grey lets out a sound of disapproval. Karter remains quiet for a moment, looking between my eyes.

"Grey," he begins, turning to him, "did you know I just got my degree in behavioral science a couple weeks ago? I wanted to expand my mind so I

decided why not?"

My breath lodges in my throat. I turn my head towards Grey to see his eyes already on me. His eyes trail up until they stop on mine.

"That sounds lovely," I whisper to Karter.

"What um, what does that entail?" I question nervously.

"Human interactions, expressions, thoughts, lies," I drag my eyes back to his. I'd think that's the coolest thing in the world if I hadn't just lied to his face. Maybe I'm just such a good liar that he didn't notice. I'm CIA trained after all.

"That's super-duper fun," I smile, "I should go." I sit all the way up, keeping my leg straight.

"I would recommend staying off your leg. Go home, get rest, and if it doesn't ease up, go to your orthopedist," he informs.

"Of course," I give a nervous nod to which he smirks at. He knows he made me nervous with that. Sudden strong arms under my body shock me out of my nervous trance. Grey's rippling muscles tense underneath me as he stands straight up, carrying me like I weigh no more than a feather. Which is false. I weigh 2 tons of feathers. Well actually, two tons of feathers would mean they *weigh* two tons. So, I weigh 111 pounds of feathers.

"I weigh 111 pounds of feathers," I blurt out as Grey carries me to the front door.

"How often do you feel you blurt things?" Karter questions, tilting his head respectfully.

"Fuckin' often," Grey grumbles for me and I giggle softly.

"I'll take that as an all-the-time," he nods. I say my goodbye to Karter, Grey stays mostly silent.

"You're quite dramatic," I whisper to him, and he halts his steps as he arrived at the passenger side of his Jeep that I honestly love so much. He grips my chin, pulling my face so that I'm looking directly at him. Closely, might I add.

"Don't test me, Lilah," he grounds out, but I hardly listen to his words, too focused on his mouth as he talks. That is until he jerks my chin up so that I'm not looking there anymore.

"*Don't*," his voice goes dark, and I roll my bottom lip into my mouth. His conflicted eyes leave mine and I keep my eyes on him as he stares away almost as if he's having an internal battle. About what? Maybe about what to have for dinner tonight. Chicken or steak? Maybe even spinach or regular lettuce?

"You need to go home," he finally says something, and my heart deflates in disappointment and fear.

"I don't want to go home," I whisper to myself. He sits me in the passenger seat before going over to his side. I keep my emotions at bay although I'm terrified to go home. And to make things worse, I can't even run away from him. That sends tears swarming in my eyes.

"Can you take me back to the store?" I keep my voice strong.

"It's closed," he answers shortly and my eyes flick to the clock to the front of me above the radio.

"Do you want a milkshake?" I question him, my voice taking on a new, shakier tone. He glances over at me.

"No."

I don't *want* to let him see how desperate I am to not go home. But I just can't go.

"Grey, please," I plead softly.

"Lilah, I have things to do," he says darkly, "the world doesn't revolve around you." I don't notice the lone tear that makes its way down my cheek. Like I said, my big girl britches have flown out the window and are missing.

"What the hell's the matter with you now?" He grumbles unhappily. I look out the window and see we're about to pass Cobblestone Park.

"Pull over," I tell him.

"The fuck are you telling me what to do fo-"

"Can't you stop being a brat for five seconds? Pull over," I glare at him, fed up with his absolute crappy attitude for right now. He pulls over and I just now realize I can't even walk. What the heck is wrong with me? Just that sends another tear running down my cheek. *I am so done with everything.*

I'm pathetic and pitiful, he's right.

"Come over here, take me out of this car, and sit me on that bench over there," I point to the bench outside my window and a little way down the sidewalk. I don't know who I think I am ordering him around but right now I could care less.

"I'm not leaving you on a fucking bench," he sneers.

"Why not? You hate my guts so why not leave me out on a random park bench to maybe get kidnapped-"

"Shut up Azalea," my name rolls off his tongue in a nasty tone.

"No, you shut up," I regret it as his eyes turn so dark.

"Why don't you want to go home?" His eyes stay deadly as his tone turns the same way, "What, do mommy and daddy not love you?"

I raise my hand to slap the living daylights out of his beautiful face, but he catches my hand in the air. Oh God, that's worse than me even slapping him.

"*Don't you fucking try me,*" he leans over to me, making sure I understand each and every word that he said.

"Enough," his tattooed hand reaches over to me, wiping the tears from my face.

Chapter Seven

Mistake

❀**Azalea**❀

I down the last bit of my milkshake, ignoring Grey's gaze. Especially when it drips down my chin, I know he's judging me. But from the way he's looking at me when I finally make eye contact with him, it seems like he's not judging me but something else. I'm not sure what it is though.

"Are you sure you don't want one? You look hungry," I say. He licks his lips as I wipe my chin with my hand. See what I mean, he's hungry, I'm sure of it. The corner of his lips turns up a bit. His jaw clenches deliciously and my bottom lip rolls into my mouth. He bites his.

"God, stop Azalea," he says in a rushed tone, "stop."

"Stop what?" My head tilts on its own accord and I feel his leg bouncing up and down underneath the table.

"I'm sorry," I apologize. For what? I don't know. I release my lip and look around the place.

I feel a hand grab my leg under the narrow table. Before I can even blink, he throws a 20 on the table. A twenty? Goodness, all the waiter did was ask what we wanted monotonously. He shoots up from his seat and grabs my hand, pulling me with him. With the large hinges and rotation controlling brace, post-operation of my first surgery on my knee, it eases some pain. I got it from my car after we stopped by Mr. Terrip's. I had left it in there after I went to the doctor one day and they told me I didn't need it anymore. Now I need it again.

I try and keep up, as well as keeping my weight off the leg because even though it's an expensive metal brace, it doesn't fix my problem.

"Grey, easy," I softly remind him but instead of stopping he turns to me and lifts me up.

"Grey," I gasp as he carries me across town square before turning down Red Street.

"Hush, Lilah," He shushes me, planting a kiss on my neck. I let out a shocked noise. Am I dreaming? I have to be. Is he drunk? Am I drunk? Was I drugged at the milkshake place? He pushes open the door at his bar and I catch sight of that bartender guy.

"Hey, buddy!" I call out and his eyes find mine. They widen at my predicament for a minute before a cute smile spreads across his face.

"How are you?" I call out before Grey grabs ahold of my chin, turning my focus back to him.

"Eyes on me, only me," he grumbles. He brushes through the doors to the back, and we end up in the same place as before. The one where they have all the alcohol stocked up. He aggressively sits me on the table before grabbing my hips with his big, strong hands. He pulls me to the edge, placing our bodies together. Me being me, all flustered and stuff, I blush and mumble incoherent sounds.

"Fuck. Look at you," His tattooed hand travels up my neck before taking a rest at the top of my throat. My skirt rises and he notices. His free hand finds my leg and he glances down.

"You can't wear these Lilah, you just can't," he mumbles lowly before pulling my skirt down to its supposed placement.

"What did I tell you about that?" His eyes find my lips and I just now notice how I'm biting it.

"S-Sorry," I stutter pathetically. Am I horny? What does horny feel like? I'm not even sure I know what that means. He presses against me harder and to create some distance, before I go crazy, my hand finds his stomach. I nearly gasp at how tense and strong he feels. When I feel his breath on my neck, I notice how heavy I've started breathing. I feel like this isn't real. Did I accidentally smoke LSD? Do you smoke LSD? Am I okay?

The type of girl you wanna chew all of my bubblegum. Why am I thinking of Paul Blart right now!?

His lips connect to my neck, and I gasp softly. No one has ever kissed me here before. He gives my neck soft, wet kisses and I sigh into him. My hand trails from his stomach around to his back on its own, feeling the way he tenses under my touch and every time he breathes. When his mouth reaches a spot right beside my throat, my hand grips his shirt harshly and I have to bite my lip to keep from making a noise.

My breathing increases as he stays on that spot, noticing my reaction. His arm reaches around me, pulling me impossibly tighter to him. His mouth works wonders on the spot, and I can't help but finally let out a soft moan. I'm pulled further into my trance even when his mouth pulls away from my neck. He places one last kiss on the spot before bringing his head out of my neck. My bottom lip returns to its hated place between my teeth, and he finally looks at my face. His dark eyes meet mine and his tattooed hand trails up from my neck to where my teeth meet my bottom lip.

"Why do you get me so riled up?" He questions, although I feel it's more to himself, so I don't answer. He pulls my lip from my teeth with his thumb, watching my mouth the whole time. Before I can say sorry for forgetting or anything, he takes my bottom lip between his teeth. He pulls at it before biting down, I let out a gasp at the sudden pinch, but he releases, placing a kiss on it before I can say a word. It's burning hot in this room, holy moly.

His lips land on mine fully and I come to the shagadelic realization that we're kissing. His taste is mesmerizing. I bet I taste like Oreos considering the milkshake I've just had.

"Damn boss, another one in here?" A male voice speaks as soon as the door to the room opens. I shoot away with a gasp before his words dawn on me. *Another one?*

"Out, Jonas," Grey sneers darkly and the guy leaves. My heart sinks and Grey turns his attention back to me. I remove my hand from his back. I keep my eyes down, too afraid to see his eyes and how he's looking at me after I've just given quite a bit of myself to him. I'd been kissed before, a slight peck actually from a truth or dare game at a birthday party Jake brought me to but other than that, I've done nothing.

"You need to go home," he decides, and I can't bring myself to fight it anymore. With his one arm that is still wrapped around me, he lifts me off the counter and places my feet gently on the ground. His strong arm supports me as I walk to the door. He opens it for me, and I'm surprised he does it.

"Thank you," I thank him softly, but he doesn't respond. Once out in the main section, I notice how empty it is. Except for the crowd of guys surrounding the bar. Now's the time to become a pimp. With all these guys here, it's a perfect setup. I walk carefully across the dark wooden floor, Grey still clings onto me, thank goodness. He's actually being very helpful. Maybe he feels bad for acting like my knee wasn't even hurt. I feel eyes on me. More like two dozen eyes on me. Where's everyone else in the bar? How come only those guys are here? Finally, we make it to the main door. Thankfully, Grey doesn't stop there. He walks me all the way to where my car is.

"Thank you for helping me," I give him a small smile, but he doesn't see it, too busy keeping his eyes away from me. He never does that. Usually, it's always him who has his eyes on me and I'm the one looking away.

"It was a mistake," his words dig into me, and it feels as if the world around us is silent. The buzzing of the streetlights pause and the crickets halt their sound-making. He's talking about the kiss and everything before it, I can feel it in my heart.

"I-Oh," is all I can muster. This time, it's me who looks away and him who looks at me. Why does that hurt really bad?

"It shouldn't have happened," he continues in a final tone just adding to the wound. I swallow the golf ball-sized lump in my throat as the back of my eyes sting. Why was I so stupid to let it happen? It's all my fault. I deserve to feel this way. Maybe it's the world getting back at me for killing my brother. The emotions I try *so, so hard* to keep at bay are released in the form of a single tear. I was hoping Grey wouldn't catch sight of it. He sees everything.

"Azalea," He starts, his fist clenching by his side, and it makes me want to cry more. His tone is emotionless, and he didn't even call me Lilah.

"It's okay," I wipe the tear with my shirt sleeve, giving him a smile, I mustered up with my last strength.

"I-um," I clear my throat to keep my voice from sounding *so* weak. I know I'm already weak enough to him. "I'm going to head home," I bite the inside of my cheek trying to keep my nose from wobbling like it always does when I cry.

I struggle to get into my car which only makes me ten times as frustrated and when I look up to see if he watched me look stupid, I find that he's already gone. It's there where I release the waterfall of emotions I was holding back.

The Niagara Falls of emotions.

~~~

"You're a fuckin' waste," my father slurs down at me.

"I pray that it should've been you; not Jake," he continues, and I try my best to crawl away from him, unable to stand up on my own from where he threw me down.

"Look at you," He sneers, bending down to me, eyeing my knee brace.

"Can't even fucking walk right. You're disgusting. You're a murderer," I feel my back hit a wall and I'm in a corner. For what seems like the nine-hundredth time today, I cry my eyes out.

I'm weak. I'm pathetic. I'm disgusting. I'm a mistake. I'm a murderer.

"You're a fucking whore," my father grips my chin painfully, tilting my head up.

"Look at your hickey you nasty piece of shit," he presses a finger against the spot Grey had his mouth on, what seemed like hours ago. He grips my face harder, and I cry in pain. He holds my face up at his, his dark green eyes bore into mine horrifyingly.

"I wish you were *dead,*" he says emotionlessly before pushing my face away harshly. I catch sight of his face as he walks away. Slight regret coats his eyes but he doesn't do anything to help me. It takes me a good twenty minutes but finally, I'm in my room. I fall onto my bed in pure exhaustion. The sound of glass plates and cups shattering reaches my ears. I place my earbuds in my ears, turning on my odd playlist of mixed music.

"Your taste in music is what's making you crazy," Jake's voice calls out and my mouth drops open.

"You're just jealous that you can't find songs as good as these on your own," I give him a little smirk. He throws a pair of pants at me. Unfortunately, they're probably dirty. Nasty dingleberry.

"If you want me to keep helping you clean your disastrous room, you best keep your dirty clothes to yourself," I point at him, and he throws blue boxers at me. I scream.

"Oh hush, they're clean...?" He trails off in question and I shiver in disgust.

"Azalea Carson!" Dad's voice travels up the stairs and Jake and I both pause our cleaning.

"Yes?" I call out nicely, afraid he'll get mad at me.

"I'm going to work," he appears in the doorway.

"This house better be spotless by the time we get back from work," he narrows his eyes at me and I give him a nod.

"Jake, make sure she does it. Love you, son," he leaves out the doorway and I feel my eyes go blurry with tears. Jake's warm arms envelop me, and he holds my head against his shoulder.

"I'll help you, it's alright," he says soothingly.

"I love you, okay?" He says the words I desperately wish my father would say to me.

"I love you too," I hold onto him tightly as if he's going anywhere.

Thank God he's not.

I jump awake and look around for Jake. It's dreams like those that make everything hurt terribly. Ones that feel so real and ones that make me think that when I wake up his smiling face will just be in the room right next door. I hadn't had a memory like that in a while. I find the clock and see that it's only three-thirty in the morning. I'm terrified of going back to sleep. I know that I'll have another dream. Maybe even a worse one.

    My mind begins to wander off to the day of the crash, but I cut those thoughts off immediately. The last time I went over what happened that day, it wouldn't stop replaying over and over again. I couldn't escape it. The pictures showed when I was awake, and they were worse when I slept. Pictures of his lifeless body are images that haunt me every single day.

    I remain wide awake until my alarm sets off. Once it does, I groggily get out of bed. I take a shower all while struggling to keep balance on my single working leg. I throw on a white sundress with short sleeves, keeping myself casual. A dress is easier to put on when you can't bend one of your knees. I open my closet, grabbing a light pink sweater noticing it's a little chilly today. I catch sight of my crutches in the back of my closet, but I internally send them the middle finger.

    Although I can hardly walk, I *will not* use those evil things. I take a seat on my bed and grab a pair of tan sandals. One goes on easily. The other doesn't. I grit my teeth in frustration and pain, and I attempt to put my shoe on my god-forbidden foot. Painful memories fly back to me as I recall having to go through this every day after the wreck. I let my hair dry, and it takes to its natural slightly wavy state.

    I almost leave before remembering something. I make my way to my bathroom and cover up the hickey on my neck.

    What a leech. I'm still incredibly upset with myself. How can I go from being angry at him to all hornish-acting? If that's even a word, heck if I know, I'm not a dictionary. Then, to make things worse, I was seen by lord-knows-who when stumbling my way out of his bar. He talks about friends of his, maybe all those guys were his friends.

    I can't help but feel jealous of him. He's got people to help him whenever he's struggling in any type of way. I had to recover from a fatal crash all on my own. I maneuver my way through the glass-covered floor to get to the front door. I grab my keys and I leave.

Lilah

K. Pope

~~~

I walk into the store leisurely; trying to keep a pained expression off my face. The last thing I want to do is worry Mr. Terrip. He doesn't deserve to be worried about me; I don't matter all that much. I find my chair and take a seat, letting out a sigh once I do.

"No 'Hello, Mr. Terrip?'" he stops right beside my chair.

"I'm sorry," I give him an apologetic smile. He takes a seat on the arm of my chair.

"What is it darling? What has got you this way?" He speaks therapeutically.

"I want him back," I keep my eyes closed so he won't see how they're watering. I've already cried in front of two people this week, I don't want to make it three.

"My heart is just, it doesn't feel right," I speak, confusing myself with where I'm going.

"It hurts; it feels heavy. It feels like there's nothing you can do to make it feel better," Mr. Terrip finishes what I'm trying to say. More like the words I'm unable to say.

"You can't keep what you've been through to yourself," he admits.

"It's haunting you, darling, I can see it," I rest my head on his side and he begins to brush my hair off of my forehead.

"I don't want it to haunt anyone else," I whisper, speaking the thoughts I've been thinking since the wreck.

"Have you considered what others think? Maybe we don't want it to haunt *you*. I know I don't. Aaron doesn't, you *know* he doesn't. I'm sure your parents don't either," he says. My *parents* make sure it haunts me. My father reminds me that I killed my brother every chance he gets.

"You and Aaron shouldn't hear it," I tell him. I only want their perspective of my brother to stay happy. I want their thoughts of him to remain as perfect as he was.

"You're too sweet," he places a kiss on my head before returning to his duties.

"How about that guy that was here? You two seemed quite close," he changed the subject, and my mood takes a turn.

"I for one saw how he couldn't take his eyes off you," he nudges my shoulder. *He was probably thinking of how annoying I am.*

"I don't think he'll be around anymore," I sigh and Mr. Terrip's eyebrows furrow.

"Well, I thought you two were friends?"

"I'm incapable of making friends," I bite my cheek.

"I think I'm done," I tell him. There's no point in trying if every time I fail.

"What happened? You two seemed fine. Especially when he was carrying you out of here," his tone turns playful causing a small smile to appear on my lips. *It was a mistake. It shouldn't have happened.*

"Our personalities didn't fit," I stand from my chair.

"I'm going to go find any out-of-place books," I turn away from him, so we won't see my watery eyes. I let my focus turn to books and before I know it, my mind has fully slipped away. Maybe it's better that Grey and I don't know each other. We're complete opposites. Plus, he's not exactly the kindest person I've met. *But why do I feel so drawn to him?*

Chapter Eight

Grasshole

❀Azalea❀

I twist and turn my torso, glancing at myself in the mirror of the bookstore's bathroom. Spending these past two and a half weeks away from the man whose name I shall not think about, has given my conscience the opportunity to develop reasons why everything was a mistake. I've concluded that I'm just...not all that fun to be around. I'm annoying and ill-favored. *At least I've still got myself to cheer myself up.*

I straighten my light denim skirt and internally curse *Grey Kingston*. Who is he to tell me to not wear skirts? He can throw himself in a dumpster for all I care. *I do care.* I actually don't. I *wish* I didn't; even though I *don't*. I turn to the toilet. I take the toilet paper off its holder, and I place it on the floor gently. I sit on the closed toilet and with my non-idiotic leg, I kick the living dookie out of it. I imagine Grey's gorgeous face on the roll, and I give it another one.

Grasshole. Big, butthead. Freakin' mood killer. Stupid gorgeous mother trucker. I let out a groan, placing my head in my hands.

Usually, after two weeks, the guy is supposed to float away from your thoughts. Especially when you take out your frustration toward him on pillows and, obviously, toilet paper rolls. I pick up the roll and throw it in the trash. What a waste, sorry Jesus. No one wants to wipe their butt with dirty TP. Unless you're into that stuff, yikes.

I grab a new one from under the sink and put it in the holder. I straighten my long blonde hair with my fingers and make my way out of the john. My knee is better. My thoughts are that I only injured my ACL, not tear it. I still walk like a pirate but a little less now I guess.

With the order of books that just arrived yesterday, I've been busy these past two days. I drag the heavy cart to the section where I left off and I pick up a book, looking at its features. The cart begins to roll away from me. *There's a ghost.* I place my hand on the handle and look up to 'see' the spirit. Aaron's mischievous blue eyes look back at me. I actually kind of missed him, he's pretty much a friend, I guess. He starts to move around the cart, and I move around it. We're at opposite ends. A smirk reaches his lips, showing off a dimple on his cheek.

"Someone's playful today," his melodic voice makes a small smile appear on my lips. He moves again and due to my slower movements thanks to my predicament, he catches my arm, pulling me against him. He hugs me to him, and I chuckle at his cuddly personality.

"I missed you A-a-ron," I bite my lip, keeping a laugh from escaping.

"You missed me?" his voice rumbles against me, "I'll have to come more often then. I missed you too, Azzy."

We pull away and he peers down at my leg.

"What'd you do, Azalea?" he bends down to my knee placing his hand just below the brace.

"I fell over a chair. I can't do anything with myself," I sigh, "I've been having a rough time." He glances up at me with a smile on his face. His dimples are so cute I just want to squeeze his cheeks. I know he sees my hands squeezing by my sides. He knows what that means.

77

"Go ahead," he mumbles, playfully rolling his eyes. I grab his cheeks and commence to being like a grandmother to her grandchild.

"It still hurts my ego that you're the only one who thinks I'm *adorable* instead of attractive," he pouts, standing.

"Your little squeezy hands," he imitates the way I squeeze my hands and I shove him lightly.

"Why're you having a rough time?" he tilts his head in question and I screw my mouth shut.

"How've you been doing at college? Good?" I change the subject, picking up books.

"Jake used to do that, don't you start it too," he says, and I look down. Jake was the champion at changing the subject. We could be talking about his game one second and then the next, about what I picked out to wear the next day. He never liked talking about himself. I had to punch him for it on a few occasions.

"We should go have lunch!" I clap my hands. I could use something to stuff my face with, so I don't have to talk as much.

"Fine," he sighs.

~~~

Not a good idea. Not a good one. Terrible idea. I should've picked where we should eat. I'm going to vomit.

"You look pale," he helps me out of my car after telling me where we're eating. Grey's freakin' bar by night, restaurant by day.

"Maybe we should go to Mcdonald's," I offer, and he scoffs.

"Mcdonald's makes me shit," he reasons.

"Why don't we go to another place?" I question as he leads me closer and closer to Grey's bar.

"Because this one is the nicest looking one that I see in my line of view," he pulls me past the bench where I met Grey. I narrow my eyes at the stupid bench.

"I don't like this place," I mumble although I know it's no use as he pulls open the door. I keep my head down, making sure that my hair is covering most of my face. I take a peek at my surroundings and instead of the usual mostly cleared floor, there are tables spread everywhere and the lights are turned up. My eyes find the door Grey and I went through, and I clench my fists. Aaron suddenly stops and I run into his back. I still keep my head down.

"Table for two?" a familiar voice asks, and I squeeze my eyes shut in frustration. I peek up and the bartender guy is giving me a sly smirk. *I need to leave.* I follow the sight of Aaron's back to our table and thankfully, we're in a back corner and not out in the middle of everything. He places our menus on the table in front of us.

"I'll be back in a minute to get your drinks," he smiles before walking away. Slowly might I add. Maybe I'm overreacting. Grey probably isn't even here. He owns the place, he can go do whatever he wants, whenever he wants.

"What's wrong with you?" Aaron's amused voice questions after noticing my head which is still down.

"I've had to sneeze for ten minutes, I don't want to look at the lights and it slip out," I tell him expertly to which he just shakes his head.

"I gotta take a piss," I scrunch my nose at him, "I'll be back Azzy, order me a lemonade." I put my face in my hands and hold back from screaming into them. I can't catch a break.

"Do you want another moonshine?" bartender dude's voice scares the daylights out of me. I shake the table when I jump in fright and the salt and pepper shakers fall to their sides.

"Yep, white lighting this time," I joke, picking the shakers back up. He takes a seat in Aaron's seat.

"Grey's not here," his lips take on a little bit of a teasing smile.

"Well, I'm glad he's not..." I look at the nametag that sits on his black shirt.

"Jai," I pronounce the differently spelled word as 'Jye.' He chuckles.

"Jai," he pronounces his own name as 'Jay.'

"I couldn't give a crap if he was here *Jai*," I almost pronounce his name incorrectly on purpose just to be petty.

"Tell him when you see him next time that he can eat dirt and belly flop on the cement," I cross my arms.

"Are you sure you want me to do tha-"

"No, don't tell him I said that, are you crazy?" I scoff.

"I'm incapable of running away, so no," I add, he laughs, shaking his head and crinkling his nose.

"You're cute," he sits his cheek on his hand, "what do you want to drink?"

"Water. And he wants lemonade," I motion to where Jai sits.

"Who is that anyway?" he asks. My dog's boyfriend's cousin's aunt.

"He's a friend, I guess," I shrug.

"You guess?" his eyebrows raise. Well, it's not confirmed if he's my friend or not, don't judge me bud. Aaron returns to our table and Jai stands up with an apology for taking his seat.

"I'll go get your drinks," he leaves with his order pad in his hand like he actually wrote down what I ordered.

"He seemed friendly," Aaron speaks up as Jai goes to get our drinks.

"Do you know him or something?" He adds. If I were to tell him that I know him because I asked him for an alcoholic beverage, he would have a heart attack, followed by a scold, followed by another heart attack.

"He's my hooker." Aaron and I both go quiet after what flew out of my mouth.

"God you're wild," he chuckles, and Jai returns with our drinks in hand. Jai bends down at my end of the table.

"I know you apparently don't want to hear this but, Grey'll be back pretty soon-"

I'm going to throw a tantrum here in front of God and everybody.

"Can I have a salad? But not one of those ones with that *kale* stuff, y'know what I mean? I don't want lettuce either, lettuce, especially Iceberg Lettuce makes me sick. So, like a spinach salad is good, if you have it. Oh! And ranch, *a lot* of ranch. I don't even like salad that much," I ramble out, trying to get my mind away from thinking of *Grey*. And I want to get out of here before Grey gets back.

"Aaron, order. What do you want?" I usher him, biting my bottom lip anxiously.

"Azzy, I haven't looked at the menu-"

"He'll take some chicken or something," I pick up his menu and mine, handing them to Jai who's trying to contain his smile. He walks off and I meet the eyes of Aaron.

"What's got you in a rush?" He grabs both of my hands in his worriedly.

"I have church to attend," I stay classy with my response, for once in my life. I was thinking of telling him I had to poop but that wouldn't make sense because there's a bathroom here.

"On a Thursday afternoon?"

"Yes, I hold my own service in my car," I nod.

"I'm a child of God," I add, giving him an innocent smile.

"Then you can have it anytime, right? Since *you* run the service?" He teases.

"Listen, God is a busy man, okay?" I start.

"He and I have a schedule," I sat with finality in my tone. We wait. I look out the window nervously for any signs of a jerk. Or shall I say *the* jerk. Part of me would love to see him and give him a big ole piece of my mind. The other part of me wants to pee my pants at the thought of his dark eyes looking at me so maliciously, as they do every time he sees me. *How long does it take to put some spinach in a bowl?*

"How're your parents?"

"*Wonderful,*" I try and keep my voice as strong as I can. I'm *so* tense. I feel like I'm waiting for my doom. After a good fifteen minutes, here comes the slow-poke, Jai. He places the salad down in front of me with a lot of ranch. Three little cups of it. Then he gives Aaron his chicken. It's got some sort of seasoning and sauce in it and I frown. I should've got that. I pour all the cups of ranch into my bowl and Aaron shakes his head at me. *I'm about to inhale this food.*

"Want some salad with that ranch?" He teases.

~~~

I tap my foot under the table. I chew on my bottom lip and wait for the world's slowest eater to finish his chicken that's not even that big of a serving.

"I can feel your eyes on me," he smirks, looking away from his food to look at me.

"Aaron, *please,* stop talking and stuff your face," I plead.

"Azzy, I know something is wrong," he puts his fork down.

"Is it because Jake used to come here?" He questions softly and I don't show my shocked reaction. *Did he use to come here?*

"Yeah," I put my head down so he doesn't see the guilt that I'm fully aware is clouding in my eyes. For the next five minutes, he actually does shovel the food into his mouth. Jai soon comes to our table and Aaron being the kind person he is, pays for the both of us. I also forgot that I only had three dollars. And finally, we leave.

I sigh in utter relief as we walk outside. All my stress flutters away and I close my eyes, breathing in the cool air of the afternoon. I go to pull my phone out to check the time only to conclude that it is no longer with me. I stop in my tracks and almost take a seat on the ground to sadly soak in my own defeat.

"Are you okay? Is your knee hurting?" Aaron stops with me.

"I forgot something at the restaurant," I speak softly.

"I can go get it for you," he places his hand on my shoulder and I give him a grateful smile. Until my eyes find the back of Grey Kingston. Right as he's turning a corner, I see him.

"No, no," I assure Aaron quickly, "I'll go get it, don't worry!"

"But your knee-"

I walk away from him, although I feel bad. In the restaurant, there are booths to hide in, out in the open of town square, I can only hide behind Aaron in the predicament I was in. Once I make it back, I slip inside and steer straight to the table Aaron and I were sitting at. I only find that it has since been cleared and cleaned. *These people are quick.* I look around for Jai and I finally see him coming out some doors that most likely lead to the kitchen.

"Jai!" I call out to him and his head snaps to mine. A little smile crosses his lips and I finally make my way over to him.

"I left my phone here; did you see it or pick it up maybe?" I question, fidgeting with my fingers. Any second now Grey is going to walk through that door, and I cannot stress enough about the fact that I can't physically run away.

"I've got it here for you," he smiles, walking over to the same counter where I asked him for moonshine, which feels like forever ago. He sits the appetizer in his hand down before reaching in the front of his black waist apron. My familiar lilac-colored phone case comes into view, and I sigh a little in relief. At least no one stole it.

"You better hurry before he gets here-" he cuts himself off.

"What happened anyway? After you left, he was a dick," his nose flares as he remembers what Grey must've been like after he told me what he told me. I love the way he talks about his boss.

"He was a male re-productive part *before* I left," I grumble, and he barks out a laugh. I turn and look out the window near the front. The coast is clear, I better go now.

"I'll see you later, Jai," I give him a little wave, "oh! Thank you for keeping my phone for me!"

"Of course," he picks up the appetizer thing and I start to feel bad again. What if the poor people's food got cold because of me? I push the door open right as someone else is pulling it open from the other side. A strong person at that, I almost go flying. Not only do I almost fly, but I crash right into the freakin' Hulk. A familiar and unfortunately extremely wonderful scent hits my nose, but it's gone when I ricochet off the chest. I brace myself for the fall and make sure to keep my injured knee straight. I hit my butt on the step right outside the entrance and it's going to leave a hefty bruise.

   My hair flies around my face and I'm actually glad that it covers my face.

   "Shi-i-i-i-t," a voice drawls out, but it isn't Grey's. *There are more people. Am I okay? No.* I move my hair out of my face, needing to see. Scared to look at the scene in front of me, I just raise my palm, which caught my fall. Unsurprisingly, it's scraped. I look up to see not only Grey but a group of about five or six men. And they're all *not only* looking at me but *directly* at my skirt.

   I look down to see how far it has risen to my upper thighs. My cheeks flush and I feel the need to slam my head into the concrete. The next thing I know, I'm lifted directly up by my underarms like a child. I fix my skirt immediately once he sets me down on my feet. I look up to glare at Grey only to see him scowling darkly at the group of guys. I'm sucked into a trance looking at his face for the first time in over two weeks. His jaw clenches harshly.

   "Excuse you," I gather my courage and push past his large frame. I don't get very far. His large hand grabs my arm and I feel my eyes narrow. Pulling me back to him, my eyes connect with that one guy who walked in on Grey kissing me. What's-his-face gives me a knowing smirk and if Grey wasn't holding onto me, I would've slapped him silly.

   "Inside," Grey nearly growls out and the guys begin filing in. I try to follow them but once again, I'm held back by Mr. Brat. Once the door closes, Grey pulls me away to a more desolate place, still near the restaurant. I try to keep my place though. Key word, try.

   "Grey," I huff out, "let go of me."

   He doesn't say anything, and I find myself getting frustrated.

   "What are you doing here?" he all but sneers and I try to ignore the sharp pain that travels through my chest.

"Leave me alone," I turn to walk away from him but he grabs the waist of my skirt, pulling me back.

"Don't fucking walk away from me," he growls out, his hand still resting against the waistband of my skirt. I'm going to punch his nose off. I *hate* myself for liking his touch. I glare up at him as darkly as I possibly can.

Chapter Nine

Friends

❀Azalea❀

"Don't look at me like that," he glares darkly right back at me.

"Where'd this confidence come from?" he questions darkly, "you didn't have it a few weeks ago."

My facade crumbles. As so do my big girl britches. He *knew* what he did hurt me. I go to walk away from him again. I'd hate it if he saw the tears gathering in my eyes. He already thinks bad enough about me.

"I told you-" he starts angrily but I cut him off, jerking my arm away from his as hard as I can at the moment.

"I don't care what you told me," my voice turns shaky.

"Lilah-" I cut him off again, turning around to shove my finger right in that stupid gorgeous face of his, not caring anymore if he sees the new tears slowly rolling down my cheeks. *What happened to me never crying in front of people?*

"Don't call me that," I let my voice waver.

"I can call you whatever the fuck I want," he keeps his eyes away from me, not looking at me once. I don't even have to worry about him seeing me crying. He's not even looking at me.

"I can too," I'll probably regret this later.

"You jerk," his darkly glaring eyes snap to mine only to soften a bit when they see me. Like I care.

"You're mean, you're rude, you don't care about anything, you only think about yourself, you have no manners, you-" he cuts me off jerking me to him softly.

"Shut *up*," his voice rumbles against me.

"You don't think before you speak, and you have no idea how your words affect other people," I begin to cry harder, shaking my head.

"You're *cruel.*"

"I wish you weren't so mean," I finally let out a sob. He crushes my face to his chest, his strong arms holding me impossibly close to his warm body. With all the feelings taking over my body I sob into the chest of the man who has made me feel this way. When the words I spoke to him finally register, I regret them. I was mean. No one should be talked to like I just talked to him. That thought only makes me continue to cry.

He smells so good. That makes me cry. He's holding me. That makes me cry. He's mean to me. That makes me cry.

A good little while passes with me just crying into him while he holds me to his chest. But then he pulls me away from him. With softer eyes than I'd ever seen but his eyebrows still pulled together, he wipes the tears from my face.

"Don't cry over me," he speaks in a tone softer than I've heard from him ever before.

"Don't make me," I reply softly, my heart still in pain. His hand goes to my hair, it drifts through my locks before lightly grabbing it and tilting my head up to his.

"*I don't know how to be good to you,*" he finishes and my heart falls.

"I grew up with no mother. No sisters, no grandmother, no aunts," he starts, his dark eyes fixed on my green ones.

"No one was there to tell me how to do it," his other hand brushes against my shoulder blade. *What about his dad?*

"But I never did anything to you," I whisper. I hate to make myself seem full of myself, but I don't think I deserved this.

"I know," his head falls downward and I find myself wanting to keep seeing those eyes of his.

"You shouldn't have acted like you wanted to kiss me if you actually didn't," I tell him. More like a scold but he deserves it I guess. His eyes raise back to mine.

"I wanted to," his voice remains quiet as if someone could hear us if he talked too loudly. There wasn't really anyone around. The hand not in my hand comes to rest on the side of my neck, his thumb brushing against my jaw. *I can't do this again.*

"Grey," I allow my hand to reach up to him. I gently pull it away from me, a little shake to my head. I look up to see his jaw clenched a bit. Nowhere near how it usually is. We're getting somewhere.

"I-I can't do that," I say softly. *Please don't let this backfire on me.*

"Friends?" I question trying to keep the hesitancy out of my voice. He slowly takes his hand out of my hair. The same hand grabs onto the hair tie on my wrist. He fiddles with it, keeping his eyes downcast. He better not think I've forgiven him. I have not. *God, he looks so cute.* His jaw clenches twice like he's holding back from saying something. I think we're definitely getting somewhere.

"Friends," he utters as if tasting the word on his tongue. Then, his eyes come back up and meet mine. He lets out a little sigh looking between both of my eyes. I give him a little nod. His jaw clenches once more.

"Alright," he finally agrees, and a small smile lights up my face. We can be *friends*. No romantic things. No romantic thoughts. No romantic gestures. And if everything goes okay, perhaps I can teach him what he never was taught.

"Hello!" I greet and his eyebrows furrow in a cute, confused face. Stop, no romantic thoughts.

"I'm Azalea!" I smile.

"Azalea..." he drawls out, waiting for the rest of my name, now understanding that we're starting over. A second chance.

"Azalea Delilah Carson," I fill in for him.

"Lilah," he decides, just as the first time. Although, it was in a much nicer tone this time. And there was no glare. I can definitely deal with this.

"What's your name?"

"Grey," he says shortly, his eyes not acting as if we're strangers. He can't keep his gosh darn eyes off my legs.

"My legs don't have eyes, Grey," I remind him and his eyes snap to mine angrily before they simmer down.

"They're looking at me," he mutters under his breath, I guess forgetting that we're supposed to not know each other.

"You can't-" he cuts me off. 'You can't say that when they don't have eyes' went down the drain.

"It rose to the fuckin' heavens and the guys saw it," his voice turns dark, but I have a hard time figuring out if it's toward me or *the guys*.

"Free show, amirite?"

"Not funny," he grumbles, gripping onto the top of my waistband. I've decided that a grumbly-Grey is just his personality.

"Friends," I remind him softly and he lets out a harsh sigh releasing my waistband in a more than touchy way, dragging his hands along my waist. He opens his mouth to say something only to be closed a second later as he finds something over my shoulder.

"Azalea Carson! What the hell?" Aaron's voice fills my ears, and my eyes widen a bit. I forgot about him. *I left him waiting, didn't I?*

"Who's this?" he questions as he nears Grey and me, his eyes taking on a slightly widened state as they peer at the man beside me.

"Who the fuck's that?" Grey questions down to me although his scowl stays on Aaron.

"Aaron, this is my friend Grey," I hear Grey's knuckles crack as he clenches his fist. Holy cow.

"Grey," I grab his clenched fist and place it behind me so that Aaron can't see it. God knows he'd freak and probably call the police or something.

"This is my friend Aaron," I look between both guys. Aaron's eyes are narrowed at Grey and Grey, well, of course, he's glaring at him. The fist behind me unclenches and grips onto the back of my shirt as if it acts as some sort of calming solution. The two don't say anything. They're sizing each other up. Losers. If I was Aaron, I would be extra friendly to the large man beside me. It's quite obvious the size difference between the two. Aaron may be fit but Grey is one heck of a *man*.

"Um," I break the silence.

"I should head on back to-"

"I haven't seen you around here," Aaron chides. He grew up here, he knows a lot of people.

"I haven't been around here," his deep voice grumbles from beside me. We've got a Knoxville boy over here.

"Is that so?" Aaron asks like he's some sort of FBI interrogator. Excuse me, Aaron, I'm the one with the qualifications here, not you. Why so suspicious all of a sudden, anyway? I can feel that Grey doesn't like Aaron's words by the way he releases my shirt before grabbing a bigger bunch of it and leaning closer to me.

"What's your fuckin' deal?" I look up to Grey as he scowls darkly at Aaron. Aaron raises his arms in surrender.

"We should head back to the store," I interrupt them. Gosh, these two are stressing me the heck out. I walk out of Grey's grip and toward Aaron. I turn back to him.

"Goodbye, Grey," I tell him softly before grabbing Aaron's arm and pulling him with me.

"I trust that guy as far as I can throw him," Aaron lets out as we walk back to my car.

"That's not very far," I laugh, "he's a lot bigger than you!"

"That hurt my ego a bit, don't say it again," he grumbles back.

"There's no reason to 'not trust him.' You don't even know him enough to decide that," I shake my head at him.

"He's a dickhead."

What, can he just see that through Grey's stance or something? He's spoken two sentences to him.

"I've already established that he's one of those, but you haven't so don't judge," I point my finger out and he lets out a defeated sigh.

~~~

* Grey *

I slam open the door to the bar. People look my way, but I shrug them off. I push open the door to the back and walk down the hallway. At the last door, I push it open.

"Bossman, did you just have a quickie?" Jonas smirks my way from his seat on the brown leather couch. I grab him by the front of his shirt, lifting him to me.

"Fuck off 'fore your nose gets broken," I sneer, and he backs down. Fucking idiot. I release his shirt and he sinks back into the couch. Just the thought of them seeing anywhere near under her skirt makes me want to knock them all the fuck out.

"What's got you all riled up?" Maxon inquires, his blue eyes glistening like he already knows the answer. I ignore them. *She's got me fucking riled up.*

"Aaron," I say suddenly, "did Jake ever say anything about an Aaron?"

They look down at the mention of his name. He was one of us.

"His best friend," Theo speaks up, "he was his best friend."

Fuck. My hands fidget like they always fucking do when I'm stressed. Lilah's face flashes through my mind. I shouldn't want to do the things I want to do to her. Like hell, I could be friends with her. Not even five minutes after she said we can only be friends, my hands couldn't stay away from that waist of hers.

Kissing her once has given me a feel of what I could have. It was a mistake getting so close to her, I know that. Kissing her and holding her like I was put dreams in my head that shouldn't be there. I shouldn't be glad that they're there but I am. After that little taste, I felt like I could never be away from her. The way her hands held onto me I could've stayed there forever.

She's too good for me. She's *sweet*. But I can't stay away. I'm drawn to her. Every time I see that damn store, I have to see her. She's got a smart mouth, she annoys the shit out of me, and she's wild but fuck if she hasn't grown on me. It's bad that she's Jake's little sister. And it's even worse that she doesn't know how he was involved with us. Jake made sure no one went near his baby sister. She was off-limits even though none of us had ever seen her.

Except for me. I was the only fucking one that he ever showed a picture of her to and now I can't quit imagining what she'd look like naked. *Fuck me. I wish she would just get this childish crush over with.* Because that's all it is. Anyway, I just can't treat her right. I don't fucking know how. That's what comes with having a shitty father and a nonexistent mother.

"I can't do this anymore," Jai comes into the room dragging his hands through his hair and down his face.

"I hate taking orders, I hate handing people food, I don't like the way people treat waiters like shit, Grey, get someone else to do it, I can't anymore," he breathes out. I tilt my head back and look at him.

"Suck it up," Jonas starts until I stop him.

"Jonas," I grumble, and he turns toward me. I nod my head to Jai who lets out a loud laugh.

"Are you kidding me?" Jonas questions, his mouth open wide.

"I'm not a people person," he adds, and I feel my teeth grit together.

"Get the fuck out there before I *put* you out there after beating your ass," I glare at him and he stands and yanks the notepad from Jai.

"Have fun buddy," Jai calls out as Jonas leaves. I hate this fucking restaurant but it's a nice undercover base.

"What time are we leaving?" Jai asks. I look up at the clock on the wall.

"Now," I watch as the clock hits five. We all rise from our seats.

"Do you think he'll give up at a million?" Theo questions, tucking a pistol in the back of his pants. I pick up the file on the coffee table in front of me.

Lilah   *K. Pope*

<u>David Anthony Morris</u>
Documentation from the Federal Bureau of Investigation
DOB - 8/14/76
Birthplace - Griffin, Georgia
Sex – Male
Height - 5'10
Eyes – Brown
Previous Criminal Offenses - Two Counts of Assault and battery, Three Counts of Statutory Rape, Two Counts of Kidnap, and One Count of Domestic Abuse.
Reported Offenses - Human Trafficking
Location of Warehouse - 359 Marly Lane, Greer, Tennessee
Relatives - Ex-wife, Marina Carnite

Fucking psycho. I give Theo a shrug and we continue loading up.

"You guys seriously are going to leave me here by myself?" Jonas questions as we walk out to the main floor.

"George and the chefs are still here," Jai points to the kitchen and Jonas glares at his big brother.

"You'll get in on the next one," Roman looks around the place, his calculating eyes searching for anything out of the ordinary. At the coat rack in the closet near the door, Jai passes out the padded leather jackets. He hands one out to me but as usual, I refuse.

"One of these days you're going to regret not putting one of those on," Jai sighs, and I glare at his head as he pulls on the jacket. If they really wanted to kill me, they'd shoot me in the head.

~~~

I lean against the outside wall of the warehouse as the guys spread out as they're supposed to. Jai takes his place to the right of me at the entrance.

"You look like a fuckin' idiot," I grumble at him as he places a pair of sunglasses on his nose. It's fucking dark outside.

"No, I look official," he argues before knocking loudly on the door. I lean my head back against the wall and let out a sigh. I hope one of these motherfuckers tries me. My fist has been itching to punch somebody. After a minute, the door swings open.

"Who the hell are you?" a gravelly voice questions and I can only imagine him to be David Morris.

"We've come to make you an offer," Jai says smoothly, which is exactly why he's constantly put in the negotiating position of what we do.

"We?" he questions, and I push myself off the wall. I stop at the edge of the doorway, slightly leaning into it. David takes a step back.

"I'll give you a million for the property," I take a look inside, over his shoulder. Half-naked women lay on and around men. They look scared for their fucking lives. I look back at David and try to keep my face emotionless. This motherfucker deserves to die.

"And everything that comes with it," I add.

"A million?" he questions, looking surprised to hear it.

"A million," Jai nods, "cash if you want."

"You want in on the trafficking world?" David smiles and I grit my teeth. My knuckles crack at how hard they're balled in a fist.

"We definitely want in," Jai smirks before holding out his hand, "Michael Jackson."

Fucking dumbass.

"Michael Jackson?" David asks, shaking Jai's hand.

"My parents named me after him," he replies coolly, and David looks over at me.

"That's Cruz Marshall," Jai answers and I send him a harsh glare.

"David Morris," he extends his hand toward me. I only glance at it before returning my gaze to his face. I don't shake hands with fucking rapists.

"He's a germaphobe," Jai explains and as soon as we're done with this bust, I'm breaking his fucking nose.

"Oh that's alright," David waves it off, his long greasy hair shaking as he does, "why don't you come inside and look around while I consider your offer?"

"We would love to," Jai smiles as the plan executes itself easily. Jai enters first and I follow. The smell of weed and even a hint of the awful chemical smell of burning cocaine hits my nose. Walking through the main floor I look around at everything and everyone. Counting, finding exits, windows, doors, everything. I hear a crunch under my foot. I stop in my tracks and look down and the crushed meth pipe.

"Hey man," a slurred voice calls out to the left of me. I turn my glare to him.

"You crushed my pipe," the man calls out, quieter this time. I look at the girl on his lap. She can't be older than fourteen. Jai walks back beside me. He sees my stare on the two.

"We'll come back to him," he assures knowing damn well that I'm fixing to throw our whole bust away because of one guy. I shake the thoughts away and continue through the main floor.

"How many girls do you have?" Jai questions. I've counted thirteen only in this room.

"Thirty in total," he answers proudly, "but tomorrow we're getting a 'shipment' of about ten more."

He leads us into another room. He shuts the door behind us and my senses heighten.

"This place is nice," Jai lies through his teeth.

"Only the best for the bitches," David chuckles, turning. My hands itch to wrap themselves around his neck. He opens one more door and a dimly lit room is on the other side. Jai walks in first and I follow. Hardly a second after entering, he comes to a sudden halt. He turns around quickly to me, and a look takes onto his face. He's furious.

"Fucking get him," he tells me quietly, and usually, I'd beat his ass for telling me what to do but with the look on his face, I understand. Feeling David's presence right behind me, I send an elbow to the side of his head. He falls into the wall and before he can yell out to the stoned guys in the main room, my fist connects with the center of his face. I feel his nose crack under my knuckles, and he falls to the floor. I barely hear Jai call the guys in with the radio too busy beating this sick motherfucker's face in. Before he dies, unfortunately, I pull him up, shoving him against the wall. Jai tosses me the cuffs and I crank them onto his wrists as tight as they'll go before letting him fall back to the ground.

"Grey, come help me with her," Jai calls out and I finally get a look at what had him so fucked up. A naked child lays with her hands and feet wired to a bed. I avert my eyes immediately and I wish, I fucking *wish* I could kill that motherfucker. Both Jai and I untwist the wires holding her wrists in place, followed by her feet. Jai quickly takes off his jacket, followed by his sweatshirt. He gives his sweatshirt to the girl, and she puts it on.

"Thank you," she cries, "are you going to help me?"

"We're here to help you," Jai helps her stand and she does so shakily, the sweatshirt falling down to her knees.

"We work with the F.B.I," he explains, knowing it's easier than telling her exactly what we do. We're *not* the F.B.I. We're an independent organization. They pay us for the jobs we do for them, and we get the full percentage and ownership of the properties from the criminals we bust. Great fucking pay.

"How old are you?" he questions, helping her to the door. She wipes her tears and sniffles.

"Twelve."

"Fucking hell," I send David's body a strong kick, most likely breaking a couple of his ribs.

"He-He almost touched me," she explains, "but someone knocked on the big door before he did."

"Did anyone else try to touch you?" he questions and she shakes her head.

"He told them not to," she whispers, "he said he wanted me for himself."

This fucking kid is going to be terrified and scarred for the rest of her life. He opens the door we came in and I grab David's foot, dragging him behind us. We make it back to the main floor and every guy is cuffed and sitting against a wall. I count only fifteen guys. There were sixteen. I drop David's leg and walk to one of the guys that looks the least stoned or drunk. I bend to his level.

"Where the fuck is he?" I question darkly.

"Who?" the guy questions back but I can see in his eyes that he knows exactly what I'm talking about.

"Don't fucking play with me," I press my fist into his sternum and his eyes widen in pain. He throws his head forward and he headbutts me, his forehead only connecting with my bottom lip. I spit the blood out and sneer at him.

"He went to a backroom before all your fucking pigs came in here," he answers and I rise.

"Shut him up," I tell Roman who smirks, and I go to find the sixteenth guy. I find him in a room at the end of a long hallway, the door cracked open, a girl on his lap, and his back faced toward me. I stalk toward him, and the girl sees me. This one is older than the last two and she's actually got clothes on. Her eyes turn wide in fear, and I shake my head at her mouthing an 'I won't hurt you'. I begrudgingly take the gun out of the back of my pants. I like to use my fists but whatever. I press it against the back of his head, and he freezes. I click off the safety and he hears it.

"Hands off," I tell him, and he raises his hands from her. She runs off as soon as he does.

"Stand up," I growl at him, and he does. I see him grab something to the side of him and I internally let out a sigh. He turns and points the gun at me. I tilt my head a bit. He can't be older than eighteen.

"Put it down, kid," I tell him gruffly. A kill is a lot of fucking paperwork. He clicks the safety off his own gun, and I roll my eyes. I lower my gun, I grab onto the end of his, and I send my knee up to his elbow, breaking his arm and he drops the gun in my hand. He lets out loud shouts in pain and I grit my teeth at the dramatic loud noise. I drag him harshly back into the main room and Maxon cuffs him as a few of my other guys bring in the remainder of the girls from isolated rooms. I count all thirty. The guys begin the protocol on each of the girls. I find the closest one to me.

"Name?" I ask her as Jai hands me a report to write her information down on.

"Anna Terri," she whispers, still obviously scared to death.

"Date of birth?" I finish writing her name and look up at her.

"10/11/03," she says, and I grip the pen harshly. She's fifteen for fucks sake, what the fuck is wrong with these motherfuckers?

"Birthplace?"

"Chicago," she says, and hope fills her eyes as she realizes she's going to go home. This is going to be a long night.

Chapter Ten

Hugs

❀Azalea❀

    I'm seriously considering becoming a stripper. Very seriously. But without actually stripping, I would get one of those shirts that has a really fit body printed on it. It's a win-win-win. Win 1) I get paid as much as a regular stripper. Win 2) I don't actually have to show off my body (thank goodness because it's nothing to really see and I probably wouldn't get much money). Win 3) I can literally dance all day.

    On the downside, I have little to no arm strength so I may have to stay off the poles. What am I even saying? At twelve in the afternoon, I'm walking through the town square. Usually, if Grey comes to see me, it's around eleven or so but today he didn't show up. So, I figured I can go to his restaurant or whatever, maybe see him, and I could get some food if I wanted with the money Aaron gave me. Two hundred whole dollars. I told him that I didn't want to take his money, but he insisted, and I can't turn down money like that so I took it.

    He's like my sugar daddy. Never mind. After getting myself a caramel iced coffee, I turn down Red Street. I open the door to Grey's bar and instead of seeing my favorite waiter, I see another one. He's leaned against a small counter where the menus are stacked, and the cash register sits in front of him. He looks quite unhappy.

"Can I help you?" he mumbles like he doesn't really want to help me. I'm sure that's not very good for Grey's business.

"Can I have a table for one? Or like a table for two I guess since I don't think there's such a thing as a table for one," I ramble a tad bit before realizing that the guy that walked in on Grey and me kissing. Isn't that just fun? He grabs a menu and hands it to me. My eyebrows furrow a bit and with the wave of his hand, he tells me to go sit wherever. I giggle a little bit at how much he obviously hates what he's doing. I find a table for two and sit on one side of it opening up my menu. Oh my gosh, they have waffles. I shimmy in my seat excitedly and crack my thumbs when I make a fist. It takes a while for the waiter guy to get to my table. A good thirty minutes actually. Good thing I'm not that hungry or he'd have to be hustling more than that.

"Drink?" he mumbles.

"Sweet tea, please," I tell him, and he shuffles away. A good ten minutes later, he comes back to take my order, still not have given me my drink.

"Belgian Waffles," I smile, "with syrup!"

He shuffles away once more. I'm not too sure if he even wrote down my order. Forty-five minutes later, I'm given some delicious-looking waffles. No syrup. I'm going to sue. I still never got my drink. I'm going to sue again.

"Here," he throws the bill down on my table. I almost throw it back at his face, but I don't. Thirty dollars?! I don't recall getting a gold-plated waffle. I look down at the bill and see that there's a cheeseburger, fries, and chicken on it. I go up to the cash register to pay.

"My bill isn't right," I tell him, and he looks at me as if he doesn't care. I pay the thirty dollars, figuring that I can just treat a family and they can treat me to my waffles. Guess who's not getting a tip?

"No tip?" I watch as he rolls his eyes. My eyebrows raise.

"Maybe if I would've got my sweet tea, I would give you one," I give him a little nasty smile.

"Bitch," he mumbles as my actual favorite waiter comes up beside him.

"Wouldn't call her that if I were you," he slaps him on the back. Dang right, Jai knows how dangerous I am.

"He sucks by the way," I point at whoever the heck that guy is.

"You swallow," he narrows his blue eyes at me. Wow, what are we? Eight years old. And for his information, yes. Yes, I do swallow my food.

"Well, you know what? I hope you fall off your high horse and break your *little* butt. You don't even have a butt. It's nonexistent, I hope you know that" I narrow my eyes right back at him.

"I hope you know that you have *no* boobs," he crosses his arms over his chest. *Excuse me? I have a strong C-cup. Almost a D. He's just being a brat. Am I going to go there? I certainly am.*

"Your peepee is tiny." Jai breaks into a fit of chuckles but me and the crappy waiter fella just stay in our stare-off. The waiter guy shoves his order notepad into Jai's chest before walking through the door to the back. *That's right, walk away.*

"He deserved that," Jai chuckles and I nod. I know.

"He's my brother," he adds and I visibly wince.

"You poor soul. If you'd like me to come any time to put him in his place, I will," I assure him.

"Do you want to see Grey this time? Are you two better?"

"We're friends now," I nod and his eyebrows raise.

"Friends, huh?" he questions a little tease in his voice.

"Yep," I nod.

"Go through the door to the back, then go through the door at the end of that room, follow the hallway and go in the first door on the right," he says and I blink. I lost concentration when he said door for the second time.

"Yeah, okay," I smile, picking up my half-drunken coffee. I walk through the door and then through another door, the only other door I saw and then I come to a hallway. I stand there for a good five minutes. I try the first door on the left. It's a closet with nothing in it. I try the first door on the right. I see Grey.

  His eyes dart up to mine and I give him a little smile walking more in the room. He sits behind a pretty big wooden desk with an iMac on top of it. Once upon a time, I wanted one of those. I looked at the price and nearly had the biggest heart attack ever recorded. The rest of his desk is filled with paperwork and a coffee cup.

  "Hi, Grey," I close the door behind me. I watch as his eyes run over my attire. A pair of shorts and an off-the-shoulder light blue top, paired with my *gorgeous* leg brace that I love *so* much. I take a seat in the chair in front of his desk. He sits his chin in his hand, his eyes trying to keep themselves open. I smile softly at him.

  "Are you tired? You look a little tired," I question, a little tilt to my head. I walk forward and hold my coffee out to him.

  "I drank quite a bit of it, but you can have the rest. Or I can go get you some," I stop by his desk, and he turns in his wheely chair toward me. I feel like he might yell at me if I suddenly start spinning him in it. My eyes zero in on a cut on his lip. A pretty big one. I gasp, getting closer.

  "What happened to you? Does it hurt? Did you get jumped?" I grab my heart. Oh God, he did, didn't he?

  "The fuck are you talking about?" he grumbles. I set my cup on his desk and go closer to him, bending at my waist. I grab his face and tilt it up to me. I get a good look at his lip. It's busted which tells me that he got it by blunt force trauma. *I watch way too many episodes of Cops.* I run my finger over the cut on his bottom lip lightly before realizing that I'm just holding his face. I feel my cheeks heat up, but I keep my cool. His dark eyes look up at me and I'm surprised to see that he's not glaring. He's just looking. Holy mackerel, did my talk with him yesterday actually work? I'm sure it's because we talked about this yesterday and now, he's realized that he's been mean.

  "I got headbutted," he answers quietly, and I feel my eyes narrow. Aren't you supposed to headbutt somebody on their forehead, not their lip? What a can't-get-right.

  "Where are they?" I question, fired up.

  "They're about to get got," I assure him, and his lips pull up into the most gorgeous smirk I've ever seen in my whole entire life.

"Here, here," I pick up my coffee again, holding it out to him.

"I'm not drinking that shit," he scowls at it. I'm offended at the way he looks at it. And I'm sure teenage girls everywhere would be too.

"Why not?"

"What's that shit?" he reuses the curse word, pointing to the caramel in the side of the cup. *Dirt that I mixed together and then put in my cup.* Getting tired of standing, I drag the chair in front of his desk to right beside his. I sit down and hold the cup out to him again.

"It's only caramel," I giggle and his eyes dart back to mine.

"You don't want it?" he questions, and I shake my head. Finally, he takes it. I watch his lips as he takes a sip, gauging his reaction. He doesn't say anything, but he keeps drinking. I knew he'd like it.

"Your chefs make really good waffles," I say out of the blue as he picks up a pen and begins writing more on what looks like a form or something.

"Your waiter fella out there got me so fired up you don't even know. He never gave me my sweet tea. *And* he had the *audacity*," I speak every syllable of the last word.

"To say that I had no boobs."

He turns back to me. I watch as his eyes fall on my chesticles. After quite a while of him just looking at them, his eyes find mine again. He raises a single eyebrow.

"He lied."

My heart flutters and I nearly fan myself.

"Why was he looking?" his head tilts, and I notice how his fingers crack when he balls them into fists.

"You've got me on that," I shrug, "he's probably just looking at what he could never have."

"Damn right," he mutters, his eyes lighter than before.

"I told him he had a small peepee," I hold my chin up proudly. The corners of his mouth rise. *I made him smile a little.* I feel my heart swell. He leans forward, cutting my thoughts off by grabbing both armrests of my chair and dragging me until I'm right in front of him.

"Next time come get me," he grumbles lowly, and I nod, my eyes set in on his lips. No romantic thoughts. He pulls my chair even closer before his arms wrap around my waist pulling me to the edge of my chair.

"Friends, Grey," I whisper.

"Do you always stare at your friends' lips?" he questions back and my eyes dart to his dark ones. *My imaginary friends don't even have lips. They talk with their feet.*

"Y-Yes," I stutter, and his eyes darken as his eyebrows furrow into a little scowl. His jaw clenches and I figure that the answer I gave him was not one he wanted to hear. His tattooed hand comes to rest on my cheek. He leans closer to me and my eyes flutter as he presses his lips against the opposite cheek, his hand pressing my face closer to his lips. He pulls away and looks at me.

"Was that good?" he questions genuinely. I give him a soft smile. He's actually sweet when he's not glaring at me. Gathering my courage, I straighten my torso and lean up to him. I place my hand on his cheek, just as he did to me. I press my lip against his opposite cheek, pushing his face closer to my lips with my hand. Good gosh he smells like heaven. My heart speeds up as I pull away and meet his eyes.

"Was that okay?" I question him and hardly any time passes before he's nodding, his eyes trained on my lips. He moves his knee, and it bumps into mine, jerking it more than it has been moved in a while. I let out a little hiss.

"Fuck," he mumbles.

"It's okay," I assure him, but his eyebrows are still drawn together. His jaw clenches and I realize how hard he is on himself. I also realize that he used to do that really, really often. Especially when he would snap at me and I'd get upset. He really *doesn't* know how to do this. Does he *want* me to kiss his cheek again? Because I definitely will in order to get his mind off of things. Am I a horn-dog? For him, I guess I am.

"Do you like hugs?" I only slightly curse my blabbermouth. He opens his mouth only to close it a second later.

"Hm?" I hum after he doesn't answer.

"I don't know," he answers, his eyes softening. My heart turns heavy. He doesn't know. We're about to find out. I have to hold back from wiggling in my seat excitedly. I stand, grabbing onto him and pulling him up with me. Standing it is. He stands tensely in front of me. Poor thing.

"Relax," I say softly, placing my hands on his shoulders and slowly dragging them down his arms. He relaxes and I can hardly catch my breath at feeling his muscles on my fingertips. His hands come around my waist before dropping very close to my behind. I gasp.

"Not friendly," my voice raises an octave. His hands raise themselves back up and I calm my wildly beating heart. I liked it but I shouldn't have.

"Do you know what friendly things are?" I question because I genuinely think that he doesn't.

"Not around you," he grumbles, and I suck in a breath. I fully step away from him to set up the hugging plan. He's taller than me by *quite* a bit. I raise my arms and go in for the kill.

"Bend down, please," I murmur so that I can reach around his neck like I need to, unable to stand on my tippy toes. He bends a little at the waist. Noticing his arms still down by his sides, I grab his hand and direct it around my torso. His other one follows. He lets out a little huff before standing up straight and just lifting me up as he does it. I let out a surprised squeak as my feet dangle. He holds onto me tightly and I bite my lip to keep the smile off of my face. *I think he needed this. I have to pee.* After a couple of minutes, his arms loosen. One of his hands goes down to the back of my thigh as he lowers me back down carefully. He keeps my injured leg off the ground with his hand until I'm fully standing on my other leg. Then, he lowers my hurt one.

"Did you like that? There's another hug we can try," I tell him. He doesn't answer so I step forward and I wrap my arms around his strong torso in the hug form number two. Holy freaking cow, he's a solid fella. On his own this time, his arms wrap around me. Am I a great teacher or what? I pull away after a little while, he's slightly scowling at me. My eyebrows furrow. Did he not like that one?

"Why are you mad at me?" I question and he better be open with me or I won't hesitate to go through everything I called him yesterday. Jai's brother already got me fired up.

"I'm not," his eyes soften.

"Which one did you like better?"

"The first one," he grabs both of my hands, directing them back around his neck. A small blush heats up my cheeks.

"I wouldn't really try this hug on your guy friends," I advise him.

"I don't think you should try it on another guy either," he grumbles.

"Do you hug your guy friends?" I question, although I feel like I already know the answer. He doesn't necessarily seem like the hugging type. He seems more like the if-you-touch-me-I'll-punch-you-directly-in-your-throat-type. He steps away from me, and he holds out his hand. Confusedly, I take it. He chest bumps me like the typical 'bro shake' and I ricochet off his chest.

"You're too small," he mumbles, and I squint my eyes. Too small my butt, I'll have him know that I'm the perfect fun size.

"You're too big," I grumble back to him, raising my head to see his bottom lip rolled into his mouth. *That's what she said.* Stop. *I have to pee.*

"Is there a bathroom anywhere around here?" I question, lowering my arms from around his neck, his eyebrows lower unhappily at my movements.

"Across the hall," he motions toward the door with a nod of his head.

I open the door and walk out into the hallway, closing the door behind me. I open the door right across from where I am and it's the same closet as before. I open the door beside it and there's a pooper. I commence to tinkling. The bathroom is kind of plain. After doing my business, I wash my hands and open the door. I walk out and the squeaking of shoes brings my attention to the person right at my side. A tall guy stands beside me, looking down at me. He's kind of scary. A scar sits on his forehead and his dark green eyes bore into mine. Aw, his eyes are pretty.

"Sorry," I mumble, getting out of his way. His calculated gaze stays on me. He must be intimidated by me, who wouldn't be? I could intimidate

The Rock.

He walks past me, and I look at his butt. I don't know why I look at everyone's butt but his is pretty nice. A gun sticks out the back of his pants. *Oh, dear Jesus Christ in a handbasket.*

I quickly open the door to Grey's office before the gun guy turns around and sees me seeing his gun. He probably has eyes in the back of his head though. For the first time, I notice a walkie-talkie at the end of his desk.

"Is that a walkie-talkie?" I gasp. Jake and I used to have those when we were little. We would go to opposite ends of the house and talk for hours. We kept them for a long time. When I was sent to my room and not allowed to come out, he would always call me on that to talk. He always made me feel better. I wonder if Grey has it to call the chef whenever he wants to tell him that he wants food. That's something I would totally do. I look up expecting to see Grey sitting at his desk but he's not. I look around the room like caveman SpongeBob and he's not here.

The gun guy had to have kidnapped him. With quite a bit of difficulty though, because Grey is a bit bigger than the gun guy. Then again, he has a *gun* so. I nearly poop my pants when the door behind me suddenly opens. Grey comes into view, and I sigh in relief. Then a sweet tea comes into view as he closes the door behind him. He hands it to me, and I bite my lip to keep from smiling. He got this for me. He was actually listening when I was rambling off?

"Thank you," I say softly, releasing my lip before he sees it. I basically chug the sweet tea. I can feel his eyes on me as I do. He's probably thirsty. I pull my lips away from the glass and catch my breath a bit. His dark eyes find mine.

"Thirsty?" I hold the glass out to him. He averts his gaze from me, closing his eyes, and clenching his amazing jaw. My phone suddenly rings. I haven't heard that thing ring in a good year or so. No one ever calls me. Grey scowls at the source of the loud noise. I hurry and answer.

"Hello! I am calling about your car insurance policy!"

"Hi!" I say, quite frankly excited someone is calling me.

"It seems that your car insurance needs to be upgraded!"

"Does it? I didn't know it could be upgraded," I answer back, and Grey narrows his eyes at me.

"Of course! We only want the best for our customers! Now all I need is your credit card number and everything will be fixed!" She says happily and I wince. Does she even know my name?

"Well, I don't have a credit card-" I'm cut off when Grey grabs my phone from my hands.

"Why don't you fuck off?" He grumbles into the phone before he hangs up on the lady.

"I was having a nice little talk with her," I mumble and he turns to me, "she wanted to upgrade my car insurance."

"The number is from North Dakota."

Maybe that's where my insurance office is.

"I don't know where my car insurance place is," I furrow my eyebrows.

"Are you stupid? It's a fuckin' scam," He growls out and my mood falters. I thought he was getting better.

"I didn't know," I say quietly. How was I supposed to know it was a scam? I never get those calls. *He's right. I am stupid. She didn't even ask for my name.*

"How do you even take care of yourself?" He grumbles, his face set harshly, his jaw locked. I bend, placing my sweet tea on his desk. He watches me with a calculated and slightly confused look as I do. I give him one last unhappy look before I open the door and walk out. *He really was doing well.*

Chapter Eleven

Jake

❀Azalea❀

This morning, I've successfully hidden from Mr. Terrip's sight. I made sure to wear my hair down in front of my face to keep extra precautions in case he did see me. Dad lost his job. So, he drank. And drank. He 'accidentally' pushed the side of my face into the wall. Then he drank more. I hardly slept last night. *I'm not sure how much more of it I can take.* The bruise that sits right on top of my cheekbone was not-so-easily covered by makeup. My foundation is light and not full coverage. Thank goodness I only get pimples rarely. Or hickeys. Why hickeys? I've only had one hickey in my entire life.

Grey. The man who I've decided to not talk to until he gets his stuff straight. But it's not actually like I can keep my big trap shut. A book called *Satan* comes into my view. I didn't know Grey Kingston had a book written about him. I feel utterly terrible for comparing Grey to the Devil. An hour and a half into dusting the top of the tall bookshelves, the bell above the door rings. After a minute I feel a presence behind me.

"You're going to hurt yourself," a low voice mumbles behind me and I sigh. How does he know? Maybe I was a circus balancing act in a past life. I adjust my footing on my ladder and peek down at him a little. He's looking up at me, a sweet tea in his hand. My heart melts a bit, but I suck it up and turn back around. Did he bring that for me? I finish dusting the shelf that nearly reaches the ceiling and now I've got nothing to do up here. What do I do? I dust that boy again.

"How many times are you going to dust it?" he questions, and I figure that if I throw one of my legs back, it could possibly hit him in the face. But then I'd probably fall so I get rid of that thought. I hear him set the tea down in a space on a lower shelf. Then I feel his hand on the side of my thigh. I look down and he's standing right under me, his dark eyes staring up at me. I'm glad I'm not wearing a skirt toda-*I'm wearing a dress.*

"Are you looking at my goodies?" I question down at him, and he doesn't move his eyes from mine as they take on a mischievous glint.

"You want me to?" his thumb rubs against my thigh and I nearly shiver. *I'm supposed mad at him, remember?* I begin climbing down. Struggling a bit due to my leg and he sees that. He grabs me by my waist and places me gently on the ground. I walk away from him, going to dust a short bookshelf that only reaches to my chest. I feel him come up beside me and I let my hair fall, covering my face. My heart begins beating wildly when he wipes it away, tucking it behind my ear. I untuck it and let it fall again. He lets out a harsh sigh.

"Want a milkshake?" he attempts, and I huff, staying quiet although he's making it hard.

"Talk to me," his hand rests on my hip. I move out of his grasp.

"How do I know you won't be mean?" I question quietly, not looking at him. He grabs my arm and pulls me to him gently. I make sure my hair stays in front of my cheekbone just in case.

"You're not stupid," his dark eyes bore into mine, recalling his words yesterday.

"I take care of myself just fine," I murmur, also recalling his words from yesterday.

"I know you do, look at you," his voice takes on a certain tone. Not necessarily a friendly one.

"I'm fashionable ain't I? You like it?" I hold out the bottom of my pale pink sundress, showing him. I notice his bottom lip roll into his mouth. Woah. He gives me a nod and his hands reach to grab me. I grab them before they get to my waist. His jaw ticks as his dark eyes stay fixed on my torso.

"I'm not one of your guy friends," I tell him, leading his hands back down at his own sides. His eyes fall back on mine.

"You're not," he agrees, an emotion swirling in his eyes. It makes me happy that he doesn't hold that emotionless mask up.

"So, you can't just say things that are mean y'know?" I finish. *And you can't kiss other girls in the spot where you kissed me. Or anywhere.*

"I'm trying."

"I know that," I nod. I can see how he's already trying to fix what he did and how he acted before. I mean, he brought me a sweet tea! His hands fidget before they grip onto the tan hair tie around my wrist. I've noticed he does that quite a bit.

"Can-" he cuts himself off, shaking his head as if the thing he was going to say was dumb.

"Hm?" I hum, tilting my head up at him. He looks between both of my eyes. *I want to smack his butt. Stop.*

"C-, hug?" he mumbles, and a smile takes onto my lips. *He's trying.* I wrap my arms around his neck, and he lifts me in a hug. He lowers me after a minute and hands me my sweet tea.

"I left mine on your floor yesterday," I mumble, feeling bad.

"It showed me I was a dick," he mumbles, "to you."

I take a sip of my tea.

"Are you doing anything today?" I question, admittedly quite shyly. I'm a little nervous he may turn on me any time. He shakes his head and I almost laugh. Doesn't he own a restaurant?

"We should go somewhere," I tell him. I haven't been on a good little drive to anywhere in a long while. Although riding makes me nervous, the destination can always make me look forward to something.

"Don't you have a car?" he questions before muttering a quiet curse.

Dad took away my keys last night. I was too scared to ask for them this morning. I had to walk here. At least it was a nice day today.

"I didn't mean it in a- that wasn't supposed to be...mean," he struggles, and I let a small smile reach my lips at him.

"Let's go," he gives up, gripping my free hand. Little butterflies flutter in my belly. Mr. Terrip sees us walking out. He gives me a smile and a little wave. Crazy old man. Grey opens the door for me and I'm a bit shocked. Who taught him that? He helps me a bit after I struggle to get my injured leg in the Jeep. When his hand grazes my butt, I feel a little turned on. Stop. I feel like it would be difficult if I was a guy. How do you stop a boner? When you get turned on, it shows. I get turned on by looking at his hands, I'm thankful that I don't have a penis. I'm not too sure he would be thankful if I *had* one. Or maybe he is. I hope not though.

"Do you like peepee? A little?" I ramble out. It sounds idiotic when it leaves my lips. I need to quit calling it a 'peepee'.

Before he can say anything, I rephrase my question.

"Do you like peters?" I think that's still really bad. I finally look up at him. He's leaned against the side of my seat, the door wide open. His head is tilted back and to the side, his eyes watching me intensely. He places his hand on the top of my seat and he steps forward before placing his other one on the space between me and the armrest console.

"You know I want to fuck you, right? Only you," he says and I intake a breath as his eyes dart down to my lips. This is the furthest thing from friendly he could say. But gosh darn it if what he just said doesn't make me want to think unfriendly things right back.

"That answer your question?" I give him a nod, still in a bit of a trance. A little smirk graces his lips and I grow wings and fly to heaven. He backs up and grips the seatbelt, pulling it across my body.

"Not friendly, was it?" he leans close to me as he clicks it in.

"No," I say a little breathlessly. His eyes return to mine before dropping down. His tattooed hand reaches up and takes my bottom lip away from my teeth. I didn't even notice I did that. He shuts my door and I let out a breath I didn't know I was holding.

Only you.

~~~

I mentally trace the intricate designs of his tattoos before lifting my gaze to meet his cold, dark eyes as my mouth continues on its non-stop ramble. "Shut up," his deep voice startles me, stopping my consistent chatter.

"Sorry," I smile sheepishly as his cold stare burns through me. I should consider hushing. The light turns green, and he continues. I'm not sure I've stopped talking our whole thirty minutes on the road. I don't even blame him for telling me to shut up.

"Sorry," he apologizes after a minute of silence which shocks me a bit.

"I was talking a lot, it's okay," I shrug my shoulders and he shakes his head.

"I was thinking," I begin again, a little giggle escaping my lips, "is your favorite color gray? that would be funny." He doesn't laugh but I laugh enough for both of us.

"Don't have one," he gruffly replies, and I let out a soft gasp. I look over at him, seeing his strong inked arm resting on the armrest and his other one steering effortlessly. I admire for a second the veins in his arm.

"I'll help you then," I decide.

"What color do you find yourself most content looking at?" I question like some sort of therapist.

"Green," he says shortly.

"Poop green, tree green, traffic light green, light green," I list off as we come to another light. He looks over at me. He peers into my eyes for a minute.

"Emerald."

"Oh, like the birthstone?" I smile. His eyebrows furrow in the littlest of bit before they return to normal.

"Sure," he answers. My stomach growls a little bit.

"We should eat somewhere," I say, "If you want. My stomach is going to start sounding like a baby whale soon."

He turns off the road and we come to a pizza place. I'm glad he didn't ask me where I wanted to eat. I wouldn't know what to tell him quite frankly.

"Good?" he unbuckles his seatbelt and I smile giving him a nod. He gets out and I open my door. I slide to the edge of my seat, bracing myself to make the jump. I don't get to as he comes to my side.

"Don't do that," he warns me grumbly, "your knee."

He places me on the ground, and we walk in. The smell of pizza hits my nose and I almost break out in a dance. Following the sign that tells us to take our own seats, we do. We sit in a booth and there are already menus on the table. His foot bumps into mine. He's got some gosh darn long legs.

"How long are your legs?" I blurt and he looks up at me from his menu.

"Never mind," I mumble, looking down at my menu. I want a pizza. *And Grey. Stop.*

"What are you getting?" I start up a conversation.

"Steak and cheese," he mumbles, "everything on it."

"Order for me," he says, closing his menu, "Please," he adds.

"Drink?"

"Sweet tea," his eyes meet mine and I give him a little smile. I don't mind ordering for him, I like talking to new people. I think he sees that. A waiter comes to our table. He's wearing a 'Bears, Beets, Battlestar Galactica' shirt and I love it with all my heart.

"Drinks?" he asks.

"Two sweet teas," I answer him, and he shuffles away.

"Why're you looking at him like that?" Grey questions gruffly, his eyes unhappy for some reason.

"Did you see his shirt?" I bite my lip, keeping a laugh in, "It's funny."

He just lets out a grunt, his hands fidgeting. I take off the hair tie around my wrist and I hand it to him since he fusses with it whenever his hands do that. He looks up at me with a cute confuzzled face.

"You mess with this when your hands do that," I tell him, and his lips pull up at the edges. He almost smiles as he takes it, now messing with it. I watch him, a small smile on my face as he peers down at the hair tie in his hands, twisting it in different ways, stretching it out into squares and triangles. The waiter comes back shortly, setting our drinks down on the table and taking out his notepad for our orders.

"How big are the small pizzas?" I question and the waiter whose name tag reads 'John' looks over at me. He gives a shrug.

"I'll have one of those with just cheese," he writes that down before turning to Grey who still fidgets with my hair tie.

"He'll have the steak and cheese, with everything on it," I say for him and the waiter turns back to me, writing it down.

"I like your shi-" he begins walking away. Not before Grey grabs the back of his shirt, pulling him back. *I would have most definitely pooped my pants if I was the waiter.*

"She was talking to you," he almost growls out as the now frightened waiter looks back at me.

"I like your shirt," I smile a little apologetic smile for Grey's actions.

"Thank you," he waits for a second this time before leaving.

~~~

I dip the sixth and final piece of my pizza in ranch before taking a bite of it like it's still the first piece. Grey finished a while ago. I look up at him. His chin sits on his hand, his eyes fixed on me. I blush a little bit.

"Did you want a bite?" I question, feeling a little bit bad about eating a whole pizza by myself. A little smirk takes over his lips.

"I'm good, Lilah."

You're also *fine*. Stop. I finish the whole slice, then finish the rest of the little bit of my tea. Grey slides me the rest of his tea and I drink that too. I've got a big appetite today and I'm fully embracing it. I'm fully embracing this food baby too. At least my dress isn't tight or anything. It's a girl and her name is Tubs. I lean back in the booth and let out a sigh. The waiter guy comes back with the check and a pizza box for the pizza. I guess he thought I wasn't going to eat. His eyes widen once he sees the empty pizza tray. Grey's eyes narrow at the action. I was hungry, okay? I pick up my phone to get the money out of the back of the case but before I freaking can, Grey hands over his card.

"I thought we were paying separately or something," I say as the waiter walks away and Grey just looks at me as if what I just said was a stupid idea.

"Well, thank you," I smile at him and he just nods, his fingers messing with my hair tie again. After leaving the restaurant and getting back on the road, I give Grey a few directions to a nice lookout halfway up The Smokies. Mr. Terrip told me about the place once. He said it's where he proposed to his late wife so I figured it must be pretty there. *God rest her soul.*

When we get there, it's gorgeous. It oversees the greenery down below us and the mountains around us; it's all pure nature below, no towns or houses. Grey gets out and helps me out. We walk to the edge for a second, me staying back a little being frightened by heights. After a little while, he lifts me onto the flat hood of his Jeep before climbing on himself. *Good gosh those muscles as he climbs.*

"Tell me about you and your family," I say softly. I know he has no mother, but I really want to know about his dad. He pauses for a minute, leaning his back against the windshield, so I do the same.

"Mom died giving birth and dad's a deadbeat," he gives a one-shouldered shrug. A sorry in his situation wouldn't do a single thing.

"I moved out when I was seventeen," he looks out into the mountains, "been on my own ever since."

"You seem to be doing well," I murmur, and he looks as if he's thinking about it. I mean, he's got to be doing well. He's got a *nice* Jeep and he owns a restaurant.

"Your turn."

I bite my lip nervously. I don't even know what I should tell him.

"Um," I begin, sensing his eyes on me, "y'know, I have just a normal family," I feel emotions creeping up on me. Mr. Terrip's words begin to sink in. The ones where he said that I need to tell somebody about Jake. Grey doesn't know Jake. His thoughts of him won't change because he never knew him. I can tell him, and he won't be hurt by it.

"I lost my brother," I start, and his eyes don't waver away from me. My chest constricts and I take a deep breath.

"We were in a crash, just me and him," I look down at my lap.

"Is that how you got hurt?" he questions about my knee, and I nod.

"I begged him-God, I *begged* him to take me to see an ice cream shop that had just opened up nearby. I had heard people at school talking about all the crazy flavors that were there. He kept telling me it was raining too hard, but I kept *on*."

"Jake. Please. Please. I want to see it so, so bad. It's all I want," I beg him. I want to try the pumpkin ice cream everyone has been talking about.

"Azzy, it's torrential downpouring right now," he shakes his head, but I continue with my pleas. My eyes go blurry with tears.

"Eventually he gave in."

"Jake, please. Jake, please. Jake, please. Jake, please. Jake-" he cuts me off by standing from the couch.

"Let's go," he sighs, and I squeal happily jumping onto his back, hugging the daylights out of him.

"Thank you so much," I squeeze him.

"On the road, we could hardly see anything in front of us. He was going slow, there was no music or anything. Then I heard screeching tires. The initial impact was on his side. The car hit us, and we rolled. We rolled off the road."

Only the sound of the rain fills up the car. Jake watches the road extremely carefully. Then I hear screeching tires. A car slams into the side of us and my shouts fill my ears and the car. I feel us roll once and a shattering pain broke out in my leg. I scream in pain as I feel the car continue on what feels like the scariest coaster ride of my life. The window on my side shatters and I see and single glance out of it. A scream bubbles out of my throat upon seeing the huge hill we're about to go down.

"Azzy-" Jake shouts just before we tilt and then fall completely down.

"There was a hill. A huge hill that we rolled down off the side of the road. Steep, it was so steep," a tear rolls down my cheek.

"I don't remember how long it took us to get to the bottom of the hill, the doctors said I went unconscious," I feel my face scrunch up as I try to keep my crying silent.

"But I woke up when we got done rolling and were just sitting there. I don't know how long I was out for. But I woke up and we were upside down."

My eyes peel open and the excruciating pain all over the right side of my body makes me want to go back away. I try to take a breath but the pain in my rib makes me almost unable to. I start wheezing. Jake. I turn my head over to Jake. He's going to be okay. He's so tough. His eyes are open, they look right at me. Blood covers him, glass is stuck in his arm, his face is mostly covered in blood. But he's okay. He's looking right at me. He's probably waiting for me to wake up already.

"Jake," I croak out, wheezing and trying my hardest to take breaths. He doesn't respond. He doesn't blink. He lays at the roof, his neck bent in an odd direction as he looks at me. Why isn't he responding?

"Jake?" I wheeze out for a final time as it hurts too bad to breathe. I let my eyes close knowing that he'll be here later to tell me that everything is okay.

"I thought he was alive," I choke on a sob, "he was looking right at me, his eyes opened. He had blood all over him, but he was looking at me."

I finally let the cry leave my lips. I put my face in my hands, hating to cry so hard in front of him. *I thought he was okay.* I finally control myself for a bit before taking my hands away.

"He was DOA. His neck was broken, he severed his spinal cord. He was gone before they even got there."

And what do I get? Broken ribs, collapsed lung, dislocated shoulder, shattered patella, torn ACL, broken tibia and fibula, and grade three concussion? It should've been me. It was all my fault it should've been me with the broken neck.

"I'm sorry," I whisper, realizing that he probably didn't really want to hear any of that. I wipe the tears from my face and for the first time, I turn to him.

His eyes look right back at me. His face sits at a calm rest. He looks at me as if he's trying to read me.

"You blame yourself, don't you?" my heart holts at his words. My eyes fall to the tatted hand that rests lazily on the hood beside me. A new round of tears fills my eyes at hearing him ask me. I roll my lips into my mouth to keep them from wiggling. I look back up at him, my eyes begging to let the tears fall. His eyes soften as he looks at me. Just looking at me, he can already tell the answer.

His strong arms wrap themselves around me. I'm lifted onto his lap like I weigh no more than a slice of pizza. With my legs on either side of him, he pulls me close to him, his hand coming to rest on the side of my face. At the moment, it doesn't register to me how unfriendly we're sitting but neither of us cares. Whenever I'm upset, I turn to ice cream. It makes me feel better. He's starting to give me the same feeling. He's the ice cream, my Sugar. He best learn to deal with me calling him that.

He pulls me further to him and his forehead comes to rest on mine. He gives me his silent support. His actions speak louder than any words could. He's here for me. *He smells like my greatest dreams that have been dipped in heaven's pure waters.* I let my eyes close, basking in the feeling of him. Then I get confused. Why is he comforting me when it's my fault? Why am I letting him? I pull away. I don't deserve to be comforted. Or to be happy. I deserve to take Jake's place.

"Please don't cry," he uses his manners and I almost hold my heart. His hands find my cheeks and he wipes the tears away.

"I don't like it when you cry," he says, looking one-hundred percent truthful.

"I deserve to feel sad."

"You don't," he says in a final tone, gripping my chin so that I'm looking right at him. *That's not what my father tells me.*

"But I killed hi-"

"*Don't.* Say that," he says sternly, his eyebrows furrowed unhappily, "you didn't kill Jake."

How did he...? I must've mentioned his name without realizing it.

"No more of that," his hands come to rest on the sides of my torso, "no more crying either."

He jerks me flush against him, wrapping his strong arms all the way around me. He's hugging me.

"Good?" he questions about the hug. I feel a little smile creeping up on my lips.

"Good."

Chapter Twelve

Destroyed

❀Azalea❀

I don't remember my bed ever being this comfortable. I actually recall it feeling like a rock on my back. I open my eyes and for the first time, it feels like I actually have energy. I let out a little evil giggle. I'm not going to be needing coffee today. I stretch my limbs letting a groan out as my back arches and my buttcheeks shake from how good the stretch is. I look around. I'm met with an unfamiliar room. The last thing I remember from yesterday was sitting on Grey's lap. After I told him about Jake. Is this Grey's room? Gray, white, and black cover most of the room. Fitting. *Thank the good Lord he didn't take me home.*

I look down at the black comforter and catch sight of how big this bed is. I could spend all day in this bed. I look at the foot of the bed and see a door, most likely leading to the bathroom. I have to brush this God-forbidden bad breath away. I don't necessarily want to get up though. Or rummage through his bathroom. Good Lord only knows what I could find. Preparation H? I hope not.

A wig? His hair better be real. What if his toilet paper isn't Charmin

Ultra Soft? I'm sorry but I cannot wipe my butt with sandpaper.

I look at the other end of the room. The door to go out sits cracked open. *I could never live by myself.* I can never make an executive decision or any important decision at all. I always think of worse case scenarios. If I go to the bathroom, who knows, Grey could be taking a poop and I'd walk right in on him. If I go out the door, Grey might faint from either my breath or how I must be looking at the moment.

The door to the room bursts open. For a second, I think it's the S.W.A.T coming to get me so I let out a frightened squeal. Next thing I know, a friggin monster jumps on my bed and looks me dead in the eye. I'm left speechless, my eyes wide. Maybe if I stay still, I'll survive.

"Bear," Grey's voice fills the room. Dang right this pup looks like a bear holy guacamole. 'Bear's' black fur almost perfectly blends in with the comforter and he towers over me even when I'm sitting up. Bear doesn't listen to Grey, and I can't take my eyes off of him. His puppy-like face lets out a little playful whine. He jumps like a fox in the snow, and I let out a little giggle. He's like a big fur ball. He plops his big body down on the bed and rolls over.

"He wants a rub," Grey's deep voice reaches my ears, and I don't hesitate to rub Bear's belly.

"Is this your puppy?" I smile excitedly and for the first time look up at Grey. He's looking back at me, leaned against the doorframe. He gives a curt nod. Growing up, I'd always wanted a dog. We never got one though. Both my dad and Jake were allergic. Bear sits up suddenly and licks my face with his huge tongue. I wince a little at the force of it when his tongue goes over my bruised cheek.

"What kind of dog is he?" I giggle as Bear comes to sit right on top of me. And he's no small dog at all.

"Newfoundland."

I pull down my dress after realizing that Grey is getting a little bit of a show.

"Whatever you need is in the bathroom," he nods is head over to the door that I had spent quite a while deciding to go in or not. *Does that mean he'll be in there too?* I nearly slap myself in the face for thinking that. I make my way out of the bed, now noticing my knee brace isn't on my knee. Thank gosh, that thing is not comfortable to sleep in. I feel Grey's eyes on me the whole time I do. I look over my shoulder at him. *He was checking out the goodies in my trunk.* His eyes travel from my butt up to mine. My eyes fall to his lips when his tongue meets the corner of his mouth.

The corner of his mouth turns up in a little smirk before his eyes dart back to Bear. He gives him a little whistle and the two exit the room. I let out a breath I didn't know I was holding. He makes me *way* too hot and bothered to just be a *friend*. *I just don't want to get hurt.*

Within twenty minutes of the time we kissed, he called it a mistake and I felt like crying for a week. I just don't want that to happen again. I mosey/limp into the bathroom and come to the conclusion that if this place is Grey's, then he's got some gosh darn *money*. Can owning a single restaurant really give you all this? I might have to become an owner. Oh my gosh, what if a stripper bar could get me *even more*?

I look at myself in the mirror. My hair is a wild mess. My blonde locks stick up with static and quite frankly, I just look like a lion. After controlling the front, I turn to look at the back. My eyes catch my butt and the way my dress is slightly bundled in the back leaving the bottom of my cheeks fully open for viewing. Grey's viewing.

I feel my cheeks burn bright and I fix it quickly like that will make some sort of difference. He already saw it. I fix the back of my hair, combing through it with my fingers. I look at the nice granite sink in front of me and spot a toothbrush in its package. What a doll, getting me a toothbrush out. I brush my teeth and wash my face before seeing the obvious bruise on my cheekbone.

"Crud," I curse, looking around like he's going to have foundation in here or something. Of course, I find nothing. *Just keep your head down.* I tinkle before washing my hands and exiting the bathroom. I put my brace on that was sitting on his dresser then I walk to the door. I poke my head out and there's a pretty friggin big hallway. I go left because why not? Not really any pictures are on the walls, and I feel like it's a little bare. I count a good place where there could be a little table with some flowers on it. I should be an interior designer.

I take a couple of turns, come across one living room with no one in it and so I turn around and go the other way. This must be an apartment or something. I finally come to a living room that actually looks like someone has been in it. The television is on and playing some sort of show. I walk further into it, and I see a huge kitchen to my left. Bear comes running at me full force and I almost brace for impact before Grey whistles one short time and he's halting.

"He's a puppy; he's hyper," he comes into view from the kitchen. Just seeing him makes this place almost homely. And Bear of course.

"How old is he?" I pet his humongous head.

"Nine months," he looks down at him, his eyes soft. I nearly squeal at the thought of Grey being soft for a puppy. I can't imagine he's only nine months being as big as he already. I look at the clock over his shoulder and see that it's nine-thirty. That's later than I usually wake up but I'm not complaining, I slept so well. I see him take a step closer to me and I turn my attention back to him. His eyes are set harshly, his jaw clenched, and his eyebrows furrowed pretty angrily.

"Grey-" I begin to question him, but I stop when his strong hands grip my face. I feel myself heat up when his finger brushes over the bruise on my cheekbone softly.

"Where the *fuck* did that come from?" his voice rumbles and I search my brain for a lie.

"I sleep wild, I probably hit myself in the face," I shrug, keeping my voice from shaking. I'm not sure it's possible to hit yourself in the face hard enough to get a bruise like mine but whatever. Thank gosh I had makeup on it yesterday so that my lie fits. He doesn't really look like he believes it.

"That wouldn't leave a bruise like that," his voice stays tense and strained.

"Well, I'm just super-duper strong," I assure him, "Imagine the damage I could do to other people."

"It's okay," I give him a nod when he still doesn't look happy. At all. He leans forward, placing a gentle kiss on the bruise. My heart swells up and my breath gets caught in my throat. *That's friendly, right? Sort of. I don't care.*

"Good?" his deep voice rumbles against me quietly. Speechless at such a gentle action, I just nod.

"Is your restaurant successful?" I question. Looking around, nothing that I've seen in this whole apartment looks cheap. I bet his shirt costs more than me and it's only a dark blue long sleeve. *I kind of miss seeing his tattoos. And those forearm veins.*

"Can you take your shirt off?" my eyes widen slightly at what just flew out of my mouth, "so your restaurant?"

"You want my shirt off?" he asks and I feel like he's just saying it to make me want to jump out of the window even more than I already do.

"Well, your restaurant and bar I guess," I keep the subject directed away from the whole shirt ordeal.

"Yes or no?" his eyes narrow in what seems like a *teasing* way as he tilts his head. One hundred percent yes.

"Yes or no? I don't know how to answer that question," I avert my eyes from his.

"I know you were looking at my gluteus maximus," I change the subject. Now who's turn is it to be embarrassed?

"Mhm. I was," he owns up to it looking the furthest thing from embarrassed. Now I'm at a crossroad.

"You liked it didn't you?" I blurt out before rolling my lips into my mouth to keep more idiotic things from coming out.

"Of course," he says without any shame whatsoever, a little bitty smile on his lips that nearly knocks the breath out of me. I look at Bear for help. He just gives me a doggish smile back.

"Don't you have a restaurant to go to and do nothing at?" I question and if Bear could understand what I just said, he'd laugh.

"Where'd you sleep?" I question. I would've known if he slept in the same bed as me. I would've been hot all night. He motions his head over to the couch and I feel bad. He lives here, he shouldn't have been the one to sleep on the couch.

"I feel bad," I wince.

"I'll sleep with you next time then."

Wait, with me? Wait, next time? Wait, I'm fine with that? Wait, sexy time or sleep?

"Sex?" I blurt, "Don't answer that, it's not friendly."

"Whatever you want," he shrugs, ignoring the fact that I told him not to answer. My face heats up.

"Hungry?" he questions like he hadn't just suggested that we have sexual sexy time.

"For what?" Food duh, I cannot believe myself.

"You talk about sex a lot," he inputs, a smirk on his face as his hands come to rest on my sides. If he keeps on, I'm going to have a heart attack.

"I have sex a lot."

With who?! His grip tightens and his eyes turn dark as his eyebrows furrow almost unhappily.

"Do you" he states, not even in question form, pulling my body closer to his.

"No," I catch sight of my hair tie on his wrist and smile a little. It's a little tight on his large wrist considering the difference of our wrist sizes. He's no small guy. He lifts me up and I gasp. I feel my butt sliding onto his kitchen counter and my heart palpitates. He grips my waist, pulling me flush against him. Memories of the time we kissed floods my brain as he starts leaning forward, his eyes set directly on my lips. *Another one.* I don't want to be another one in here too. I wrap my arms around his neck and just hug him. He tenses for a second before relaxing and wrapping his arms around my torso.

"I'm sorry," he rumbles.

"For what?" I question softly, pulling away to look at his mesmerizing dark eyes. They're actually not black. Being so close, I see that they're only brown.

"Everything. I was bad to you," his thumbs draw circles in my side, admittedly tickling me a little bit but I try not to show that it is.

"That was before we re-introduced ourselves," my fingertips feel the strong muscles of his back and I almost blush. He *was* mean.

"For saying that kissing you was a mistake," adds, "it fuckin' wasn't." He tucks a piece of my hair behind my hair, now seeing my whole face.

"For not being friendly ever," he refers to how he almost just kissed me. And a few other times.

"You deserve better," he says.

"We started over, remember?" I remind him.

~~~

"I'll only be a couple of minutes," I give him a smile, climbing out of his Jeep carefully.

"Are you sure you don't want me to come in?" he asks, his eyebrows furrowing when I shake my head automatically.

"N-No! I'll be quick," I shut the door and make my way to my front door. Now that dad has lost his job, I'm guessing he'll always be here. That only adds to how much I never want to go home anyway. I open the door nervously before stepping inside. I look around the living room and the kitchen for any signs of him, but I don't see him. *Maybe he's sleeping in his room.*

I walk up the stairs carefully, making sure not to make too much noise just in case he's not sleeping. I walk into my room and find it completely trashed. My bed is off of the frame, my covers strewn all over the place, my dresser is turned over and the mirror built into it is shattered on the floor. My closet doors are broken off their hinges and the clothes that were once inside, are all over the ground. Stupid tears flood my eyes. *The only safe place I thought I had is destroyed.* I find my father sitting on the ground, a bottle of some sort of alcohol in his hands.

"Where've you been all night?" he mumbles. I stay pressed up against my door frame, too scared to go near him.

"A friends," I answer quietly.

"A boy, wasn't it? Don't think I've forgotten about that hickey you had," he sneers, and I flinch closer into the doorframe.

"Your brother would be so disgusted by you whoring yourself around." A tear falls down my cheek at the mention of Jake. He starts standing up, falling over himself twice before actually standing straight and towering over me.

"Exactly," he slurs, "you smell just like a man."

He bumps his large body into mine walking out, knocking me to my side. I hurriedly shut my door behind him and lock it, letting out a deep breath. I look around my trashed room and bite my wobbling lip. Not wanting to keep Grey waiting for long and also worrying that my dad will see him in the driveway, I quickly pick out clothes to wear.

I put on a pair of black shorts, a white sports bra because my boobs need a break from wearing a tight bra all night, a hoodless, slightly large Tennessee sweatshirt, and my beloved pair of flip flops. I step into the bathroom, grab another hair tie and a scrunchie to put on my wrist, and blink my eyes rapidly to make them less red from crying.

I find my charger meddled in with my comforter on my floor and then open my door. I take a peek around and say freak it. I walk down the stairs and catch sight of my father laying on the couch. As quietly as I can, I walk to the front door and let out a relieved sigh once I'm closing it behind me. I open the car door and climb inside carefully, letting out a breath as I struggle slightly.

"Where're your pants, Lilah?" he questions sincerely. I just walked out here without them.

"I'm not wearing any," I tell him, shrugging my shoulders a little bit. He stays quiet, I think surprised or something. I just turn up the radio. AC/DC reaches my ears and I bite my lip excitedly. I mouth the words to *You Shook Me All Night Long*, a classic but still one of my favorites by them. My favorite by them is, without a doubt, *Big Balls*. Not just because of the name, but because the actual lyrics are dirtier than the name. The whole song is an innuendo. It's not about the male part, it just sounds like it is. Got to love *Big Balls. That's what she said.*

We come to town square and Grey parks. He climbs out smoothly, and I get a little jealous. Next thing I know, my door is being swung open. He unbuckles my seatbelt and turns my body to him. He lifts my sweatshirt looking down at my legs.

"What if I wasn't wearing any shorts?" I raise my eyebrow and he looks up at me, a little smirk pulling at his lips.

"I'll just keep my thoughts to myself," his tongue swipes over the corner of his mouth. His hands grab the top of my shorts, and he tucks a little of my sweatshirt into my pants.

"You're skinny," he observes my stomach which is more on the flat side (except for the fact that I'm sitting and there's a little roll I've graciously named Pat) and I find myself blushing a tad bit. Gosh dang if that's not what a lot of girls would love to hear.

"You're hungry a lot?" he questions and I let out a loud laugh.

"Let's eat," he decides, lifting me and placing me gently on the ground. With burning cheeks and his large hand swallowing mine, he leads me to his restaurant making sure to walk a little slowly so that I can keep up.

"I ate a whole pizza by myself, I eat enough," I smile, remembering that delicious pizza.

"It was a small," he offends me.

"Is that a challenge?"

He takes a glance down at me, raising one of his shoulders. I might have to shove a few slices in my bra, but I'd still finish it. He holds open the door to his restaurant/bar and I walk in. Jai sees me immediately and gives me a smile. Then he sees Grey and his eyebrows shoot up in surprise.

~~~

Eating my amazing waffles, with the syrup this time, I watch as Grey's hands stretch and fiddle with the hair tie I gave him yesterday. The hair tie snaps, and he just looks at it in his hand like 'what do I do now?' I eat the last piece of my waffle, a little smile on my face. After sitting down my fork, I stand from my seat. His eyes dart up to me and he watches me as I come to sit right beside him in the booth, never once taking his eyes off me or moving the hair tie in his hands.

"Did you break it?" I already know the answer but I'm kind of curious to see what he'd say.

"I didn't mean to," he replies quietly, his jaw clenching as he visibly becomes annoyed with himself. I literally have them all over my room. *My once neat and tidy room.*

"It's okay," I smile. I take it from his hands gently and remove the scrunchie from my wrist. *Good luck breaking this one buddy.*

"This won't break and look," I move closer to him showing him the color, "It's gray!"

"It's pretty soft too," I run my finger over the fabric of it and then turn my attention to him. He already looks at me. *I've probably got syrup on my face.* I hold it out to him, and he takes it. I watch as he feels around it, getting used to the difference between the scrunchie and the regular hair tie.

"All done?" Jai's voice comes from beside me. I look up at him, the smile from looking at Grey still present on my face, and I nod. He picks up the plates, gives me a sly little wink, and returns to the kitchen.

"You can have that," I nod to it, "and if you put it on your wrist, it won't make a mark like the other one; it's not as tight."

I picture Grey with a scrunchie on his wrist and I smile a little. I find the neckline of his shirt. Just barely over the edge of it, on the very top of his collarbone there lies a part of a tattoo. *A tattoo that I want to see more than anything.* How many tattoos does he have? Does he have more than just his sleeve?

"I used to want a tattoo on my butt," I blurt out. I recall being twelve and wanting a tattoo of a little butterfly at the top of my butt. Of course, I would never actually get it. Or an actual tattoo. After all the needles and IV's I've had in my arms, I've definitely had it with any sort of needles.

"Show me where?" he glances at me, his eyebrows slightly raised. *Is he teasing me?* Lost in my own world called 'what-the-heck-just-occurred' I didn't notice Jai come back until he speaks.

"Bill?" he questions. Grey owns this place.

"Fuck outta here," Grey waves his hand, his eyebrows scrunched. I giggle a little when Jai chuckles.

"Tip?" he questions.

"You're not getting shit," Grey nudges my side and I stand as he gets out the booth. I start feeling bad, but Jai's smile doesn't falter. I sneakily grab a twenty dollar bill out of my phone case. When Grey is turned the other way, I nudge Jai, handing him the money.

"No, no," he shakes his head, not taking it.

"I'll cut it into tiny pieces and shove it down your nose," I give him a shy smile, "take it."

His eyes widen a slight bit before his lips form an amused smirk. His eyes dart over to Grey. Jai shakes his head and finally takes it. Walking away, I hear him mutter something almost inaudibly. Something along the lines of: *'God, what a match.'* Whatever that means.

Chapter Thirteen

Drugs

* Grey *

The door to the office opens and I feel myself grow unhappy at the interruption. *I told them not to when she's here.* Her blonde hair flies as she whips her head to the doorway where Roman stands. He glances down at her, his eyes taking on a curious state. I reach forward to the computer on my desk and pause the movie she was watching while I was filling out paperwork for the bust that'll go down tonight.

"What?" I question, my voice serious enough to make him understand that I'm not in the mood for bullshit.

"Look at the time," is all he says before closing my door back. I raise my eyes to the clock.

"Motherfucker," I curse quietly, and I feel her eyes come to rest on me.

"You okay?" she questions softly, her hand coming to rest on mine. I ignore the fucking feeling it gives me and only send her a nod. *God that question is one she constantly asks.* It should get on my nerves but it fucking doesn't. It makes me feel...I don't fucking know just...good.

"Do you need a ride home?" I question and her eyes fall to her fingers. I start fiddling with the scrunchie she gave me nearly a week ago.

"No," she gives me a fake smile and I feel a scowl on my face. *What the hell is she upset for?*

"I'm just going to drive," she suddenly smiles up at me and my scowl deepens.

"What's wrong?" *She* asks *me*. I don't think I could ever get used to someone asking me what's wrong. There's never been someone who gave enough of a fuck. It's new. It's all new.

"Nothing," I grumble out, unable to help it and being so unused to the question. She lets out a quiet sigh just like whenever I get an attitude with her.

"I love that," she points to the scrunchie that I put back on my wrist. It's sat there all week. For some fucking reason, it relieves my stress. Unlike Roman and even a few other guys, I never turned to Marlboro Ultra Lights to keep me from going off the deep end when I get nerve-wracked or stressed out. Because what's it going to do for you in the long run? Absolute shit. I'd rather punch an asshole in the face. Or fucking fiddle with a goddamn scrunchie.

"*I love it when you call me big poppa*," she wiggles in her seat, and I feel a little smirk reach my lips watching her. *God, she's a wild child.*

"Okay, okay," she giggles, stopping herself. She gets out of her seat and drags it back to its spot in front of the desk. My eyes never once leave her little frame. I never can keep my eyes off her.

"I'm leaving now," she grabs her phone and I stand. I walk with her. A slight wind blows around us once we get outside. Her blonde hair blows onto my chest and her dress raises against her tan legs. I clench my jaw. *Friends. Fucking friends.*

"Oh," she says suddenly, "give Bear a good pat for me."

I fucking struggled harder than I ever have before when she slept in my bed. I don't mind sleeping on the couch, it's comfortable and I didn't want her to think I was being 'unfriendly' if I would've slept there with her. But It took me hours to actually go to sleep. I couldn't stop thinking about her. On my bed. Where no other girl has been before. In her fucking dress that had risen up to the top of her thighs. *God, I'm trying so hard to be good to her.* We make it to the parking lot, and she stops in front of her car. She looks up at me, that *smile* on her face. That smile.

"Bring it in," she raises her arms and I find myself getting excited. Excited for a hug. I bend and her arms wrap around my neck. I stand straight up and her legs dangle. Then, she raises her legs and wraps them around my torso. I tense at the feeling, not used to this position not being sexual. She pulls away and just looks at me. I look back into those emerald, green eyes of hers.

"I'll see you later, Grey," she scrunches her nose making a funny face, "try not to get headbutted again."

"Y'know what I mean? Like do this," she jerks her head to the left quickly, dodging an imaginary headbutt. I walk to the driver side of her car, opening the door and sitting her in her seat.

"I'll try that," she still looks at me for a few seconds. I lean in and place a kiss on her forehead. *That's friendly, right?* I've got to experiment sometime. I can't just fucking go on without touching her. The hugs are purely friendly. I'm not a *purely friendly* type of guy even though she's got me hugging for the first time in my life.

"Good?" I question quietly, pulling away and leaning down to be closer to her. Her cheeks flush a light pink, and my heart does a stupid fucking twitch. *Damn.* She leans up and I feel her lips on my forehead. My eyes close at the feeling and my heart does something funny again. The fuck is going on with me?

"Goodnight Grey," she smiles, buckling her seatbelt. I back away and close her door still fucked up from her kiss.

~ ~ ~

"What's with the face?" Jai questions as I walk back into the bar. He wipes down a table from the last customers that came in before we closed.

"Nothing," I mumble, clearing my face of whatever emotion that was on it. I walk into the back and to the room at the very end of the hall. I close the door behind me, and my eyes catch sight of the picture hung on the wall of all of us. I glance at Jake in the picture and run my hand through my hair.

DOA; severed spinal cord.

I let out a harsh sigh and shake my head from the thoughts. And she fucking blames herself. Not only did she have to live through the hell of seeing her dead brother's eyes open and staring at her when he was dead, but she blames herself.

"Roman mentioned the chick in your office," Jonas claps my back and I feel my shoulders grow tense.

"Also said he'd seen her another time," a smirk reaches his lips.

"Is the boss man keeping around a fuck-budd-" I grab him by the collar of his shirt and slam him into the wall in front of me. I hear the guys on the couches jump up at the sudden loud noise and seeing him up against the wall.

"Shut the *fuck* up."

I take my hands off him with a jerk and turn around.

"Her tits aren't even shit anyway," he tries as a final blow. Hearing someone talk about her like she's a piece of shit oddly sets me the fuck off. Before I even know it, my fist is flying at his face. I don't stop. Not until they grab me and pull me off him.

"What the fuck?" Jai says confusedly, finally arriving probably after hearing all the yelling from the guys behind me.

"I swear to fuck," I turn to Jai, "control your little brother."

"And don't you *ever* fucking talk about her again," I can't even control the words as they spill out of my mouth. What is she doing to me? I'm turning into a fucking blabbermouth just like her. Not paying attention to any of the widened eyes in the room, I walk up to the bulletin board. *Stop fucking thinking about it. Her. Everything.*

"Timothy Wells," I get their attention and they don't say anything else about what just happened.

"He's holding an auction three hours away from here," I speak loudly, pinning up a picture of him for all the guys to see. Jonas can't see through his swelling eyes but it's not like he's coming to a fucking bust any time soon. He needs to mature up.

"An estimated fifteen girls will be there tonight," I look around at them. They all looked pissed. These busts are the ones that no one wants to go to. They take a toll on everyone. We see the kind of shit that no one wants to see. Little women and kids being sold to be raped, tortured, and eventually killed.

"We have to blend in," I nod at them, telling them that the jeans and shirts that we're wearing is what we're keeping on.

"Three exits," I put up a map of the place where the auction is being held up on the board.

"Grey," Maxon nearly fucking giggles.

"What?"

"Is that- Is that a scrunchie on your wrist?" they laugh and I look down at the gray fabric on my wrist.

"The fuck does it look like?" I grumble. So fucking what? Fuckers'll never get what I have.

"Definitely a scrunchie," Linc smirks, popping a piece of gum in his mouth.

"Then it's a fuckin' scrunchie," I deadpan, "kiss my ass motherfuckers."

"Roman and Theo," I continue, nodding toward the two of them, forgetting their snickering, "Y'all stay outside at the back entrance; expect most of those who are trying to escape going out that door."

"Reed and Maxon, take the side exit," I point to where that is.

"Blaise and Linc, get the front exit," I motion to it.

"Everyone else, you're inside with me." I look out at all of them, "we're going in blind. We don't know how many people will be there. Watch each other's backs."

"Let's go."

"What about me?" Jonas asks, holding a towel up to his nose.

"Clean the fuckin' toilets for all I give a shit," I sneer at him. We suit up. Guns go in waistbands, around ankles, in boots, and in jacket pockets. We head to the front and Jai opens the closet. He hands out padded leathers to everyone. For some reason, I think about actually putting one on. Why? I've never put one on before. *'I'll see you later, Grey.'* What if I don't see her later? What if something does happen and she can't see me? *I can't see her?* I fiddle with the scrunchie on my wrist thinking about it. I shake my head, taking the scrunchie off and putting it in my back pocket. I need to focus.

~~~

❀Azalea❀

"I feel like I'm seeing you a little less nowadays," Mr. Terrip greets me as I walk into the store.

"I'm sorry," I give his frail figure a hug. He needs some meat on his bones, I swear. It took a couple of days to clean my room. Especially the floor where glass from the mirror was everywhere. Plus, Grey has taken me up on the challenge of eating a full pizza. I got to the last piece before I had to stop. He sat and watched me with those gorgeous, amused eyes of his after he finished eating his food. At least he doesn't judge me. If he did, I'd pizza slap him. But I'd make sure the pizza slice wouldn't fall on the floor so that it doesn't waste, and I can still eat it.

He lets me watch movies all day and if that doesn't just tickle my pickle, then I don't know what does. *He kissed my forehead. I pooped my pants. Nearly.* I couldn't help but kiss his back. I mean come on; it was right in my reach. My assumption for why the gun guy said 'look at the time'; they were planning to go party. Or to a club maybe. I mean, I'm only nineteen so I'm basically three years old so I get why he didn't invite me. I probably wouldn't have gone anyway. That's a lie, if Grey is there, I'd pretty much go anywhere with him.

I begin to work with the books in the store, catching up on everything I haven't been doing since I've been all over the place lately. *Gosh,*

Grey gives the best hugs for not being very experienced with them. His big arms just know how to wrap all the way around me and it ruffles my truffles like no one else. The man radiates body heat better than a hot sidewalk in the middle of summer on a day where it's hotter than Satan's actual butthole. Goodness knows how long passes before I feel a hand on the small of my back. I turn and see Grey. Automatically, a smile reaches my lips.

"What?" he questions, looking at my too-wide-of-a-smile and I bite my lip. His eyes follow my action and I release my lip, remembering how he hates when I do that. I quickly put away the last few books in the cart and then I look back up at him. His eyes are on my bottom half. Aka, my buns. My biscuits. My money maker. My butt.

"What are those pants?" he asks, and I furrow my eyebrows in confusion.

"They're leggings," I smile. His butt would look phenomenal in a pair of leggings. But he doesn't look like he'd wear them, unfortunately.

"Mm," he hums, grabbing my arm and turning me sideways and backward a couple of times.

"Fuck *me*," he mumbles under his breath and my eyebrows furrow again. He places his hands on my hip. One of the hand trails to my stomach.

"You hungry?" he questions, and I throw my head back in laughter before letting my forehead fall against his chest. We've already gone over this.

"I'm not hungry," I shake my head. He places a kiss on my forehead and butterflies flutter all the way down to my toes. As soon as he pulls away, he's leaning down for me to kiss his. I do so with a smile before catching sight of his bruised knuckles.

"What happened?" I lift his hand.

"I punched a shit in the face," he says like it's a normal thing, but my eyes widen.

"I did too," I nod, showing him my completely clean and unbothered knuckles.

"I'm just so good at punching, it's not even bruised or anything," I give him an I'm-totally-telling-the-truth smile.

"I could teach you some time if you'd like," I raise my eyebrows twice, meanwhile he's still looking at my knuckles for bruises. My mind wanders off as I catch sight of a book with a maple leaf on it. I thought it was a weed thingy leaf or whatever the heck that 'herb' is, if it is even a herb.

"I also took weed."

His eyes come back up to mine. I've never even seen a real live weed that you do. I'm just blabbing by now.

"You *smoked* weed," he fixes, and I nod.

"I smoked weed," I don't know why I keep it up.

"How'd it go?" a single eyebrow raises.

"Why don't you tell me?"

I don't have a clue what weed will do to you. Literally two seconds ago I thought you *took* weed, not *smoke* it.

"I wouldn't know," he leans against the bookcase beside us and I roll my lips into my mouth. At least he doesn't do drugs. Unlike me, I do the hard stuff. That's what she said. Stop.

"I smoked LSD once," I inform him and he nods, tucking a piece of my hair behind my ear that had fallen in my face after I nodded harshly to make sure he understands how well I do the drugs.

"You *took* LSD," a small smile graces his lips.

"I think I'm on it right now," I gush over the smile on his lips.

"I bet you are."

"What does crystal meth look like?" I question. Do people collect the crystals? Because they're crystals, so wouldn't they be pretty? What if someone found a crystal somewhere, and then they kept it because it was pretty only to find out that it was meth?

"Little white crystals," he says and I give him a little smile.

"I love it when you talk drugs to me," I bite my lip to keep the laugh that is bubbling in my throat contained. He chuckles. Like, actually chuckles. I sigh internally and replay the sound in my head.

"I still haven't seen you shirtless," I blurt and then proceed to ignore my cheeks that are starting to tinge pink. He looks around the store and I begin to get my hopes up. He spots a window though. Instead of forgetting about it, he grabs my hand and leads me to the bathroom. He shuts the door behind us, and I take a seat on the closed toilet, shimmying happily.

"I have to warn you," he says. Warn me about what? 'Azalea, I have to warn you. You might die from how freaking attractive I am.' That might actually happen.

"About...?" I question, looking up at him.

"You won't have a fit?" he says, and I look up at the ceiling for the answer.

"Oh gosh, you have an extra nipple?" I gasp and his eyebrows furrow.

"I got stabbed last night but it's patched up," my eyes widen to the size of freaking Jupiter. I stand from my seat on the toilet and pace around the bathroom. Here I was thinking about how I'm going to deal with an extra nipple and he's actually freaking stabbed?

"I tell you not to get headbutted," I say, "and you don't. Which is great!"

"But you went and got stabbed?!" I look up at him. Do I need to show him the CIA videos I watch? Maybe that'll help him get his stuff together. Doesn't he own a bar?! Why the heck did he get stabbed?

"Did you stab him back?" I question, making an odd jabbing motion with my hand. He pauses as if he's thinking about the answer.

"He's dead," he hesitantly says unlike everything else he has always said. He's very straightforward. *I'm in the bathroom with a man who has just committed a kill. Or done a kill. Or killed someone, whatever or however you say it, I can't think well when I'm nervous.*

"Do I need to hide you from the po-po?" I question him. Is he a criminal? A convict? *Konvict, Upfront, Akon, Slim Shady. Stop, this is serious. Smack that, all on the floor Smack that, give me some more.* I take a deep breath.

"You know what? My trunk has a lot of space so you can stay in there," I nod to him therapeutically.

"Lilah," he says, "you don't need to hide me in your trunk."

"Oh no," I run my hand through my hair, "that's because you've already been arrested and they set bail, but you paid it and now you're out until trial, right?"

"I'm a fed."

"I'm proud of you for being a fed-ex worker or driver or whatever but we're talking abou-"

"FBI, Lilah."

"You're an FBI-er?" I gasp, my eyes wide.

"Of sorts," he shrugs a single shoulder and then realization dawns on me.

"I told you I did drugs!" I hold my heart, my mouth wide open.

"I watched movies on an illegal website!" I continue, "for the record if your computer starts going slow, it may or may not be because of that site."

I ruined a fed's computer. Oh, Jesus help me please Lord, God. I close my eyes tightly for a minute and pray.

Dear God and Jesus, I need both of you right here, please. I've just basically ensured that I will be sent to prison so if you can, watch over me while I go to prison. Please help make my sentence not that terribly long. Maybe even help make my bail only about a hundred dollars. When I get to the prison place, help me make decisions to not get beaten up by the scary people there. And help me not get Polio. Or Hepatitis A, or Hep B, or Hep C. I'm not sure how many letters of the alphabet Hepatitis has after it but none of the Hepatitis'. Just please God and Jesus, you too Mother Mary, and Joseph. Even you too Noah, Abraham this goes for you too, even you Moses. I love you all, I promise, I'm a faithful child so please help me out here, Amen.

"Take me away," I tell Grey after finishing my prayer.

"Hm?" he hums confusedly. I look up at him. There aren't any cuffs in his hands. Not like I need them anyway, I won't struggle. Even if I did struggle, it wouldn't take much to get me controlled. I hold my head in my hands. He's just made his investigation worse by actually getting me to like him. Oh gosh, what else have I done that can make me get a longer sentence? Is telling someone they have a small peepee a crime? I'm the worst lawbreaker I've ever met.

I feel him move close to me. He bends down but I keep my head down. His hands come to take mine away from my head before resting on the sides of my face.

"Take me to prison already," I whisper quietly. He doesn't say anything, he just leans forward and presses a soft kiss against my cheek. *He's just making it worse. But please do it again.* He pulls his hands away. Most likely to get the handcuffs now. I get confused when I feel his strong arms lift me up. He turns and sits on the closed toilet seat, before situating me on his lap.

"You're not going anywhere," he mutters.

"So you're turning this store into a prison and this bathroom into my cell?" I sigh.

"At least I have a pooper," I look at the bright side. It's a clean pooper too.

"You haven't done anything," he rests his tattooed hand on my thigh.

"But drugs," I remind him.

"You didn't do drugs," he shakes his head and I narrow my eyes at him.

"How would you know?" I ask a freaking *fed*.

"Call it intuition," he rolls his gorgeous eyes. Was that sarcasm? I follow the trail of tattoos up his arm.

"Can you take your shirt off?" I question again and that beautiful smirk appears on his lips once again and I yawn. All this freaking out has got me tired.

"Let's go to my place," he offers, and my eyebrows rise up. Don't have to tell me twice.

~~~

"I'm ready now," I sit on his couch, surprised at how comfy it is. He comes to stand in front of me.

"Why do you want me to?" he questions, gripping the bottom of his shirt and pulling it up to below his belly button. I get eager as heck.

"I'll take mine off," I offer although I won't actually. Well...maybe.

"No you won't," he grumbles, lowering the shirt back down a bit.

"I'll take my pants off," I offer. His eyebrows raise a bit as if considering it but then he shakes his head.

"You won't," he says, lowering it even further with a teasing look on his face now.

"I'll," I struggle, "um, um. What do you want?"

"Stay the night."

"Like a sleepover, done deal!" I smile, happy I won't have to go home tonight. His lip turns up at the word 'sleepover.'

"And I need your number," he looks at me, a little smirk on his lips.

"You're a fed, you can figure it out," I tease and his eyes narrow. He lets go of his shirt.

"I'm joking, you know I'm joking," I say immediately, "I'll give it to you."

We went this long without contacting each other by text. We talked just like the olden days. He grabs the bottom of his shirt again and I smile a little.

"Y'know," he steals my word that I use all the time, "this isn't very friendly as you say."

"I don't care at the moment. I have the chance to see someone shirtless besides my brother and his best friend, so I'm going to take it."

I'm not experienced in the *slightest*. With hardly *anything*. All I know is school health class and sex ed. His eyebrows furrow and his head tilts a tiny bit.

"You mean-"

"Yes," I interrupt and he gives me a little smile that I read right through. Aw, kiss my grits. He lifts his shirt off his head and the breath is knocked out of me and thrown out the window. The room's temperature rises a good twenty degrees. In front of me stands not a man but a *man*.

Never have I ever seen a real live six pack. It's not *so* defined like those models that only eat dry spinach leaves right off the tree or wherever they come from, but gosh darn it if it isn't obvious. His muscles are purely man-ness and not from weights but from hard work. He's thick, I have to admit, he's not some skinny guy. He's truly a wall of muscle.

I feel myself gaping at him. I think Bear is doing the same thing. Probably not but I pretend he is so that I'm not the only one. I was right that there are more tattoos. I stand and go to get a closer look at them. I feel his gaze on me as I come closer to him. On his bicep, which is always covered by his shirts, there's a battle.

There's a person with wings who stands with her foot over a man with horns. Devil horns. She holds a sword to him, but it doesn't pierce his skin. He's defeated. Just on the other side of his bicep, which holy freaking heck is strong and built and as big as my leg, there's a very realistic skull with tons of details and all. I swear Vincent Van Gogh did his tattoos. Then spreading over to the one side of his chest, there's a huge lion head roaring which also has a crazy amount of detail.

On his back, spreading over his shoulder blade, there's another angel. She reminds me of those old statues that they have in Greece. She wears a robe, and she looks to her left where she lays her hand on a man. A cross sits in her other hand. Shading fills in space behind them making the two of them really come to life.

I look down at his hand. A bunch of small tattoos litter his hand. From more realistic skulls to daggers and even to nicer things like a small pair of praying hands, his hand is full of tattoos just like his arm. There aren't any flowers. Which is odd. Everything is dead pretty much. Usually, in sleeves that I've seen on celebrities, they like to fill up space with flowers like roses. Wherever there was space needing to be filled on Grey's arm, I feel like he used skulls or other...scary things. But I *love* it. It's *him*.

I look at his other arm and see where he was talking about. On the bandage that has been wrapped around his arm, there's a little blood seeping through. It'll need to be changed soon. *I'll also need to get out of my trance soon.*

Chapter Fourteen

Nothing

❦Azalea❦

"I'm going to throat-punch you if you don't let me do it," I cross my arms at him, pausing the movie on the tv.

"Don't threaten me," he grumbles.

"It's a promise, Sugar," I flex my bicep. He's literally bleeding through his bandage all while saying 'I'm fine, it's fine.' He's been stabbed for crying out loud, he's not fine. Gosh knows how deep it is anyway.

"It's fine."

"Well, if it's stitched up and *still* bleeding then you could have opened the stitches," I scoot closer to him on the couch. I feel the heat radiating off his bare chest and I nearly have to fan myself.

"And if you've opened the stitches then it could get infected more easily and if it gets infected then you could get really sick and then you could maybe die or something and I don't want that to happen," I explain, "Bear doesn't want that to happen either."

I pat Bear's head and he licks my fingers. Grey lets out a frustrated sigh. He instructs me where to find all the bandages and disinfectant in the closet in his hallway and when I come back, he's sitting upright on the couch. I bend down to his level and feeling his eyes on me, I take the bloodied bandage off.

I nearly gasp at the sight. The stitches haven't been busted but on the end of the wound, there could have been one more stitch but there's not. I clean around the wound, trying my absolute hardest to keep it from hurting him. When his body tenses though, I know I have.

I place my other hand on his strong arm giving it a sympathetic little squeeze. Then I give it one more squeeze, feeling the amount of muscle he has. In response, the arm wraps around my waist and pulls me closer to him. I put another clean bandage on it and as soon as it's done being taped, I'm pulled onto his lap. I hold in the gasp that wants to escape.

He lays his head down on my shoulder and I feel my heart say 'aw.' Bear gets jealous. He comes over to me and claws at my leg. I let a little giggle out and I rub his belly when he turns over for me.

I feel lips on my neck and a soft sigh comes out of my mouth. I forget about how unfriendly what he's doing is. I keep telling myself that I don't want to get hurt again. I'm terrified of going through heartbreak. Terrified. Of all the things that have happened to me and are happening, I want to stay friends with someone because I'm scared that if he hurts me, then I'll go back to having no one except Mr. Terrip and my pillows. I feel his finger trail down the crease in my back and I shudder under his touch. He kisses up my neck, over my jawline and he stops on my cheek.

"I can feel your spine," he grumbles. I swear I eat a lot. I swear I do. I eat an unimaginable amount when it's given to me. I reach my hand around his side and press my fingers into his spine gently. I can just faintly feel his spine and I grin.

"I can feel yours too," I return my eyes to his only to see them trained on my lips.

"Are you mad at me?" he suddenly asks, and I feel my eyebrows furrow.

"For..." he trails off, his hand coming to rest on my neck where moments previous, his mouth was. *It felt too good to be wrong.* I shake my head.

My eyes find the clock and I see that it's already almost five in the afternoon. I climb off Grey's lap and watch as his jaw clenches unhappily at my action. I sit next to him and lean my head on his tattooed arm. Soon, I feel myself drifting off.

~ ~ ~

"Let's go to bed," Grey shakes me gently awake and I just give him a little sleepy nod. I feel his strong arms under me, and I relish in the feeling of his warm chest under my hands. He opens his bedroom door, and he sets me on my feet.

"Can I have a t-shirt?" I question a little shyly. I don't necessarily want to sleep in the sweater I'm in unless he wants a puddle of sweat on his bed. Ew. He opens a drawer and grabs the first thing he sees. He tosses it over to me and it hits me in the face. I fall back onto the bed with a groan as it does. I get over my fit and stand up, taking off my sweater. I look at the shirt he gave me. It's a plain white t-shirt with a whole bunch of black words on the back. Something about the FBI. I'm *not* an FBI agent because I'm wearing this. I'm *not*. *I am*. I pull the shirt over my head and then my eyes lock with Grey. *I thought he left.* He runs his hand through his dark, thick hair.

"Give me a break Lilah," his jaw clenches, and I turn confused.

"I'm trying to be good for you. You're making it *so fucking hard*," he stresses, walking closer to me. *That's what she said. Shut up.*

"Stop biting your lip," he glares, and I release it, not even realizing I was doing it. He grabs my waist and pulls me flush against him. His tattooed hand rests at the top of my throat as he tilts my head up to him. His eyes travel down the shirt on my body and he whispers a curse.

"I'm getting in the shower," he grumbles before letting me go and walking into the bathroom. A good fifteen or so minutes later, he comes back out, his hair wet and water dripping down the ripples on his chest. *I need to go to church.* I watch him with slight pervert eyes as he comes to the head of the bed. He grabs a pillow to take with him.

"Grey," I call out as he begins walking out the room. He turns and looks at me. I look at his torso. He sees that. He wipes away a water droplet on his abdomen. I wipe the drool coming out the corner of my mouth.

"Take the bed," I start getting up.

"I'm not sleeping in that bed unless you're in it."

My heart flies out the window and ascends to say hi to Jesus.

"Okay," I say pathetically. I stretch my legs in front of me. I take off the brace on my leg and he sits on his side of the bed. I massage my knee gently and let out a sigh. I hear a little scratch at the closed door and a soft whine. I hold my heart and stand up. I walk carefully over to the door.

"He's not allowed in here," Grey grumbles and I gasp. How could anyone resist his whines?

"Please," I plead, and his face remains blank.

"Grey."

We hear another little whine. I look back at Grey.

"How can you just listen to that? Poor Bear feels left out," my voice goes soft for Bear.

"He just wants to spend time with us," I explain, edging closer to the door. *I won't give up on this Bear.* On the other side of the door, he lets out the world's cutest little 'awoo' and I send Grey a pretty please look.

"Goddammit, fuck," his jaw ticks, "whatever."

I smile excitedly and open the door. Bear rushes in and his tail wags very happily. He rubs up against me, nearly knocking me over and I rub through his black hair.

"Look how happy he is," I cup Bear's face and tilt it up to me. He licks my nose and I giggle. I walk over to the bed and Bear runs over to Grey on his side of the bed. He puts his paws up on the bed and nudges Grey's arm continuously. *Bear loves him so much.* I climb up on the bed and Bear pushes his lower half up onto the bed.

"Bear," Grey warns, a scowl on his face. I'm guessing he's not allowed on the bed either. Even though the first time I was here he jumped up to see me. Bear jumps on the bed like a Fox in the snow and I fall deeper in love with him.

He goes crazy. He chases his tail in circles, jumps all around, and pounces at Grey who looks unamused, although I can see a little twinkle in his eye. Once he's done, he plops his big body down, and pants with his tongue hanging out of his mouth.

"You're such a good boy, Bear," I scoot closer to him and he turns all the way over on his back to get the belly rub that he deserves.

"I don't want him sleeping with us," Grey grumbles.

"You won't even know he's here, I'll keep him on my side," I explain before patting the other side of me and Bear plops directly in that spot. I pat his head.

"You don't want to snuggle him then fine; I'll give him the snuggles he deserves," I look at Grey and he looks unhappy.

"Your face will stick like that," I say, fixing a part of his bandage that had rolled over. He gets up grumbly and turns the lights off before coming back to bed, lifting the covers for us, getting in, and he turns away from me on his side. *I don't need him. I've got Bear.* I turn on my side away from him too and throw an arm around Bear's big body. He turns around and licks me in my face before settling back. Hardly even feeling Grey's presence as we're on either side of the bed, I drift off.

~~~

I wake up to the sound of the bedroom door opening. The first thing that registers is how crushed my whole entire body feels. And it's not Bear who's on top of me. Grey's hand rests *on my bare stomach* and the rest of him is completely on top of me. His head rests on the pillow above mine and his long legs aren't even tangled with mine, they're in between mine. I'm holding this man like he weighs only thirty pounds. He weighs twice as much as me. *Wait. Then who's at the door?*

"Grey," a deep voice calls out. At least the covers are still us because goodness knows how far my shirt has risen up. Plus, with Grey's body crushing my small frame, I'm sure the guy can't even see me. Grey doesn't move a single muscle at the voice. *Oh god. There's a dead man on top of me.* I can't even move, he's so heavy.

"Grey," the voice calls out louder and he finally moves. He moves his hand up to the bottom of my bra. My heart hammers against my chest.

"Grey!" The voice shouts and Grey lets out a dark groan before his head moves and I figure he's opened his eyes.

"I like you underneath me," he grumbles quietly, his thumb caressing the wire at the bottom of my bra. *He likes me to not be able to breathe?*

"Get up man," the guy calls and Grey lets out a grunt. He finds the top of my shirt all the way bunched up at the top of my breasts and he pulls it down for me before rolling off. I intake a deep breath, finally getting the air I need.

"Wh-" the guy makes a little bit of a surprised noise once I'm revealed. I decide to keep going with the idea of acting like I'm still asleep to avoid awkward confrontation. So, I turn over on my side away from the door and hope for the best. Bear isn't even here to help me get through it. I feel Grey sit up from beside me, his arm brushing against my back.

"Almost all of us are out here so..." the guy trails off, most likely looking over at me.

"Stop looking at her," Grey grumbles out as I feel his hand grab my shirt and pull it down to cover my exposed back that I didn't know was exposed.

"Alright, alright," the guy says defensively, "whenever y'all are ready to come out, we'll be here. I think one of the guys is cooking so we'll be here for a while."

"Yeah thanks for just fuckin' showing up," Grey's voice stays unhappy.

"Well San has news about the last bust," the guy says. *I feel like an agent listening to this. Is this illegal?*

"Tell Sanfred that I'm kicking his fucking ass for bringing all you fucks," Grey responds unhappily and the guy chuckles.

"Will do," he closes the door, and considering how long I've already been acting asleep, I'm tired again. I fall back asleep as Grey is getting off the bed and walking to the bathroom. I'm woken up hardly ten minutes later.

"C'mon," Grey's voice coaxes me as he takes one of my hands and pulls me to a sitting position. With the lights now on in the room, I keep my eyes closed.

"Lilah, open those eyes," his amused voice says, and I squint them open. He helps me out of the bed and walks me to the bathroom. My heart flutters seeing the toothbrush I used from last time now in the holder he puts his in. I brush my teeth and still squint my eyes. *How freaking bright does this guy like his lights?! Gosh darn.* I wiggle on my feet, and he sighs before wrapping an arm around my waist and stepping behind me, holding my body still by letting me lean my back against his still bare chest. His other hand comes to rest on my stomach. 3.. 2..1

"You hungry?" he questions, and I groan a little. I brush my teeth and then throw water on my face to wake me up. Grey grabs me a towel and he puts it directly on my face. He doesn't wipe the water off, he just holds it on my face.

"Thanks," I mumble against the towel and finally he actually wipes my face. Is he even going to speak about sleeping literally right on top of me or not? But it's not like I'm bringing it up, I was "asleep." I look at his butt. I raise my hand a slight bit to smack it but then I lower it back. *Ooh, I want to.*

I put my hair up in a bun but halfway through twisting it my arms get tired, and I have to lean over against the sink to rest my arms for a second. I have noodle arms. I finish with my hair and look at myself in the mirror. Then I look at Grey who is looking at me in the mirror with a little smirk on his face.

"What?" I question a little smile now on my face. He just shakes his head, rocking back on his heels. I take the extra hair tie on my wrist off and tie the back of his shirt so that it fits me better and doesn't drown me. Once back in his room, I put on my brace with a long sigh. Grey doesn't make a move to put a shirt on and quite frankly, I'm glad. I could stare at his goodies all day long. He opens his door and leads me out. I hear talking. A lot of talking.

"Grey, how many people are here?" I stress. He turns around and gives me a one-shouldered shrug.

"Probably fifteen," my eyes widen, and I shake my head, stopping in my tracks.

"I'm not going," I announce, and he rolls his eyes.

"Don't act like you're shy," he says, knowing I'm the furthest thing from shy. He grabs my hand, but I plant my feet in the ground like that'll totally stop him from taking me anywhere.

"I'm not going," I repeat as if those are the only words I'm programmed to say. What would I even do in a room full of people who I don't know? I'd try to talk but they'd only ignore me like everyone else. It's pretty much a given that they'll hate me. Everyone does. Grey did when he first met me. Probably still a little actually.

"Fine, stay there," he begins walking away and I smile a little in victory. He gets a good four steps away before turning around and storming back toward me. I try to get away but I'm not all that fast considering my predicament in the knee region. He grips onto my hand and begins pulling me. I dig my feet into the ground and that does one hundred percent, absolutely nothing at all. So, I fall to the ground like a dead weight.

"God, you're a child," he grumbles and I, fully on my back, stare up at him. He lets go of my hand only to grab onto my non-injured leg and continue to drag me.

"Grey," I warn, "I swear if you drag me in there, I'll..."

"You'll what? Huh?"

"I'll dognap Bear," I say my threat and he narrows his eyes at me. I bet a hundred dollars that it'd be the easiest dognap ever. He'd probably just follow me wherever and be happy and excited while doing it.

"I'm not scared of your threats, Lilah."

"Ooh, you should be," I warn him, "I'm a dangerous little person."

His grip loosens, and I take that as my chance to escape. I turn over on my stomach quickly and use my little arm strength to grab onto the door frames and drag myself back to his room. He grabs my foot and pulls me back, effectively riding up my shirt to right under my bra. He turns me back over and I'm lying there, my stomach all out and exposed.

"Now look," I motion toward my stomach and his eyes look there, "you've gone and got my belly button cold."

I lower my shirt back down and he raises it back. I get goosebumps and they're kind of obvious, which is *fantastic*.

"What's that?" he points to the scar on my ribs where I had surgery on the stupid things.

"A scar."

"No shit."

"Oh yes."

"Where'd it come from?" he questions and I let out a little sigh.

"I once saved a child from a train," I sigh dramatically

"Shit," he draws out sarcastically.

"The crash. I have metal plates in my ribs," I explain.

"I didn't mean to bring it up."

"It's okay," I offer him a smile, sitting up. He grabs my hands and helps me stand.

"Now c' mon," he urges, and I plant my feet again.

"What's the deal?" he huffs out and I fiddle with my fingers. He grabs them to get me to stop.

"No one likes me," I start quietly, "those people won't either."

"And I'll punch them in the fuckin' dicks. Quit being bashful because you know you're not, let's go," he says, and although he threatened a whole bunch of peepee's he made me feel a bit better. I sigh and unplant my feet. I keep my head down as we walk into the loud living room. I almost whine when the room suddenly gets quite a bit quieter.

"Goddamn, I thought you were kidding," a voice near me says.

"I told you,' The voice from this morning responds.

"Azalea?" Jai's voice questions and a breath of relief escapes my lips. I look up to see him sitting on the couch beside the guy I told he had a small peter. My eyes narrow a little at him. Faint bruises cover his face, and I would high-five the person who did that to him if I knew who it was. I look around the room and Grey was right. Fifteen or so guys look back at me.

I've never been surrounded by so many guys in my life. They all look perfect for my pimping business. Grey pulls me into the kitchen, and I hear Jai follow, and some other people.

"Are your lungs deflated?" Karter, the guy who I called Dr. Weiner when he checked out my knee, asks.

"Grey was laying right on top of you. Fully on top of you. I didn't even see you until he rolled off," a guy with the prettiest hazel eyes I've ever seen says. Am I lost in his eyes? Yes.

"You have really nice eyes," I blurt, "the color."

A little smile reaches his lips, and his cheeks tinge the lightest color of pink. I hold back an aw. I want to hug him because he's so cute.

"Thank you," he clears his throat and Grey gives my hand a rough tug, pulling me closer to him.

"I'm Theo," he smiles.

"She's Azalea, now enough," Grey grumbles and Jai smirks a little from beside Theo.

"Have I seen you somewhere before?" another guy asks. I'm mesmerized by his butt. It's very nice. And round. I'm a pervert.

"No," I shake my head, "I would've remembered you."

"Why is that?" he tilts his head a little smirk on his face.

"Because your butt is very nice," I blab, and the smirk grows.

"How's that knee?" Karter asks. *Wouldn't you like to know, weather boy?* He moves to touch it. I move it away.

"I swear, you're going to get kicked in the face-hole," I warn. I feel Grey's eyes on the side of my face. I look at him through the corner of my eye and see that he's looking at me with a little smirk on his face.

"I swear she's my favorite person," Jai gives me a wink, nudging nice-butt-guy. I'm lifted like a child by my underarms and sat on the marble kitchen counter. I look at Grey's face to give him a 'really' look but he looks unhappy.

"What's the matter?" I question quietly and he shakes his head although I see his jaw ticking.

"You need to change that, Grey," Karter nods to Grey's bandage which covers the horrific stab wound. Karter moves forward and grabs the items we left out from me doing it for Grey last night. He only takes it out of his hand.

"You're not fuckin' touching me you rough fuck," he glares icily at

Karter and my eyebrows raise in surprise.

"C'mere Lilah, " he walks over to me, handing me the stuff.

"And you're not supposed to be lifting-" he refers to Grey lifting me onto the counter but is cut off.

"Kiss my ass," he says to Karter who seems pretty much unfazed. It's now that I realize that even from the beginning Grey was on the *nicer* side to me.

"You're gentle," he speaks softly to me, and I bite my lip, keeping the huge smile off my lips.

"I still hurt you though," I begin taking the bandage off.

"Not enough to make me kick your ass," he mumbles and my eyes widen as I meet his.

"Not that I would ever, " he recovers quickly, "that didn't come out right."

Karter must've gotten his butt whooped then. Speaking of that, I do see a little cut on his lip and a slight bruise on the bridge of his nose. I change his bandage carefully and gently and as soon as I'm done, he grabs a plate and sticks it in my hands.

"Eat," he demands. I sigh unhappily at his tone.

"Please eat," he fixes it real quick and I give him a smile. He helps me off the counter and leads me to the dining room table where a few other guys sit and eat or talk. I take a seat and before I can even dig in, my eyes find the hair of the guy in the seat closest to me. I fall in love with his curtain-style haircut and soft light brown hair. His hair reminds me of Jared Leto's on the show *Camp Wilder*.

"Azalea," Jai comes next to me, getting the attention of the amazing-hair guy who looks at me.

"You going to eat that?" Jai points to the bacon on my plate. I lean forward, closer to Jared Leto's hair clone.

"I love your hair," I smile, looking up at it. I bite my lip at it. I want to play with it. I bet it's soft.

"Thank you," he leans his chin on his hand, grinning widely and I watch as a piece of hair falls over his eye.

"I love your smile," he says, and I hold my heart. No one's ever told me that before.

"Thank you," I gush sincerely.

"You're a cutie," he chuckles, and I hold my heart again. No one's ever told me that before either. *Did I make a friend?*

"Linc," Jai calls out but Linc ignores him, keeping his eyes on me while I watch his hair.

"Lincoln!" Jai calls louder, finally getting his attention, "you better watch yourself, you horny bastard. Grey ought to whoop your ass for flirting with her."

He was flirting with me? I turn to where Grey was standing but he's gone. Why would he even be that upset about it? *Yeah sure, just leave me here with all these guys, that's fine.*

~~~

At six-thirty at night, Grey finally gets all the guys out of the house. He hasn't spoken to me since I bandaged him up earlier and I'm slowly planning to kick him in that nice butt of his. He closes the door and with the glare that's been on his face for *hours*, he sits on the couch scowling at the tv.

"What's wrong?" I ask him for the fifth time since earlier. He only shakes his head. He doesn't even say *anything*.

"Grey," I deadpan, knowing he's lying. He directs his glare toward me. *Excuse me, sir.*

"*Nothing*," he says darkly. I stay silent, my hand rubbing up and down Bear's back. I don't even remember doing anything to him. To make things worse, he won't even tell me if it was me and what I did or did not do.

"Fine," I huff. A good ten seconds pass.

"If you would just tell me then we could solve whatever is wron-"

"Fuck," he curses, standing from his seated position and pacing around the room slowly, his hands fussing with my scrunchie harshly.

"You're messing with me Azalea," he says my actual name, and I know something is serious.

"What do you mean?" I ask softly.

"You're fucking with my head," his jaw ticks continuously.

"I don't understand Grey," I say quietly, furrowing my eyebrows in confusion.

"How do you think it makes me feel when you're off telling those fucks that you like their hair? Or their eyes? And goddammit Azalea, Maxon's *ass*? Are you serious?" he goes off and I watch him as he does. *Maybe I'm not the best at giving compliments.*

"Well-" he cuts me off.

"I'm not fucking done," he says deeply, and I shut up, "you hug *me*, you kiss *me*, you sleep with *me*, you're showing *me* how to do this, you don't say my eyes are pretty, why the fuck are you saying it to them?" I recall my attempt at making a friend to those few guys. I guess the approach for making guy friends and girl friends must be different.

"I can't do this if all you are is another thing to worry about. I don't need that shit and I sure as hell don't need some girl to be fucking with my head," he shakes his head.

"Grey you're like my best friend-"

"For fuck's sake Azalea," he lifts his head to the ceiling. I thought he wanted to hear that I *am* his friend. That I'm here for him and that I'm not something that he should worry about because I'm his *friend*.

"*I don't want to be your fucking friend.*"

My heart falls and I look down at my hands, swallowing the lump in my throat. Are we really going back to the old way? I hear him stop in front of me and bend down. He grips the sides of my face and tilts my head up to his.

"I can't be your friend when every time I look at you, I want to fuck you. I want to touch you in places only I should be allowed to. I want your eyes always on me. I want to kiss you not here," he leans his forehead against mine.

"But here," he runs his thumb over my lip, and I shudder. *Frick everything friendly.*

"I know you think I'll hurt you. I know you do," he pulls away looking into my eyes, "I've already done it way too many times. And I've got a lot to learn about this, but I *want* to learn it from *you*. I need you to straighten me out and help me get my shit together and I promise I can be more than just your friend."

"Grey," I start as soft as a whisper placing my hand on the side of his face.

"I want to fall in love with you," he whispers.

Chapter Fifteen

Selfish

❀Azalea❀

"Almost two days Azalea," my father's voice reaches my ears as soon as I step foot into my room. *My 'safe' place.*

"I've been waiting for you. I need 'shine," he glares up at me from his seat on my bed. *I can't do this again.* He sees my hesitance and he rises to his feet coming to stand directly in front of me. My heart pounds in fear of him.

"Fine. You don't want to," he shrugs, and I think he's going to let me go. I shouldn't have thought that. He undoes his belt and my heart falls to my feet.

"Dad please," I beg, and it doesn't stop him, "I'll get it!"

Seeing that he's not even thinking about stopping, I turn to go get out of my room and hopefully out of the house. Maybe Grey is still here. My father grabs my arm, and he jerks me back, striking my back harshly with his belt. I fall onto one knee as a cry escapes my lips. I don't count how many times he does it. With each hit, I get weaker, and eventually my back is numb to the point where I don't cry out anymore. At that point, he stops. Without a look at me, he leaves my room. I'm left on the floor unmoving.

I stay for a week laying still. A week of me alone in my room, my door locked, and in constant fear that Dad will come back and do it all over again. I guess it really is a form of his punishment. Maybe I should just stop being a baby and I should get used to it. I feel utterly terrible for ignoring Grey's calls and his texts, but I know if I don't then he'll convince me to see him and I *do not* want a *fed* to see what Dad has done.

It's even worse than telling Aaron. Friday, exactly a week and one day after receiving the welts on my back, I can finally move around and do things with less struggle or pain. After cleaning my closet out, I get in the tub and take a nice warm and relaxing bath.

My phone rings from the sink where I sat it. My heart hurts at the thought of me ignoring Grey. *I want to fall in love with you.* Those words buttered my biscuit in an unimaginably perfect way. To even think that someone, anyone, would even like me like that is wild to me. After my bath, I feel refreshed and content for the first time in a week. And I know I smell amazing. I throw on a lilac-colored sports bra and a huge, oversized T-shirt.

I walk into my room running my fingers through my wet hair and I have a full-blown heart attack upon seeing the man in my room. I grasp my heart and gasp loudly. Although my heart fills with happiness as I see him for the first time in a week, his face is not happy. *Wait, he can't be here.*

"Grey you can't be here, you have to leave," I rush out. If Dad sees him here, gosh knows what he'd do to me after he'd leave. How did he get in anyway? *Oh, what if he's the type of fed that sneaks into houses to catch people?*

"The fuck do you mean I can't be here?" He asks unhappily.

"You ignore me for a week and as soon as I *finally* see you, you tell me to leave?"

I feel terrible. I'm a terrible person.

"I know, I know," I nod completely taking the blame. *Am I selfish for not wanting to get hit with the belt again?* I wouldn't want Grey to feel upset. Maybe another whipping for him to feel better is okay.

"I'm sorry Grey," I tell him sincerely and he softens.

"I don't know how I haven't ruined this thing," he lifts up the scrunchie, "stressing over you."

I walk to him and wrap my arms around his waist. He moves to wrap his arms around me, but I catch them before he can touch my back and I place them back down by his side. He tenses.

"Why won't you let me touch you?" His voice goes unhappy.

"How'd you get in?" I redirect the conversation. I release his waist and walk over to my window.

"The door was open," he says, and I look down into our driveway. *Dad's car isn't here.* I breathe a breath of relief turning back to him.

"What's going on Azalea?" His jaw ticks as he searches for answers.

"Nothing," I avert my eyes away from his. He steps forward and tries to wrap his arms around me. Before they can touch my back, I step out of his reach.

"Why won't you let me touch you?" he grows frustrated and I only feel worse.

"Here, here, I'm sorry," I grab his arms and direct them to wrap around my very lower back. His arms relax and I'm tenser than ever. Lord knows when Dad will come back.

"What is it, hm?" His hand reaches up and he brushes a wet strand behind my ear. I lean into his touch even though my mind tells me not to.

"Let me see you," I hear the want in his voice, and I let him tilt my chin up to meet his eyes.

"You need to leave," I attempt one last time.

"Spend the night with me," he says, "come back with me."

I'm so selfish, aren't I?

"Grey, I can't. I'm sure there's some other girl that would love to though. I can't," my words hurt my heart. *Like that girl he kissed in the same room he kissed me in.* His eyes turn dark, and he gives me a glare that I hadn't seen in a while.

"Bull-fucking-shit. You can. You're an adult. You can do what you want to. Is your dad telling you shit? Your mom? I don't want some other *girl, I want you,"* he furrows his eyebrows. I'm hardly an adult.

"You fucking *know* I want you. Only you," he grumbles. *What am I supposed to say now?*

"My Dad doesn't...he doesn't *want* me to be around...um...you..." I struggle and he lets out a scoff.

"Fuck what he says."

"I can't," I say softly. I live under his roof. And I have no idea what he'd do to me if he found out that Grey was here and that I'd left with him. His other hand begins raising on my back. I grab it before he can get too far up. His jaw clenches.

"I haven't touched you all fucking week and when I finally have you in front of me, you barely let me," He grumbles out and I feel bad again, looking down at the ground. He lets go of me and he slips his boots off. I watch him with slightly confused eyes as he walks over to my bed. He grips my hand suddenly and pulls me into his lap, facing him.

"Do you *want* me to touch you?" he asks, his soft eyes traveling down to where my body meets his. *Of course, I do.* I give him a little nod and his hands come to rest on my thighs before trailing up and then going back down. He repeats the action in a soft soothing rub on my thighs.

"Just there, okay?" I make sure he won't touch my back again.

"Just here," he agrees softly, and I let out a quiet hum. His hands progressively trail a little bit higher, and I rest my head on his chest. When his hands reach under my shirt and up onto my upper thighs, he tilts me away from him. He grabs the bottom of my shirt and before I can stop him with 'Woah, I ain't got no britches on' he lifts it up. He gets a view of my favorite pair of pink and purple striped underwear. He lets out a throaty groan before lowering my shirt back slowly.

"It's funny because this time I actually *don't* have pants on," I let out a little laugh he doesn't laugh. He only grips my legs harder and pulls me closer to him, resting his forehead on mine.

"God, I want you Lilah. More than I've ever wanted anyone else."

"Aw, Grey," my heart flutters and he pulls his head away from mine, a little confuzzled look on his handsome face.

"You want my hugs? Is that it? Well, guess what? You can have all the hugs you want," I smile happily. *I love that he wants me. I guess my hugs are better than I thought.*

"C'mere," I wrap my arms around his neck but his stay by his side.

My great hugs shock him apparently. I rub my hand up and down his strong back for a few minutes before pulling away. He's still got the same look on his face.

"Do you want another, Sugar?" I tease and his face turns unhappy. I go in for another.

"Don't call me that," he mumbles against my shoulder. *He'll like it eventually.*

"Then don't call me Lilah," I propose, and he stiffens before letting out a harsh 'No.'

"I'll go put on pants if that's what you wan-"

"No," he grips my legs, holding me to him. I lean against him, and I get a whiff of his scent. He smells so good. *Dad doesn't agree apparently.* I pick up the front of my shirt and smell that too. It's beginning to smell of him. *Dad wouldn't like that either.* I lean over to my bedside table and grab a nice, scented perfume. I spray a little in the air and let it fall onto us.

"What's that for?"

"Now you can smell as much like me as I do you. And my dad won't be able to smell that you've been here. You smell very good, but he says you smell like a *man*."

"The guys already tell me I smell like you," His eyes fall over every inch of my face. Now he's going to smell more like me.

"Well, I just don't want to get in trouble," I put the bottle back. He sighs harshly before sliding one hand under my butt and lifting me with him as he stands. *Good gosh, what does this guy bench? 800 pounds?* He lays down on my bed, with me fully on top of him.

"What's wrong with your back?" He asks seriously.

"I hurt it."

"How?" He asks and I search my brain.

"Sex," I blurt. He tenses before relaxing after a few seconds.

"Goddammit, Lilah."

~~~

I wake up casually and instantly feel Grey's hand brushing my hair out of my face. I realize I'm still directly on top of him, but I don't feel bad because he did the exact same thing to me, and he weighs a good 23,583 pounds more than me. Or at least that's what it felt like. I roll my head over to the clock, feeling his eyes trained on the side of my face, and nearly have a heart attack when I see that it's almost time for mom to come home. Plus, who knows when dad will be home?

"Grey, you really have to go now," I tell him. He lets out a harsh sigh and he lifts both of us out of my bed. He grasps my chin gently but firmly.

"You don't deserve to be treated like a fucking child," He sneers but not at me. *But I'm living under his roof.*

"You do whatever the fuck you want," he adds. *But he'll probably hurt me.*

"And for you to not be allowed to *smell* like me? That's bullshit."

"Tell your dad that he can kiss my ass," he releases me and goes to put his shoes on. *I would never speak out against him. I can't.* I'm actually excited to hear Grey talk this much.

"Let me guess," he finishes putting on one shoe, "you can't?"

"I could treat you better than these fucks and I'm still learning how to."

"You're nineteen, not ten," he grumbles.

"You don't understand," I sigh.

"Why? Because I don't have parents?" He asks and I feel bad.

"No, no. My dad, he's just..." I hesitate and he notices narrowing his eyes.

"He just what?"

"He just parents in a different way that's all."

I suppose.

"And your mom?" He asks.

"She doesn't have much to do with me," I mumble. *Except for the occasional telling Dad that I've had enough.*

"We all were affected by Jake's passing in a different way," I shrug a single shoulder.

"Don't ignore me anymore," he says sharply before adding a softer 'please.'

"Okay," I agree opening my door to walk him out now that he's got his shoes back on. We make it outside and to Grey's Jeep. He leans against the side of his car and grabs my arm pulling me flush to him.

"I've got to go away for a while after tomorrow," he says, and I feel a little myself shrink in disappointment.

"How long?" I question.

"Four or five days," he sighs, and I bite my lip in the thought of who the heck I'm going to talk to when he's gone. His hands fall to the back of my upper thighs, and he pulls my lower half closer to his. Holy mother of Jesus. Am I okay? I don't think I know how to breathe anymore.

He lowers his head to my neck and gives the skin right under my jaw a little bite. *Woah, baby.* Thoughts fill my head and I remind myself to give an extra-long prayer tonight. Me being me, aka a slight idiot, I grab onto his hands and move them up to where I want them. My booty cheeks. I no longer think about the fact that I don't have pants on, all that registers is his warm hands on me. He brings his head out of my neck, a gorgeous smirk on his face.

"You like that, hm?" He gives my hind end a little squeeze and I get hot. I love you Jesus, and I'm sorry.

"Are you going away for work?" I clear my throat after starting the sentence and my voice coming out slightly higher. He gives me a nod, his eyes traveling all over my face.

"Don't get stabbed. Or headbutted. Or hurt. Please," I say, and his eyes soften. If it happens again, somebody is going to get got. And if someone gets got, then I'm going to have to go on the run from the po-po.

"Are you catching a bad guy, or what?" I smile. He rolls his eyes a little before giving me a small nod. I wish my life was nearly as exciting as his. He gets to manage a restaurant, which I don't even know why he does, and also catch bad guys for a living. What do I do? From time to time, I put a new shipment of books away on bookshelves. I wonder if he was chasing a bad guy the first time we got milkshakes together? When he basically kidnapped me in the backroom.

"Who were we hiding from the first time we got milkshakes?" I speak my thoughts.

"No one you need to worry about," he says dryly, and I bite my tongue. He can't just say that to me. I'm way too curious and my mind wanders off. A lot.

"Was the person a local pimp?" I could learn the ways.

"Sure," he rolls his eyes again. I hear a car pulling into the driveway and I quickly move his hands from me and back up. I feel his scowl on the side of my face, but I ignore it as I watch mom's car drive up the driveway. *Still no pants.* She won't tell dad, right?

"You should go, Grey," I tell him quietly. I feel him lean down to kiss my cheek. I stop him before he can, my heart feeling heavy. He could get hurt and I'm not even letting him kiss my cheek, being too scared that mom will tell dad. I really am selfish. I watch as his jaw clenches and his eyes take on a dark essence. I whisper the world's quietest 'I'm sorry' to him but I'm not sure if he heard it. I hear mom's car door shut as Grey opens his. I feel her hand on my arm as I watch his car drive away.

"Go inside, Azalea," she says, and I do as she says with her following right behind me. She shuts the door behind us as soon as we're both inside.

"You shouldn't be bringing him around like that," she says and I look down at my feet.

"If your father would've found out about him being here, we don't know what he'd do," she says and I'm thankful that she's fully sober at the moment.

"Make my back welt up with his belt? Or lock me in Jake's room again?" I question out looking up at her. Her dark brown hair lays flat, and her eyes look back at me tiredly. I notice a faint bruise on her cheek, and I grow upset. It's one thing to put his hands on me; I understand his violence against me. But mom did nothing.

"When did he start hitting you?" my voice cracks.

"I don't know," she breathes, shaking her head slowly.

"Please," I plead, my eyes tearing up, but I don't let them fall.

"Please stop drinking," I whisper out, watching her dulled blue eyes well up. I turn and go up to my room, not giving her time to answer. *Please.*

Chapter Sixteen

Miami

* Grey *

A day after touching down in Miami, we've settled in where we've been put to stay and have been introduced to the unit we're assisting for the rest of the week. It pisses me off the looks we get because we're young. If we were bad at what we did, we wouldn't have the job we do. It doesn't piss me off as much as the fact that Azalea is obviously hiding something from me. And not letting me touch her. And the way she had ignored me for a *full fucking week. And one day.*

The girl doesn't understand that I've thrown everything I used to do all away for her. It's not like I did shit with a girl every night or anything, but I had the occasional hookup and 'fun.' It's different going as long as I have without hooking up and not even *wanting to. Unless the girl is her.*

And I know that Jonas catching me and her in that room together hurt her. Him being the idiot he is just had to add the 'another one?' The only other one beside Azalea that had been in that room with me was a random girl that had followed me into the back room. Did we do shit? Hell no, I kicked her drunk ass out. But did Jonas just happen to walk in there? Yeah. But I'm not a liar and I *do* want to fall in love with her. Who wouldn't want to? I don't have a damn clue what the feeling is like to love someone. I don't even think that word has ever left my lips before but with her, I can feel it being a possibility. *If I don't fuck things up first.*

Even now, for the first time in my life, I think I miss her. I think; I don't know what that feeling is. But I feel like I'm missing something, and it isn't the fucking scrunchie on my wrist or our weaponry. *Her stupid random comments.* Even her laugh has my heart feeling like a dumb blubbering bitch. I take another sip of my fucking milkshake. *Goddammit.* Roman looks at me with a calculated gaze. I glare back at him.

"Are you mad at your milkshake?" Jai asks from beside me and I loosen my grip on the cup in my hand.

"No."

"They're ready for us to be there," Roman chimes in.

"They can fuckin' wait."

"They've already been waiting for almost an hour now. You've got a long-lasting milkshake," Jai chuckles. I feel my jaw tick as I rise from my seat. Arriving at the unit's HQ I walk into the meeting room and they're all there. Jai and Roman follow soon after and take their seats along one of the tables.

"Joshua Vander," I speak out, picking up his file.

"He's been on the run since early last year," I continue. *And apparently you fucks can't catch him, that's why we're here.*

"Hold up," a guy sitting at one of the tables say suddenly. I feel a scowl form on my face at the interruption. A guy, probably in his mid-thirties, leans forward at his table, his eyes on me.

"They expect us to listen to some twenty-something year old who's wearing a scrunchie and drinking a milkshake?" he asks out. What the fuck is everyone's deal with the goddamn scrunchie? I sit my milkshake down. I guess the title FAA that rests on the board behind me doesn't mean shit to him.

"If it bothers you that much," I keep my voice calm, "go ahead and don't listen to me. Then get your fucking ass killed, see if I care."

"It'd be under your mission," he tries back. Everyone else remains quiet. Like that would hurt me.

"Not my responsibility. You don't follow my orders, that's your own fucking fault. I'm only here to win the chase that you couldn't," I look down at the ring on his ring finger. I'm embarrassed for his wife.

"Who says we couldn't catch him ourselves?" his face turns redder and redder as he gets mad.

"The time limit between the date the warrant was set and now," I look at the original warrant date, "almost two years ago."

"Fuck you," he sneers. Being as old as he is, I would've thought he'd be less of a prick. Guess not.

"What the fuck do you know? I've been in this unit for over ten years, I know what the hell I'm doing!" he stands up and I pick up my milkshake, taking another sip.

"Well damn!" Maxon chuckles. The one Azalea said had a *nice fucking ass*.

"Why didn't you tell us that!" he says sarcastically, "If you're so good, where is he?"

The room remains quiet.

"Oh, don't tell me you don't know," Jai chimes in, shaking his head.

"Now sit the fuck down and shut up," I give him one more glare before going back to explaining what we're going to do to catch the guy.

~~~

In a quick two days, we find his location and have our means of catching him planned and memorized. Jai hands out the padded leathers. Her voice fills my thoughts. *'Don't get stabbed. Or headbutted. Or hurt. Please.'* I grit my teeth and yank a jacket from Jai's hands whose eyes widen in surprise. I pull on the jacket and sit her scrunchie down on the table, pushing the thoughts of her out of my head.

"You're wearing-"

"Shut up," I cut off Theo as we get into the SUVs. On the ride, my mind drifts off to her. Her soft sighs when I kiss her neck. Her body shimmying excitedly when she sees me. Her soft skin. *Fuck.*

I get a surge of adrenaline when we pull up to Joshua's hideout. A shack in the middle of the goddamn swamp.

"If I get eaten by a damn 'gator, I'm going to be pissed," Jai mumbles as we get out of the cars and sink our boots into the deep mud.

"Is now a bad time to admit I'm scared of reptiles?" Theo's voice comes from behind me. The guy she said had *pretty eyes. I hope one bites him in the ass.* We execute our plan exactly as it was written. Being nearly soundless, we walk through the front part of his shack. Guns lay all over his shabby couch. Not taking any chances, I motion for them to be taken out before we head into the back of the run-down place.

We find Joshua and a hooker both asleep on a mattress that sits on the floor. I walk in the room first. The woman's breathing catches my attention. She breathes at an abnormal pace for anyone who's sleeping. Or awake; it's way too fast. I look at Joshua. I just barely see his arm twitch and I know that they know we're here.

I hold my arm up to the guys behind me. His lower arm twitches and he shoots up in a flash, a gun positioned in his hand. Instead of firing, he grabs the barely clothed girl beside him and holds the gun to her head. The guys fill the room, and he looks at us all.

"Drop your guns, o-or I'll kill her," he warns shakily, obviously shaken up by the fact that he's been caught. He won't hesitate to kill her, he's already neck-deep in records and charges; he's got nothing to lose. I nod to the floor, and we place our guns down slowly, kicking them to the bed.

"She doesn't have anything to do with this Josh," Jai speaks and with the silence in the room, we hear the safety on his gun click off.

"I don't give a fuck," he shakes his head, pressing the gun further into the girl's temple. I flit my eyes toward the window Josh is standing next to. Roman can barely be seen through the bushes at his position on top of the run-down building beside the shack Josh lives in. A long rifle sits in front of him.

"You don't want to do this, just let the girl go," Jai warns, knowing what will happen if he doesn't let go of the woman. With a small nod of my head, Roman takes the shot. Joshua falls limply to the ground, the woman falling with him. As soon as she's down, she's back up sobbing with horror.

My eyes find the guy who loved to fucking argue with me earlier.

"Clean this up," I nod at the body on the floor and his face falls as my lip rises in a small smirk. Clearing the shit-shack of paraphernalia and guns we leave the swamp.

"We're in Miami, let's party," Maxon groans, climbing up into the dark SUV.

"I'm up for it," Theo nods, along with the rest of the fucking people in the car. They don't have a shit ton of paperwork. It's not like I have a desire to fucking 'party' in the first place. Five and a half hours later, the finished paperwork sits on the table and the fucking idiots stare back at me.

"Now we go," Theo smiles and I scowl at him. I look up at the clock and see it's already three-thirty in the morning. The sooner I fucking sleep, then the sooner I can go home, and go to Lilah. My mind wanders off to her. Sleeping in my bed. *Fuck.*

~~~

Six beers in, I'm a little buzzed. That doesn't change the fact that I still want to *fucking leave*.

"Look," Linc slaps my shoulder, "you're having a good time, aren't you?"

Ass.

"Don't fuckin' touch me," I glare at the fuck. I sink down on a couch in the VIP section.

"I think you need a good lay," Linc says, and I hold back from punching him in the *fucking face*. I finish my seventh beer, grabbing another. I feel someone sit beside me and my jaw ticks. I look to my left to see a blonde-haired girl staring right back at me.

"What are you doing all by yourself?" she asks seductively. Her hand slips to my arm and she runs her fingers over my tattoos. I *don't* like to be fucking touched.

"I think I should join you," she whispers, her lip rolling into her mouth. All I see is someone who is *not* Azalea. And that's *not* what I want. This girl's hair is too dark of a blonde to be Azalea's hair color. Her eyes are bright blue instead of that fucking wild green. The girl beside me is too tall and too leggy to be who I want. This girl's smile can't make my heart beat faster than it's supposed to. And she sure as hell can't turn me on by using that voice or showing me what's down her shirt. I stand up and walk away from her. *Not what I want.*

    I fall onto my bed at the hotel and with my clothes on and everything, I sleep. I wake up with a slight headache and a pissy attitude. We all pack up our shit and board the plane, hangovers and all. No one talks to anyone, and I wish they had hangovers all the fucking time. We land in Nashville and split from there. Most of the guys go home. I go to Mr. Terrip's. Walking in the front, I'm met by the frail old man that Azalea loves so much. He peers up at me from his desk.

    "Your Azalea is near the back," he nods to the back of the store. *My Azalea.* I see the back of her as she picks up a handful of books, rearranging them on the shelf that is eye level with her. My heart does weird shit when she lightly shakes those fucking hips. She turns suddenly and the books fly out of her hands. She shimmies happily when she sees me before extending her arms out, a wide smile on her face. Her body finally touches mine.

    "Did you miss me, Sugar?" That *damn* name passes her lips. It pisses me off how easily that name can make me get goosebumps. I'm pretty sure I did miss her. I just give her a little nod to which she giggles.

    "C'mere," her hand falls to my back and I'm put in a fucking trance when her bottom lip rolls into her mouth.

    "Did you catch your bad guy-fella?" she questions, sitting down on a couch in a clearing of the shelves, pulling me down with her.

    "Or girl!" She says suddenly.

    "I could just as easily be a wanted person. I've done so many illegal things, it isn't even funny," I watch her intently as she talks. The fact that she talks so much used to annoy the living shit out of me. Now I just like the sound of her voice. And the wild shit that comes out of her mouth. *God, why did I miss her so much?*

    "Why are you being so quiet?" she asks, tilting her head in curiosity.

Lilah   *K. Pope*

A blonde lock falls across her face and barely a second passes before I'm getting it out of the way, scowling at how it was covering her from me.

"When do I ask for you to be my girlfriend?"

Being so close to her, I feel the intake of air she breathes in when I ask the question.

"I'm just slightly confused on why it is that you still want to be...um," she hesitates, "with me?"

Hell if I know. In case she hasn't noticed, I've never been in an actual relationship. I steered clear of the whole relationship thing. If you can't treat a girl right, why put her through your shit? But I can't stay away from the girl in front of me. And I hope to God she's already been through the worst of my shit. I'm learning. I watch the ways she talks to me, and I try my hardest to mimic the softness. Except for times when I get pissed off.

I've gotten my first fit of jealousy. Still haven't gotten over it actually. I'm *drawn* to her. So fucking drawn to her and I don't know why. My hands always need to be on her. I always need to see her. And I'm pretty happy hearing her voice. I look down at my hands that lay on the smooth skin of her bare thighs.

"Whenever you would want," she explains. I stay quiet.

"Don't ask me now," she blurts, "I'm a simple child, but I'd rather be asked without knowing you're going to ask me."

"You're not a child," I grumble.

"Right."

"I missed you," I admit just leaving out the 'a lot' part. Her mouth opens and a little gasp leaves her lips. Then her face morphs into the same one she has when she sees Bear. Her hand comes to rest on the side of my face and before my heart can do that shit it does when she touches me, she opens her damn mouth.

"You're so cute."

Are you *kidding me*? Theo's got pretty eyes, Maxon's got the perfect ass for her, Linc's got the hair she *adores,* and what am I? Oh, I'm pretty fucking cute.

"What?" her voice turns into a teasing one which only makes my scowl deepen, "you don't like being called cute?"

I can't tell.

"At least she doesn't think you're ugly," Mr. Terrip's weathered voice sings as he strolls by us which elicits a giggle from her.

"So, where'd you go?" her words barely register as she presses herself up against me on the couch.

"Miami," I grunt out. She looks at me for a minute, her eyes taking me in.

"I think you need a little hug," she says softly before leaning forward and wrapping her arms around my neck. I trace the waistband of the back of her shorts before casually slipping my arm under her, picking her up, and pulling her onto my lap. *She fits right on top of me so fucking well.* My hand trails up the back of her shirt and she lets out a soft breath.

I run my fingers down that *sexy* crease in the middle of her back, making sure to keep my eyes trained on her, taking in the way she tenses and slightly digs her hips down into mine. *Fuck.* She slightly leans closer to me, and I press a kiss on her soft cheek.

"What are you doing Azalea?" A guy's voice says, and she pulls away from me. I scowl.

"Giving Grey a hug," she explains simply.

"Yeah, while he's feeling you up?" the guy asks unhappily, motioning to my hand which is still under her shirt. *Who the fuck does he think he is?*

"Aaron. He's not feeling me up," she rolls her eyes. I was *slightly* feeling her up. I glare at him. She slides off my lap and I glare at him harder.

"The dickhead-" he starts, and I start standing. She grabs onto the back of my shirt and keeps me down. Why the fuck is her grip strong as hell?

"Don't start," she mumbles to me, and I give her a scowl. She narrows her eyes at my look.

"Aaron, don't call him that," she tells him, and my heart does stupid shit at her being the only person to ever defend me.

"You *said* he was a dickhead the last time I said he was," Aaron argues. *She said I was a dickhead?*

"*What the fuck*," I turn to her.

"I only said that because that was when you *were*," she says apologetically. I deserved it. I still do. I treated her like shit just because I was too caught up in the fact that I could never be deserving of a girl as perfect as her. Also knowing that she's Jake's little sister. I took out my anger on her. I deserve to be called worse than just a dickhead.

"He still is!" Aaron exclaims like he knows shit.

"He's taking advantage of you, Azalea. You're young and he just wants to get in your pants. How old is this guy anyway?" He hits a pretty big nerve in saying that I'm *taking advantage* of the one person who is my only chance at having it for longer than a night.

"Who the fuck are you to say I'm taking advantage of her?" I stand, getting up real close to him.

"You don't know shit," I sneer down at him.

"Just because some guy shows interest in you, that doesn't mean he wants anything other than sex," he looks at over at her.

"You can't act like you know him, Aaron," she comes up close to him, the most serious look I've ever seen on her face. He pissed little Lilah off.

"You're naive, Azalea," He stresses.

"And you're being a freaking jerk! What is wrong with you?" She shoves at his chest. He pissed her off bad.

"You're going to get fucked over," they have their own conversation about me, acting like I'm not even fucking here.

"He's old and he only wants one thing," he adds. Goddamn, what am I? Fucking fifty? *Shit.*

"He's twenty-four!"

"Twenty-five," I lightly nudge her, and she gasps, turning to me.

"Did you just have a birthday?" She asks.

"A couple weeks ago," I shrug a single shoulder. She furrows her eyebrows at me.

"And you didn't tell me, that's not nice."

"Azalea, focus," Aaron says and she turns back to him.

"He's twenty-five," she says.

"Yeah, and look at him!" He motions to me and my eyes narrow.

"He's got a fucking sleeve! Drug addicts, criminals, and gang members have sleeves," he stresses.

"What the fuck do you know?" I look at his polo shirt. Some fucking rich boy.

"You've been sheltered your whole fucking life, I can see it now," I sneer at him, "you wouldn't know the difference between real life and the shit your parents put in your head."

"And what? Let me guess? You don't have parents?" He mocks. *Is this guy for real?*

"Aaron, why would you say that? That's terrible to say," she places her hand on my back.

"Azalea, Jake wouldn't want you around people like this," he obviously hits a strong nerve when I feel her whole body tense. If only this fucker knew. *Who brings up a dead family member like that?*

"You know what your problem is? All you do is judge. Grey is nothing like you think and *don't* bring Jake up to win an argument against me. Sure, he may be rough around the edges and a little scary looking because he's a big guy, but I bet you *didn't* know that he gives the world's best hugs, he's got a darling puppy named Bear, and that he finds bad guys for a living!"

"He fiddles with my scrunchie when he's stressed," she lifts my wrist where her scrunchie sits.

"He's not very good at dodging headbutts," she says. I frown.

"But he's considerate and he listens to me, and he hugs me when I'm sad and he doesn't judge me, especially when I eat a whole entire pizza by myself," she finishes all in one breath and my eyes don't stray from her. *So, I'm doing things right, I guess.* Her hand falls to my ass. She gives it a continuous pat that could nearly send me to fucking sleep. I don't even think about stopping her.

"I don't want you to get hurt, Azalea," Aaron's voice takes a softer tone.

"I know Aaron, I'll be okay, I promise. But if you don't want me hurt, then don't be mean to him," she says sternly. I can't believe I was ever so terrible to her. She's the one person who least deserves it.

"Same goes to you Grey," she says and my eyebrows furrow. I did jack shit to this fuck.

"Fighting in my store does nothing when it comes to me trying to get customers," Mr. Terrip walks by us, a couple of books in his hands.

"Sorry," she apologizes as he saunters away.

"What are you doing here, Aaron?" she questions.

"I came to see you Azzy," Aaron steps forward putting an arm around her. I feel the glare return full force along with a strong ass feeling of wanting to punch him in the fucking face. She lifts her head, smiling up at him. Glad that I'm just sitting here watching them be all goddamn loving toward each other.

"I'm going," I walk forward, fed the fuck up.

"Wait, Grey," she calls out, but I ignore her and Mr. Terrip's knowing eyes as I pass by him. *I can dodge a headbutt just fucking fine.*

Chapter Seventeen

Childish

❀ Azalea ❀

"I haven't seen you for a long time," I tell the sweet homeless man that I gave that money to all that time ago. Aaron gave me two hundred more dollars.

"I remember you," the man smiles up at me from his seat on the curb.

"I got a new pair of shoes with that money, thank you very much," he says sincerely, and I smile.

"Well, I have even more for you," I take out a hundred dollars. So, what if I need it? This guy doesn't even have a home, he needs it more.

"I can't take this, it's too much!" he exclaims, his eyes wide.

"Don't be silly," I place it in his slightly dirty hands, my smile never faltering.

"Thank you very much," he nods. I walk away feeling happy. Until I remember where I'm walking to. Grey's restaurant. Is it even his? I don't know. He started ignoring me a little. Which has not made me the happiest person in the world considering he's been doing it for three whole days. Who am I supposed to talk to? Mr. Terrip and books? *And who does he think he is ignoring me?*

I realize that I'm the one that probably taught him that since I did it too but that was different. An end is coming to this immediately. If one of us is upset, we need to talk it out. Especially if I don't even know why the man is mad. I make it there and see the 'Closed' sign on the door. Like that'll stop me. I open it and walk in. *I'm such a bad-butt.*

"We're closed," the small pee pee guy stops in front of me.

"I don't care," I send him my best glare as a group of guys come through the doors to the back. I see the beautiful hair guy and even the nice butt guy.

"Leave," he glares down at me.

"Do you want to get got? 'Cause you're about to," I warn, and he rolls his blue eyes.

"I'm not scared of some little girl," he sneers. Oh, he should be. I'm crazy, he doesn't know what I'll do.

"You think you're so big and bad just because you're taller than me. Is that it?" I narrow my eyes at him.

"You're a little shit," he growls out like that'll offend me or something. Well, guess what? He's an even bigger one. I feel a presence behind me and before I can get my last word in. I'm yanked back by the belt loop on the back of my shorts. I give him the I've-got-my-eyes-on-you motion, and he doesn't take his glare off of me as I'm dragged backward. I smack the hand holding onto the back of my pants away and turn around. I narrow my eyes up at the man in front of me.

"You," I poke his chest, then poke it again because he feels really nice and solid, "and me, need to have a serious talk."

He looks down at me unhappily like *I* did something wrong. Jai chuckles from beside us and I send him the look I'm giving Grey. He stops and I come to the realization of how insanely intimidating I really am. I'm *so* intimidating.

"Come with me," I lead him to the back like this is my restaurant and not his. The door closes behind us.

"Hurry this up, I've got to go," he says quite emotionlessly. I give him a deep sigh at the attitude he's showing me.

"Why are you ignoring me, Grey?" It's times like this I wish his name was short for something. Then I would use his full name so that he knows I'm serious. Like if someone's name is Joe, then when you're serious with him you can be like, 'Joseph.' But Grey's name isn't short for anything and Greyseph doesn't sound right.

"Like you can say anything about ignoring someone," he grumbles.

"That was different. I was sick, I didn't want you to catch it," I explain and his eyebrows scrunch as his eyes narrow.

"You told me your back hurt."

"Same thing," I shrug and watch as his jaw clenches.

"What, so you thought your back pain was contagious?" He grumbles out.

"We're not questioning me here and I'm not a scientist," I tell him. He slightly glares.

"We can't do this childish ignoring thing, got it? It's only going to hurt us," I say, and he scoffs.

"You started it," he grounds out and I give him a 'really' look.

"Well, I'm sorry for 'starting it,'" I mock childishly.

"Childish," he grumbles. This whole thing is childish, what are we doing?

"Stop, we're done," I cut it off and his face falls from the glare.

"What?" he asks quietly.

"No more," I say simply. We had an argument about being childish all while being childish, we need to be serious. And I need to figure out why he's ignoring me.

"I don't want it to be no more," his voice stays soft and my eyebrows furrow. He still wants to be childish?

"Grey, I'm not fooling with you," I cross my arms. Can't this man be not childish for a second? He talks about *me* being childish, heck.

"You can't say we're done," he says, and I scoff. I can say we're done being childish if I freaking want. Does he not understand that I need to know why he was ignoring me?

"The heck I can't!" I exclaim.

"We just started this, you can't just leave me," he mumbles, and I furrow my eyebrows before realizing what he means. He thinks we're done *done*. I let out a soft sad gasp. Oh, the poor thing.

"No," I draw out as softly as possible, walking toward him. He leans back against the counter.

"You and me aren't done," I explain shaking my head, "the whole childish thing is done. Not us."

"Come here," I open my arms, walking to him. We hug in our way and pulling away before he puts me down, I press a soft kiss on his cheek.

"I didn't mean it to sound like that," I tell him softly and he leans his forehead against mine. I wrap my legs around his waist so hopefully, I'm not as heavy. He grabs my hand gently and places it on his heart. It's beating wildly.

"You scared me," he mumbles and my heart falls, feeling bad.

"I'm sorry," I trail that hand around to his back and rub it, hopefully soothing him a little bit. Everyone likes backrubs.

"I was jealous. That's why I ignored you. Aaron and you seem close," he grumbles the last sentence and I come to a realization.

"*You're* mine, not him," I blurt. His eyes fall on me, and they're oddly lit up. The most heart stopping smile takes onto his lips. A real smile. I nearly fall out of his arms. Gosh, he's absolutely gorgeous.

"I'm yours," his lips make contact with my neck. I pull away solely due to the reason of him having another girl in here. *I'm* jealous.

"I never had another girl in here, I promise," he sees my hesitance. He's telling me I fussed for forever about nothing? Goodness.

"Okay," I whisper, and his lips find my neck once more. I let out a soft sigh at feeling his mouth on me. It feels too good. His hand reaches down to my butt, and he gives it a squeeze. I am *so* squeezing that booty of his once he lets me down. He sets me down on the counter.

A sound leaves the back of my throat and I feel his smirk against my neck. He pulls away and places his hand on my cheek. His eyes fall to my lips, and I get excited.

"Goddamn, I blew up that bathroom," the door that leads even further to the back bursts open and some guy walks through, fanning the air behind him. Grey lowers his head and lets out a sigh and a curse. I reach up a little bit and kiss his forehead seeing it in my reach.

"Oh shit," the guy says, "my bad."

"Reed, get the fuck out," Grey turns and glares at the guy. Reed hurries and exits out into the main room.

"We can't do shit in this room," he grumbles, and I let out a breathy laugh. He holds one side of my face and kisses the other. He pulls away and then kisses it again. He slides me off the counter and helps me land carefully on my feet.

"You can go watch a movie," he leads me further into the back where his office is.

"You have to get a bad guy?" I ask as he opens the door for me.

"I'll be back soon," he nods, and I smile up at him. He leans down and my heart falls to my toes when he kisses my cheek, near the corner of my mouth.

"Be careful," I whisper, still mostly in shock. He gives me a small smirk before closing the door behind him as he leaves. *Would he ever find out if I watched Magic Mike on his computer?*

~~~

I didn't have the heart to watch *Magic Mike*. In all honesty, I was a little scared to. I read the reviews on the movie. From there, I decided that I was not prepared to see the things mentioned. So, I stuck to the cartoon version of *Hercules*. Then *Mulan*. After that movie, I watched *The Green Mile*, and I cried my eyes out. *The Green Mile* is no short movie. After finishing that movie, I realize that it has been nearly six hours since Grey left. And that it's also two in the morning.

So, I pause my movie-watching marathon and I begin to have a worry-fit. *I mean, he's a big guy, he's fine, right? But what if there are bigger guys? Oh gosh. He's okay.* But what if he's not? What if someone headbutted him extra hard and since he's got a headbutted-deficiency issue, it knocked him out or something? He said he'd be back soon, how soon is *his* soon?

I'm better than most at minding my own business...*sometimes*. I don't touch any of the drawers in his desk or open the closet he has in the room. I stay where he told me I could be, although he didn't say I wasn't allowed to go to other places. But I've seen way too many movies where someone goes to explore and they either find something they shouldn't, or they get caught. *I could find freaking molded cheese in this restaurant.* I shiver at the thought and pull my sweatshirt over my head.

With the hood up and all, like a total bad-butt, I sit in his comfy spinny chair and decide on one more movie. I decide on the most heartbreaking children's film I can think of. *Up*. Mid-crying, the door opens and Grey walks in, looking unharmed. I let out a little breath of relief and his eyebrows furrow when he sees me.

"You stayed this late?" he questions.

"I was a little worried about you," I admit, wiping under my eyes. I watch him as he walks closer to me. He pulls something out of the back of his pants. At first, I thought he was scratching his butt but nope. He sets a real-live gun down on the table and I scoot my chair away from the table a little bit.

"That's real?" I question softly as he takes his jacket off. I swallow the drool in my mouth as his strong arms come into view. He sits the jacket down in the chair at the front of the desk before bending over down to his foot. He comes back up with another gun in his hand. This man is seriously going to make me have a heart attack. What happens if the gun suddenly goes off while it's on his ankle and his foot gets shot? Then he can't walk, *and* he can't catch the bad guy. It's a lose-lose situation. What's next? He pulls a freaking shotgun out his butt? Or maybe he even takes a knife he carries around out of his nostril.

He opens the closet that I looked at but never touched and there are *more guns in there*. Thank Jesus I did not open that closet because I would have fainted.

"What took so long?" I question, looking away from the weapons.

"The woman threw her bags of fucking crack at us, threatened to kill herself if we moved, and after four hours, she passed out," he grumbles, and my eyes widen. And I call *Grey* a crackhead. Oh no, I'm sorry Jesus.

"Did you save a bag of crack for me?" I blurt. He turns around and shoots me a glare.

"There's some on the bottom of my shoe if you want it," he recovers and I throw my head back in a laugh.

"We went through all that shit just because she's a known crack dealer," he comes closer to me.

"Never get high on your own supply," I mumble and he rolls his eyes, "that's why I buy mine. Or get it off the bottom of your shoe."

"You need to sleep," he says like I'm acting crazy or something. I'm wide awake. Oh no. What if the crack particles from the bottom of his shoe flew into the air and accidentally got into my bloodstream? *I do have a little cut on my finger.* I begin standing. And only then do I realize how tired I actually am. I've been awake for 19 hours. How is Grey even functioning? And looking gorgeous while doing it?

"You look like a kid," he mumbles, coming over to me and taking the hood off my head. The hoodie does kind of drown me.

"Well, I'm not perfectly super tall and filled out," I say softly. I mean, I've got a little bit of a booty. He pulls me around and we become pressed flush together. I look up at him and he looks down at me. He trails his hands down my sides and stops them on my hips.

"You feel perfect to me," he grumbles, his eyes set hard in seriousness. I feel my cheeks flush at his words. Then again, he's been around crack particles all night and it's really early in the morning. Plus, I'm sure if I talked to a dietician, they would say that I'm a pig and only a single lettuce a day would save me from all that I've already eaten. I know I'm not perfect. Grey knows I'm not perfect. But I guess to him, he likes whatever I've got. And that sends me on a whirlwind of crazy emotions that I've never felt before.

"Are you trying to get in my pants?" I whisper up to him, a little smile on my face. His lips turn up at the corners.

"It must be working if you're thinking about it," he leans down closer to me, and I let out an amused gasp.

"Are you flirting with me?" I question him softly, my eyes on his lips. I feel his hand tilt my chin back up so that I'm looking into his eyes now.

"I think you're flirting with me," his voice gets quieter with his free hand, he lifts me up onto his desk. I let out an unflattering snort and I wince internally. I'm literally a pig.

"You're sure you want to fall in love with me?" I question. It's odd that he can sit here and listen to me snort. And eat a whole pizza. And listen to all my talking. And my nonsense.

"I'm already too far into it," he presses a kiss to my chin, "and I'm not slowing down anytime soon."

He raises my head, and his lips are pressed against mine. Unlike the first time, this time is completely surreal. His arms wrap around me, holding me as close as humanly possible, meanwhile, my heart has shapeshifted into butterflies. His lips are softer than I remember and he's more gentle than I remember. Like he's nervous he'll mess up somehow.

I grip the side of his face and kiss him deeper. He needs to know that he shouldn't be all nervous all the time. Our lips come together in a way that creates more sparks than fireworks. I push away all the nerve-wracking thoughts that hit me.

He's much more experienced, that much I can tell. He's older, which plays a factor in the whole experience part. I know that he doesn't just want me for what Aaron thinks. Or thought. I've never looked at Grey as that type of person. He's always been truthful with me. And I may not know what he was like before we met, but that was before. Before he wanted to fall in love. As much as I've thought about it. I want to fall in love too. I've never been in love, and by the way, he talks about it, he never has either.

It definitely wouldn't hurt to fall in love with the crackhead in front of me. He's already come so far. He's learned things from me that I didn't even know he needed to be taught. I don't think he understands that we're learning together. He and I are quite the teachers and students. *That sounded illegal and not right.* And even though he's still got his bratty moments, and his manners have never been existent, I wouldn't rather have any other best friend. *Even*

Lilah   *K. Pope*

though he doesn't like me to use that term when talking about the two of us.

      He already means a lot to me. And especially considering the kiss that is taking place exactly right now, I'm pretty far gone. And these kisses are going to happen *more* often.

Chapter Eighteen

Karma

❀ Azalea ❀

"Grey," I groan.

"Shut up," He responds, and I scoff.

"You're heavy," I wheeze, trying to wiggle my body that is one hundred percent under his.

"You're fine," he mumbles and I let out another sound of frustration.

"You don't know how I feel."

He's not the one with someone as heavy as him on top of him. What? Whatever.

"Why are *you* the one on top of *me*? You're heavier," I complain. He gives one mischievous chuckle.

"I'd rather be the top," he grumbles amusedly. The top of what? That doesn't make sense. Is this man sleep talking?

"Well, I don't like being the bottom," I whine, and he raises off me. He props himself up on his elbows and looks down at me.

"You're so fucking oblivious," he shakes his head, rolling off me.

Finally.

"Oh, thank you, Jesus!" I take a deep breath.

"I can breathe!" I arch my back up, stretching and breathing.

"Dramatic ass," he walks into the bathroom.

"Sugar," I get up, walking into the bathroom behind him, "one of these times, my ribs are going to collapse."

I pick up my toothbrush and follow him in brushing my teeth. It doesn't matter whichever position we fall asleep in, he ends up directly on top of me. To my surprise, he doesn't say anything about me calling him Sugar. *Is he warming up to it?*

"You like being called Sugar, don't you?" I tease, placing my toothbrush back after finishing. He does the same and gives me a side-eyed scowl. He grips my chin harshly and he kisses me. My body temperature rises a good ten degrees, and my right leg starts wiggling. He pulls away.

"You like it when I kiss you, don't you?" He teases the same way I did to him and I'm left blubbering.

"I think both of our questions are rhetorical," I lower my voice up at him. His lip curls up into a smirk. His hand slides to right above my hip bone. He gently squeezes it and I jerk, a squeal leaving my lips. He covers the last half of the squeal with his lips. His arm goes under my butt, and he scoops me up. He deepens the kiss and I pull away in shock. *Woah, baby.*

"Baby steps," I breathe out, "don't rush into things, okay?"

"I'm sorry, I know better," he kisses the side of my face.

"It's just new, right? I know, it's okay," I assure him, kissing his cheek as he had done to me.

"I can still kiss you?" he questions, his eyes searching mine for an answer. A little smile reaches my lips.

"If I can call you Sugar," I bite my lip, trying not to laugh, "and slap your butt," I blurt.

"Whatever you want," he pulls my bottom lip from my teeth and he leans forward and kisses it. I swear, he's a very affectionate person and he never knew it. His hands haven't left me all morning. *Heck, I'm not complaining.*

Lilah   *K. Pope*

~~~

Pancakes? I think yes. Am I the world's best pancake maker? Absolutely. Did I have to make them from scratch because Grey has no pancake mix or anything? Yes. Did that make them any less freaking amazing? Heck no.

I kind of have to fend for myself when I get hungry. Mom doesn't really make any food anymore and dad sure doesn't either. And I'm not necessarily the richest person; I can't just buy food. And I can't starve. My appetite needs to be filled because even though I'm not growing, I like to think I am.

"C'mere Bear," I call him over. I feed him one of the smaller pancakes and he eats it without chewing. Finishing the pancakes on his plate, Grey gets up to put it in the sink. I take that as my chance. I hop out of my seat and CIA-style sneak up to him. I draw my hand back and just like I told him I would, I slap the booty. And it gets me fired up. I feel pumped up like a football player before a game. I feel oddly masculine and like if I spoke, my voice would be deeper. *Oh, I'm so going to do that more often.*

"You liked that way too much," he shakes his head, turning around to look at me.

"It turned me on, bro," I say deeply.

"Don't call me bro."

"Dude," I try and his eyes narrow.

"Dawg," I smirk.

"Fella," I love that one. A dish rag gets thrown in my face, my neck gets kissed, and my butt cheek is slapped off.

"I didn't hit you that hard!" I remove the rag from my face, wincing at the pain in my butt.

"I didn't hit you that hard," he rolls his eyes playfully. I twist my torso, lifting my shorts up. I look at the huge five-star on my butt. *I'm hitting him as hard as I can next time.*

"I have a five-star!" I exclaim. I turn around and show him the mark on my cheek.

"I can't see all of it. You should take off your pants so I can," He offers, and I consider it before realizing he's teasing. And I'm wearing a pair of one-of-a-kind peach-colored underwear that tends to ride up my butt. So, he's *definitely* missing out.

"Did you go to college?" I question, changing the subject as my cheeks tinge.

"I got my associates in high school," he grumbles. *Jake was doing that too.*

"My parents-well, my dad didn't let me do that. He said...never mind," I decide against telling him what Dad told me. His eyes fall into a scowl, and I wince. I turn around and go back to my seat at the table, shoving my face with pancakes.

"What'd he say to you?" He questions, his voice serious.

"It doesn't matter," I smile, pretending what he said didn't affect me.

"Azalea," he says harshly, and I sigh.

"He said I should leave the success to Jake and that I'd never do good in college anyway." The worst part about it: I believed him. If no one liked me in high school and even strangers don't, college would be no different plus hard schoolwork. *But I wanted to go.*

After the accident, I missed the last part of my school year and even a quarter of the next one, too busy trying to heal everything and going to PT. I spent the rest of my high school year, including the summer, catching up and getting everything I needed to graduate and maintain a good GPA to get into college. And then Dad told me I wasn't allowed to go.

It broke my heart. I wanted the experience. There was always the chance that college would've been better for me. But I guess everything happens for a reason.

"Jake was very good at sports," I explain further, figuring he didn't know what Jake was successful at.

"Azzy. Try it," Jake encourages. I huff and shoot the basketball up into the hoop or basket or net or whatever the heck they call it. It bounces off the top and hits me square in the face. I groan and dramatically fall onto the floor. He lets out a bark of laughter.

"Is my nose still there?" I question out and he pulls me up.

"Try again."

I try a good twenty more times. It doesn't work.

"It's just not your sport," he shrugs. *I don't think any sport is my sport.*

"Softball?" he questions, tossing Aaron's sister's softball at me. *It hits me in the boob and then proceeds to fall onto my toe. I dramatically cry out.*

"That's not even soft," I whine, ignoring his chuckles.

"Soccer?" he asks.

"You honestly think I can run that much?" I respond. He thinks about it before shaking his head.

"Tennis?" he asks.

"That's a scary sport," I chide, *"do you hear all the grunts and stuff they do on tv?"*

"Sports aren't for you," he decides, and I agree with him. I really have no desire.

"That's okay," he smiles.

"You know your dad is fucked up?" he questions seriously. I look up at him.

"I know," I admit softly.

"I'm going to get in trouble for spending the night here," I tell him honestly and a glare settles on his face.

"It's okay," I dismiss it, waving my hand in the air.

"Why don't I have a talk with your dad?" he crosses his arms and my eyes widen a little bit. I shake my head.

"Oh no, that'd only make things a lot worse," I explain.

"What does he expect from you? Does he want you to wait until you're thirty to have a relationship?" he grumbles. I honestly don't know why it bothers dad so much.

"I don't know," I mumble. He only sighs.

"And your mom doesn't say anything?"

"When you came to my house, she said I shouldn't let you be there much," I look up at him. His face sets unhappily.

"I should actually probably go home. The last time I stayed for long, Dad got mad," I tell him honestly, picking up my plate, and putting it in the sink.

"Do you want me to wash those?" I question sincerely, nodding to the dishes in the sink. His face scrunches as if it was stupid to ask that.

"Quit asking stupid questions," he warns me, gripping onto my arm and turning me the opposite direction of the sink.

"Kiss my butt," I send him a scowl over my shoulder. The look on my face drops when he starts coming for me. He grips the top of the back of my pants, and I'm pulled back into him.

"Right now?" His hand slides over my booty.

"Grey," I scold. He isn't serious, is he?

"Think heavenly thoughts Sugar," I imitate the praying hands that he has tattooed on his hand, with mine.

"Where'd you get this scar?" His finger brushes over a scar on the very top of my shoulder.

"Sex."

"That was my first guess," he chides.

"A couple of years ago, I was in the shower- aren't you already *so* interested?"

By now, Mr. Terrip would've already tuned me out.

"A couple years ago you were in the shower," he repeats.

"Tell me about that shower," his voice gets lower.

"Oh well the shower was nice and warm. I think I was really tired, so it was supposed to be a really quick one," I tell him about it and after I finish he sighs.

"I-Okay," he starts but cuts himself off.

"Anyway, I fell and busted my shoulder up on the faucet," I recall the pain in my shoulder. I feel him lean down and place a kiss on it. *Sweet as sugar.* Bear whines in jealousy.

"Are you still hungry?" He asks. I ate six pancakes.

"Is this why Bear is just a little chunky? Do you always give him food just because you think he looks hungry?" I turn around to face him.

"He's not chunky," he looks over at him. He's only a bit chunky. But that's perfectly okay because it means that there's just more of him for us to love.

"He eats when he's hungry," he says.

"Dogs are always going to eat if you give them food," I smile.

"Then he eats a lot."

He lifts up my shirt and looks at my belly. He places his big hand on my stomach.

"I'm so full," I promise him, "can't you feel how tense my stomach is? That's cause it's full of pancakes."

"It's barely tense," he grumbles, and I raise my brows.

"Are you just saying that because I don't have muscles there?"

"I wouldn't care if you had a fuckin' potbelly. I don't want you hungry," he takes his hand off my stomach and lowers my shirt back. He's like a grandma, always worried about if Bear and I are eating enough.

"Would you care if I had better stomach muscles than you?" A little smile touches my lips.

"No. As long as you're not hungry," he keeps up his reasoning. I'm not sure that would look right to have better muscles than him. It'd be like The Rock with my face.

"What is a no-go for you? Like, a type. Do you have a type?" I ask. Am I his type? He gives a single-shouldered shrug.

"Light blonde. Green eyes. Fuckin' talkative apparently. How tall are you?"

"5'2," I furrow my eyebrows

"5'2," He continues, "pretty smile."

"Cute fucking nose," he kisses my nose. Is he talking about me? He's got to be, duh Azalea.

"You think I have a pretty smile?" My voice raises an octave in awe. He rolls his eyes.

"Step in front of a mirror once in a while," he grumbles. Usually, that's an insult but not right now.

"I like guys around 5'5-5'8," I sigh 'dreamily' and just barely catch sight of his face growing unhappy.

"Blue eyes are a must! And he's got to be very skinny. Like a stick. Oh! Light brown hair would be nice. Or a bald guy," I describe the opposite person to Grey. I look up to see his face set in a harsh glare. His jaw tense and his shoulders the same.

"That's *not* me," he says bluntly.

"I'm only teasing," I wrap my arms around his strong torso. He stays tense and I let out a breathy laugh. So tense he won't even hug.

"Grey," I say. He keeps his eyes away from me.

"What did we talk about ignoring?" I remind him and his eyes dart down to me.

"C'mere," I wiggle my finger for him to lean down to me.

"Not to," He grumbles quietly.

"You're my type, I promise. Look," I lean up as tall as I can and I press my lips softly against his.

"You're getting some confidence, hm?" He pulls away just an inch.

"Hush," I tell him.

~ ~ ~

"Mr. Terrip?" I call out after I've finished putting all the books that were brought out back in their correct places.

"What do you think about Grey?" I ask him the question that has entered my mind on a couple of occasions. Of course, I know what I think about Grey, but I just want to know what pretty much my only friend thinks of him too. I watch as a little smile spreads across his lips. He removes his glasses and peers up at me from his seated position.

"He's got a soft spot for you," he says, "and as long as he doesn't treat you poorly, or hurt you, I think positively about him."

I bite back a smile.

"That makes you happy, honey?" his grandfatherly smile returns.

"I like him a lot," I explain, "and it does make me happy."

I wouldn't want Mr. Terrip to not like him. I may not be that important to him, but he's important to me. I also wouldn't like for someone to not understand that Grey really is a good person. He may be a little...rough and vulgar. And he may not have any manners at all but there's a reason I call him Sugar. He worries about whether I always eat or not and his touch is gentler than anyone else's touch I know. He likes to be held in his sleep, even as large as he is, and gosh darn it if it doesn't make me all fluttery in the heart. *I miss him.*

When I got home yesterday, thank the Lord above, dad wasn't there, and I never got punished for being away for the night. And when nothing happened to me, I felt bad for leaving Grey. *Well, maybe he wanted me to go.* What if I'm around him too much and then he gets tired of me? Then again, he should know that I'm not the type of person that should be left without socialization. I'll be even crazier than I already am.

I'm going to see him. If he's got a problem with it, I'll tell him to shove his words where the sun doesn't shine and I'll even smack his butt as hard as he smacked mine yesterday.

"I'm going to go get me a sweet tea," I tell Mr. Terrip who nods. I walk out the main entrance and begin the journey.

Halfway there, I look down at my halter-neck swing sundress. Will he like it? Why am I being so worrisome today? I think I was poisoned.

I love sundresses. And it's a pretty color; baby blue. I only sigh softly and hope for the best. The dress has an open back and it allows the warm air to seep into my skin. I made sure the healing lashes weren't visible before going out. I wouldn't want anyone to see. I finally bust through the door in Grey's restaurant. Jai welcomes me with his always bright and contagious smile.

"Grey came in this morning, not as moody," he starts, "did you have something to do with that?"

I internally giggle.

"I tickled his pickle," I blurt, "can I have a sweet tea?"

Where's my mind at?

"What?" he leans against the counter where the register sits, his eyes laughing.

"I'm kidding," I explain a bark of some sort of odd laughter leaving my mouth. I don't know how to tickle a pickle. But mine gets tickled a lot. Not my *pickle*. But my metaphorical pickle. I don't have a pickle. I don't think. He leaves to get me my sweet tea and I take out my money while he's away.

"Here you go," he hands it to me gently. I shove the money at him.

"Grey told me you aren't allowed to pay here," he smirks. I scoff.

"Tell him this money is from 'Fernando'," I instruct him. He shakes his head. My eyes narrow.

"How would he know anyway?" I question.

"Jonas would probably tell him if he found out," he shrugs.

"Who's Jonas?"

"The guy you said had a small dick," he smiles, and you know what? I don't doubt that he'd tell Grey that I paid when I wasn't supposed to.

"And then I'll get my ass beat," he adds and my hand flies to my heart. What a turd Grey is.

"Look Jonas is coming!" I point to the other side of the room. He turns his head and looks while I amazingly sneak the money into his thingy. Not *thingy* but waiter apron thingy. 6He turns back around and pulls it out the pocket I put it in.

"You're not very sneaky," he holds out the money to me.

"Don't lie to me Jai," I smile. He chuckles.

"Fine, I'll keep it," he finally gives in, and I smile wider.

"Grey is in one of the back rooms," he nods to the employees only door.

"I promise I won't tell him I gave you money," I cross my fingers. Don't blab to Grey. Don't blab to Grey. *Don't.*

"Are you sure?" he tilts his head. I think about it.

"...Yes...?" I offer a smile. I walk to the back, convincing myself that I don't have to blurt anything to feel better. I feel like I'd be a terrible crime committer. Or criminal, whatever it is. I'd probably confess before the po-po even caught me. I open the door to the first back room I see at the end of the hallway, and it looks like a meeting room. I walk in further and Grey stands at a table near the corner, pictures and documents in his hands.

I go to shut the door behind me, and I feel something tickle my neck. I bring my hand up and I pull the exact same five-dollar bill I gave Jai out of the strap of my dress. I feel my mouth open. Not only has he made me look unprofessional, but he's made me look like a stripper. He never even touched me! What CIA video did he watch? I scrunch my nose in the thought of getting him back as the door finally shuts. I see something in the corner of my eye.

My eyes find themselves on a picture placed on the wall. I look through the faces in the picture. I smile when I see Theo's beautiful eyes and Jared Leto's hair clone. Then I narrow my eyes at Jai's face but my smile returns larger when I see Grey. Goodness, he looks good in pictures. The smile gets wiped off my face when my eyes fall on Jake. Jake. My brother. *What?* I've never been so confused in my *entire* life.

"I was just going to come see you," Grey's voice reaches my ears but I just barely hear it, trying to figure out what is going on. *Grey knew him.* I'm an absolutely terrible, horrible, and atrocious human being. I feel a large tear trickle down my cheek.

"Lilah?" I hear his footsteps draw closer. I'm left in the same spot. My heart breaks at what I've done to Grey. I feel him stop beside me and I just know he's looking where I'm looking.

"Azalea," he whispers regretfully. I've *ruined* it. I've completely destroyed his last image of Jake. The one reason I never told anybody what happened during the crash was that I didn't want to hurt anyone else. But I've done it. I've succeeded in doing the one thing I promised I'd never blab about.

Now Grey's image of Jake will never be the same. He knew him. *But he didn't tell me.* But that shouldn't even matter, I shouldn't have ever told him. Or anyone. *I'm so destructive.* I knew karma would strike me from being selfish eventually. I swallow back a cry. I open the door, in an attempt to push through the heartbreaking realization of what I've done. The hallway is blurry as I start walking down it.

"Azalea, I'm sorry," Grey grabs onto my arm, turning me back around to him. He grips onto my face and tilts it up to his. I can't even look him in the eye, scared I'll see how badly I had to have hurt him.

"I fucked up," he says, his voice taking on a soft tone which makes me even more upset.

"I should've told you," his thumbs brush the continuous tears that run down my cheeks, "please don't cry my Lilah."

"I'm sorry," he places two kisses on my forehead, "I'm sorry I didn't tell you I knew him."

I'm nowhere near upset at him for not telling me he knew him. I'm upset and I despise myself for allowing my mouth to spew out *details* of everything. And it can never be undone or forgotten. *He* shouldn't be apologizing to *me*. I pull his hands from my face and back away, and by the look on his face, I can only think that I'm just hurting him more. I turn and try to flee once more. He catches me in the room we first kissed in, what seems like forever ago.

"I'm sorry I hurt you again. Don't go," he slips his arm around my stomach. It's even worse that he thinks *he* hurt *me*. I did this to myself.

"I was going to tell you. I had to figure out how."

"Let go, Grey, it's okay," my voice comes out very quietly. He releases me just as I say it and I turn around.

"I just need to be alone," my voice cracks and my eyes fill up and go blurry once more.

"What does that mean?" his voice turns only slightly desperate. I only step away from him. He grips onto my hand.

"*I'm sorry*. What do I do? What do you want me to do to fix it?" he speaks genuinely.

"Let me go," I whisper, and he does. I just need to think for a minute.

~~~

I walk all the way home. I walked to Mr. Terrip's this morning and I slightly regret it. I regret it, even more, when I see dad's car parked in the driveway. I open the front door and watch him rise from his laid down position on the couch.

"What's got you crying?" he slurs. I only close my eyes wishing to be anywhere else.

"Huh?" his voice raises to almost a shout.

"Did one of your little boyfriends leave you? You shouldn't even try," he turns up a bottle of some sort of alcohol, getting the very last bit in the bottom.

"God you're the worst thing that's ever happened to me. To all of us," he sneers. It hits me pretty hard. I think hearing that could hit anyone pretty hard. I try my hardest not to cry at the verbal punishments he gives me but at times like these, I just can't help it. He knows just what to say sometimes.

"Weak little shit," he growls out. I yank my car keys from the hook and dart back outside. I climb up in my car and stop. I calm down as best as I can. When I do, I drive to the only place I can think about.

I order four tacos from Taco Bell. Then I drive up The Smokies and stop and eat the tacos looking over the overhang down into all the pretty green trees. I let my mind wander off away from everything. Dad, Jake, Grey, everything.

But the thought of me causing someone to feel terrible hurts beyond the point of forgetting about it for a second. Maybe it's because I know what it feels like to hurt. And I wouldn't wish that upon anyone. Especially Grey. He's one of the only people still on Earth that actually makes me smile. And makes me happy. And I could've taken my source of happiness' happiness away. I never want to come close to doing that *ever* again.

As the sun finally falls below the horizon, I figure I should get up. A poop is stirring which played a factor in the decision but it's also getting chilly. *I should have only gotten two tacos.*

Chapter Nineteen

Yours

❀ Azalea ❀

 I spend two days thinking, well actually, trying *not* to think about things. He's done exactly what I asked of him, and it warms my heart to know that he lets me have my time and space to think. But I've thought enough, and he's waited for me long enough. If I hurt him as much as I thought I did, he wouldn't be apologizing to *me*, right? It still doesn't change the guilt that sits with me, but it doesn't matter about me, as long as he's happy. I'm just *me*, nothing special. He's special.

 I climb out of the bathtub and wrap a towel around me. I drain out the now cold water from the hour-long bath and mosey back into my room. I pull on a pair of shorts and a hooded sweatshirt once I realize that it's rainy out today. And as something different, I pull my hair back into a single French braid.

 I take a good three or four breaks, only now realizing how long my air actually is. Once I finish, the braid reaches just to the middle of my back. I confine my feet in my pair of basic white converse that is only worn in the winter and on rainy days.

Lilah   *K. Pope*

I press my ear against my door, listening for any signs of Dad. When I don't hear any, I open it softly and walk quietly down the stairs. I pass by him but thankfully he's still passed out from all the drinking he did last night. I could hear him up at three stumbling over furniture and turning the tv up loud.

I grab my keys off the hook and sigh in relief once I'm out. I park near Grey's restaurant and get out carefully. Unlike every other day, I don't walk nearly as fast as I can to get to him. Lord knows what'll happen when I see him. He may be mad at me for leaving him.

Over the past couple of days, I think I've thought of every scenario. And as I open the door, I turn just a little nervous. My eyes meet Jai's, and a concerned look takes over his face.

"Are you okay?" He asks, "you look sad."

For the first time in two days, I give a little smile.

"I'm okay," I nod.

"If you're looking for Grey, he's not here," he explains, and my eyebrows furrow.

"Where is he?"

"I'm not sure," he gives me a shrug.

"On Tuesday he left not long after you did. He hasn't come back since until today, but he went out a while ago," he says, and I nod. *Does he want me to see him?*

"Since when has the cat got your tongue?" He gives me a sweet smile.

"I'm sorry," I mumble. He opens his mouth to say something but closes it when the door behind me opens. A tall figure looms over me and Grey's wonderful scent envelops my nose. I feel his hand travel up and under the back of my sweatshirt. Warmth radiates from his large hand onto my back.

"Can we talk?" I whisper up to him. He gives me a slight nod before taking his hand off my back and gripping onto my hand. I offer Jai a tight-lipped smile as Grey drags me away. We finally come to a stop once we're in his office. He shuts the door behind me before turning to see me. Before he can say anything, I do.

"Grey, I'm sorry. I'm not mad at you for not telling me or sad about that. I promise," I try to stop my eyes from being watery, but it doesn't work.

"I've never told anyone what I told you about the crash. No one but you know what I saw because I never wanted anyone to picture Jake looking the way I saw him. He deserved to stay in the minds of people he knew as the funny and nice guy he was. I was *so* upset because I thought I ruined that for you," I keep my eyes away from his entire form.

"You can't take the blame for everything," he says, seriously.

"I can if it makes someone else feel better," I reply quietly. He grips my chin not painfully but hard enough to get my attention.

"You can't live like that Lilah," he says sternly.

"I knew how Jake was. I knew the type of person he was. That'll never change no matter what. You haven't ruined anything. You've helped. And you've helped yourself," he says, and I only shake my head.

"Helping myself is selfish," I say softly.

"Not when it's something you need."

It's silent for a while. I feel his eyes travel all over my face.

"They blame you, don't they?" He asks quietly. My heart falls a little and my breath halts. I just know he's talking about the crash. He pulls me closer to him.

"Is that what's hurting you so badly?" His voice stays soft as can be. That's the only thing I've heard from Dad about the accident. That it was all my fault. And no one has ever told me differently or known about how he blames me. Except for Grey.

"When something is drilled into your head, it's hard to believe someone else when they tell you the opposite," I tell him truthfully indirectly referring to how he told me the accident wasn't my fault. Realization crosses his features. His hand falls under my butt and he lifts me up to him.

He sits down on the floor with me in his lap, facing him. With my heart feeling heavy and all he lets me lean the side of my head against his shoulder. He waits a while as if searching for words. I already know he's not great with his words but I'm not looking for some sort of crazy, deep, and meaningful speech. Him just holding me to him can be enough.

"You need to see that it wasn't your fault. Things like that are out of control, out of *your* control. You can't blame yourself," he makes sure I'm looking right up at him, "And don't listen to the bullshit that comes out their mouths."

"Because *you*," his hand comes to rest on the side of my face, "don't deserve to be treated any less than fucking perfect."

I begin shaking my head.

"Don't argue with me."

"But-" I get cut off.

"I said don't."

"Okay," I agree softly. He leans down and places a feather-like kiss on the corner of my mouth. He places his hands back under the back of my sweatshirt and I sigh contently.

"You like that?" he questions quietly. Who doesn't like backrubs? I offer him a small nod and he places his other hand under my hoodie too.

"Can I make a rule?" he asks suddenly. I nod against him.

"We can't keep anything from each other," he says, and I feel my muscles tense. What muscles? Not the strong ones that I don't have. I automatically think of dad. I *can't* tell him. Thankfully, he can't see my face because I'm nearly in tears at the thought of breaking a rule already.

"Good?" he mumbles and I pause.

"Good," my voice just barely cracks.

"Jake talked about you a lot," his voice rumbles against me. A slight frown etches onto my face.

"He never talked about any of this," I refer to the whole 'fed' thing. I'm still not even sure what is going on.

"Or whatever you do is."

"I work as the head of the FAA," he explains, and my head turns confused, "Federal Assistance Agency."

"So that's why some of those guys call you 'boss'?" I come to the realization, now looking up at him, very interested. He rolls his eyes and nods.

"I thought you were in the FBI?"

"We're branched off from the FBI. We hold our own regulations, separate from them. We're independent," he explains, "But we're trained the same at first."

"You really do catch bad guys and stuff?"

"We assist in failed cases, our own federal cases, fucked up ones, particularly dangerous ones, and some regular shit sometimes," he shrugs.

"Oh. You do the dirty work," I smile. His eyes find my lips and the corners of his raise.

"There's that smile," he pulls me closer to him, resting his forehead on mine.

"I don't want you to go that long without that smile anymore," he throws a big blush on my face. I pull away in thought and try to get the attention off of my red face.

"Why didn't Jake tell me about this? Was he in it too?" I furrow my eyebrows.

"He was young but already eighteen. He wasn't allowed in fieldwork, being so young, but he did a lot for us. He worked computers with our main tech guy, he helped Theo with the weaponry, and he trained harder than anyone I've ever known. He deserved to go out with us on cases more than anyone."

"He never wanted you to worry about him," Grey's thumb brushes over my cheekbone. So, Grey knew about me all along?

"You knew who I was from the beginning?" Grey hesitates at my question. Then why was he so mean to me?

"I had only ever seen one picture of you, and it was for a split second, years ago," he explains, "I thought you only looked familiar until you told me your name."

"But" I sigh, "why were you mean to me."

"I was guilty."

"Why were you guilty?" I question softly.

"Your brother did everything he could to keep your name and your face out of this place. He never wanted you involved. I was the only person who ever saw your picture. I felt guilty because when I first met you in person, I was so *fucking* attracted to you. I felt like I owed it to him to leave you alone but there I was, not being able to walk away from you and with a slight hard-on," he says. My mouth falls open a bit. My body temperature rises and my heart pumps faster. I've only known what the term he used for boner was because of Aaron. He uses it when talking about dark-haired girls he meets at college parties. Nasty boy.

"Horny?" I blurt quietly.

"Very fucking horny."

"And I knew I couldn't treat you right, so I wanted you away. But guess what? My *horny* ass couldn't stay away from you," I watch as his eyebrows scrunch, recalling how he felt then.

"So, I kissed you," he speaks of our first kiss.

"And I've never felt so fuckin' shitty about everything I said leading up to it. And I hated how much I wanted to keep doing it. So, I went and said that stupid shit about it being a mistake," his fingers dig into my back, trailing down and I swear he could've been a masseuse because it feels heavenly.

"And now here we are," I say softly.

"Here we are," he places his lips on mine in a soft kiss.

The door bursts open and the small peepee guy walks in looking around for Grey.

"Get out loser," I scrunch my nose at him, and he turns to us, hearing my voice. His eyes narrow and his lip curls into a sneer. I stand from Grey's lap, being as tall as I can be compared to Jonas.

"Small titty bitch," he growls and I'm not even offended because Grey told me that my boobies are fine.

"Say that shit *one more time*," Grey's voice sounds scary as heck as he now stands behind me.

'Say it.' I mouth to Jonas who still glares at me.

'Whore,' he mouths back to me so quickly that I'm one hundred percent sure Grey never even saw it. I feel like me and Jonas hate each other but we thoroughly enjoy being terribly mean to each other. Or that's just me.

"Hold me back Grey," I say, and he doesn't.

"Grey, I said hold me back," I repeat myself.

"You haven't moved," he replies, and I sigh.

"I'm about to, that's why I'm telling you to hold me back," I say. Come on, who doesn't know this? He sighs and grips onto the back of my hoodie. *Like that little grip can hold back my dark side.* I pounce.

"Grey, a little looser, I can't move," I admit. I mean, goodness he's strong. I ignore the little baby smile that now sits on Jonas' face. Well, he doesn't look like a brat when he's smiling.

"Are you done being a little shit?" Jonas asks like he's talking to a child. I feel Grey release me and start storming forward. I grip onto his arm.

"I've got this Grey," I assure him before clearing my throat.

"You," I point to Jonas. Before I can even *think* of an insult, people walk into the room.

"Hey!" one of them shouts *very* loudly, "why wasn't I invited to this party?"

"Get out Sanfred," Grey grumbles.

"Who's this lovely lady?" the guy Grey called Sanfred asks, smiling down at me. Don't compliment his dimples. Don't. Don't. It's physically hurting me. Badly.

"What's your name doll baby?" Grey lets out a loud scoff, throwing an arm around my shoulder, nearly knocking me over.

"Oh, do we have a protective boy here?" Sanfred smiles wildly.

"Mhm," Jai winks at me as he walks into the room, past Sanfred. I feel a tug on my hair, and I turn to find Linc, Jared Leto's hair clone, looking down at my hair in his hands. Grey grabs my hair from Linc's hands.

"Don't fucking touch," he grumbles, a glare clearly present on his face.

"Can you teach me how to do that?" Linc ignores Grey. I smile wildly and nod. *I wish I had met these guys when Jake did.*

"Oh," I remember Sanfred asked me a question, "I'm Azalea."

"Are you a new recruit? Are you gonna take my job or are you good with guns?" he smiles. Grey grips onto me and pulls me to his chest, holding the side of my face squished against him.

"*No*," he says sternly.

"Mama Bear is *coming out*," Sanfred laughs.

"Tell me all his secrets and I'll give you a hundred dol-" Grey covers my ears from Sanfred's offer and I giggle. I like Sanfred.

~~~

"Would you like to be my model?" I place my hands on my hips, staring up at Grey. His upper lip curls up unhappily.

"No," he grunts, and I roll my eyes, leaning against the wall in his hallway.

"Then I don't want to hear it," I inform him and his face doesn't change.

"Sanfred just wants you to touch him," he grumbles out. Oh, what*ever*. Using someone with long enough hair to help teach Linc how to braid means nothing. It just so happens that Sanfred has a flow haircut that is long enough.

"Then get me a doll," I offer.

"What do you just want me to pull one out my ass?" he asks sarcastically.

"Grey," I start, "I hope you don't do that in your free time."

"Use your own damn hair," he speaks still unhappily.

"In case you haven't noticed, my hair is down to my butt. It takes a long time to braid it and I'm not going to throw all the hard work I put in this morning away," I scoff. My arms were jelly after braiding all my hair this morning.

"It's not like I'm going to catch feelings for him by braiding his hair," I raise my eyebrow at him. I've only got those feelings for one person and he's standing in front of me. In a black shirt that makes me want to jump him. He grabs the pocket in the front of my hoodie, and he pulls me to him. Our bodies hit and he looks down at me as I peer up at him.

"*I'm* yours," he makes sure I know. He grips my jaw, and he roughly kisses me. I heat up when his hand travels under the front of my shirt.

"When did you eat last?" he mumbles against my lips before continuing the kiss. Two days ago, why?

"A couple of hours ago," I say strongly.

"What was it?"

"A pepperoni pizza," I answer. His eyebrows furrow into a frown.

"You don't like pepperoni," he responds expertly, recalling how I told him the last time we went to the pizza place I didn't like pepperoni.

"I took the pepperoni off," I shrug.

"Then it would be a cheese pizza, not a pepperoni," he acts like he's an apparent pizza expert.

"I'm not talking to you anymore if all you're going to be is a smart aleck," I narrow my eyes up at him.

"Fine," he says, pulling away from me, "like you can actually keep your damn mouth shut."

Somebody peed in his Cheerios. I give him a slightly unhappy look to which he only emotionlessly looks at.

"When you're done being the way you are right now, come talk to me," I tell him before turning and walking down the hall and back into the living room. Right as I'm entering, he grips onto the back of my pants and turns me back around to him.

"I'm done being a shit now," he assures me, "I'm sorry."

A little smile creeps onto my face and he bends, kissing me.

"Azalea, can I have a kiss too?" Sanfred's voice breaks our kiss.

"Fuck off," Grey sneers at him. Both Jai's and Linc's chuckles fill the room. I plop my booty cheeks on the couch and Lincoln sits down beside me. Sanfred gives me a wink before sitting down on the floor in front of me, in between my legs. I feel Grey's eyes on the both of us. And Bear's. I find his eyes and he mouths 'kick him away'. I just roll my eyes and give him a little smile.

I look at Sanfred's soft looking hair. I brush his hair back with my hands right before I have to show Linc how to part it to braid it. A tapping noise fills the room. It stays continuous. I find the source of the noise to be from Grey's bouncing leg which shakes the chair he's sitting in. His face is very unhappy and beside him, Jai's face is happy as can be, smiling and everything.

"You start at the very top, okay?" I instruct Linc who nods. I tilt

Sanfred's head back. I show Lincoln how to part it in three ways all while he watches, contently paying attention. Hopefully, he's paying attention. Sanfred suddenly lets out a groan. I wince. Bear perks up at the sudden noise.

"Did I pull too hard?" I question.

"No baby doll, you pulled just right," he answers, and my eyebrows raise.

"You're a piece of shit," Grey sneers.

"Grey, you're missing out man," he says, "it feels really good."

"I'm getting horny," he adds at the end and Grey shoots up from his seat.

"Protect me tiny woman," Sanfred shrinks back into the couch.

"You're done," Grey's voice announces darkly. He grabs Sanfred's shirt, and he lifts him off the ground. He pushes him in the direction of the chair he was sitting in.

"I was kidding!"

"I don't give a fuck," Grey glares back at him. I keep my glare on Grey as I take the hair tie out the very bottom of my braid. *I'm mad.* I truly don't think Grey understands how hard it will be to braid my *own* hair while *teaching* someone how. It's not that simple. His eyes take on a horny look as I unbraid my hair. *Why is everyone horny?*

Over the next hour and a half, I show Lincoln the braiding ways, demonstrating on my own and explaining thoroughly. *And glaring at Grey.* And now, as I sit in front of Lincoln as he braids my hair, Grey watches the man behind me's movements. I hiss softly when my hair gets tangled in Linc's fingers. Bear lifts his head from my lap and looks back at Lincoln.

"Easy motherfucker," Grey scowls.

"It's okay, Linc," I assure him. Two- or three-times Lincoln practices on my hair before he figures we should call it a day. I'm not sure how his arms haven't fallen off. The three guys pile out at about five in the afternoon.

"Have a good night baby doll."

"I'll see you later Azalea."

"Thank you for the help, Azalea," Linc smiles before leaving and closing the door after him. Grey brushes my now wavy and pretty frizzy hair away from my neck before bending and placing soft kisses under my ear. Bear sits his butt on my feet. I love this dog. I lean back into the world's most jealous person and his hand slips under the front of my shirt.

"We're getting pizza," he pulls away gruffly, and I groan.

"I'm not even hungry," I cross my arms and his eyes fall to my chesticles.

"Not the time to look at my goodies," I inform him.

"Lincoln got to," he grumbles unhappily and I hold my heart.

"What are you talking about?"

"You can't act like you don't know he was peeking down your fucking shirt every once in a while," his jaw ticks. Come on, I know I've got pretty good goodies, but Lincoln needs to control it for Grey's sake.

"I didn't *know*. I was too busy focusing on trying to teach him how to braid hair *on my own head,* because *somebody* took away my model in a fit of jealousy," I uncross my arms and place my hands on my hips.

"He said he was getting horny because of you!" his voice raises.

"He was joking Grey," I keep my voice quiet to keep him calm.

"You don't know that shit," he scowls.

"Well, then I just ignore it."

"Are you fucking kidding me?" he questions like I'm not serious. I just sigh and plop my booty down on the couch. Bear watches the interaction like a counselor.

"He calls you *baby doll.* I don't even call you anything like that, that's not fucking friendly," he insists. It's not like they'd actually like me. I'm still shocked Grey does. Very shocked.

"Well Grey, I'm not an expert on friendly things, okay? All I know is the textbook stuff. The 'friends don't kiss' type stuff. Give me a break, okay?" I stress.

"And you think *I'm* an expert on *any of this?* You must think so shitty about yourself to not understand that you're fucking beautiful. The guys are coming at you left and right and neither of us understands who's joking or not. Don't cancel out the possibility of one of them actually liking you just because you don't think they ever could," he says. *He thinks I'm beautiful?*

"And you're mine just as much as I'm yours so don't even think about giving some other fucker a chance," he says sternly, and I have to bite back a smile. I stand back up and he looks up at the ceiling, not watching me, his jaw set tensely. I'm not sure if *he* knows this but he's pretty much the only chance at something I've got. Whether he says I've got guys coming at me left and right or not.

"I'm positive that you shouldn't worry about me giving some other guy a chance," I assure him.

"You're so fucking friendly with everyone Lilah," he sighs, finally looking down at me.

"I'm only trying to make friends," I mumble. He gives a small nod of understanding.

"And I promise It's only you," I grab his tattooed arm and wrap it around my torso, pulling him closer.

"I'm *not* a cheater," I say with finality. Cheaters are the worst of the worst.

"That means we're together now?" he asks, and I smile softly before giving him a little nod.

"You didn't ask me," he says expectantly. I feel my smile grow wider.

"Grey," I start, "would you like to be my boyfriend?"

He remains silent, and I feel my mouth drop open, the smile never leaving.

"I would like to be asked without knowing," he quotes my words and I throw my head back in laughter.

"But I guess it'll do," he leans down and kisses me. I slap his booty. Not hard for the time being but later, it will be hard. That's what she said.

"Now call the damn pizza place," he shoves his phone at me. I shake my head at the constant unwillingness to talk to any type of server or worker he has. I look at the plain black lock screen and I scoff. That's going to change immediately.

"Password?" I ask, expecting him to take his phone back and type it in himself.

"834953," he says, and my eyebrows raise.

"Put your recognition-shit thing in," he mumbles, his attention focused on the channel check. My heart falls to my cooter and my smile never falls. I bend down, take a great picture of Bear and me, and change his plain black background. I swear Bear is a much better model than I'll ever wish to be. I call the pizza place and order what we want before going into his settings and setting the recognition-crap thing as he called it. Aka, face recognition.

"Oh look," Grey's extremely sarcastic voice says, "Aaron's fuckin' calling you."

He hands me my phone and I answer it.

"Hey A-a-ron," I smirk.

"Hello sweet Azzy," I can basically hear the smile he has on his face. The call is definitely a little unexpected. He usually just shows up to see me, he doesn't really call.

"I wanted to check on you," he says, "especially after what happened the last time I was there."

"Oh. Well, I'm perfectly good, thank you," I say.

"How's that asshole with the tattoos?"

"Who?" my eyebrows furrow.

"Fifty-year-old dude," he adds, and my eyebrows furrow even furrow. If he's talking about Mr. Terrip, we're going to have some issues. And he's just going to have to get got.

"Silver," he adds another.

"You mean Grey?" I question, unsure. Grey turns toward me at the mention of his name.

"Bingo. He hasn't done anything has he?" he questions.

"Aaron, I told you he's not like that. He's done nothing," I sigh and watch as Grey's face turns into a scowl. Aaron sets off on a whole entire twenty-five-minute lecture of what to do if Grey does anything. He starts by reminding me that 911 is a thing and he ends by wanting Grey's number or to talk to him. I hung up on him. The doorbell rings and Grey drags me to the door with him.

"Hello!" I greet her once he opens the door. A girl probably around

Grey's age stands on the other side, the pizzas in her pizza-warming-pouch-thingy. She pops her bubble gum once before setting her eyes on the large man beside me. Her stern look drops, and she pops her hip out. Grey remains quiet.

"Uh," I interrupt her staring, "how much for it?"

I watch her as her eyes travel down Grey. Her bottom lip rolls into her mouth and my stomach churns. I look over at him to find his eyes set intently on me.

"How much?" I ask once more only to be ignored again.

"This is fixing to be free if you don't answer me," I tilt my head. Grey opens his mouth to say something, a scowl on his face but I speak again before he can. She's *not* getting a tip.

"Wipe your drool before it drips onto my pizza box," my voice comes out oddly stern. Her eyes jerk away from Grey and fall on me.

"$45.95," she finally answers. I chuckle evilly at the amount of food I got. But it's okay because I haven't eaten in two days and I'm going to pay for it. I *was* going to pay for it. Grey shoves money at her, grabs the food, and shuts the door before the girl can say anything else. He sets the food down in the kitchen before turning to me and leaning back against the counter.

"Now you know what it feels like," he says.

"Oh, come on!" I throw my hands in the air, "it's not that obvious. She was so, *so* obvious."

"It's *that* fucking obvious," he says truthfully. You know what, I still don't believe it. I mean, it can't be. I'm me.

Chapter Twenty

Drunk

❀ Azalea ❀

"Get up."

"No," he grunts. I grunt back.

"Get up," I repeat, and he doesn't even respond this time around. I arch my back up as far as I can and he finally rolls off me.

"Fuckin' strong ass," he grumbles as I walk to the bathroom to pee. When he's lying on top of me, bladder and all, it really makes me have to pee ten times as bad. I tinkle and as I'm brushing my teeth, he waltzes in. I finish up and turn to him.

"What if I had no clothes on?" I raise my eyebrow at him. He finishes up and turns to me. He just gives me a smirk, his eyes darting down then back up my body. Why was that the most attractive movement I've ever seen?

"Don't answer it," I predict that his answer wouldn't be a good one. Walking out, he climbs back onto the bed. He gives me the "c'mere" finger and I mosey on over to him. He grabs onto my hand and pulls me onto the bed. He doesn't stop pulling until I'm standing on my knees on either side of his legs as he rests his back against the headboard. His eyes stay dark as he looks at me. His hands come to rest on my back, and he leans forward, placing a single kiss on my lips. He pulls away, his eyes light with mischievousness, and his lips form a gorgeous smirk.

His hands slip under my pants, and he grips onto my butt. I gasp and he covers it with his mouth. I lurch forward at the feeling, and he groans into the kiss, sliding his hand from my booty to right over my hip bones. He slips his tongue in my mouth and my hands find his amazingly soft hair.

Maybe it's Maybelline. Stop. I break away, out of breath before him and he watches me as I take deep breaths. He licks his lips and his eyes drift to my neck. He leans down and kisses it before leaning back part of the way and looking at my reaction. Which is, 'holy moly this is wild.' He trails his lips all the way down to the neckline of my shirt. From there, he pulls it down further and he looks back up at me.

"Your dad won't see anything here," his voice comes out husky and it makes it harder for me to breathe. He lowers his head, and his lips find the top of my breast. *My boob.* A sudden sigh leaves my lips, and his lips don't stop. He gently but firmly gives the spot a bite and I gasp. He pulls away and pecks my lips.

"So flustered, hm?" the smirk returns full force onto his lips as he stares at my probably pink face.

"First of all, your hands are down my pants," I remind him breathlessly and he drags his hands up to my back again.

"And second," I pull down my shirt, looking at the hickey that lays on my chest.

"You did *that*."

"Want the other one to match?" he offers. Someone woke up on the horny side of the bed this morning.

"Y'know," my voice nearly squeaks, "I think I'm pretty good."

I'd probably faint if I'm being honest.

"Let's go out to eat," he says, grabbing the back of my pants and *lifting me* like I weigh nothing.

"Not necessary," I grumble.

"I hope you want me to see down your shirt because I can," he lets go and I fall onto my back on the bed, looking up at him.

"You've already seen all there is," I sit up. There isn't much left to my boobies. After all, even though Grey said they're fine, they may be a little small.

"Not all."

"Want to?" I blurt.

"Fuck," he curses under his breath.

"Where are we eating?" I recover but his heated eyes don't leave my frame as I stand up. Oh, Lord help me.

~~~

"And then, you know what he did?" I rant to Mr. Terrip who currently has his deaf ear pointed right at me.

"He spilled the syrup all over my lap and I had to go home, shower, and change. And by the time I was done, he had to leave to go to work. So now, I haven't seen him since yesterday and I'm telling you, he's going to get *got*."

Oh, how I missed the so-called conversations between Mr. Terrip and me.

"I'm going to hit him so hard, he'll think it was The Rock," I assure him. I sigh.

"But it'll probably have to wait until later today. The bad guy was being difficult I guess, and he has to work a little bit today too. He texted me a couple of hours ago."

"You've been talking about this man for an hour now," Mr. Terrip informs me.

"He's very easy to talk about," I bite back a smile. I would like to tell Mr. Terrip about how Jake was involved with Grey and everything, but I figure that since Jake never told anyone, then he just didn't want them to know.

"A flippin' pizza delivery girl flirted with him yesterday!" I suddenly remember and apparently this gets his attention because he turns his other ear

Lilah

toward me, the working one.

"He didn't flirt back, did he?" he raises a wary eyebrow.

"I'd leave if he did! He didn't though," I smile. My first ever physical altercation would be with a pizza woman if she would've been touchy. And she most definitely would have lost. I mean, she was a good eight inches taller than me, but does she have my skills? I'm not sure but for my sake, yes. Plus, she's probably got some pretty big guns with carrying that heavy food all the time. Well, guess what? I'm pretty sure I was a weightlifter in a past life.

My phone dings with a text and I pull it out of my boob. Or my bra, wherever. It falls to Mr. Terrip's desk, and he shoves it back over to me with the book in his hand. It's not like I've got cooties. *'Drive your ass to my place'* Grey's lovely text reads and my socks are just blown off by the amount of charm that man has. He could be a prince, I'm convinced.

'Only because you asked nicely' I reply.

'Kiss my ass' he responds oh-so-sweetly. I'll smack it. I laugh evilly internally. I peer at the clock on my phone and find that most of the day has already faded away. I'm pretty sure I was talking to Mr. Terrip for way longer than just an hour.

"I'm retiring Mr. Terrip," I tease, turning my phone off. His eyes flit over to me for only a split second.

"For today," I add, and he nods as if he's saying, 'that's what I thought.'

I bid my goodbye and head to Greys. He must've seen me get here because he opens the door right as I'm walking up to it. Loud talking sounds behind him and he shuts the door as he comes out.

"Is that a party?" I hold back a laugh.

"We've got a new recruit assigned to our unit," he grumbles unhappily, "and they fucking showed up."

What a poor thing he is.

"I already want her out. She won't stop fucking trying to talk to me. And she stares," he rants.

"And you want me here, why?" I tilt my head in question.

"Why the fuck not? And she needs to see that I'm not available for her bullshit. I'm only available for your bullshit," my heart jumps at his words and I bite back a smile.

"You couldn't have told her that?"

"No point in telling her when I can show her and spend time with you all in one," his arm wraps around my torso.

"I missed you Sugar," I hug him, pressing the side of my face to his chest and wrapping my arms around his torso.

"I've missed my pillow," he grumbles, placing a kiss on the crown of my head. He enjoys crushing my bones and suffocating me. I smack my hand down on his booty. It's been a few days since I've done it and it feels *good*. He doesn't really react, but I feel him lift his hand above my booty.

"No!" I squeal, unwrapping an arm from around him and covering my butt. Thankfully, he pulls his hand away and just leans down to kiss me. He pulls away after a little while and he looks down.

"Let me see it," he pulls at the top of my maroon halter neck top. He finally sees the hickey he freaking left and his lips pull up at the edges.

"Did you actually want to see that or did you want to look at my goodies?" I question.

"The hickey. I'm lying," he kisses the corner of my mouth. You know what, at least he's truthful.

"You're wearing pants?" he peers down at my black skinny jeans. I'm not the biggest fan of wearing pants due to the fact that my legs feel confined, but I didn't want people to see the horrific bruise on my leg.

"I have a bruise the size of Jupiter above my knee," I explain truthfully.

"I was putting folded clothes away in my dresser and I slammed my knee right into the open drawer. I was paralyzed for five minutes, and I thought I wasn't going to make it but I did," I recall the horrific event that occurred just yesterday.

"Not your already hurt one?" he makes sure.

"No, the other one. Thank goodness, I just took my brace off last week," I thank Jesus again really quick.

"So," I rock on my heels, "is the new girl pretty?"

"Pretty as a mule's ass."

Oh, that's just terrible.

"Grey, that was a horrible thing to say," I bite my lip, "I bet she's beautiful and very nice."

"You want me to lie to you?" he pauses and we just stand there as he thinks for a minute.

"She's *so* pretty," he says dryly and sarcastically all mixed in one.

"That's even worse."

"She's not my type. I wouldn't've fucke-"

"Don't you dare say what you were just about to," I cut him off, raising my hand to him.

"It's true," he shrugs.

"I bet you would've said the same about me before you got to know me," I scold. His eyebrows furrow.

"I would've fucked you within the first five minutes we met if you were up to it," he pulls me against him and my cheeks blaze.

"That is *not* where I wanted my point to go," I take a deep breath.

"Oh, but you talk about sex all the time," he pulls my lips up to his.

"I joke," I blubber.

"I don't," he kisses me.

"Want to make out?" he kisses under my ear and my eyes nearly bulge out of my head.

"Are you okay?"

"You just look fucking *good*," he keeps my head tilted up to him. I step away and look down at my outfit.

"Aw, you like my outfit? I don't remember where I got the shirt, but I like it too. I thought it went together wel-"

He cuts me off, pulling me to him and kissing me roughly. His hands travel under my butt, and he lifts me. I gasp and notice how hot and bothered I really am. The door opens behind Grey, and I pull away.

"The party host isn't supposed to leave the partay- well goddamn, if it's to make out with a sexy mama, then I can't blame him," Sanfred's head comes into view.

"Hey, baby doll."

"Go inside motherfucker," Grey glares and Sanfred rolls his eyes before closing the door. He gives me one more kiss before placing me back on the ground, gripping my hand, and opening the door. He pulls me inside. I find the girl he was talking about immediately. *I didn't know models worked for the FAA.* What was he talking about? A mule's butt? Is he joking?

Suddenly I feel like I'm back in high school and feeling extremely self-conscious. Her legs are as long as me. Her hair is thick, beautiful, brown, and it lays in perfect loose curls. I stop there, I don't even want to look at the body difference between her and me. It'd probably make me want to leave. Grey gets tossed a beer and I almost jump out of the way when the can seems like it's going to hit me. I should've stepped in front of it though, I could've sued and got millions.

"Want one?" he asks me.

"No, I'm good," I give him a tight-lipped smile, slightly eyeing the same can that I see strewn all over my kitchen most of the time.

"You won't get arrested," he reminds me.

"I don't drink."

I've promised myself I would never. He pauses and looks down at me, his eyebrows furrowed.

"Why'd you want moonshine then?" he recalls something I totally forgot about. *Crap.*

"I was taste-testing," I recover.

"You were specific," he counters, and I sigh internally.

"I searched that they were flavors that tasted good," I lie. I almost tear up at lying after we had specifically agreed to not keep anything from each other anymore. *I wish I was as bad of a liar as him.*

"Who's this?" a feminine voice asks. Is it Jonas? I laugh internally at myself. I know it's the new girl. Neither Grey or I answer I guess thinking each other was going to say something.

"Hello?" she slightly laughs. I look up at him and he looks at me. He narrows his eyes a slight bit once which says 'talk.'

I narrow mine once back which says, 'no you crackhead.'

"I said hello?" she continues and Grey's eyes fall to my lips when I roll my bottom one into my mouth nervously. I feel bad for ignoring her, I really do. But I just can't seem to talk.

"These are my two mute buddies," Theo pops up between us.

"He's not mute," she points to Grey.

"Whoop-"

"You're wrong," Lincoln joins in, "Grey has selective mutism."

"He talks when he wants to? Everyone has that," she rolls her eyes.

"Uh-"

"He has one of the worst cases," Jai comes up to us from behind me. Grey's jaw ticks at the situation that I kind of got us into.

"His girlfriend is on a no-speaking strike. She's also a politician. She wants to be the president of the United States. She's a vegan right now though," he says like being a vegan is a job. Then he loudly hiccups.

"I just ate four shots," he mumbles, "I mean drinked. Or drank. Or drink-ted. Maybe it's drunk. No, *I'm* drunk. Actually no, I'm tipsy. *Errybody in this bitch gettin' tipsy*."

"Azalea, keep doing you, honey bunches of oats," he pats my head. Honey bunches of oats? He's definitely not just *tipsy*.

"And Grey?" he says.

"What?" Grey grumbles.

"I'll tell you what I was thinkin' when I remember it," he starts walking away, attempting to give the peace sign but instead he sticks out his thumb and pointer finger. At least he's not a mean drunk. I wish dad was a funny drunk. Or not ever drunk at all.

"We're going to go make sure he doesn't drink anymore," the two guys leave and Grey, the girl, and I are left alone again.

"So, girlfriend?" she looks over at me and I feel intimidated by her gaze.

What am I saying? I can't be intimidated by her, I'm the one who intimidates The Rock. I'm a badbutt.

"Yes," I smile looking at her, "I'm Azalea."

Her eyes are like freaking ice. Is she from Earth? Oh gosh.

"Cute," a forced smile reaches her lips. I would like to leave please.

"Younger girls, huh?" she turns to Grey, and he tenses. Why is it that she's making me feel so utterly terrible about myself? I mean it's not like she's the only one to do that.

"You like your job?" he asks, his eyes set hard. Her eyebrows furrow a tad.

"Yes."

"If you want fieldwork, shut the fuck up," he says simply and her eyes widen in surprise.

"I-I didn't know you were the head," she struggles, her eyes darting everywhere.

"Shit," drunk Jai drawls out as he's being dragged somewhere by Theo and Linc, "now you know he's boss man. You tried to flirt with the boss man. Did you know that Azalea?"

He breaks free from Lincoln and Theo, coming over to me.

"I don't think I like Jaqueline very much," he attempts to be quiet but everyone around us heard it.

"Okay Jai," I speak to him more or so like a child. Drunk people are like children, at least that's what I've learned from when mom gets drunk. Dad, not so much at all.

"I'm going to go sneak some more tequila," he attempts to be quiet once more before sneaking away. Grey pulls me away from in front of the door where everything went down and we end up at the kitchen table where Jai is being put in 'timeout.'

"I was hoping she was going to be a little nicer, y'know?" I mumble, sitting down in the seat at the head of the table.

"Younger girls," I grumble. I bite down harshly.

"I'm fired up Grey," I grumble unhappily.

"Six years. That's hardly anything. Nineteen and twenty-five. It's not even bad!" I exclaim.

"My parents are sixteen years apart," Lincoln chimes in, keeping a close eye on Jai who's currently trying to slide out of his chair and under the table. Theo grabs the back of Jai's shirt to keep him from sliding completely under the table. I look over at Grey to find that he's looking at me already.

"Send her to a different unit, give her to the DEA," Lincoln proposes.

"I've already sent out her file," he says, bringing his hand forward and gripping onto my chair. He slides my chair to right beside him and then picks up my legs, placing them over his lap. He runs his hands up and down my legs and I lean my head against his shoulder. He grabs an unopened beer from the table in front of us and he starts drinking. With a kiss pressed to the top of my head, he basically chugs down the rest of it. *Yikes.*

~~~

I watch him repeat the action a good four more times before deciding that I should go to bed. Jai escaped twice and was caught both times. Although the second time he was brought back, he had a hidden mini bottle of tequila. It was pretty funny. I probably shouldn't be, but I'm just scared to see what drunk Grey is like. Is he mean? Is he nice? I don't want to know.

I know he'd never hurt me and he's nothing like dad, but I'd rather not see what he's like. Plus, Bear and I can snuggle. So once in the room, I remove my pants and shirt, grab one of his, and jump into bed with Bear following.

I give Bear a wonderful belly rub that he deserves, and he and I watch *Treehouse Masters* on the mounted TV. *I want a freaking treehouse.* After *Treehouse Masters* goes off, I watch half of the movie *Grown Ups* before drifting off. I wake up when the door to the room opens, not so quietly. I sit up and the light is turned on. I take a couple of seconds to adjust my eyes and the door is shut. *It's three-thirty in the morning.*

I recognize Grey's figure and then the chicken leg in his hand. He nearly trips over himself trying to take his boots off. *He's drunk.* I stay quiet, just watching him as my heart pounds nervously. He pulls his shirt off his head, and he meets my eyes.

"Want me to strip the rest of the way for you baby?" he says and my eyebrows shoot up. Baby? *Uh, frick yeah.*

"Hm?" he adds.

"No, it's okay," I respond quietly, "Where'd you get your chicken leg?"

He looks down at the chicken leg in his hand. His eyebrows furrow and he examines it.

"I think I found it," he mumbles and I wince. Good Lord knows where that thing came from. I wrap the blankets tighter around me and he moseys over to me, swaying a bit. The nervousness has died down more now. Bear still lays asleep at the foot of the bed. He climbs onto the bed, looking at me.

"You're my burrito," he refers to all the blankets wrapped around me, and I giggle.

"Kiss-Kiss," he says leaning forward. I place a little kiss on his lips, and he pulls away.

"You taste better than any burrito I've ever had," he licks his lips.

"I think you taste your chicken leg," I motion to it and he shakes his head.

"I taste you through the chicky," he climbs on top of me and I groan. *Chicky?* He bites the chicken and rolls too close to the edge and onto the ground. I wince.

"Fuckin' fuck," he groans. This man can get stabbed and hardly wince, but he falls off the bed and whines?

"You okay?" I uncover myself and scoot off the bed. He lies there and doesn't move when he sees me. I bend down next to him, and he throws an arm around me, pulling me the rest of the way down.

"Grey," I mumble, "we can't lay on the floor, it's hard."

That's what she said. Stop.

"Hold this," he hands me the chicken leg. He slides his hands under me and stands with me in his arms. He tosses me back onto the bed and takes the chicken. I look up at him and he smiles. *Aw.*

"You're so fucking cute," he makes my heart beat faster, "I just want to hold you all day."

"Sober words speak drunk-" he pauses and starts over, "drunk words speak sober thoughts."

He once again climbs on top of me. He hovers over me and looks all over my face.

"You're beautiful," he kisses my forehead, "are you falling in love with me too?"

I smile softly back at him.

"I am," I nod.

"Remind me when I'm sober," he places his chicken leg on my pillow, making sure it's straight and that it won't roll off.

"Don't put it there, it's greasy," I tell him.

"I'll eat it okay? Want some?" he takes a bite out of it. Bear leans up to us and he tries to sniff it. Grey holds it to himself, possessive over it. Drunk Grey isn't bad. *Thank God.*

~~~

I wake up before him. It takes me twenty minutes, but I pry him off of me. He's *passed out.* I brush my teeth, tinkle, and throw my hair up with Bear beside me. I walk into the kitchen and clean all the red solo cups and beer cans, out of habit. I straighten everything out of place and make Grey a *big* glass of water when he wakes up.

I grab Ibuprofen and take out two for him because I know that his head will be hurting. Or his back will because that's where he landed on it when he fell off the bed last night. He doesn't do this often though. I know that for a fact. This is the first time I've ever seen him drink and I think it's okay for him to let loose occasionally. Toast helps too. Mom always eats toast and fixes dad things like that the mornings after they're up drinking almost all night.

So, I fix him some toast. And some for myself. I eat my toast and then grab his, walking back to the room. I don't turn the light on and I set the plate and his glass of water on the bedside table. He stirs and rolls over to me.

"Are you awake?" I keep my voice soft, to not hurt his head more. He doesn't respond, only grips onto my bare thigh with his hand.

"You okay?" I question softly, gently rubbing the arm that's attached to my leg. He pulls the chicken bone from last night out from under the covers and I laugh as quietly as I can.

"Why is this in my hand?" he grumbles, his voice dark and husky.

"You came in here last night with it," he hands it to me, and my nose scrunches up as I take it. He sits up slowly and I can't help my eyes that are drawn to his chest. I sit beside him as he eats the toast and drinks the water. When he's done, he leans over and lays his head down in my lap. Little flurries erupt in my stomach.

"Thank you," he says.

"You're welcome, Sugar."

"Did I call you a burrito?" his eyebrows furrow and I giggle.

"*Your* burrito," I nod.

"You have something to remind me of," he says expectantly, and I bite back a smile.

"I'm falling in love with you," I tell him.

"Mhm."

If I'm not already.

Chapter Twenty-One

Sway

❀ Azalea ❀

Sometimes I wonder why bad things happen to me. And why they happen quite frequently. And why they have to be *the worst things possible*. I'm panicking. Grey's trying not to judge but I feel like that's a very hard task. I knew that sometime this would backfire. *Oh, God.*

"What's wrong with you?"

"Grey, dad's here. He's downstairs," I stress. At least Grey parked across the street.

"I'll just leave," he mumbles like it's no big deal. And I can't even explain to him that it *is* a big deal.

"No! Unless you leave through the window," I wince.

"Like some fuckin' spider monkey? Who do you think I am?"

"He can't see you," I add, and his jaw ticks.

"The window? What are you so scared of?" his eyebrows furrow.

"What's the worst the guy's going to do? Come on, Azalea. We're together, is he ever going to find out?"

My head hurts from my mind conflicting with *itself*. I don't know what to do, what to say, or anything.

"You're going to make me cry," I whisper, and he sighs. He pulls me to him, and he kisses the side of my head.

"I don't want to get in trouble. I don't like getting in trouble," I say metaphorically. I don't like getting welts on my back.

"Why don't I just stay here until he leaves again?" he tries.

"He won't leave until late tomorrow," I shake my head, "and you said you have to work in a little bit."

"You really want me to leave out the window?" he grumbles.

"I'm really, really sorry, and I know it's selfish for me to not want to get in trouble but I just-" he shuts me up with a kiss.

"It's not selfish. It's okay," he nods, and I sigh. He licks his lips.

"Give me one more 'fore I go," he leans in, his eyes focused on my lips. I lean in the rest of the way. I shoot away from him upon hearing my bedroom door being opened forcibly.

"I knew I heard someone else in here," dad's sober voice enters my room. *He's sober*. My heart falls. He glares at me evilly and I attempt to calm my breathing.

"I-I'm sorry," I whisper loudly enough for me to hear him.

"You *should* be sorry," his nose flares in anger. He turns his attention to Grey who sits beside me, not knowing what to do. But his face is nowhere near happy. Dad's tone is far from how a father should talk to his daughter. He's trying his best to not glare at dad.

"You, get the hell out of my house," dad points his finger in Grey's face which only irritates him more, "you goddamn *punk*."

Grey takes his time as he pulls his boots back on. Who knew Grey was a petty man?

"This is the guy? This lowlife?" dad sneers down at me and I shrink away. *Too scared to even defend Grey*. Why does everyone think so terribly about Grey? He's nothing like they think.

"Stay away from that child," not his daughter, but *that child*.

"She's not a fucking child," Grey sneers right back, standing up and looming over dad's 5'11 height.

"What gives you the right to curse at me in my own home?" dad tries to stand his ground.

"The same right that allows me to not give two shits," I wince at Grey's response.

"Get the fuck out of my house!" dad grows even more irate. Grey looks back at me.

"I'll text you," he tells me before walking to my door.

"You will not!" dad demands and Grey turns around.

"Yes, the fuck I will," he nearly growls out before leaving me and dad alone. He's sober though. He won't hurt me, right?

"You are to never see him again. Where is your phone, give me it," he demands.

"I don't know," I lie. He can't take my phone. Grey said he'd text me, he can't take it.

"Don't you lie to me Azalea Carson," he glares.

"I really don't know," my voice comes out shakily, "it's been lost for a couple of days."

He walks closer to me threateningly.

"And don't you *ever* think about telling anyone shit," he gives me the meanest tone, one that sends my eyes watery.

"Okay," I whimper and he leaves, slamming my door harshly behind him. And then I cry.

~~~

At this point in my life, I'm the furthest from alone I've ever been. But I'm also a liar and I keep things from the people most important to me. So I feel alone. My phone lights up with a call but I ignore it, having a feeling I know who it is. Grey cares. He cares a lot and he's not the only one but I *can't* tell him about dad. I just *can't*. I don't want to lose my father too. He'll get better. *Right?*

Why is it that I don't want to let Grey worry, but at the same time, I'm making him worry by not answering him? *I just want it all to stop.* I want to stop worrying about dad. I want to stop worrying about what to do. I want to stop feeling selfish about everything. I want to stop thinking so much. I want to stop being scared to death of my own father. I want to stop lying to the one person who I *know* cares about me. I want to stop saying 'I can't.' But I *can't*.

On one of the call's last rings, I pick up the phone.

"I was wondering when the hell you were fixing to pick up the damn phone," his unhappy voice says through the phone. I bite my lip as my eyes water. I guess he's done working for today.

"I'm sorry," I tell him softly, looking out into the sea of trees over the overlook.

"What's wrong Lilah?" his voice softens which only sends a tear down my cheek.

"I don't know," I admit defeatedly, my voice breaking.

"Where are you?" he asks softly. I calm myself and swallow the lump in my throat.

"That overhang we went to," I mumble softly.

"I'll be there in a minute," his voice remains quiet. Most likely because he can hear my shaky voice. The call ends and I hug my knees to my chest sitting on the rock edge of the overlook. At least if I fall off this thing, there's a grass patch on the other side before it really drops off. *Like it would matter. Shut up. It does matter.*

It takes Grey ten minutes to get here. It should've taken him around fifteen, but *somebody* must've been speeding. He stands to the side of me, holding out his hand. I place my hand in his and he helps me to stand, and he pulls me to him.

"What is it?" he holds me to his chest as his hand rubs my back soothingly.

"I'm having a mental breakdown," I tell him truthfully.

"I'm sorry about my dad," I whisper. He lifts my chin up to him.

"I don't want to hear it," he says sternly.

"That's enough," he wipes my damp cheeks.

"Don't be sorry about anything. Nothing is your fault," he adds.

"Is it 'cause I'm an ugly crier?" I sniffle.

"Shut up, you could never be ugly," he grumbles. *I bet I could prove him wrong.*

"Do you think I'm an unlucky person or it's just karma?" I question quietly.

"It wouldn't be karma because you never did anything in the first place," he drills into me sternly.

"And so what if you're unlucky? I'm lucky as fuck, I've got enough luck for the both of us," he places a slow kiss on my lips, one that makes my heart speed up.

"Everything happens for a reason," I remind myself softly and he nods, tucking my hair behind my ear.

"Would a tattoo on your forehead hurt? I'm thinking about getting one there that says, 'I'm sorry you have to hear me talk', what color should I get it done in, blac-"

It's wild how quickly he can cheer me up just by being near me.

"Shut up."

"See, exactly what I mean. I'm sorry you have to hear me talk. I could get another one on my chin that says, 'ignore me'," I explain.

"Oh! I've got a good one. This one I can get under my eyes like Post Malone, and it'll say, 'Turn off your hearing aids old people,' that's a good one," I can imagine it now. That's a lot of words on my face though. I look up to see him scowling right back at me.

"I'm sorr-"

"Stop saying that," he grumbles and I internally say I'm sorry. Suck it.

"Did it hurt," when you fell from heaven, "when you got all these tattoos?"

"Some," he says, and I sigh.

"Have you ever thought of getting one on your forehead?"

"One that says leave me the fuck alone," he mumbles. Is he kidding or not?

"That would fit you," I smile.

"Get your ass in your car," he lightly pushes me away and I laugh at him.

"Come home with me," he opens my door for me and watches as I climb in the driver's side. Home? *His* home, he meant.

"Aw. Do you like spending time with me?" I lean up and kiss his cheek as he hands me my seatbelt. He leans into me, and I kiss it again before he pulls away.

"You've got a pretty face," he shrugs a single shoulder and the corner of his lips turns up in a little baby smile.

"You're so cut-"

"Don't call me cute," he cuts me off. That's like me telling him to not call me Lilah. It's never going to happen. I buckle my seatbelt and turn back to him.

"Were you listening to Mötley Crüe?" He looks at my radio where the screen reads the name *Kickstart My Heart*. I listen to hard rock when I cry sometimes to make me feel like a badbutt. It didn't work this time even with one of the hardest rock songs I have.

"I love how heavenly their music is," I say sarcastically with an innocent smile on my face. He leans his arm on the outside of my car and I hold back from swooning. My eyes find his lips that are beautifully resting in a small smirk.

"Are you going to kiss me or just look at me?"

I blush slightly and lean up to him. He leans down the rest of the way and kisses me. He pulls away only to look at me.

"God you're sweet," he kisses me again with a bit more force. He grips my chin and I gasp when he bites my lip. Then he pulls away and I'm left blushing.

"Okay," I blurt for no reason, and he kisses my forehead. He leans down and I kiss his softly. He's *cute* and he can kiss my grits if he doesn't like it.

~~~

"Why are you like this?" I sigh, looking up at him.

"I didn't ask for this," he responds.

"You're not trying at all," I narrow my eyes up at him.

"Yeah 'cause I'm going to step on you," he looks down at my bare feet. I step back away from him, and he reluctantly releases my waist from his grip. Grey doesn't know how to dance. Such a cutie. *I'm quite the dancer myself.* I specialize in many different types. Ballroom, stripping, salsa, I'm not very good at break dancing, and I'm *super* great a ballet. And I'm actually pretty good a slow dancing. Grey never asked to learn but I'm teaching him, I don't care what he thinks.

"Sway," I instruct him.

"The fuck do you mean, *sway?*" he mimics.

"The *frick* do you mean you don't know how to *sway?*" I mimic him right back.

"Sway like you did the other night when you got drunk," I tilt my head and his eyes narrow slightly. He doesn't move. I return to my spot in front of him. I wrap my arms around him.

"Don't move your feet, just sway with me," I begin swaying and the freaking crackhead is stiff. I squeeze that booty of his.

"Stop being stiff."

"Well, your hands are on my ass," he mumbles, and I chuckle evilly. I move his hands down to my butt. Now we're equal.

"You don't feel me being stiff, now do you?" I question.

"No one just touched my ass before you," he grumbles, and I let a smile grow on my lips.

"And you think people have touched mine?" I tilt my head.

"'They' better not have," he scowls.

"Look. You're swaying and not tense," I chime in, noticing how he's not being stiff and he's actually moving with me.

"I'm going to step back, you step forward," I instruct.

"What foot?"

"Um." I've never actually taught anyone how to slow dance. I kind of thought it was something everyone already knew.

"Your right one."

I grab one of his hands from my booty and I hold it up in a classic slow dance move. Then I let go of it because my eyes fall on his nice chest. So, I place my hand on his chest and he moves his hand back. I almost squeeze his peck, but I refrain. *Goodness, he's strong.*

"Now move your right foot to the right," I say softly, and he does so. And then my heart swells when he presses a kiss to my temple. I give him a few more instructions and tips and soon enough, he's got it down and we're slow dancing. And Bear is very jealous. I sense an intruder when the front door opens suddenly, and I expect Grey to pull away and react, but he doesn't. And then I see Sanfred walk into sight.

"Aw, look at my parents," he says with a little smile on his face. I *feel* Grey rolling his eyes. Bear attacks him with love and jumps on him and everything.

"Grey, please. Your mammoth of a dog is going to make Bella jealous," Sanfred moves out of the way of Bear.

"C'mere Bear," I call him back over to us.

"Do you have a dog too?" I gasp.

"Yes. And Bella won't come near me if she smells Bear on me."

"What kind of dog is she?"

"A dachshund-"

"Oh my gosh, you have a wiener dog?!" I squeal. I love those little wieners. *That's probably not what she said.*

"Bella is *not* a *wiener dog*. She is a princess," he argues. Grey pulls away when I stop moving. I grab his butt and pull him back to me.

"Well-"

"Azalea, I'm on a mission to retrieve this guy from his house because some old guy is being held hostage in some shack two towns over but when I get back, I will argue with you for hours on how my Bella is more of a princess than actual princesses. Now Grey, get your guns and get your ass in my car," he says all in one breath.

There's an old man being held, hostage?!

"Try again," Grey sneers.

"I meant: Azalea, I'll tell you about Bell later on and Grey, please gather your weaponry and accompany me in my car...please," he fixes his phrase.

"That's what I fuckin' thought," Grey grumbles, releasing me to go get his 'weaponry.'

"Don't touch," he points to Sanfred then back to me. As soon as he's out of view, Sanfred runs to me.

"Let's dance baby doll," he rushes out, grabbing my hand and giving me a twirl.

"Is your name really Sanfred?" I ask the question that's been on my mind for a while.

"My name's Oaklee San*ford*. Whoever gave these guys my resume said my last name was Sanfred, and it stuck with them. I'm not even sure Grey knows my first name," he shrugs.

"Can I call you Oaklee?" I question.

"You can call me whatever you want, baby doll," he winks.

"You remind me of someone," he suddenly says.

"Jake Carson?" I question. They all knew him, and it was only a matter of time before someone found out. I'd rather tell them firsthand.

"How did you...?" he says, surprised.

"He was my brother," I say softly, and his movements pause. He just looks at me for a second.

"I gave you one rule," Grey's voice grumbles as he comes back into the room. I step away from Oaklee.

"She's irresistible," Oaklee shrugs. I'm probably going to forget to call Sanfred Oaklee, but I'll enjoy it while it lasts.

"Go wait in the car."

"Fine," Oaklee leaves and after a second, the front door opens then closes. Grey sits two guns on the couch, and I feel my eyebrows raise. I feel him grab onto my waist and pull me to him. He turns my chin to him. He kisses me harshly and my breath is knocked out of me. *Woah, baby.* He kisses down my neck and I'm sure he can feel my wild pulse with his lips. He pulls away and gives me one last gentle, sweet kiss.

"If anyone tries to break in and kill you, there's a gun beside the bed. And don't try to be their fuckin' friend," he kisses my forehead. *Like I'll know*

Lilah   *K. Pope*

how to use it.

    "And if anyone tries to headbutt you, um," I think of something that he'd be able to do.

    "Just don't get close enough for anybody to reach you like that since you don't know how to dodge them," I give him an assuring nod.

    "I know how to," he mumbles.

    "You just lied to me, okay? Be careful," I wrap my arms around him in a hug.

    "I'll be home soon," he bends down, and I kiss his forehead.

    "Okay Sugar," I smile.

<p align="center">~~~</p>

* Grey *

    "Azalea is Jake's little sister?" Sanfred asks as soon as I get in the car.

    "Did she tell you that?" I sigh.

    "Yep. She's beautiful. I guess that's why Jake never let us see her," he mumbles.

    "Shut up," I warn him. Goddammit.

    The forty-five-minute drive goes by slowly. Everything goes slowly when I'm with Sanfred. I dread being in his company. Or anyone's. Except Lilah's. And it *pisses* me *the fuck off* when someone has to get in the way of us spending time together. Who holds an old guy hostage anyway? Dumb motherfucker. *I hate everybody.* Arriving at the location where everything is taking place, I'm handed a leather and the file of who's holding the old guy hostage. Police cars and our SUV's surround the place. I get stopped as I walk closer.

    "Can I see some identification, sir?" the cop asks, resting his hands on his belt.

    "Talk to him," I brush past him tossing my ID at Sanfred who follows behind me.

"This is so exciting," whatever her name, new girl, says as I finally see our group. She holds her gun pointed at the bushes. *Watch out for those damn bush critters. For fuck's sake.*

"He's been holding him in there for a good hour and a half now," Jai informs me as I stop beside him.

"It's his grandfather, apparently," he adds.

"The fuck's her name?" I nod to the new girl.

"Jacqueline," he smirks, "I left a spot open right next to her just for you."

"Fuck you, piece of shit," I grumble and he only chuckles. I rest against the SUV beside her.

"So," she starts, and I already want her to shut the fuck up.

"Why'd you get here so late? And why isn't your gun drawn?"

"Two things. One, shut up. Two, don't ask me questions," I scowl. Theo's phone dings with a text from a few people over from me. *Idiot.*

"Grey, you're *fucking* Jake's little sister!?" He yells out. *I'm going to kill Sanfred.*

"I'm not *fucking* her," I turn to him with a glare.

"Is it Azalea?" Jai asks, "oh my god!"

"You're having sex with some girl?" the new girl who's name I already forgot again, asks. I choose to ignore her.

"No way you're fucking that man," Jonas' voice says. He knows just the right shit to make me so mad.

"Who the *fuck* brought this *motherfucker?"* I glower.

"Why are you with her?" Theo asks me. He used to be the closest one with Jake.

"It wasn't on purpose," I grit my teeth.

"So, you knew who she was?" He asks confusedly.

"No, not really. Sort of," I sigh.

"And what? You just thought she's hot and probably hurting from Jake dying, 'lemme slide right in?'" He grows angry. I do too. What kind of motherfucker does he think I am?

"I didn't fucking want her Theo," I glare, "I knew it was shitty. Do you think I don't know that? I don't need you telling me this shit."

"But you're with her-"

"I tried fucking pushing her away from me," I sneer. I tried everything to stay away from her, but I couldn't. And not staying away from her was the best decision I have ever made.

"If I wasn't fucking serious about her, why would I bring her around? Why would she be with me all the time?"

Why would I be constantly thinking about when I get to see her next? I'm not even able to keep my eyes and hands off her. He remains silent.

"We've got movement at the front door," some random officer tells us. I glance at the window beside the front door of the house.

"That's a cat," I glare at the officer. He winces. I turn back to Theo.

"Don't act like you know shit about us because you don't," I glare at him one last time before turning to the door where the damn cat is still rubbing itself against the window beside it.

"Are you okay Grey?" the new girl's voice asks. I feel her hand come to rest on my arm and I jerk it away from her.

"Don't touch me," I scowl. What, does she think she's privileged or some shit? She's not Azalea, she doesn't have free rein to touch me whenever she wants. Or at all. *Only Lilah.*

Chapter Twenty Two

Enough

❀ Azalea ❀

    I'm calling it now; Grey is going to be not-so-happy. Last night when he went out for the old man hostage situation, he was supposed to come right back here. Turns out, they got another call and he got back here at seven in the morning. So, he's been sleeping for *forever*. What's a girl supposed to do? Just watch tv or something? Not me. I painted his nails.

    He's a heavy sleeper. And it's not like it's bright pink on both hands. It's *purple* on *one* hand. He'll be fine. I painted Bear's nails too. He looks fabulous. I think he likes it too. Yeah, I could've left and gone to Mr. Terrip's but now that I've painted his nails, his reaction is going to be a must-see.

    Finally, at three in the afternoon, sleeping beauty awakens. More like the beast from Beauty and The Beast. Because he's not necessarily a morning person. Or an any-time-of-the-day person. He at first stirs in his sleep and I look away from the driving game on my phone, to see him. Then his beautiful dark eyes open and squint over at me.

    "Good afternoon, Sugar," I smile. I lean forward to him and kiss his cheek. I pull away to see his eyes closed and the sweetest little content look on his face. He sticks his hand underneath the covers and from what it looks like, down his pants. My eyes widen just a bit.

"What are you...?" I trail off, not even knowing what to ask.

"Making my hard-on less noticeable before I stand up," he grumbles, and my eyes widen even larger. I follow his line of sight to my shirt that has gotten bunched up around my waist, showing him my beautiful pair of magenta underwear, which just so happen to be my favorite pair. He got quite the peek.

"Oops, sorry," I laugh pulling down the shirt.

"Fuck," he swears quietly. He sits up and looks over at me again. I peer back at him admittedly a teensy bit shyly.

"Are you okay?" I ask.

"Don't talk to me, you're making it worse," he doesn't take his eyes off me.

"Then stop looking at me," I chide.

"I'm not going to stop looking at you, you look sexy sitting there," he lets his eyes travel up and down my frame. Azalea and 'sexy' have never been used in the same sentence before. I'm not even sure I've *said* the word sexy before.

"You think I'm...sexy?" The last word comes out a little higher pitched than the rest.

"If you can give me a hard-on like this, you're more than sexy," his eyes find my lips. I release my bottom lip I never knew was being held by my teeth. I grab the comforter around my knees and pull it all the way up to my shoulders.

"And you're *so cute*," I tease. His face contorts unhappily. He gets up without another word and disappears into the bathroom. I continue my driving game, hitting only a couple of pedestrians. Following the demolition of seven cars, Grey opens the bathroom door harshly and he walks back into the room, coming straight for me. His wet hair sends water droplets down his defined chest, and I give him an innocent smile.

"What're you looking all riled up for?" I question just as he stops right beside me. He doesn't answer, he only throws an arm around me and lifts me from the bed, holding me over his shoulder. I let out a screech.

"My buttcheeks are out!" I shout, noticing how his shirt that I'm wearing is slowly riding up, being in my position.

"Ha!" I realize something, "but you can't see them because I'm *over your shoulder*!"

He smacks my butt. Pretty hard.

"I'm going to get you back for that when you least expect it Sugar," I assure him, the sting still present. He brings me into the bathroom and now he can see my butt in the mirror. I don't even care anymore.

"Yeah Grey, take a good *long* look at my booty because you'll never see it again," I ramble as he lowers me from his shoulder and sits me on the counter next to the sink. I watch as one of those gorgeous smirks forms on his lips. He lifts my chin up to him.

"We both know that's not true," he says softly. Someone needs to turn the AC up higher because this is getting ridiculous.

"You know what? You're just *so cute*. You're the cutest thing in the world," I tilt my head to the side and his smirk falls.

"And so sweet. You're such a cute sweetheart," I grip onto his cheeks. Buttcheeks? Ha not yet, it'll be coming soon though.

"Tell me how to get it off," he shows me his hand and I dramatically gasp.

"Where'd that come from?" I keep my eyes wide as I look back up at him.

"Where *did* it come from?" He asks sarcastically.

"Oh goodness, someone broke in and did that didn't they?" I grasp my heart. He grips my chin firmly and tilts it directly up to him.

"Get it off," he grumbles, his eyes only flitting to my lips for a second.

"What's so wrong with it?"

"It's purple and on *one* hand," he rolls his eyes. I always keep extra nail polish in my car. If I mess one nail up, then I don't have to worry. But what I don't have is a remover. And the polish just so happens to be gel.

"Well," I start, "technically it'll come off if you scrub it for a while." He only stares at me. No emotion rests on his face.

"I'm not even surprised you did this shit."

"Grey! I didn't even-" I'm cut off when Bear jumps up onto the counter beside us, his purple toenails in view.

"Oh my gosh! They did it to him too?!" I gasp. He rolls his eyes at me. I look down at his arms that rest on either side of me on the counter. Veins run up his forearms and I don't even hold back from dragging my finger along one near the middle. How does he get it to do that? He leans closer and I keep from shivering upon feeling his lips near the shell of my ear.

"Don't tease Lilah," he spreads my legs and steps between them, pulling me closer to him by my waist.

"You're getting me wet," I wipe a water droplet from his bare chest in front of me. His hair is still dripping. His hands roam up the shirt on my body. I look up to him and see how dark and sinful he looks.

"Wet, huh?" He questions lowly. I swallow thickly. He leans into me and kisses my lips once. He kisses down my neck and his hands roam. One hand stops at the top of my underwear. Near the front where my goody of all goodies is.

"How wet?" He kisses along my jaw, and I realize how heavily I've started breathing. My heart beats faster like I've just run a marathon. *He's giving me breathing issues.*

"Uh-um," I struggle, and I feel his lips curve into a smirk.

"I'll just have to see myself then," his lips return to mine as his hand travels under my underwear. *Woah, baby.*

~~~

* Grey *

"I'm not even surprised to see you with painted nails," Jai sits opposite of me, organizing the files of cases we've completed this week.

"I mean a couple of months ago, I'd be shocked beyond belief but knowing Azalea, this is probably going to be one of the least surprising things she'll do," he adds. *She's killing me.* But do I hate the control she's got over me? Fuck no, she can do whatever she wants. I'm just along for the ride. And she's a wild ride.

"You're wrapped around her finger," he chuckles.

"I know," I keep my eyes trained on the files that cover the table in front of us. She's the *one* person who I let tell me what to do. It pisses me off how I can't win anything around her. Arguments? Absolutely not.

"You admit it?" He places a couple of papers down, his voice a little surprised. I encourage it. I need someone to keep my shit together when I can't. I wake up drunk: she's there with medicine and food. I'm in a pissy mood: she calls me out for it and *makes* me get my shit together.

"It's fuckin' obvious," I grumble. I'm fully aware that my eyes never stray from her when she's around. I'm fully aware she's obsessed with my ass. I'm fully aware I'm obsessed with her.

"You're damn right it is," he chuckles.

"Where's she at anyway?" He questions, "I hardly see you two separated."

She's acting all shy after earlier. After she came down, she could hardly look at me without blushing. *Fuck she's perfect.*

"Around here somewhere," I decide as an answer.

"Y'all aren't talking about me, are you?" Whatever her name is walks into the room. Jai gives me a look and I scoff. She moseys over to the table we're sitting at and leans her hands down onto it, her arm brushing against mine. I grit my teeth and lean away from her. I hate people and I hate them even fucking more when they *touch* me.

"So, do we have anything scheduled for tonight?" She asks all fucking jolly. I look up at the time. Seven.

"Grey's got a few things to write up but other than that, the bar's open tonight," Jai pushes from the table and stands, gathering the files in his hands.

"Paperwork?" She shoots up, "Can I help?"

Jai turns to me, a sly smirk on his face. Motherfucker. I gather the rest of the files on the table and stand. I walk back to my office, away from the girl whose name I still don't know. I close my door behind me and walk to the filing cabinet. My door opens and I grow even more irritated.

Get the fuck away from me.

I close the cabinet back after putting them all away and I turn. What's-her-face stands directly in front of me, peering up at me. I glare back at her and she bites her lip. Jesus Christ, I'd rather stare at a cow's ass.

"Jai left; he's out serving drinks now," she steps closer.

"And why *the fuck* would I give a shit?"

"I don't know," she breathes deeply, a smile still on her face. I don't like her. I never will. Not if she was the last person on earth, besides me.

"I bet your little teenager can't give you all you want," she smiles up at me, looking through her lashes.

"Sugar!" Lilah's voice calls out just before she opens my door. I give the woman in front of me one last sneer before moving away from her. Lilah opens the door and walks through. Her eyes light up and she smiles when she sees me. Then that smile falters a bit when she sees the girl.

"Hi, Jacqueline," she gives *Jacqueline* a small smile.

"Hey girl," she responds, and I feel my jaw clench. Azalea stands there awkwardly. I take in the sight of her and ignore the things she does to me without knowing.

"I'm going to go tinkle," she mumbles, walking back out the door.

"She still acts like a-"

"Keep fucking talking," I warn her, "keep trying to talk yourself up because you only sound like a fucking idiot."

Her mouth drops open a bit.

"Because no one could come close to being better than her. So quit making a fucking fool of yourself because if you aren't her, then you don't have a chance," I glare. She better not fucking dump me. She's just about the only thing I can talk good about.

"Oh yeah!" Azalea's voice comes from the cracked open door of the office. She walks in proud. *Good god this woman.*

"He told you!" She walks toward me and throws her arms around my torso.

"Suck my balls, Jacqueline!" My eyebrows raise. *Wild*. I know for a *fact* she has no balls. I *felt* for a fact.

"No means no!" She continues all while Jacqueline gives her glares. She presses her cheek against my chest.

"Now if you'll excuse us, my Sugar and I have business to attend to," she speaks sharply. Jacqueline rushes out, a glare on her face, closing the door behind her.

"I was so nervous about talking to her I thought I actually was going to tinkle," she breathes out in relief. And then her cheeks go pink.

"Are you thinking about something?" I tilt her chin up to me, leaning down and kissing those lips.

"Um," she struggles.

"Something earlier today?"

"You're making my cheeks blow up Grey," she leans her forehead against my chest.

"You weren't this shy when I did it," I chide, and she gasps. The sounds she made. *Fuck*.

"I did have polish remover, but I guess I don't now," she pulls away, her cheeks still a little pink.

"Don't play."

~~~

🌸Azalea🌸

"Stop moving!" I groan when, for a fourth time, he moves away from me.

"It smells like shit," he grumbles as I use the remover to get the polish off his nails. And he's got an advantage because he's in a wheely chair.

"Would you rather leave it on? I can leave right now," I pull away only to be pulled back by my waist.

"That's what I thought," I humph and he squeezes my hip bone causing me to thrash. I continue getting the purple off his nails and I feel his eyes trained on me.

"The longer you look at my face, the uglier I get," I warn.

"Shut up."

"You hush," I grumble back. I'm thinking logically here. The longer he looks at my face, the more time he has to see all my flaws and then to think 'wow, she's not pretty at all, what I am doing, I deserve better.'

"Hyper."

"Crackhead."

"Loud-mouth."

"Baboon."

"Flighty." My mouth drops open a bit at that.

"Buttnugget."

"Simpleton." My jaw drops again. He leans forward and kisses me like that'll make up for his words. He bites down on my bottom lip when I don't kiss him back. I pull away.

"Bear needs to probably take a poop when you get back home," I remind him. Before we left his place, I may have slipped him some greasy bacon. I can only hope he hasn't pooped already.

"When *I* get back home?" he questions grumbly.

"Yes...?" I furrow my eyebrows.

"And why aren't you coming home with me?" his face sets unhappily and I tilt my head, a small smile on my lips.

"You know why," I sigh. Then I lurch forward, pulling his head under my chin.

"Are you going to miss me Sugar?" I hum teasingly and his arms find their way around my torso, pulling the rest of me closer to him. He doesn't respond, only holding me close. I take it as a 'yes wonderful woman I'll miss you more than anything in the world because you are the greatest funny person ever.' The little smile stays on my face until I realize he's not letting go anytime soon.

"What's wrong?" I ask softly, he pulls his head away from me and looks up at me.

"I don't know," he mumbles, and I know he's lying. He sucks at lying. And he's fiddling with the scrunchie on his wrist so he must know that I know that he's lying. For a federal dude or whatever, he's not good at lying.

"You can tell me," I assure him. I mean, I tell him everything. Like, probably too much. He knows when I'm tinkling and when I'm pooping. *Yikes*. His reaction never differs. It's always either 'hurry up' or 'I'm not pausing the movie, hurry the *insert f-word* up.' He doesn't *judge*. I mean, it is only a dookie so it's whatever.

But of all the things he hears me say, and of all the things he sees me do, never once have I looked over at him and found a judgmental look on his face. And that's crazy because I don't think I'm very normal. And as many times as I play the song *Cherry Pie* by Warrant when we're driving somewhere, it surprises me how he doesn't even care. If I had a theme song, it'd be that one. And I scream my lungs out when I play that song. I look over at him, he doesn't care.

If Grey had a theme song, it'd be silence. Or *Paint It, Black* by the Rolling Stones. I even played that song for him once. He didn't have a reaction. It still makes me wonder if he even listens to music. Or his dancing is not moving. Or smiling. Does he breathe? What if he listens to classical music? I'm going to have to test that theory.

"I don't like it when you're not with me," he finally says.

"Aww, I knew it. You do miss me," I hug him tight, "you're so cute. I miss you too."

He doesn't deny it, so I giggle evilly.

"Fuckin' cute," he mumbles just a little bit unhappily.

"Would you rather me say adorable? Because you are adorab-" he cuts me off, kissing me harshly.

"Fuck off," he mumbles against my lips.

"Are you sure?" I tease, he pulls me onto his lap.

"You're really about to see up my skirt the way I'm sitting," I warn, looking down at my slightly spread legs and my black skirt.

"I'm about to? Does that mean you're going to show me?" I watch as the corner of his mouth rises.

"Oh yes," I nod, "and once I've taken my skirt off, I'll be sure to dance on the table."

"Now you're just putting thoughts in my head," he trails his hand down to my waist. That backfired a bit.

"If I'm going to be a stripper, I'm going to need you to pay me," I say. He leans back fully against the back of his chair.

"You wouldn't enjoy stripping for me?"

"That doesn't mean I won't enjoy it," I wiggle my eyebrows, "after it I'd probably need money for food. I'd put my heart into it."

"You've thought about doing it before?" he tilts his head in question. Oh yes. I've thought about him doing it too.

"I think about a lot of things," I shrug.

Food, shoes, Grey, Carebears, Cap'n Crunch, Silly String, ceiling fans, and Grey.

"What things?" he grips onto my hips.

"I feel like you're tricking me into saying 'sex.' But sex," I wince. I stand from his lap.

"I just adore our lovely conversations," I bend, kissing his forehead. I stay down and he kisses mine.

"You have to go?"

"It's getting late," I nod, "and when it's dark, there's a better chance to hit an animal I can't see and I don't feel like crying tonight."

"Natural selection," he grumbles, and I gasp.

"That's horrible," I place my hands on my hips. He gives me horny eyes.

"Stop it," I warn.

"Stop what?" he acts clueless.

"You know what," I raise my eyebrow.

"You stop," he shamelessly continues looking at me. I take my hands off my hips.

"I'm not doing anything!"

"You're doing it again," he says, and my mouth drops open.

"I'm standing!"

"Quit," his lip curls into a smirk. I place my booty cheeks on the floor and narrow my eyes at him.

"Goddammit, you keep doing it."

"No, I don't! Do what? I'm sitting! You're crazy," I stand again, and his eyes never leave me.

"Fuckin' keep on," he nods. *I'm going to throat-punch him.*

"Keep on what? Grey, I'm going to kick you in the face," I warn.

"Do it," he nods, "that won't make you stop though."

"Stop what?!"

"Stop."

"I'm leaving! Have a wonderful night you donkey," I scold, opening his door and walking out.

~~~

I sink down in my bath slowly, letting the pain of the lashes on my back stiffen my body. *Because I wasn't home yesterday.* I honestly have no clue how I'm going to keep Grey from touching me. Nowadays, he's always touching me, wanting my amazing hugs, or lifting my shirt, feeling my stomach to try and convince me I'm hungry. I pray that sometime soon dad will get tired of all the alcohol, and he'll quit drinking. Drinking all the same stuff has to get tiring and old sometimes, right?

I soak for a little while just relaxing and trying not to move in any way that would cause my back to hurt. I wash and carefully step out, draining the tub. I slip on a big baggy shirt and a pair of cotton shorts.

From twelve to four in the morning, dad plays the tv too loud for me to go to sleep. My only pair of earbuds I left at Grey's place. And my pillows only block out so much. After I can hardly hold my eyes open for any longer, I eventually drift off into a light sleep. At exactly three-nineteen in the afternoon, I wake up. My back is sore, and the pain has set in even further. It's always worse the second day. My stomach growls loudly, sounding like a whale's cousin.

I slowly rise out of bed and walk over to my mirror. I carefully take my shirt off and only turn my head to see the damage done to my back. Long stretches of belt marks are spread sporadically across the surface of my back. I put on the largest sweatshirt I have and certainly no bra. The worst thing I could do is put a bra on. I throw on a pair of black ripped jeans feeling out of the ordinary today. And it's rainy so why not? I put on my furred moccasins because they're comfortable and I don't give a fudge. I pick up my phone and see messages from Grey.

One telling me good morning. Good f-ing morning, to be exact. Another one stating my butt better answer him. In other words. Two more stating unhappy thoughts of me ignoring him. With more choice words, of course. One telling me he got a case a couple of towns over. That one was five hours ago. In it, he said two choice words. Another saying that he's back from the town. With one choice word. And one last one asking if I had eaten yet *and* stating that I'm going to have a long 'talking to' when I see him again. In a lot of choice words.

I let a little smile onto my face. Before I get the chance to text back, I hear a loud crash downstairs. My smile falls and I look toward my door. *Better now than later.* I open my bedroom door and start down the stairs cautiously. Nearing the bottom of the steps, I look around the living room for him. When I don't see him, I figure he's in the kitchen. I step down the last step and a loud noise resounds from under my foot when I step on an empty beer can, never seeing it.

I close my eyes, visibly wincing and my heart begins pounding as I hear his footsteps nearing. I could go back up the stairs, but I wouldn't get very far. But maybe he's sober? What am I saying? He's not sober, it's already nearing four in the afternoon. My breath holts when he suddenly appears from the corner beside me, his eyes bloodshot from the amount of sleep he probably hasn't been getting.

"Where the hell are you going?" he slurs and I'm terrified to answer, worried that my answer won't be the right one no matter what I say.

"I-I was going to the bookstore," I fib nervously, keeping my eyes away from his.

"No, you're not," he sneers, "you're going to see that *boy*, aren't you?"

"N-No-" he cuts me off.

"Is he treatin' you like you deserve?" he pulls me off the steps by my hood.

"Like a murderer should be treated? Are you cleaning for him and cookin' whatever he wants? He should be smacking you around, you deserve that," he adds, and I bite back tears.

"I *should* let you go out on these wet roads," his voice turns even more sinister, "maybe then you'll wreck just like you caused your brother to. That way you can get what you caused, and you won't give people here anymore issues."

I let a single tear fall, too scared to move and wipe it away.

"Why're you crying? You're a pussy of a killer," he growls.

"I didn't kill him," I say so softly I didn't think he heard me at first. And then it registers that I said that aloud to him. *I just couldn't take it.*

"What the fuck did you just say?" he grabs the front of my sweatshirt, and he pulls me up to him. The alcohol on his breath digs into my senses and I hold back a wince.

"Nothing," I whisper, my eyes slightly widened as he forces me to look up at him.

"You said you didn't kill him," if possible, he grows twice as irate, "yes you did."

Before I can even blink, he does the one thing I thought he'd never do. He jabs his fist right into the side of my face, the class ring he always wears on his middle finger digging into my cheekbone. I'm sent backward, my head spinning, and my cheek pounding searingly. My vision goes hazy, and I feel something drip down my cheek. I blink rapidly to get the haze out of my eyes. Busy focusing on trying to keep myself from blacking out, I don't see his knee until it's right in front of my face. He knees me in the mouth and blood soon coats my lips, teeth, and tongue. I don't even know what all is coming down my face. Blood mixed with tears.

Through my still hazy eyes, I look up at him. His eyes switch from malicious to only slightly concerned. The concern being the tiny bit of sober left in him. I thank God when he walks past me and up the stairs, done.

I stay on the floor for a while, letting my tears mix with the blood on my face. Eventually, the haziness fades away and my head is only left pounding. My cheek stings wickedly but adrenaline still courses through me keeping the pain of my mouth and cheek to a minimum. But eventually, adrenaline will wear off. On the floor, my gray sweatshirt covered in my own blood, the coppery taste of blood in my mouth, and the pain of the welts on my back, I come to a decision.

Enough is enough.

Chapter Twenty-Three

Retaliation

❀ Azalea ❀

  I rise from my position on the floor slowly making my best attempts not to fall over and injure myself further. I grip onto the railing of the stairs once I can reach it and on my way to the kitchen, I hold onto anything that I think will keep me standing. I grip the paper towels on the hook they sit on and only just now realize how bloodied my hands are. I turn and look at the trail of blood I left behind on the railing of the stairs, the wall, and even the couch. *How much am I bleeding? Can you run out?*

  I catch my reflection in our mirror-like, shiny microwave and I gasp. The left side of my face is *covered* in blood, my teeth are red stained with the blood that drips down my chin, and it breaks my heart all over again. How could a father do this to their child?

  I grab the paper towels and try to wipe the excess blood from my cheek. I can't even get half an inch away from the cut from his ring on my cheekbone; it hurts too bad. I wipe my chin but the blood from both places still doesn't stop, and my tears don't either. Blood soaks the paper towel and I go to grab another. Every slight movement of my cheek makes me want to stub my toe on something just to have pain somewhere else to take my mind off it.

My movements stop when I hear him coming back down the stairs. Moving as quickly as I can, I grab my car keys off the hook and rush out the door. *Where am I going to go?* Taco Bell. Shut up, I can't go there. Can I? No. The hospital is an absolute no-go. Who's got the money for that? Not me. I would if I was a stripper though.

I did conclude that I need to tell someone. Grey. *I never wanted to break my family up worse than it already is.* But I wasn't wanting to do it so soon. I wanted to not look like I do right now, but I guess I don't really have a choice. I can't necessarily cover this up with makeup. And I think I need some Jesus and medical assistance because my cheek is still gushing.

I turn on my car and wipe the tears from my eyes to see the road as best as I can. I probably *shouldn't* be driving at all in my predicament *and* considering the wet roads. But if I *do* wreck, it sure wouldn't hurt Dad at all. He said the opposite. *Whatever happens, happens.* My adrenaline decreases and harsh pain begins to set in. When tears fill my eyes, I blink rapidly to get them cleared.

Whenever I feel my blood dripping off my face, I make sure to wipe it with my sleeve. Why not? This sweatshirt is already covered anyway. I try to stay calm at red lights, praying that no one will see me and freak out. I haven't fully seen myself, but I know there's blood everywhere. Before I left, I should've gotten paper towels, but I was just too terrified of Dad seeing me again and maybe continuing.

I park in the closest parking spot you can get to Grey's restaurant/bar/flippin' headquarters for his drug cartel. I stay wiping my face as close to the gash as I can handle, mostly covering it so people won't see and freak out. Then again, I do have blood all over my sweatshirt but maybe they'll think it's like, tie-dye. Yeah right. I successfully make it to the entrance. I pull it open and just barely catch the eyes of Jonas.

His eyes widen, and he actually looks…really concerned. He's going to be really concerned when he gets a face full of my bloody sweatshirt sleeve.

I ignore him and walk as quickly as I can into the back, I'd hate to ruin someone's meal by seeing me look gross and bloody. I wipe my hands as best as I can on my sweatshirt before gripping Grey's door handle and pushing open the door gently, I turn my body away from Grey's desk. I close the door behind me and stay facing away from him, looking at the door.

"It's about damn time you show up," his voice reaches me, and I feel tears leave my eyes.

"Why haven't you been answering?" I hear his spinney chair roll back as he most likely stands. Then I hear his footsteps. I take the few seconds I have until he reaches me to figure out how I'm going to go about this. What I'm going to say, that is if I don't break down crying. Which I have a feeling I may do. I might even be doing that right now. It may be tears and blood that's still gushing. *I need some Frosted Flakes.*

"Why are you facing the door?" he questions, nearing even closer. I feel his hand on my back and I flinch forward.

"Lilah...?" he grips onto my arm, "what the fuck is on your sleeves?"

I flit my eyes down to my blood-soaked sleeves. And then I turn to him. He takes a couple of shocked steps back, his eyes widening and his mouth opening a bit. His eyebrows furrow like he can't believe what he's seeing and then he visibly snaps out of it, surging forward to me. He places his hand on the side of my face without all the damage and he looks all over. My cheekbone, my mouth, my shirt, my sleeves, my tears.

"Oh my God," he whispers in shock. He moves to touch my cheek and I flinch away.

"It hurts," I mumble quietly, "please don't touch it."

"Who the fuck did this to you?" his voice changes drastically from concerned to deadly. I stay silent, afraid to open my mouth and suddenly ugly cry. He wipes away the blood about to drip from my jaw.

"You're touching my blood without knowing if I have diseases," I breathe out. Hepatitis or something, I don't know, I'm not a scientist.

"Who fucking did it Azalea?" he demands and I verbally freeze. After so long of keeping it to myself and not telling a single soul, I find it hard to just *say it*. He pulls away from me. I catch his tensed body, clenched jaw, and bawled fists. And I feel bad about not being able to just say it. I hold back a gasp when he suddenly grips the edge of his desk and flips the entire thing. *Oh no, the iMac. What about my movies?*

He picks up his chair and he throws it clean across the room. I flinch as it hits the wall loudly, breaking into dozens of different pieces. Watch out, we've got Hulk over here. Except he's gray instead of green, 'cause his name is Grey- stop. He walks back over to me, his chest rising and falling quick. He pulls me away from the door and in front of him. He wipes more blood only for it to return not even a second later.

"You need to tell me that it is who I think it is," he says lowly, and I let out a sob. Of course, he pretty much already knows.

"I can take care of it, Lilah, I promise. You need to tell me. I can't do anything if you don't tell me," he pleads just before the door to his office opens harshly. Jai steps in looking at all the damage. His eyes find me, and they widen in great concern. Then they fall on Grey and Grey's bloodied hand from wiping my face.

"What the fuck did you do?" Jai sneers to Grey and my eyes widen. Oh gosh, it does look bad.

"You think I did this to her?" Grey growls out.

"It doesn't look to be in your goddamn favor, Grey," Jai walks toward us.

"That's fresh," he tilts my face to him, pointing at it. *Pointing is rude.* My blood drips onto his hand and I internally cry harder. He grips Grey's arm and lifts his bloody hand and bloody knuckles from where the excessive blood dripped onto all parts of his hand. Grey jerks his arm away. *He doesn't like people to touch him.*

"He didn't do it," I speak up, shaking my head softly.

"Azalea," Jai starts, "you don't have to defend hi-"

"What the shit?" Lincoln walks in, "What are you two fucking doing?!"

Lincoln pulls me to him, seeing a scene that looks even worse. My face all fudged up, Grey with my blood on his hands, *and* Jai with my blood on his hands.

"Linc," I start, and he places his hand on the side of my face, searching over the gash and my lip, "they didn't-"

"Oh my God!" Theo runs in, his eyes darting all over the place, "what the hell are y'all doing to her?!"

This is getting ridiculous. I should probably be getting some type of medical attention, but everyone is too busy trying to blame someone else.

"Shut the fuck up!" Grey sneers loud enough for everyone to hear.

"Like you can say shit, you woman-beater!" Jai shouts and I gasp. I caused them to hate each other. Everything's my fault. I should've just never come here and waited for these injuries to heal themselves.

"Excuse me Jai!" Theo yells, "you can't say shit! Look at you, blood all over your fucking hands!"

"I came in here after I heard that loud noise and here Grey is, he flipped the whole damn place upside down and his knuckles are all bloody!" Jai points an accusing finger at Grey. *Where's Dr. Weiner, or whatever his name is when you need him?*

"I would *never* put my *fucking* hands on her," Grey shoves him back into the wall.

"He didn't hit me," I attempt but it can't be heard over their arguing. I begin feeling lightheaded and I try to take deep breaths. If I pass out and hit my head on the way down, I'm suing everyone in this room.

"That's not what it looks like!" Lincoln inputs, "both of y'all have bloody knuckles, you both hit her."

Have I lost too much blood? It feels like I have.

"Hell no! It looks like all three of you hit her," Theo chimes in loudly.

"No," my voice only comes out as a whisper as I start feeling even fainter.

"Grey," I try calling out, but he doesn't hear me the first time.

"Grey," I say as loud as my body will let me. His head whips over to me as my head struggles to stay upright. I fall back against the wall behind me, barely being able to react to the pain it causes on my back. Grey rushes over to me and the conversation stops.

"Call Karter," he demands.

~~~

I wake up to the sound of my own stomach grumbling. My face hurts, my lips hurt, my back hurts, I have to fart, I have to pee, I'm hungry, I need to crack my butt-bone, and my mother trucking fingernail polish came off a little bit on one nail. I'm *driving* the struggle bus.

I open my eyes and find what looks like a hospital room. I look to the side of my bed and see the blood pouch thingy that I remember vividly from the accident standing beside me. *I knew I was losing too much.* At least this room isn't nearly as ugly decorated as hospital rooms. It's got style.

The door opens and Grey walks through. It takes him a second to look up at me and when he does his face visibly relaxes. I move my hand up and touch my face, I nearly throw up at the pain that explodes in my cheek when I do but I feel stitches. *Stitches. What a bad-butt I am.* I run my tongue along my bottom lip, the lip which got most of the blow, and I find it's got a huge bump from where it was busted open.

"Am I *so* pretty?" I mumble sarcastically, pronouncing the t's in 'pretty' so goodly. Obviously not. I look like Frankenstein I bet. Well actually, Frankenstein's monster. Frankenstein was the doctor who made the monster.

"Always," he takes a seat on the side of my bed, tucking my hair behind my ear.

"That's the nicest thing you've ever said to me."

"No, it's not, shut up," he lifts my hand kissing the top of it.

"Who got to see my amazing bod' when they put me in this?" I wiggle my brows looking down at the new sweatshirt that I'm wearing. *Oh my, Jesus Christ in the morning. I'm not wearing a bra.*

"Somebody got to see some seriously good stuff, let me tell you, was it you, you little hooker? You got to see it all. I mean *all*," I ramble.

"Karter's wife," he says, and I nod. He missed out. And I missed out on making a mother trucking friend, too busy being stupidly passed out. I feel like my legs could run a mile. Just my legs.

"What drugs am I on? Can we turn the dosage up? My face hurts like an elephant just stomped on it," I groan.

"Karter get in here," Grey's lovely voice just lights up my life. Karter, aka, Dr. Weiner, waltzes in.

"Which amazing drug has my mind feeling *great*? Did you give me crack?"

"Are you an addict?" he questions.

"I like drugs."

I look at Weiner. He looks at me. I wink at him. Then wink nonstop about 11 more times.

"Is she having a seizure?" Wiener questions.

"You're the doctor, Weiner Man," I tell him, winking once more and making a clicking sound with my mouth.

"Baby, what the hell are you doing?" Grey grips my chin, turning my face toward him.

"I'll wink at you too," I wink at him. Then make the same clicking sound four times. Grey smiles. He smiles at me. A real good smile. It bakes my flipping beans.

"Hey Weeny," I look at Weiner. He looks at me. I wink at him, make the clicking sound, and kiss my middle finger then show it to him.

"Jesus, Lilah," Grey grips onto the finger and pushes my hand back down.

"What?" I question. I didn't do anything wrong. With my other hand, I raise my middle finger to Grey. I draw a heart in the air with the finger. If I drew the heart on paper, it would be purple because I would like it to be. He grabs that finger, releasing my other hand. His face breaks out into a smile, and he lets out a beautiful, deep, and melodic laugh.

"You gave her some *good* shit," he leans to me and kissed my temple.

"He did give me good *shit,*" I nod, holding my fist out so Weiner can give me a fist bump.

"Azalea!" Grey looks at me, his eyes wide, "I thought you don't say those words?"

"*Shit*, my bad," I tell him.

"I can't believe you said that" Grey chuckles then pauses, "*don't* say *that* word, got it?"

"Got it fu-" he places his hand over my mouth. Weiner appears to be appalled. I pull away from Grey remembering my face hurts.

"Listen here Dr. Wenis, my face hurts, give me some more pain meds please, and thank you. And you should throw in some LSD."

"Dear God," Karter shakes his head, pinching the bridge of his nose.

"Oh hey, can I sit up? My back hurts," I grunt.

"I guess-" Karter starts.

"You guess? Oh gosh, you aren't even a real doctor, are you? Are my stitches on the correct side of my face Grey?"

"No," he tells me seriously, but I can tell he's kidding because I'm on drugs. Hopefully.

"On a scale of one to ten, how would you rate your pain?" Karter asks. I don't even know who *I* am. Let alone what numbers *are*.

"Who's asking?" I narrow my eyes suspiciously.

"What? - Azalea, do you hurt?" he chuckles.

"I'm about to have a heart attack if you don't let me sit up," I warn.

"You can sit up," Karter nods. I try to sit up, it may not look like it because I don't move, but I tried.

"Somebody pull me up," I reach out and Karter pulls me up.

"My back is on fire," I groan, and Karter's eyebrows furrow.

"Why?"

"You didn't see it?" I furrow my eyebrows.

"See what?" Grey asks suspiciously.

"My killer boobi-" Grey grips onto my hipbone and I thrash.

"Ouch, Greyseph," I raise my fists like I'm going to fight him. *Man, I feel good. Tired, weak, and sexy.*

"Grey, look," I motion to my back. He pulls up the back of my sweatshirt and I feel him tense. Karter moves to the side, and he looks too. I just close my eyes and let a sigh escape. After forever hiding that, it feels kind of relieving to show it.

"I'll be back," Karter leaves the room and Grey lowers my shirt. I look over at him.

"Azalea, tell me," Grey sighs.

"You already know who Grey," I say defeatedly.

"Your dad," he states. I feel stupid emotions creeping up on me.

"I'm sorry," I bite my wiggling lip, "for keeping it from you after we made that agreement to not keep anything from each other. I kept the biggest possible thing from you."

He leans over and kisses the side of my head.

"I don't want my dad to go to jail. My family is already messed up enough, I don't want it to get worse," I sniffle.

"But you know what's going to happen now," he keeps his voice calm and quiet.

"The fucker's going to prison," he nods, and I sigh.

"I know," I whisper.

"You need to tell me what happened," he smooths down the back of my hair from where I was laying. I squeeze my eyes shut.

"He calls me a murderer," I start, "he says that I killed Jake. And that it should've been me who died, instead of him."

"For some reason, I just couldn't stand hearing it anymore. I told him I didn't kill him. He went off."

"He's never punched me before, but he did. He always wears his class ring on his middle finger and that's what did that," I point to the stitches on my cheekbone.

"And then when I was on the ground, he kneed me in the mouth," Grey wipes the tear under my eye.

"You didn't blackout, you remember it all?"

"He's a weakling, he couldn't even knock me out. Loser. I'm The Rock, you can't knock me out," I pat my chest. Grey's dating The Rock remade as a small woman.

"I almost passed out," I simmer down.

"What about your back?" he says, and I sigh, looking over at his beautiful dark eyes.

"He started hitting me with his belt about a year ago. It's gotten worse. Harder, and more hits for smaller things," I explain.

"Like when he finds out you're with me," he whispers.

"Yeah," I hesitate.

"I should've fucking seen it before," he curses, and I shake my head.

"Don't shake your head," he argues, "that time when you wouldn't let me touch your back. How fucking stupid could I have been?"

"Grey-"

"And that bruise on your cheek the first time you stayed at my place, fuck," his jaw tenses.

"I don't want to talk about it anymore," I crisscross applesauce my legs.

"I'm hungry," I grumble.

"Jonas' bringing pizza," he shoves his hand under my sweatshirt. Is he going to feel me up? Go ahead.

"Jonas? He'll probably poison my pizza," I groan.

"You'll be fine," he kicks his boots off and gets the rest of the way onto my bed. I'll be fine? Excuse me? Tell that to the poison control center.

"Yes, go ahead, take up more than half of my bed, you're welcome," I pat his back. He scoots right up next to me, and he lays down. Trying my best to get comfortable, I lay my head where his arm meets his shoulder. His cold, gargantuan hand comes to rest under my sweatshirt and on my bare stomach. I wiggle a bit and sigh at the uncomfortable feeling my jeans are leaving me in. *Who the heck let me sleep in these?* I force my hands under the covers and unbutton my pants, and I let out a sigh once they're unbuttoned.

"Is that an invite?" his hand travels lower.

"An invite to where? Can I come?" I get a little excited. We best be talking about a party. I'm ready to *party*.

"Fuck," he whispers. He places a gentle kiss on my non-Frankenstein-monster cheek.

"Why'd you unbutton your pants?" he sighs.

"I'm a bit of a chunk so they were digging into my stomach," I pull up my sweatshirt, showing him the mark my pants made on my stomach.

"Shut up," he glances at me unhappily. I lay down carefully and sigh.

"I'd never hurt you; you know that?" he kisses my temple.

"I know," I smile softly, "I can't believe Jai thought you did this to me."

"Just wait 'till he comes in here," his voice takes on a playful tone.

"I won't hurt you either, y'know," I chime, "I'll make sure to never headbutt you since you don't know how to dodge them."

"Goddammit."

"It's okay Grey, we all have weaknesses," I speak therapeutically.

~~~

I finish the last slice of pizza and Jai applauds me, his bruised face and all. I guess that's what Grey was talking about. Grey hasn't moved since he got in my bed. I still don't know where I am, but I could care less as long as he's here with me. I'm in love. No question. No 'right?' at the end of the sentence. I'm fully in love with him.

There was no big realization. I just took a huge bite of my pizza and looked over to see him giving me a little smile and I thought it was a normal thought. 'I love him' was all there was to it. Of course, I haven't said it aloud yet. I'm still a little droopy in talking but not in thinking. I wouldn't want him to not believe it.

Anyone who still wants to be around me after seeing what I'm like when I'm by myself deserves an award. In Grey's case, that award is my wonderful love and affection, and butt smacks, and sex jokes, and all my body's scars, and my odd music taste, and my pizza-eating skills, and most importantly my boobies that are maybe a little small, but fine to him.

"How're you feeling Azalea?" Karter questions, stopping beside the bed. He leans down and raises his hand to my face.

"If you touch me, I'll rip your hand off," I scrunch my nose.

"What she said," Grey nods his head in my direction. *I love you.*

"Y'all are an evil couple. Evil," he stresses.

"I'm not," I give him an innocent smile.

"It's five-thirty," Jai peers over at the clock on the wall. Grey's demeanor changes completely and a glare settles onto his face. Not at anyone in particular but it's just there. I know what has to happen now. And I know that my life will never be the same. *Dad's going away.*

"You have to go?" I question softly. Grey's features lighten a bit when he looks down at me.

"Only for a little while," he begins putting his boots back on.

"I don't want to sit here anymore," I say, "I need to be active."

"You need to rest," Grey deadpans and I scrunch my nose at him.

"I *need* to get my hyper energy out," I explain.

"Run horizontally," Jai chimes in the idea.

"She's not talking about that kind of active," Grey grumbles, knowing me too well. My 'active' is walking around and interacting. Other 'active' is running and working out. Ew. I sit up fully. I can't just *sit here*. I start getting up, Grey pushes me back down gently by pressing his monstrous hand on my forehead.

"Grey," I groan, sitting up again.

"Azalea," he warns, pushing me down again.

"I'm going to throat-punch you," I glare.

"Do it," he gets closer, his eyes narrowing. I crack my knuckles.

"It's going to hurt," I warn, nodding my head.

"Go ahead," He keeps on. *I love you.*

"I don't want to hurt you," I let a smile on my lips. He places his fingers under my chin, and he brings my lips to his. I melt. Even though my lip feels like it's falling off, I could care less.

"I wouldn't recommend kissing," Karter mumbles. Grey pulls away.

"Fuck off."

"Hush wiener," Grey and I speak at the same time. I *really* love him.

~ ~ ~

* Grey *

Jai knocks on the front door of the house. The fucks all came to a decision to not let me be the first person her dad sees. Like they own me or some bullshit. But I agreed when they brought Lilah up. *Goddammit.* The door opens.

"Can I help you?" He slurs but tries to hide as drunk as he is. He's drunk as fuck. He's so drunk he doesn't remember who I am.

"Oh yes you can," Jai plasters on a fake smile. Jai reaches around to the pocket of his pants.

"Goddammit. Where the hell did I put my handcuffs?" He curses. Dumb motherfucker. Jackson Carson turns, and he starts running. Which is to be expected. Slow fuck. I grab the back of his shirt and I yank him back into the wall beside the door.

"This is illegal!" He shouts. I send an elbow to his face, and he falls, leaning up against the wall.

"I did nothing!" He sneers, blood dripping out of his nose. He sends his head forward and it clashes against my nose. *Why the fuck can't I dodge a headbutt?* I feel my nose start to bleed and that only makes me angrier. And then he freezes.

"I know you," he says.

"You aren't cops. You're a gang!" He shouts, "You're that punk who's been messing with my child!"

"The woman you've been putting your hands on?" I sneer.

"She's no woman," he scoffs.

"You're no fucking father," Theo starts to charge for him, only to be pulled back by Jai. Theo's been through shit with abusive parents. He grew up an orphan and he'd gone through some fucked up houses. That's how we found him and how he came to join our shit. But he's also a fucking dumbass at times. Not at times, most of the time. So is everyone else. And Lilah, she's just fucking oblivious to what the hell is going on, bless her goddamn heart.

"What's going on?" A quiet voice asks, walking down the stairs. Azalea's mom.

"Mrs. Carson," Jai speaks, "we're a part of the FAA, and we're here to bring your husband into custody."

"They don't have a fucking warrant, Marianne!" He shouts. If I had a dollar for every time a motherfucker said this, I'd be richer than the richest man on earth.

"They've pulled their guns on me! Call the real police!" he continues his pitiful shouts. I look around at the two other guys in the room. Obviously, their hands are empty. Marianne continues walking down the stairs and the closer she gets, the more visible her bruises are.

"Sick motherfucker," I toss him on the ground.

"I'm not resisting," he resists, wiggling around like a fucking fish out of water. I back away from him, making him look even more like a fucking idiot. If I could kill him, I would. Theo walks with Marianne outside just as Jackson is jumping up.

"She snitched, huh?" he catches his breath.

"Nah, the fucking gash she had on her face told us all we needed to know," I glare.

"How'd it go again?" I ask.

"Wasn't it a punch that did it?" Jai goes along.

"Yeah," I nod, taking the Jai's class ring he lent me just for this occasion, "and the ring was on which finger again?"

"Pretty sure it was the middle," Jai nods and I slip it on my middle. In the corner of my eye, I see him start to try and run. Well, that's not fair. Lilah couldn't run. I kick his back and he falls into the railing. He grabs onto his leg and lets out a shout of pain. I look along the railing and the wall. Dried blood remains on the walls, and I know it's hers. I grab him by his shirt and lift him to his feet.

"Now you can't run, motherfucker."

As soon as he turns his head and looks at me, I drive my fist into the side of his face. Not hard enough to knock him out. But he'll need stitches. I let him fall. I wouldn't want to knock him out. If he's out, he won't be able to feel the pain.

"What'd you do next, Jackson?" I hum. He grumbles unintelligibly. I look up at the ceiling in thought.

"K-Kneed her," he finally utters.

"That's what I thought," Jai chides, "It was either that or another punch."

I knee him in the mouth. Harder than he kneed her. Good. In prison, he'll be missing a few teeth. I bend down next to him.

"You're going to rot in prison," I grip the hair on his head and tilt his head back, "and after that, you'll rot in fucking hell."

It's not about just sending this motherfucker to prison. It's fucking retaliation. No one will *ever* lay their hands on her again.

"Do you know what they do to men who beat women in prison?" I ask him, a delightful look on my face.

"No," his eyes turn frightened.

"No? Well, don't you worry," I pat the side of his face with excessive force, "you'll find out pretty quick."

I send the side of his face another jab, following it, I slam his face into the ground. Azalea should have never had to go through this. I'd give up whatever she wanted me to just so I can still see her smile and to hear her voice when she calls me Sugar. Fuck that name. But she's happy when I let her call me it. *What am I feeling?*

Chapter Twenty Four

Amazing

❀ Azalea ❀

A week and two days, Grey has been acting like an overprotective mother. He won't let me move. I've told him many times, 'Grey, if you keep feeding me and not letting me walk it off, I'm going to be confined to this bed for the rest of my life and I won't be able to walk ever again.' He usually does one of three things each time I tell him that.

1) Shut up. 2) Do you want more food? (my answer is usually yes, obviously) 3) Shut the *insert F-word* up.

He really is such a sweetheart. I mean come on. My face is fudged up, not my legs. My showers are my only time to stand and so I do tons of physical activities during my showers. My activities usually consist of three things.

1) Staring at the wall and pretending I'm in a sentimental and dramatic movie while my shower water runs over my face. 2) Dancing wildly, although it's hard in the small space. 3) Telling Grey to leave me alone after he bangs on the door for ten minutes.

My back feels better, which is great. It's still a bit tender at times but that's whatever. I guess I'm just not used to someone taking care of me.

Usually, it's only me nursing myself. I'm trying to adjust but it's taking a while. A couple of days ago, I got my stitches removed. Grey wasn't allowed in the room because once again, he's a little crazy. Finally, Grey had to go to work for some type of murder thingy. Yikes. So, I escaped.

    I burst into Mr. Terrip's bookstore, and I find him almost immediately.

    "I haven't seen you in forever," he stresses, "I was beginning to get very worried."

    "What happened to your face?" he grips onto my chin, tilting it all around looking at the bruise and still visible, but healing, cut on my cheekbone. *I've got to tell him sometime.*

    "Well," I hesitate. He gives me the 'hurry up or I'm going to lose interest' face.

    "I just got the stitches out and I've been bedridden. Forcefully," I keep the cause of the stitches out of it.

    "And how'd you get those stitches?"

    "Uh. Dad hit me," I hesitate.

    "Oh Goodness, honey," he hugs me to his frail frame. Thank gosh his frame is different from Greys. I was getting tired of Grey's freaking bear-hugs that aren't meant to be bear hugs but just are. Oh wait. *Bear* hugs. I love Bear. I love Grey too. I didn't *forget* to tell him I love him. I just...am nervous and I've taught myself not to blurt it. It's been rough. It's been hard. *That's what she said.* I'm *not* tired of Grey's body. He can hug me all day. I'd be living it up with him pressed against me. But Mr. Terrip's hugs are pretty darn good too.

    "Did you get help? Did the police get him?" he questions, his eyebrows drawn together.

    "It's taken care of," I repeat Grey's exact words he told me that day when he came back from 'dealing with' dad.

    "You poor thing," he hugs me again and I smile.

    "Have you been staying at home? Is your mom okay?" he asks.

    "I've mostly been staying at," I look down shyly, "Grey's place."

    "Who?" Good Lord this man.

    "Grey, y'know," I hold out my arms and flex my biceps.

"Oh! Him, okay," he recalls, and I roll my eyes.

"I've been staying at his place mostly. I haven't been back to my house since dad did what he did," I explain.

"And you trust him, right? He's good to you still?" He asks just to make sure.

"He's such a sweet little cutie," I laugh internally at what Grey would say if I would've said that in front of him. Most likely it would be something along the lines of, 'You try to get on my (effing) nerves with that bull(shiz), god(darn it)'.

"What about Aaron?"

"I'll uh, I'll come around to it," I nod unconvinced with myself.

"I don't believe you," he gives me a look.

"I will," I nod, "I just have to figure out how to tell him. He used to be so close with my whole family, I don't want to just spring it on him."

"You're right," he nods.

"I've got a lot of books to put away, I bet," I smile, and he nods.

"I've put away some but I'm not as quick as you. I don't have it all memorized," he smiles back.

"I'm here to rescue you," I give him one last hug before going and starting on the huge stacks of books that I need to put away. The thing is, Mr. Terrip's bookstore isn't just a bookstore. It's also like a library. People can rent books. Kind of like a library. So, there's always things to put away. Also considering this place is the only bookstore/library around for the next thirty or so miles. I feel in the zone after getting the tenth book into its correct place. And then, I go on for hours. After finishing putting all the books away, I see a box of new ones.

I check my phone that I left on the table and see quite a few texts from Grey about my escape. From the time of his last text, I've got about ten minutes to begin putting the new books away and to look as innocent as I can while I'm at it. And if he's mad, I'll jump off the ladder and see what happens. I get to work. Sure enough, ten minutes later, I hear him come in. I *hear* him. That's not a great sign.

I consider flashing him to get his mind off the subject but I'm right in front of the windows at the moment. The second I see his tattooed hand wrap around my waist and yank me off my little ladder, I know that I've tickled the beast. And he didn't like the tickle.

"What in the world are you doing here?" I gasp innocently and he glares down at me.

"Thanks for telling me where you were," he nearly growls.

"Well, I was but I didn't want to bother you," I smile.

"You never fucking bother me, you know that," he tenses his jaw.

"I know that you *tell* me that, I don't know that it's true," I chide.

"Well how much more do you want me to say it?" he questions, "You don't bother me. Other motherfuckers do. You don't. End of it."

"Jesus would wash your mouth out if provided a bar of soap," I nod. He rolls those beautiful dark eyes.

"How do you feel?" he cups my face, dragging his eyes over my cheekbone.

"I feel like I just got out of prison," I smile. I walk away from him, chuckling at the unhappy look on his face.

"Jacked and free," I smile. I grip onto the box of all the new books, and I call to my muscles to try and pull it out of the supply room. *Maybe not as jacked as I want to be.* It moves a couple of inches. I turn back to see Grey watching me. Not helping, just watching.

"Don't look at me. I'm not helping you," he grumbles childishly.

"You're mean."

"Mhm."

I bend down and an idea pops into my head. I evilly laugh internally. I begin pushing the box, it still doesn't move because it's a stupid box. I pull on my acting britches.

"Ow, my back," I hiss, placing my hand on my back lightly. Was that too much monotone in that sentence? Maybe I'm not the greatest actor.

"Your back hurts from using your arms?" he questions, quite unimpressed.

"Now my head hurts from your attitude," I scrunch my nose at him.

"Bullshit," he chides.

"Oh gosh, there goes my leg starting to hurt from you not believing me," I grab my leg. He rolls his eyes at me.

"Grey! My hip hurts now!" I grab my hip. Here in a minute, I'm just going to fall out on the floor. He places his foot on the side of the box, pushing it and it glides across the carpet as if it weighs nothing. *Someone does not skip leg day.*

"Now was that so hard?" I smile. The moment I begin putting the new books away, Grey follows me around like a lost puppy. He doesn't help, he just follows me. I smacked his butt a couple of times; he smacks mine one hurtful time. We made out once near the very back. He asked if I'm hungry nine-hundred times. Grey's *kind* looks sort of scared away two customers, and I crop dusted a random aisle once. I internally told him I loved him eight times.

"We should go on a date," I gasp at the idea. We've never gone on an *official* date before.

"We've never gone on a date," I add.

"Yes, we have," he argues.

"When?"

"Every time we're together," he shrugs one shoulder.

"Thank you for telling me that *now,*" I say. His finger trails across my collarbone and under my shirt just a bit. His other hand travels up the side of my skirt. He leans down to me and kisses under my ear. His hand gets extra close to my *goody*.

"Grey," I warn breathlessly. I grip the tattooed arm that's close to between my legs. *Woah baby.*

"I've got you," he bites my neck gently and then he slowly moves his hand away. I pull away from him and prop myself up against a bookcase, gathering myself.

"You're beautiful," he says out of nowhere. He's getting better at this relationship thing. *He thinks I'm beautiful?* He leans down to me and kisses my lips softly. He pulls away and licks his lips. He leans back down and me a second time, a little harsher. I wrap my arms around his torso and press my forehead against his chest.

"You're just so cute," I tease and then gasp loudly when his hand goes back down, and he cups in between my legs.

"Don't tease," He hums, holding me close to him. *Oh gosh*. When his fingers start to move, he covers my mouth with his shoulder. I bite him a little bit to say, 'excuse me, sir, this is inappropriate.' We know better than to do something like this here. At least I do, Grey has no control. His fingers slide under my nice pale-yellow underwear, and I harshly grip onto his shirt, squeezing it for dear life.

"You like that?" His voice stays dark and quiet. He grips the hair at the bottom of my skull lightly and pulls my mouth away from his shoulder and quickly replaces it with his mouth. His now free hand comes to rest on my chesticle. *My boob!* After only a few moments, I feel great. I feel his lips form a smirk into the kiss and I grip onto him tighter.

"Azalea, where'd you go?" I just barely hear Mr. Terrip call out. My eyes nearly bulge out of my head and Grey, and I shoot away from each other. I straighten my skirt and lick my lips as I attempt to catch my breath and try not to make frustrated noises. I'm going to kill Grey. I feel oddly frustrated. What is he doing to me? I tuck my hair behind my ears and Mr. Terrip comes around the corner.

"There you are," he smiles when he sees me, and I feel guilty. I glance at Grey to see him leaned back against a bookcase, looking at me with a smirk on his beautiful face. I glare at him, and he crosses his arms across his chest.

"You helpin' her?" Mr. Terrip smiles over at Grey. Grey slowly drags his eyes away from me and looks over at him.

"Yeah," he looks right at Mr. Terrip as he lies. A *sin*.

"Well, I got to close early. Bingo is an hour away today," he rolls his eyes, "pisses me off those old asses."

He's actually pretty mad.

"Sounds ridiculous to me," Grey mumbles.

"You're exactly right," he nods to Grey, "they expect me to waste my gas trying to win myself some bingo money? I mean there's a chance I'll win so I'll drive there but it's getting ridiculous."

I love how this problem perfectly explains how old Mr. Terrip is.

~~~

"You have quite the nerve," I point in his face. I take a bite of my taco. We were going to order food from a nice restaurant but all of them in town don't do takeout. Who do they think they are? So, we settled for Taco Bell.

"Doing that in the store," I add.

"Did you stop me?"

"How am I supposed to do that when…you know," I feel my cheeks tinge.

"When what?" he smirks.

"You're- You- When it feels-, I just can't," I narrow my eyes at him.

"This is a date don't fight with me," he says like he's an expert on date-going or having, whatever.

"Bear, eat his taco," I whisper over to Bear, and he only wags his tail and licks my nose.

"How's your face?" He mumbles. What a darling way to ask that.

"It's okay," I spill part of my taco on my shirt and groan. Of course, that would happen to me. My phone rings and my eyebrows furrow. I answer it and even Grey is confused as to who is calling me.

"Hello?" I answer.

"Azalea, can you please come home? I really would like to talk to you," mom's voice travels through the phone.

"Oh. Yeah, sure. I'll be there in a little bit," I mumble softly and hang up. What would she want to talk about?

"Are you ditching me?" He says dryly from beside me.

"Yes, my boss at the strippery says I need to work tonight," I lean to him and kiss his cheek.

"What the fuck was that?"

"My boss at the strip club?" I question, figuring that'd be what he was confused about. He grips my jaw and pulls me close to him.

"On the lips," he demands, and I bite back a smile before leaning forward and kissing his lips. I go to pull away, but he just pulls me onto his lap. Two minutes later here I still am, on his lap but with his fingers buried in my pants, my head resting in his neck trying not to faint, and him doing the thing he does.

"I want my face in between your legs," he says lowly, biting my ear and I'm sent over the edge. Like I *wasn't* at the store since we got interrupted. *He wants his what, where?!*

"There you go," he says softly, kissing my temple and I gather myself. And to think he used to hate everything about me. I wiggle off his lap and only catch a small glimpse of his glistening fingers. I stand on wobbly legs and watch as Grey slips his middle finger into his mouth just like he's licking off Cheeto dust or something. *I need to have a church session in my car.* I straighten my skirt and take a deep breath.

"I'll see you later," my voice raises only a bit, and he gives me a once over. I walk out of there with still wobbly legs.

~~~

Walking up to the front door, I'm nervous. What's mom going to say to me? I haven't stepped foot in this house since what Dad did, am I going to get sad or what? I open the door and walk in. My heart soars when I see no sign of alcohol. I spot her sitting on the light brown couch in our living room.

"Azalea," she smiles when she sees me. She pats the spot beside her, and I walk over and take a seat. A tissue box sits on the empty coffee table in front of us.

"I just want to start by saying how sorry I am," she whispers, and I understand why there's a tissue box because me and her both are already teared up.

"I'm sorry for so many things," she shakes her head.

"I'm sorry for all the drinking that I never should have done. I'm sorry," she cuts herself off, grabbing a tissue and wiping under her eyes.

"I'm sorry for never standing up for you when you when Jackson would hurt you, I have no excuses," she wipes a fallen tear off my face. I know why she didn't stop him. She was afraid. She knew he would do the same thing to her and eventually he did.

"And most of all," she picks up my hand and holds in both of hers, "I'm *so* sorry for not being there for when you needed me the most."

She reaches up and wipes my tears away again.

"I was too busy in my own grief to not even realize yours and I could never forgive myself for that," she shakes her head. I understand though. I understand everything. Why she wouldn't fight with dad on why he locked me in Jake's room. She didn't want either of us to get hurt. But I also know that no matter what, if he came back, she wouldn't defend me even then.

"I forgive you," I whisper and pull her into a hug. I can forgive. Forgiving, although is different than forgetting. I believe she deserves a second chance, maybe she will prove me wrong. Sure, after Jake passed everything went straight downhill, my parents, everything. It felt like the world was closing in around me and there was no way I could get out of the pain. It surrounded me. But now, I feel *happy*. And I have no worries. Everything is just amazing.

"I don't deserve that," she holds me tight to her.

"I forgive you mom," I tell her again and she cries. We stay hugging for a couple minutes before she pulls away.

"After your father lost his job," her demeanor grows sad once more and my eyebrows furrow.

"I tried my best to keep up with everything. The bills, the payments, and everything. But I couldn't keep up, I still can't," she shakes her head.

"Well, that's okay," I give her an encouraging smile.

"We can get a smaller place. Just for the two of us!"

"Exactly," she smiles excitedly too. Everything really is amazing.

"So, I looked for one," her smile stays, and I get excited. We're moving!

"And I figured it would be the best idea to get a fresh start. Tennessee holds too many bad memories, so I found a wonderful house up in

Kentucky that I know you'll just love," my smile falls a bit.

"And I've already put in the offer, and they accepted! This house went up on the market earlier today!" She smiles happily. A smile so happy I can't even remember the last time I'd seen it on her face. My smile drops completely. She already got her offer accepted?

"Pack your bags honey! We're getting a fresh start in Kentucky!"

Everything is *not* amazing.

Chapter Twenty-Five

Stargazing

Grey

It's pitiful the way I am when I'm not around her. It's ridiculous. And the longer I go without seeing her, the worse I get. I haven't seen her in two fucking days. I'm not happy. We've talked yeah, fuck that. I need to *see* her. We haven't even talked much today really at all. Whatever she's doing, is keeping her busy. I'm busy too but does that keep me from talking to her? No, it doesn't. Now four and a half hours away in the most southwestern region of Tennessee, basically Memphis, we pull up to the old run-down 18th century mansion.

Shit's piling up. We've got to bust a trafficking house, the worst type of thing we're called to deal with, and I haven't seen my favorite person in two days. *I'm about to lose my shit.* Speeding through all the basic idiotic chit-chat with the fucker that owns the place, I'm finally set free to knock his teeth out when he accidentally bumps into me. I didn't know someone could buy cologne that smells that bad. And to put it over body odor? Come on motherfucker.

"Where are they at?" Jai glares at the guy who holds his now fucked up nose. Bored, I check my phone again. She hasn't even *read* my texts. I grit my teeth and shove my phone back in my pocket.

"Who?" the crusty fuck still refuses to answer. I step on his hand. He squeals like a pig.

"Where are your workers? And where are the girls?" Jai asks. This top floor, so far, is deserted. There's no sign of anyone. But they're here. Sanfred has never led us to the wrong place even though he's dumber than a box of rocks.

"It's like you *want* to get punched in the face again," Jai rolls his eyes. The guy quickly shakes his head.

"The girls are in the basement," he breathes out, "my guys aren't here today, it's their day off. I swear, I promise."

Fucking idiot.

"Oh my God! Really?" Jai gasps, "there's no basement you idiot, we know that."

Does this guy think we just walk into houses without knowing the basics of the floorplan? That's what drugs will do to you. It's ridiculous that 'drugs' remind me of Azalea. Two long-ass hours later, he finally confesses. After both of his hands are broken, each finger, and two of his toes.

"Do I have to go first?" Maxon whines like the little shit he is.

"Your ass is the biggest, we're here to push you down in case you get stuck," Linc smiles and Maxon's mouth drops open. It's not like he's a big guy. His mom is just known for feeding him and his brother carbs.

"It's not my fault carbs go straight to my ass!" he rolls his eyes.

"Straight to your mom's too," Theo bites his lip.

"Are you really going to talk about my momma right now?"

"Your mom's hot," Theo purposefully pisses Maxon off.

"When I get out of this fucking hole, I'm going to kill you," Maxon glares.

"Hurry up and get your ass down there," Roman rolls his eyes. Maxon drops himself down into the hole in the ground in the back of a closet in one of the house's bedrooms. The place the owner says leads to the hideout. One by one we all jump down.

"I'm scared," Theo mumbles when it's his turn. The guy is scared of his own shadow.

"Get the *fuck* down there before I *push* you down there," I give him a shove.

"But I don't know what's down there! It's just a black hole," he steps away from it.

"You idiot, there's five of us already down here!" Jai calls up.

"Oh shit! There's a snake!" Linc calls out.

"I'm just kidding you bitch get down here," he adds.

"I'm scared of the dark," he mumbles. I step forward and push him down into the hole before going down.

"You could've been one man short from doing that," he tells me once I'm down there.

"Not much of a man," Linc nudges me. I give him a look for touching me and he steps away.

"This dude hates being touched so much; I don't even know how he has a girlfrien-"

"Focus," Jai hisses, "I agree with you but focus."

We shine our lights at the huge iron door that keeps everyone out of the people's hideout. I take out the key that the owner gave us, and I stick it in and turn it. Theo sneezes.

"Can you shut the fuck up?"

"God Theo, idiot."

"Theo, goddamn."

"Dumbass."

"Learn how to shut up."

"I'm allergic to dust!" he defends himself. I creak open the door and there's almost no sign of anyone. I push it open all the way and we file in quietly. Rotting couches and chairs fill up the huge main room and in the center are even a couple of poles. But there really are no workers. Which only means there's going to be more of these type busts down the road. We look around the empty place and Jai spots a hallway. We slowly walk down the hall, and more than a dozen doors are on either side of it.

"Spread out," I wave to all the doors. I grab the handle of the door closest to me and I push it open, walking in slowly. I flash my light around the room and sure enough, a small group of three girls is huddled in the corner. I find the light switch by the door and right before I can flick it on another girl, one I didn't see, throws herself onto me.

She doesn't weigh much, most likely from malnourishment and I quickly flick the light on. She does everything she can to hurt me. Kicking, punching, even tries to bite me. I don't blame her though. The shit she's been through I can't even imagine. I wish she *wasn't* touching me though.

"Don't touch them!" She yells.

"How 'bout you not touch me?" I grumble. Maybe a little harsh, I just don't like when people touch me.

"Do whatever you want with me, but not them!" She shouts. I pry her off me and she lands on her feet in front of me.

"Please," she pleads, "they're too young."

"I'm here to help you," I *try* the best *helpful* voice I can manage but most of the time when we go on these busts, I'm not the one that should be talking. It's obvious I don't come across to people as 'approachable' or 'nice'. At all.

"Help?" A girl's quiet voice from the corner asks.

"No, don't listen to him," she turns her head to them, "they've said that before."

"I'm not going to do anything to you," I shake my head.

"We work with the FBI," I explain, "we're here to help you."

The brown-haired girl in front of me thinks over my words. It's obvious she's got terrible trust issues and I can understand that.

"I think he's okay Raven," a girl walks up behind her, "I believe him. He doesn't look like them."

I almost want to thank her for saying that I don't look like a greasy-headed druggy. Raven nods.

"Girls, it's safe," she tells the rest of them over in the corner. I look over and see a redhead and a light blonde. *Way too fucking close to Lilah's blonde.* My heart drops to my stomach. She's small like her too. And she hasn't texted me back almost all day. I rush to the girl and grip her arm, turning her to me. She gasps and brown eyes look back at me instead of green. The biggest feeling of relief I've ever had in my life washes over me.

"I thought you were someone else," I let go of her and she looks relieved too. *That scared me way too much.* I lead the way back into the main room where all the girls are being asked for their names, birthdays, and everything else. We spend hours collecting all the information about all the fifty-six girls in the hideout. Each second that goes by, I grow more antsy to see her. My mind is fucked.

The more I think about it, the more ridiculous it sounds that she would be all the way over here and at this place. But it wasn't impossible and especially with the dim lighting in the room, their hair looked the same. I realize I'm clingy as fuck. God, I want her so bad. I'm vulnerable.

"On the road again," Theo sings as we pile into the SUV. I take my place in the passenger seat and my knee bounces up and down.

"You alright?" Roman questions from the driver's seat.

"Just get me home," I pick up the scrunchie I carelessly tossed on the dashboard when we first got here. For four hours, I anxiously fuck with the scrunchie. It isn't any better that my phone died ten minutes into the car ride. *I'm in deep.* Eight in the morning is when I finally make it to my place. I shower as my phone charges and as soon as I've got my damn pants on someone knocks on my front door. When I open it, Lilah stands there, the most worried look on her face.

"I've been up all night worried about you," her voice shakes, and I pull her inside, scoop her up, and hug her to me. She always smells *so* fucking good. She hugs me back just as tight, not even knowing a reason why. She just does.

"I missed you," she tells me softly. I force my head out of her neck and I kiss those lips of hers four times. I kick my door shut and carry her all the way to our room. She *demands* I wait for Bear to waltz in too and I'm not the one to tell her no when she uses that tone. *What have I become?*

I shut the door once he's in and I lay her on the bed. I take a second to admire her small pajamas before I lay on her, in between her legs.

She says she's crushed but she'll be fine. If there was one place I'd always want to be, it'd be right here.

"Are you okay?" She questions softly, running her hand through my damp hair. I only nod.

"Were you up all night?"

"In Memphis," I answer.

"Your texts woke me up at three in the morning and I've been awake ever since. I got scared when you didn't answer me," she explains. *I got scared when I saw your lookalike at a trafficking house.*

"I'm sorry," I mumble, dragging my hand up her shirt.

"Sh, it's okay, let's just go to sleep," her voice wobbles tiredly. I lean up and watch her as her eyes close before placing a single kiss on her temple and drifting off myself.

~~~

🌸Azalea🌸

"I love you," I whisper down to Grey who still lays with his head right on my chesticles as he sleeps. Sure, it's dumb I'm telling him I love him in his sleep. But I need practice. If I'm leaving, I don't want to go without telling him I love him. Google Maps told me I'd be moving five hours away. Five whole hours. And I spent the last two days helping mom pack up everything while subtly trying to tell her to get a place closer. She didn't pick it up. Maybe I'm overthinking things. I probably think this relationship is more serious than Grey thinks it is. I don't know, maybe he wouldn't really care that much that I'd be moving. *But I would. I really would.*

And I *cannot* leave Mr. Terrip. I couldn't leave Grey either. Or Bear. Oh my gosh, Bear. Maybe I could just drive back here every other day? Or every two days. That's a lot of gas though. And I don't have gas money. And Grey's busy a lot anyway. So, he probably wouldn't want to drive five hours to see me. Or my boobs. I sigh softly.

"I love you so much," I whisper.

"Hm?" He hums and my eyes bulge out of my head.

"I was just talking to myself," I try to keep my sentence from sounding like a question. On the bright side, there have been a few occasions where Grey has heard me talking to myself. He kind of just goes along with it, I don't really know how he stays with me because sometimes I can't even deal with myself. He slowly rises off me and I breathe in the great air that can now enter my lungs. He grips onto my arm and yanks me up too, I go flying into space. I swear, it's like he *wants* me to karate chop his jugular.

"Quiet game, ready go," I announce and then shut my mouth. I walk into the bathroom and begin brushing my teeth. I can shut up if something is in my mouth. That's what she said. Oh my gosh, that sounds like I'm talking about something bad. Well, maybe not bad but just...I don't even know what I'm talking about. Grey follows suit. I purposefully take extra-long when I start brushing my hair. Like one strand at a time slow. The more I have to focus on, the less likely it is for me to start talking. And I take this game *very* seriously.

From the corner of my eye, I see Grey pick up my phone. I ignore it. Maybe he'll take a picture of his muscles and then I can obsess over it later. He places my phone back down and within a second, sound emits from the speaker. My mouth drops open and he looks over at me, a smirk on his lips. *He's dirty.* He leans over to me and scrunches his nose mockingly like I do sometimes. My heart fills up knowing that he knows the name of one of my favorite songs. Sure, maybe it's because I play it a ton, but he remembered the name and that tickles my willy. I hold myself back for as long as possible.

"She's my cherry pie!" I shout. I embrace my pitiful-ness. I throw my hand back and give Grey's booty a nice 'ole smack.

"Oh yeah," I mimic the Kool-Aid man.

"What'd you have to see your mom for?" he turns his body toward me. I look down at my hands. Are they powerless or something? Does he have no feeling in his booty cheeks? I hit him hard, why the heck isn't he giving a reaction?

Anything like 'ouch Azalea, you hurt my booty' would suffice but it's like I didn't even touch him. *Buns of steel.*

"What'd you say?" I hardly even heard him. I think I need to squeeze his butt.

"What'd you have to see your mom for?" he repeats. Um, how should I do this? Firstly, I would like to tell him I love him before telling him I'm moving. And second, I don't want to do either of them inside a bathroom.

"Has anybody ever told you that you have a wonderful little smile?" I smile up at him. I could tell the funniest joke in the world, as I do all the time, and his lips would only turn up at the corners. I laugh enough for both of us. I laugh at my own jokes.

"No," he seems unamused. How could someone not compliment his little smiles? They're amazing.

"Well, they should've," I mosey out of the bathroom and away from him. I plop on the floor in the living room with Bear, giving him a nice belly rub when he rolls over dramatically. I'll really miss Bear. He's like family now. And I *love* Grey.

~~~

I wipe my sweaty palms on the fabric of my leggings, staring out the window, watching the trees go by as we drive up the Smokies. What if he doesn't love me too? We make it to our spot and Grey removes the top to the Jeep and we both lean our seats back looking up at the stars.

"Grey, we're stargazing," I smile softly. Just like people do in movies. But unlike the people in the movies, I have no clue what I'm looking at. Most of the time, movies have a character that knows where the Milky Way is at. If we were in my car, my Milky Ways are in the glove compartment. *Sometimes I need a snack.* I look over at him, wanting to see his heavenly side profile but I find him looking at me already. I smile.

"Am I missing my earring?" I question, moving my hand up to feel my ear. It's not missing. He doesn't say anything.

"Excuse me, are you using your selective mutism on me?" I cross my arms over my chest and raise my eyebrow at him.

"C'mere," he motions to his lap.

"You want me to climb-"

"Yes, so fuckin' come on," he cuts me off. I scrunch my nose at him and climb over the whatever-it's-called-thing in the middle and then finally place myself on his lap. His arms wrap around my lower back, and he leans up slightly. I kiss his lips softly. His hand slips under the back of my shirt and he trails his fingers along my back softly. He picks up the pace, kissing with more urgency. I feel emotions bubble in my throat, partly because I'm about to start my period and, I'm freaking sad.

Why can't I just have this one thing? It's all I want. I can't be happy when I have to leave him. Why can't I just be happy for more than a couple hours? I wrap my arms around him and pull myself as close as I can. He bites down on my bottom lip teasingly and I feel his little smile. *I'm going to cry.* I don't want to go away from that smile. I don't think I could. It doesn't matter if the smile is little. I can't bring myself to let go.

He pulls away for a split second and kisses my cheek. Then his lips find mine once more in a soft, delicate kiss. Slow and not harsh. His hand travels further up my back and the other one comes to rest under my jaw, his thumb on my cheek.

After a while, he pulls away. I watch his lips as that smile returns. I feel my chest contract and a feeling comes up.

"I love you and I'm leaving you," I blurt the two things I've been keeping in. *God, help me, please.*

Chapter Twenty-Six

Dumb

❀ Azalea ❀

I cover my mouth with my hands. I did not mean to blurt it like that. *At all.* I was supposed to break it to him nice and easy. I rehearsed it but that went in the dumpster because I'm an idiot. He stops moving altogether. He doesn't talk. He doesn't move and I hate myself for springing both things on him. Not even a few hours ago I was stressing about him not loving me back when I should've been stressing about whether or not I was going to blurt everything out.

"You're leaving me?" he asks quietly. My heart pounds. Not in a good way. Not in the way it does when he kisses me. It pounds in the way of hurt. *I don't deserve Grey. I only keep hurting him.* My phone dings at just the worst time in the world. I read the text from mom asking me to come home and help her finish packing the things in the garage. I climb off him and return to my seat. Grey remains quiet. I'm so sorry.

"I need to go home," I whisper quietly. He starts the car up and begins driving, the silence deafening me. I keep my eyes focused out the window, not knowing a single thing to say to make either of us feel better. 'Yeah Grey, I really love you but I'm leaving really, I'm not kidding.' I don't think so. I'm leaving. It is what it is, and I can't control it. *Did he hear the part where I said I love him or...?*

"What the fuck did I do to make you leave me?" he suddenly questions as we turn onto my road.

"It's not like that," I answer softly, shaking my head. He pulls into my driveway.

"Then what's it like, Azalea?" I almost wince when he uses my name.

"I don't have a choice, Grey," I tell him quietly.

"Yeah, you don't have a choice, are you fucking with me?"

"Grey, please don't do this," I sigh, rubbing my temple. I can't handle all this stress. I'm about to fake passing out.

"Don't do *what?* Tell you not to leave me?" I don't look at him, knowing he's full-on glaring at me. So, I make a terrible decision and I just get out of the car. I know it's a bad decision when I hear him get out too.

"Don't walk away from me," he grips onto my arm, turning me back around to him.

"What the *fuck* is this?" he points over to the 'For Sale' sign that has a red 'Sold' painted over it.

"We're leaving," I bite my wobbly lip.

"What?"

"Grey, I don't have a choice-"

"So, you're not *leaving* me, like breaking up?" his eyebrows furrow down and the glare on his face lessens.

"No, I thought you knew that?" my own eyebrows furrow.

"What the fuck? You said you were *leaving* me," his jaw tenses.

"I am leaving," I grow more confused.

"Are we both dumb? What is going on?" he places his hand on his forehead.

"I'm not dumb, you're dumb," I scrunch my nose at him.

"I'm moving to Kentucky," I explain, and he grows unhappy again.

"No," he says simply. What does he mean 'No'?

"What do you mean no? I wasn't asking a question," I grip my own forehead.

"That's too far from me, you can't go," he shakes his head like I have any control over the situation.

"Grey, *I don't have a choice,*" I stress. He throws his arms up.

"You act like I don't have a fucking place, stay with me," he rolls his eyes and mine widen. We're ready for that? I thought couples weren't supposed to move in together until they got engaged.

"I don't know," I whisper. What if he starts to hate me from being together so much?

"What do you mean you don't know? Do you want to go to Kentucky?" His face grows unhappy again.

"No, of course not! Here is everything I know," all the two friends I have are here and I feel like it'd be terrible to move to someplace new. Especially with my social issues, being weird and all. Sure, bad memories are here. Quite a few of them. But there are also good memories, great ones. I can't leave it all behind. Especially Grey.

"Then live with me," he nods. I bite my lip, still thinking about how if we live together, he might start to dislike me.

"I don't think you'll appreciate being around me all the time," I tell him honestly.

"Shut up," he stresses, "why do you think I don't want to be around you? "

"Well, you don't like people-" he cuts me off, throwing his hands into the air.

"Because they're not *you,*" I watch as he grows frustrated. This doesn't make sense. Am I dumb or am I *dumb?*

"Wait, so you *want* me to live with you?"

"Yes," he doesn't even waste a second. My heart grows. I never considered *living* with Grey. I thought it was so far out of the picture that there was no chance of considering it. And I sure as heck wasn't going to *ask* to live with him, that'd be crazy. That's like inviting yourself to someone's birthday party without them wanting you to come.

"Oh my gosh!" I exclaim, "it'd be like a sleepover every night!"

We've known each other for four and a half months. I pray this won't backfire on me like everything else has.

"Let me ask my mom," I tell him.

"You're an adult, you can do what you want," he reminds me. I don't consider myself an adult. I mean, I'm not a kid, I know that, but I just think it feels right to talk about huge decisions.

"Right," I say unconvincingly. He only rolls those beautiful eyes of his. Did he hear the part where I told him I loved him?

~~~

"Are you sure you want to do this?" she asks me. I give her a smile and a nod.

"I thought you would want to get away too, I didn't mean to try and take you away from everyone," she gives me a sorry smile.

"I understand," I bring her in for a world-famous hug of mine, "you need to get away from everything."

Grey walks past me and I slap his butt as he does. Did mom see that? Good, now she knows he's my b-word.

"I'm sorry for everything," she says, and I shake my head. She's already apologized twenty times.

"Mom, it's okay, I promise."

"And you don't need any help getting the rest of your stuff together?" she questions, and I shake my head.

"I'll make Grey carry it all," I give her a cheeky smile. And if he refuses, the only name I'll call him for the rest of the day is 'cutie.'

"Okay," she sighs before her eyes begin to water slightly, "I'll see you soon, I love you."

That's the first time I've heard someone say that to me in quite a while.

"I love you too. Be careful on your way and send me pictures once you've settled in," she brings me in for a hug and we stand there for a little while, embracing each other. We pull away and she climbs into her car and is off to Kentucky. I watch her car until it's out of sight.

"Are you ready Grey?" I walk up the front porch where he's waiting for me.

"You best pull on your working britches, 'cause you're fixing to work," I slap his butt again for good measures. I open the door and walk in. Just as I'm turned to close the door behind Grey, his freaking huge hand slaps down on my butt. Am I okay? I cover my mouth with my hand. Does that hurt his hand? It has to.

I think I need to start working out and lifting weights because the difference between our butt-smacks to each other is just too much. It feels like my butt-cheek is no longer attached. It's on the floor or something. He grips my arms gently and pulls me into him, his lips pulled up at the corners in his little smile. He slides his hand onto my murdered cheek.

"You feel it?" he asks. I nod.

"Then you're fine."

"You're a fresh cow poop," I poke his man-boob. I step away, my glaring eyes still focused on him. I walk up the stairs, well, technically Grey pushes me up the stairs from behind me. I can't walk because of my butt. *That's what she-no. Oh my.* I bust up in my room and head straight for my wild closet that still needs to be packed up and put into easily movable boxes. So, I begin.

"Grey, isn't this shirt so cute? I forgot I had it," I hold up the light blue off-the-shoulder shirt to me and show him. I've never seen someone look so unamused *in my life*.

"Don't look at me like that," I pick up a flip flop from the bottom of my closet and I throw it at him. He doesn't even blink as it misses him and hits the wall behind him.

"Oh, so now you're making fun of me?" I raise my eyebrow at him. *He's fixing to get got.*

"I would be so nice to *you* if you needed help going through your closet!"

"All your black clothes," I grumble, "you need some color in your life Sugar."

I pick up the biggest t-shirt I have. It's pale yellow and who knows, maybe it's his color.

"Try this on," I give it to him. His upper lip curls unhappily and I roll my eyes.

"Don't curl that lip at me, Grey," I scrunch my nose at him.

"It's too small," he mumbles.

"Hush, no it's not, put it on," I point to it and then watch as he stands. He pulls his shirt off and I sigh happily. Maybe I don't want him to put the shirt on, I just want to see him without a shirt.

He pulls the yellow shirt over his head and his strong arms just hardly fit. I bite my lip to keep the smile off my face when I see that it really doesn't fit him. It's too short, it's too tight, even though it does way too many good things for his muscular frame, his face just looks unhappy and pitiful. Now, I'm not saying that yellow isn't his color, all I'm saying is yellow is too *happy* of a color. It just doesn't fit physically or characteristically.

"You look so handsome!" I smile pulling him in front of the mirror. His tense body never loosens and my slap my forehead.

"It's okay," I wrap my arms around him, and he relaxes a bit. And then there's a ripping sound. I pull away to find the fabric on top of his right shoulder ripped.

"I said it's too small," he shrugs, and it rips a little bit more. Following the tragic murder of my shirt, we begin putting all my stuff into the boxes. Grey never put his shirt back on and I'm loving every minute of it. And the look of his silver chain around his neck. Who knew that was so attractive? If I'm being honest, Grey has packed half of my room and I'm sitting here and being all excited when I find things I forgot I had. Like I found a wiggly, rubbery, yardstick. Did I forget I had it? Yes. Do I need it? Who knows? Did I continuously hit Grey with it? Of course, I did until he took it away from me and threw it outside my room.

Grey held me the time I almost started crying when I found one of Jake's old t-shirts and he rolled his eyes at me when I bounced a little bouncy

Lilah   *K. Pope*

ball off his head. He threw that bouncy ball out of my room too.

"Are we going to be sleeping in the same room like we usually do?" I question and he turns his head around toward me.

"You already know the answer to that," he mumbles.

"Okay well if we are, I have nothing against the black comforter, but maybe if we add a spice of color, then you'll be more of a morning person," I reach up to the top of my closet where my extra comforters are. Of course, I just can't get a full-size comforter for my full-size bed. It needs to be big and fluffy so I can wrap myself in it. All my comforters are king size. So is Grey's bed.   He looks at me with the world's most unamused face. For the two-hundredth time today. I pick up my dullest, but still somewhat colorful comforter and hold it out to him. I glance over the baby blue and white comforter, and I smile a little.

"What do you think?"

He just looks at me for a few seconds, his eyes darting between both of mine.

"...Fine."

I lean down to him and kiss him. Beginning to pull away, he doesn't let me, gripping onto my shirt lightly and holding me to him. He tugs me onto his lap.

"Did you hear me when I told you I love you? " I blurt. What is wrong with me? God, please give me an answer as to why I'm like this. He leans back a bit to see my face in its entirety. I don't know why he'd want to do that but whatever.

"I don't think you do," he shakes his head.

"Why do you say that?" I furrow my eyebrows.

"I just, I'm not meant to be...that," his jaw ticks unpleasantly as he mumbles through his words, making them all jumbled together. He isn't meant to be *loved?* I don't get it.

"Why not?"

"I'm just not," he grows frustrated. I do too. I don't have the most room to talk but he hardly tells me anything. All I know about his past is that his mom died not long after giving birth to him and his dad wasn't a good dad.

I don't want to pry but I just want to know more about him. Do I talk too much? Is that the problem? Does he feel like maybe I won't listen? I open my mouth to apologize for my nonstop talking but before I can say anything, the doorbell downstairs rings.

"It's a burglar, hide," I whisper. *Why would the burglar be ringing the doorbell?* I pick up my phone, just in case 911 needs to be called...even though I have Grey here. The screen turns on and messages from Aaron fill my home screen. Messages like 'are you at Terrip's' and 'Terrip said you're probably at home and that I should talk to you' and 'I'm here.' My eyes bulge out of my head. Maybe I forgot that I needed to tell him about everything. Doing drugs will do that to you.

"Um, maybe put your shirt back on," I warn Grey and head downstairs. I open the door and Aaron stands there tall, proud, and with one eyebrow raised.

"Hello, beautiful," he wraps an arm around my neck and pulls me to him in a hug.

"Whose car is here-oh *that* guy," I hear his voice turn a bit darker and Grey's footsteps coming down the stairs. Aaron pulls away from me and looks around.

"What the hell's going on?" he looks around the mostly empty house. The couch and bigger furniture are still here and will be for a few more days until the movers get here to pick them up.

"What'd you do, Silver?" Aaron's eyes narrow in Grey's direction. *Silver, is he serious? And that dude still didn't put a shirt on.*

"What the fuck happened to your face?!" Aaron grips my face and examines it. The cut on my cheek has been doing much better, although it is still definitely visible.

"I knew he was fucking terrible," his face turns red in anger.

"Aaron, that's enough," I furrow my eyebrows unhappily. We've already had enough of these accusations.

"You motherfucker!" Aaron shouts, pointing his finger in Grey's face who stands there emotionlessly but I can tell he's far from happy.

"Aaron!" I shout, my mouth falling open.

"You hit a *woman* half your size you sick fuck," Aaron charges at Grey.

"Aaron shut up!" I yell as loud as I think I ever have, "dad hit me not him!"

Aaron freezes. He turns back to me slowly.

"What?" he asks.

"Dad did this," I sigh, "he's been hurting me for a while. Grey's never touched me. Well, technically he *has* touch- never mind you didn't hear that."

I feel my cheeks blush and from the corner of my eye, I see Grey biting the side of his lip, a small smirk on his face.

"Why didn't you tell me Azzy?" his voice turns soft, completely ignoring my previous comment. Thank gosh.

"I was scared. But he's away now. And he will be for a long time," I look to Grey, and he nods, as a 'you're doing great sweetie' type of thing.

"Where's your mom?"

"Halfway into Kentucky now. To her new house," I bite my lip, worried for his reaction.

"Why aren't you with her?" he asks slowly.

"I'm not moving with her." Aaron stays quiet as he thinks over my words.

"So, where are you going to go...?" he hesitates, knowing I can't pay for this house even a little bit. I look over at Grey and fiddle with my fingers nervously.

"With um, Grey," I almost wince. Aaron's eyes widen before he shakes his head vigorously.

"No. You're not. Are you stupid?" he asks, and I shrink back a bit.

"You must be fuckin' stupid to be talking to her like that," Grey's upper lip curls in a sneer.

"Do you want to take this outside?" Aaron steps up, even though he's shorter than Grey. I'm sorry but poor Aaron would get demolished if Grey would fight him. Grey doesn't get egged on very easily though. Well, sometimes. Aaron swivels back around to me when he sees the look on Grey's face.

"You can't move in with this guy!" he stresses, "your little 'friend' could be a murderer!"

"We're not friends. We're together," I should really shut my mouth.

"Even worse! This dude could be like Ted Bundy for all we know," he motions to Grey.

"Why would he be a politician?" I grow confused. What?

"Ted *Bundy* babe, not Ted *Cruz*," Grey helps me.

"Thank you, Sugar."

Did he say babe? Woah, baby.

"You're not like Ted Bundy, correct?" I roll my eyes and he shakes his head, rolling his eyes too.

"See, he's not like Ted Bundy," I tell Aaron.

"Look," I walk over to Grey and pick up his hand, "look at his nice tattoos. Not the skulls or the bones but the other ones."

"Aren't they so nice?"

"Azalea, stop changing the subject," Aaron grips his forehead.

"Whoops."

"I just don't want to see you hurt anymore. I've seen it too much. I know I've said it before but now especially since you want to move in with him," he stresses.

"Aaron, we're taking it slow; I promise. Grey would never try anything on me because he knows I can knock him out with one punch and severely injure his clavicle too."

"Where's the clavicle?" I whisper up to Grey and he rubs his collarbone. I probably saw that on a show or something, I don't know. I thought it has something to do with the pelvis but never mind. Then I sort of thought it was a part of the ear.

"Azalea, I know that you're an adult and that you should be making decisions for yourself but, I'm really nervous about this one," he says honestly.

"You already kept this whole thing from me, what would stop you from not telling me if something goes wrong between the two of you?"

"I know. I'm sorry," I tell him, "but now I promise I won't keep anything from you. I really promise."

He looks all over my face for any sign of hesitation. I'll even text him when I'm on the toilet and not. He'll love it.

"Pinky promise me," he holds out his pinky. I connect it with mine and he pulls me into another hug.

"I love you, Azzy," he kisses the top of my head. Meanwhile, I grip onto Grey's hand, trying to use all my arm strength to pull him closer to us. I pull away from Aaron and place Grey in front of me. Both of their eyes narrow at each other.

"I don't like you one bit," Aaron tells him honestly. Grey's thumb knuckle cracks.

"I don't like how you're more swole than me," Aaron's eyes narrow, "and I don't like that you're taller than me."

Does he realize he's kind of complimenting him?

"His eyelashes are really nice too," I chime in, a small smile on my face. I'm proud of myself for not saying how nice his butt is.

"But you seem to be making her happy," Aaron continues, mostly ignoring me. *Heck yeah looking at that gluteus Maximus of his all day can make anyone happy.*

"And if that ever stops," he trails off, "I *will* be hiring a hitman."

It's honestly such an *amazing* idea to threaten a fed, it's such a good idea, I don't even plan on telling Aaron that Grey's a fed.

"Why's your shirt off?" Aaron asks him. Grey looks over at me and then down at my hand. I only now notice that I'm holding his shirt. I must've just picked it up when he was trying on the yellow one.

"Why do you *have* his shirt?" Aaron tilts his head. *Don't say sex. It's simple. Just don't say sex.*

"Se- because I was going to hand it to him and then the doorbell rang," I explain.

"Right," he looks between the two of us suspiciously.

"Because sex," I blurt.

"Goddammit," Grey grips the bridge of his nose. *I was doing so good.*
"What?!"

Chapter Twenty-Seven

Tattoo

❀ Azalea ❀

    It was never my intention to...make small additions to Grey's place. And now, there are couch pillows. There are drying rags on the stove handle. There is a vase of colorful flowers at the end of the hallway, sitting on the table and there are flowers on the dining room table. The bedroom and bathroom have a matching color scheme of white and light blue. The half of the closet that's his is full of dark blues, blacks, and grays, my side is filled with all my colorful clothes. I don't think he's ever seen so many hair ties and bottles of nail polish in his life.

    It just happened. He asked what I wanted to do around the place and my mind went off. He went along with it, so I don't think he's got that much of a problem with it. He followed me around Home Depot and everywhere else we went, clinging to my hand, and wrapping his arm around me whispering in my ear 'can we (effing) leave?' I promised I'd make it up to him and we stayed for another thirty minutes.

    Now his head's between my legs.

    His strong hands hold my hips down and I *cannot* breathe. How does it make it feel *so good?* I clench the bedsheets harder than I thought was possible, proving that I'm The Rock. I cover my mouth with my free hand, concealing some of my noises. He reaches up and pulls my hand away from my mouth, sitting me up. I breathe heavily and he places my hand in his hair before letting go. I squeal quietly and lay back down, my hips moving upward. His strong hands softly grip onto my hip bones, and he pulls me further into his mouth. *Oh my gosh.* His thumbs rub circles on my hips, and I find his eyes looking up to me. He lets a slow smile onto his lips, and I lay my head back onto the pillow, my hips raising but his hands pushing them back down.

"Grey," I whisper breathlessly, and he hums knowingly. His phone rings loudly and he groans softly. I *feel* that vibration from his mouth. He never moves from me, only reaches around to his pocket and takes his phone out, declining the call and throwing his phone onto the bed. Hardly five seconds later, the caller calls again. He declines it again. The person calls again and Grey pulls away. I take a second to calm myself and catch my breath, sitting up. But he doesn't give me much time, replacing his mouth with his hand and pushing me back down. I cover my mouth keeping my noises to a minimum as he talks on the *stupid phone.*

I take a small part of the comforter and cover my face when I feel the release coming soon. Grey's quick to move it away and in only a second or two, I'm coming undone right on his hand. He ends his call and throws his phone back onto the bed. He moves his hand under the small of my back and he pulls me to my feet. I nearly fall over; my legs are so wobbly. My shirt falls all the way down to above my knees, and his hand takes place at the top of my throat, tilting my head up to him. My cheeks stay a light pink and my heart pounds. *I love you.* He connects our lips softly.

"You taste good," he mumbles against my lips, and I feel my blush deepen. I bury my face in his chest to conceal my face. He kisses the top of my head. He places his hand on my back and gently slides his hand up and down.

"That feels good," I mumble against him.

"Just like it felt good when I slid my tongue between your-"

I shoot away from him, gasping loudly, and holding my heart.

"That's inappropriate!" I squeal.

"You didn't think it was inappropriate then. Especially when you were moaning and telling me that it felt so good-"

"Grey!" I poke his stomach.

"Yeah, that's the name you moaned," he nods, and my eyes widen. He's wild today.

"I don't have pants on Grey, get away from me," I chuckle, pushing away from him.

"I know. 'Cause I'm the one who took those pants off."

"Good Lord," I shake my head at him.

"I got to go," he mumbles, his mood back to normal.

"You *got to go* read the Bible," I advise him.

"You're the one who let me go down on you," he kisses under my ear.

"You're the one who *keeps bringing it up*," I tell him.

"'Cause I can't get over how perfect you are," he kisses me. He pulls back slightly and kisses my forehead.

"I love the way you lie," isn't that a song?

"I want to fuck you," he mumbles, looking straight at me as I go off on my jokes.

"Good heavens," I clench my legs together. Why did I do that with my legs?

"I want to," he nods seriously. He grips onto my thigh.

"I saw that," his voice gets lower.

"Well, Grey," I clear my throat. What do I say, what do I say, what do I say, what do I say?

"I thought you said I couldn't keep a guy around long enough to have sex with me?"

He freezes, and I bite my lip to keep myself from smiling.

"...Bullshit," he says almost *cockily*.

"Excuse me, I recall it perfectly."

"'You couldn't keep a guy around long enough to blank you with that mouth of yours always running'," I mimic him.

"I'm not *a* guy I'm *the* guy," he shrugs. *The guy I love even though he's a hooker.*

"The guy who's a brat," I let out a bark of laughter.

"You have to leave," I remind him. He nods, leaning down. I kiss his forehead.

"I'll be home soon."

"I'll be counting on you to not get headbutted, Sugar," I pat his booty. He and I need to talk when he gets back. I have to be able to tell him I love him. He may not love me back or want to say it, but he needs to *believe* I love him. Because I really love him.

~ ~ ~

I sit in the very middle of the bed as Grey comes out of the bathroom, freshly showered, and looking amazing. He turns the light to the bathroom off, throws his clothes in the hamper and then pauses as he sees me on the bed.

"Fuck," he mumbles under his breath, "you look good."

"Come here," I motion for him, and he smirks as he doesn't hesitate to do what I've just told him to. I open my arms for him, and he closes the gap between us, lifting me onto his lap. I kiss his cheek softly. I pull back and just look at him, a little smile on my face.

"I love you," I nod.

"No-"

"Shut up," I cut him off, his eyes narrow a little bit.

"Don't tell me to-"

"Shut up," I tell him again.

"Little shit-"

"I love you and there's nothing you can do about it," I tell him in a final tone.

"Bullshit."

"You can curse it all you want," I hug him to me and rock from side to side. I don't expect him to say he loves me too. He can't even accept the fact that I love him. *I'll just have to tell him until he believes it.*

"I love you, I love you, I love you, I love you, I love you," I press kisses on the side of his head after each 'I love you.' Bear jumps up on the bed and sticks his nose between Grey and me, his tail wagging wildly.

"And Bear loves you too," I kiss Bear's fluffy head.

"Right here Bear," I point to Grey's cheek and Bear licks his cheek. I allow my eyes to travel along the tattoos on his arm.

"How old were you when you got your first tattoo?" I tilt my head. He's going to get to talking today, whether he likes it or not.

"Sixteen."

"Don't you need permission to get one underage?"

I was a little serious about getting that one butterfly tattoo, sue me.

"I told the guy if he didn't tattoo me then I'd knock him out and tattoo a fucking dick on his forehead," he mumbles seriously.

"And the guy believed that a sixteen-year-old would actually do that?" I laugh.

"I was already a head taller than him. And I was piss-drunk, and it was unpredictable what I would do," he shrugs.

"I have a similar story," I nod.

"One time, I drank too much Capri-Sun at one of Jakes' friend's house and then Jake's friend's sister pushed me in the pool. I got cramps from drinking too much and I can't swim. I almost died," I reminisce on that...lovely day. Jake's friend's sister hated me with all her might and so she pushed me in the pool, wearing my clothes and all. Jake gave her quite the speech after he basically saved my life. And then we left and got ice cream. Now that I think about it, our stories have zero similarities.

"What's Capri-Sun?" he questions, and my eyebrows shoot up.

"It's like a fruit punch pouch," I throw my head back before realizing he *doesn't know what that is.*

"You've never had Capri-Sun?" I gasp.

"I don't drink fruity alcohol," his upper lip curls in distaste.

"It's-it's a kids drink. Not alcohol," I explain.

~ ~ ~

"Do you understand how bad this is?" I drag him through the Target entrance, gripping onto his wrist over the sleeve of his gray long-sleeve shirt that hugs his arms very nicely. Target is the best. He shoves my hand away and I almost give him a few words about it until he places his hand in mine, instead of me holding his wrist. A lady turns and looks at us as we walk in. Not hardly as second later, she turns back around quicker than ever.

"Is my cheek still that bad?" I tilt my head up to him. He takes his narrowed eyes away from the lady and looks down at me. I run my finger over the cut that still lies there. It's nothing compared to what it was and it's smaller now. Makeup wouldn't cover the actual cut so there's no point in trying to hide it or anything.

"Yes," he mumbles, I hold my heart and am about to gasp.

"I meant no," he tugs me closer to him when some random fifty-year-old dude wearing a trucker hat gives me a little smile.

"I should just go ask that trucker guy, he seems like a total babe," I smile, turning my head to look at the trucker's retreating figure.

"Fuckin' funny," he grumbles unhappily, letting go of my hand and slipping his hand down the side of my pants. I almost warn him that this is not the correct place to be doing things like that but in a matter of .003 seconds, he snaps my underwear back against my hip and walks ahead of me. I groan and catch up with him. I should be catching up with that wonderful trucker guy. I bet he wouldn't do what Grey just did to me.

I should make a Craigslist account that hires people to just come here and headbutt him. I'll pay in braiding people's hair. I continuously push on his back. Solely to annoy him. I step on the backs of his boots too. And poke his sides. He stops abruptly and I clash with his back. I play it off perfectly by wrapping my arms around his torso and just hugging him.

"If it makes you feel better, you're much cuter than that trucker guy," I bite back my smile. Figuring my best option would be to get away from him, I do, walking down another aisle with him following closely behind me. He grips the back of my pants and pulls me flush to his front.

"Get away from me you crackhead," I tell him just as a nice lady walks by. She pauses and looks at me.

"Oh no! Not you! You're not a crackhead," I hope she's not a crackhead, "I wasn't talking to you, I promise!"

"I was talking to him," I point at the big guy that stands right behind me. Her eyebrows furrow and a concerned look takes over her face. She takes a step closer.

"Do you need help? How about I give you a ride home?"

Oh gosh, she actually thinks he's some crackhead.

"No," I laugh, "he's not an actual crackhead. I just call him that. I promise he doesn't do drugs. I don't either. I like to say I do but I don't."

"His name is Grey," I point to him again. I can just tell he's looking at me with a 'I'm done with being in Target' face, "I'm Azalea."

"Oh!" I almost forget, "he's actually my boyfriend."

Was I talking too much? The lady gives me a smile that says, 'this girl is a total, actual crackhead' and she walks off.

"Look what you made me do," I turn around and rest my head on his chest.

"No one told you to call me a crackhead."

"What else would I call you? Grey? I think not," I scoff.

"Grey is your regular personality name. When you're being averagely rude. Sugar is your sweet name when you're being a sweetheart. Crackhead is when you're being ridiculous or whenever I feel it's fit, it's the 'etcetera' one too," I explain. He looks unamused now. I look to my left and spot a Capri Suns pack. *Uh, freak yeah.* I pick that boy up and haul butt out of that aisle. We pay, we drive home, we take a seat on the couch, I take one pouch out for him, and one for me. He looks at it like 'what the fudge is this poop?'

"What the fuck is this bullshit?" he grips the pouch which looks too small for his big hands. *I was close to predicting what he would say.* It's actually not a hard thing to do. His vocabulary consists of every curse word, unhappy words, my name, and 'shut up'. He speaks those words and every other word slowly, lowly, and almost always like he's bored, tired, or done with the conversation. Quite the opposite compared to me. I take off the straw and poke it through the hole. He watches me and grabs the straw. He sticks the straw through the whole thing, effectively making it poke out through the other side.

"You're doing great, try again," I hand him another and watch as his eyebrows furrow in concentration. More carefully this time, he pokes it through the hole, and it doesn't come through the other side this time. I smile wildly and lean forward, hugging him to me.

"I'm proud, you're so cute," I kiss his temple like he does to me. He can't even open a bag of chips without busting open the whole thing, I'm glad he can control himself long enough to get a straw through a pouch. He takes the world's smallest sip of it and hands it to me.

"Drink more."

"I don't like it," he says.

"Because it barely hit your tongue, take a bigger sip," I hand it back to him.

"No."

"Don't think you're winning this argument, because you're not," I warn him. He narrows his eyes slightly. He slowly drags it back up to his lips and he takes a longer sip. He still hands it to me.

"Don't like it."

He's just saying that to get on my nerves. I drink both mine and his, plus two more. I sit back and watch as my stomach gets bigger. The drink baby's name is Flitzengerald.

"Let's have a heart to heart," I propose. I need to know every little detail about him. *Everything.* What's his favorite type of tissue? What's his worst habit? What's his biggest pet peeves? I'm sure he's got tons of those. What's his favorite season? What does he name his food babies? Which is better? Trailer Park Boys or Impractical Jokers.

"What happened to your dad?" that too, but I didn't mean to blurt it.

"I don't know," he answers plainly.

"What was he like?" I try. He glances over at me.

"Why are we talking about this?" he questions, not so happy.

"I only want to know more about you," I answer.

"Asking about him doesn't have anything to do with knowing more about me," his jaw clenches, "he's got nothing to do with me."

"I just wanted to know about where you came from," I tell him softly. I don't mean to pry. He knows everything about me. *Everything*.

"You don't want to know where I came from, and I don't want to talk about it," a glare settles on his face as he fixes his gaze on the wall.

"You know I won't judge you, right?" I remind him, "I'll always be here for you. I really do love you."

"No one's said that to me before," he tells me honestly. No one?

"Is that why you don't think I love you?" I whisper. He looks down at our intertwined hands before giving me a soft nod.

"And so, you've never said it to anyone?" I ask quietly and he shakes his head.

"But you wanted to fall in love with me?" I scoot a bit closer to him, gripping onto his other hand too.

"I'm getting old."

I throw my head back and laugh. Twenty-five is hardly *old*.

"And you're the only girl I've ever wanted to be around for hours at a time."

'Long periodically time'. Gosh, I love watching news interviews. He doesn't know if he loves me because he's never loved anyone before. Oh no.

"What if you only like me as a friend but you don't know the difference," I slap my cheeks, my face, not my booty.

"I ate yo-"

"And what if you're just sexually attracted to me but you actually *don't* have any feelings," I don't know why someone would be solely *sexually* attracted to me but whatever.

"Shut up," he rolls his eyes.

"How did I know you were going to say that?"

"Because you love me," he answers, and I smile wider than I have in a long time.

"You're right," I nod, leaning forward and placing a soft kiss on his lips. Bear whines from his position on the floor beside the couch. I break away from the kiss and Grey continues his path down my neck.

"I love you too Bear," I pat his head, Grey stays on the spot right under my jaw and I play with the hair at the back of his head.

"Oh wait," I said suddenly, "I want another Capri-Sun."

"Of course," he mumbles, and I slide off his lap. My foot rolls on one of Bear's bones and I go down like a dead weight. I feel a slight tug on my hair and almost slap Grey for thinking it's okay for him to pull my hair when I'm falling to my death. But the pulling doesn't stop. I sit back up and grip onto the pieces of hair that are being pulled. Grey holds the end of it trying to get my hair untangled from his zipper. The zipper near his main goody.

"Are you kidding me?" I grumble, getting on my knees in front of me. He stops for a second and looks at me.

"What?" I sigh at him stopping.

"This puts thoughts in my head," he licks the corner of his mouth. He moves my hair not attached to his zipper out of my face.

"You getting my god-forbidden hair unstuck from your zipper puts thoughts in my head so how 'bout we get on to doing that!" I slap the side of his leg. He only leans back and smirks at me.

"When I get unstuck," I warn lowly, "you're going to seriously get got."

The door bursts open and I almost pee my pants.

"Woah y'all," Sanfred's voice travels through the room, "do I need to come back?"

"Yes," Grey mumbles at the same time I'm saying 'No.'

"Oaklee, can you help me-"

"He's not coming *near* my dick," Grey grumbles and I turn to just *pulling* my hair instead of untangling it.

"I'm near it," I furrow my eyebrows.

"Oh 'cause you're *you* baby doll, he wants you always near his dick. He wants you on his dick, touching his dick, he wants to be *inside* you-"

"How 'bout shut the fuck up?"

"Am I wrong?" Oaklee chuckles and Grey doesn't give any hints to any sort of answer. My eyes start to water from the few last strands that are still stuck. It's not that it hurts so bad I'm going to cry or something but it's just since they're little strands.

"What do you want?" Grey asks him as I pull away, rubbing the sore spot on my head now.

"C'mere doll baby, I'll rub it for you," Oaklee gives me a dimpled smile, waving me over. Grey grips onto my arm and pulls me down onto him.

"Did you lock the door after we got back from Target?" he grumbles. I smile and shake my head no. He scoffs.

"Well, there's another call for tomorrow in southeastern North Carolina. Trafficking," Oaklee takes a seat on one of the recliners. *Trafficking?!*

"It's supposedly small but spread out around Tinesburg. So, multiple houses, each with a couple of girls," he explains.

"Oh, and me and you are riding together," he adds.

"I'm quitting my fucking job."

Chapter Twenty Eight

Done

❀ Azalea ❀

"I got go-go juice Mr. Terrip!" I raise my coffee in the air, smiling widely.

"Like you need coffee, you're wild enough," he shakes his head. My eyes are tired, my personality isn't.

"Did you know that Grey has never had Capri-Sun?" I sit my chin on my hand, leaning on his desk.

"Who? What's Capri-Sun?" I close my eyes and internally try to not be disappointed in his ability to never remember anything I say.

"The guy that comes here with me sometimes and Capri-Sun is a drink," I explain. *Why doesn't anyone know what Capri-Sun is?* The bell at the door goes off, signaling that someone has entered. A girl, probably around my age or a little older, walks up to us, a small shy smile on her face.

"Hi," her voice says quietly. She tucks her shoulder-length black hair behind her ear.

"Do you have any books here on constitutional law?" She questions. Mr. Terrip looks over at me for the answer.

"I think we might," I give her a smile, standing and ushering her to follow me. Oh, my goodness. We can be friends. *Don't say anything stupid. Don't say anything stupid.*

"Are you studying law?" I question her as I lead her to the section where the book would most likely be.

"Oh no, it's a general studies class at Western Oak," she explains. If not a four-year college, I wanted to go to Western Oak Community College. But neither happened.

"We're doing a presentation and I need a book on it," she says further.

"A book on constitutional law would be around this area," I show her the area of government-related books.

"I'm Abby," she smiles. *Does this mean she wants to be friends?! I need to calm down.*

"I'm Li-Azalea," I've been around Grey too much, I think. But I'm not going to stop being around him. Anyone who sets their eyes on his bootylicious butt can see the reason why. And he's a darling sometimes, I guess. She bends and picks out the exact book she needs.

"Are you in college?" She asks. I laugh a small bit and shake my head. She continues to look at me for a second and I feel her light brown eyes on the cut on my cheek.

"I play powderpuff football, it's a battle wound," I explain and then internally rolls my eyes at myself. Why do I have to say the *weirdest* things? I lower my eyes and fully expect her to laugh awkwardly and then go check out the book in her hand. Instead, she laughs. Like actually laughs, not a fake one.

"How'd you get drafted? Can you put in a good word for me?" She questions.

"Mr. Terrip, the man who owns this place is the main referee," I add, "you should talk to him."

"No, I'm not in college," I answer her earlier question, shaking my head in an attempt to recover from my crackhead episode, "I would love to be though."

Lilah *K. Pope*

It's still true. There are still things I'd love to do. I'm just not sure when. I have a list. 1) Master the lyrics to every Aerosmith and Def Leppard song. 2) Go to Hawaii and get recruited by the hula dancers. 3) Slap Grey in the face, for no reason, I just want to see his reaction. 4) Immediately after slapping him, kiss him repeatedly. 5) Go to college. 6) Dress Bear up in a Tutu. 7) Go to get a tattoo, but chicken out completely. 8) Get Grey to strip for me. 9) Write a book on the philosophy of a Clue named Blue. 10) Tell Grey I love him many times each and every day.

There are more that I can't even remember but I think I have them written down somewhere. Abby and I stay talking for nearly two hours. It took a while for me to really tell what actually happened to my cheek. I was a little nervous for a few reasons. One, she could be a cold-hearted killer. Two, she could not give a crap. Three, she wouldn't want to be friends with someone with baggage. But everything worked out.

I found out she's from the small town next to mine and that she has two little sisters. She's a sophomore this year and she just recently turned twenty. Her favorite color is pale pink, and her favorite food place is Subway. I told myself I wouldn't talk about Grey or even mention him at all. It's actually a great way to get a mental break from him. *And his muscles.* I was even able to talk just a bit about Jake. I wasn't a *complete* weirdo when trying to explain my life. Although, I definitely slipped up through from time to time.

My phone rings and listening to Abby talk about her cat Sweetie, I figure it'd be rude to answer my phone, so I click the power button, silencing the ringtone.

"Sweetie hates everyone," she laughs. *Sugar hates everyone.*

"I know a person like that," I smile cheekily. Grey Alexander Kingston. I spent two hours getting his middle name out of him and I'm fully prepared to use it in any and every situation. I even thought about changing his contact name to 'Grey Alexander' with two poop emojis and one heart emoji. But in the end, I decided that I would keep the one I have now for a while. 'Sugar' with a mean face emoji, an angel emoji, and then one kissy face emoji. One for each of his most common moods. I'm sure he's noticed by now that I've changed my name on his phone. It is now "Big Booty Judy" with the peach emoji and the heart eyes one. I'm not sure if he's changed it back yet though.

"He's not even an old cat, he just hates everyone. He *tolerates* me sometimes-" she pauses when my phone begins to ring again. I roll my eyes, pick up my phone and full-on decline the call this time.

"Maybe you should answer that," she chuckles.

"I can call back later," I assure her.

"Anyway, you said you want to go to college, you should enroll in the spring semester!" she proposes, and I sit up, interested. That actually sounds pretty great.

"I think I'll have to look into that," I nod. My phone rings again and I answer it quickly.

"Yes, my love?" I answer sweetly. 'Cause I know he is not happy now that I haven't answered two of his calls.

"What the fuck has you *not* answering me?" he grumbles like the darling he is.

"I've been busy Sugar," I tell him honestly an Abby gives me a kind smile that says 'aw.'

Yeah, if only she knew the language that comes out of his mouth. But I wouldn't want him any other way.

"Busy enough to not answer me?"

"What's wrong?" I ask softly, detecting a certain *extra* tint of rude in his mood.

"When are you coming home?" he sighs, obviously not answering my question. I furrow my eyebrows and take the phone away from my ear to check the time.

"I'll be home in a bit," I tell him.

"When's a *bit?*" he says nearly *bitterly. Someone needs to cool their jets.* I stand from my seat for a little more privacy and I walk away a small distance.

"Who am I to you?"

"What?" he questions.

"What am I to you?"

"Girlfriend," he answers.

"Okay, but the way you're talking to me doesn't make me sound like I am."

"Sorry," he mumbles.

"I'll be home soon, goodbye," I hang up on him and huff, returning to my seat.

"Is that your boyfriend?" she smiles.

"Yes," I nod, "he's just being a bit difficult at the moment."

"Oh, I know how that is," she pats my arm. So, is *this* girl talk? 'Cause it's freaking cool.

"I should really get going, I have homework and stuff that I've procrastinated enough on," she stands, and I follow.

"I can check out your books for you," I lead her back to the register where I scan her books for her. We exchange numbers and I almost have to hold my breath in excitement. Did I make a friend?! I made a friend! *Jake would be so proud of me.*

~~~

If I was physically able to skip, I would. Of course, my knee is an idiot so I can't, but I skip metaphorically. I walk into Grey's place and shut the door behind me. Bear nearly attacks me with kisses and when he flops over, I rub his belly happily. Grey moseys into the living room, and I give him a sweet smile. I walk to him, and we hug.

"I made a friend," I tell him excitedly when we pull away. He pulls me up to him and he kisses me. He lets out a small grunt and I deflate a bit. I wasn't expecting much, but a little more than a grunt.

"Her name is Abby and she's really nice," I add, following him as he walks into the kitchen and grabs a water bottle, drinking half of it, and not really paying much attention to me. I try and ignore the little pang that it sends me.

"Grey, really, what's wrong?" I question softly, placing my hand on his back.

"Nothing," he shakes his head. I remove my hand and only saunter away. If he doesn't want to talk, whatever. But he needs to not take it out on me if he won't tell me the problem. But he's kept all his feelings to himself for so long. He's used to only dealing with things by himself. But now I'm here. And I care. I take a seat on the couch and go on Netflix headed straight for the scary movies section. For some reason, it's Grey's favorite.

He shows no interest in almost any genre except horror. It keeps him interested and it keeps me freaked out. Grey follows me after a few seconds and instead of sitting right up beside me, usually leaning into me, he takes a seat beside me, not touching me.

I bite my lip in confusion. I pat the spot beside me, and Bear jumps up, taking Grey's usual spot. I cuddle him instead of Grey. I didn't even realize I was drifting off until I'm woken up by the door opening. I blink my eyes and spot Grey entering and shutting the main door behind him. I sit up and stretch my arms.

"I didn't know you left," I mumble, "you should've told me, I would've gone with you."

"Didn't know I had to tell you," he grumbles and a feeling of hurt I haven't felt in a while washes over me. *I need my big girl britches, I think.*

"How long have I been asleep?" I question.

"I wasn't counting," he rolls his eyes, "remind me next time."

I pinch my arm to prevent my eyes from watering.

"Maybe if you tell me what's wrong then it'll help, and you won't still be upset. I promise I'll listen and try my best to make you feel better," I explain softly, trying to keep my voice from wavering.

"It's none of your fuckin' business anyways," he turns and gives me a quick glare. One I hadn't seen in forever. I grasp my heart in a way to tell it to stop deflating painfully. I duct tape my big girl britches on myself.

"You're making it my business by taking it out on me," I tell him strongly, standing from the couch and walking over to him.

"Just tell me and I can help you. Why aren't you telling me?" I question.

"Just like you wouldn't tell me about your dad?" he says bitterly, and I take a step back, shocked. *Why would he bring that up?*

"Remember how you were supposed to tell me everything? You couldn't even tell anyone your own dad was hitting you, I can keep whatever the fuck I want from you," he nearly sneers.

"You're not entitled," he adds. My chest constricts in the worst possible way. I blink the blinding tears from my eyes but eventually, they're too heavy to blink away. I glare up at him and his face softens as he looks over the tears on my face.

"The one person who's here for you is standing right in front of you, caring about how you feel," I keep my voice strong even though my face is crumbling, "and you take it out on me?"

"I might have let you talk to me that way before but I'm not doing it anymore," I poke his chest only once. Not twice like I usually do but once.

"I had reasons for keeping things from you and you *know* what those reasons are so there's no point in bringing it up just to make yourself feel better."

"You *will not* talk to me like I'm nothing," I warn him, "you might do that to other people but *not* to me."

He remains quiet only looking at me. Is this what it's going to be like every time he gets upset? Is he going to take it out on me? Maybe we just need to take a ten-minute breather and come back? I pick up my car keys and my jacket.

"Where're you going? You've got nowhere to go," he adds fuel to the fire, and I feel steam coming out of my ears.

"You think I don't know that? I left my mom alone to stay here with *you*," I wipe my tears angrily.

"But I'm sure she'd enjoy my company if I suddenly decided to join her," I know I shouldn't have said it but I'm in my last line of defense.

"Don't threaten me with that bullshit," he shakes his head, the glare still present. Would I go up there with her? I don't even know at this point. I'm not regretting staying with Grey here but now my heart is halfway through a shredder.

"Don't make me."

"So, all this shit's my fault? You had no part, sticking your fucking nose in my business," he sends me a mean look. *What made him get like this?*

"What do you want from me, Grey?" I question, "Do you want me to not care about you or your feelings? You want me to not ask you about *you* or how you're feeling?"

"Stay fucking out of it," he glares.

"I'm done," I slam my keys back onto the table. I can't stay out of it. It's impossible for me. I guess he doesn't get that. I take off his sweatshirt and I throw it onto the ground at his feet. Next, I take off his shirt that I put on before taking my small nap. He watches me with no sign of a glare now. I don't even care that I'm standing in front of him in just my bra and pair of shorts.

I hope he gets a good look at me because he's only going to be reminded of this. I rush into the bedroom and grab a random shirt that's mine, not his. When I walk back out, he's still standing in the same place, looking down at his clothes that are on the floor. I yank my scrunchie off his wrist.

"You need to take a while and figure yourself out before trying to figure out how to have a relationship. I'm not going to sit here and take you talking to me like this," I advise him.

"I've dealt with things like that too much in my life and I'm not about to continue," I add.

"Azalea," he says softly, "please don't-"

"I don't want to hear it, Grey."

I don't think I could ever forget the look on his face when I said that to him. I care too much not to ask. And if he can't handle that then he's just not ready for a relationship. With me at least. I sob on the way down to my car, lifting my shirt and covering my face. I can't imagine what he's doing at the moment. Is he relieved? Is he happy? Does he care? Where *am* I going to go?

Chapter Twenty-Nine

Reassurance

* Grey *

Before

"Are you *aware* how talented I am with these drinks?" Jai boasts, twirling a bottle of whiskey in his hand.

"Are you aware of how much I don't care?" Roman turns up his shot.

"Are we going to open the bar or are we going to just sit here?" Theo pokes his head through the door to the back, "can I go home?"

Apparently, we're already open because the bell above the door rings and someone walks in.

"Isn't that..." Jai trails off and I look to see who's walking in. *What the fuck does he want?* I stand from the barstool, walking to him and meeting him in the middle.

"What are you doing here?" I ask him, cutting the bullshit.

"I came to see how everything is going," he lets a smirk on his face.

"You could've called Azalea, you don't need to see me," I send him a pointed glare.

"But I knew she wouldn't tell me the truth if things were going bad," Aaron shrugs a single shoulder.

"You just look for a way to get her to hate me," I counter. It's all he sticks around for.

"You're not wrong. I've got a good instinct. You could never deserve Azalea. She's too good for you," I feel his words dig into me and I snap my jaw shut to keep what I want to say from coming out.

"You don't fucking know me."

"I know more about you than you think," he chuckles, "you're the head of this whole thing, right?"

It's not like it was a secret, he's not a special motherfucker for knowing.

"To the guys here, you're 'boss', right? You're used to controlling these people, so you'd want to control the woman in your life too," He acts like he's some sort of fucking specialist. He doesn't know *shit*. I'd die before being controlling over her.

"Get the fuck out of here," I send him a small shove.

"Why? Because you can't stand me being right? She'd never stay with you," he raises his finger to my face. *I'm going to break that fucking finger.*

"A blind man could see you two would never belong together. Everyone can see that," he keeps his voice low.

"You're complete opposites. You could never work," he adds.

"Try saying that in front of her. You're fucking pathetic. You don't want her to see how shitty you really are," I glare at him as his little facade crumbles a bit. *I'm* the one who's always had a bad feeling about him.

"You think you know everything about her just because you've fucked her," he sneers, and I feel a vein in my neck bulge.

"She deserves better than to have you in her life, I fucking know that," I say without a doubt. Who talks about someone like that? I've *fucked* her? He's a piece of shit.

"That's where you're wrong. I'm her clutch. Whenever you fuck up, she comes to me. And guess what?" he smiles, "I'll always be there for her.

She's known me for years and I've always been there for her."

This *motherfucker*.

"You're in love with her," I feel my jaw tense. Listening to his little speech it's obvious now. I thought he was before maybe but now, I'm positive.

"And you're not," he tells me, "you'll never love her. And she needs someone who will love her."

"Get the *fuck out,*" I shove him harshly toward the door.

"There that is," he throws a hand up, "that temper is going to get the best of you. You're going to explode and she's going to come running to me."

I pick him up and throw him out the door, closing it and locking it once I shut it. I walk past the now empty bar from where the guys cleared out. I push my way through the door and head straight to my office, locking the door behind me once I'm in. I fall into the closest chair at the front of my desk, clutching my head. I feel my chest constricting and my breaths turn short. *Reassure, reassure, find reassurance.* I *can't.* Terrifying scenarios where Azalea leaves me play throughout my thoughts. Scenes that feel real and inevitable. *Fuck, is he right?* He is.

The Aftermath

I'm fucked. Utterly and completely *fucked*. Everything is my fault. Every piece of it. I don't deny it. I don't even know why I got mad that she asked what was wrong. She's always cared, why did it set me off then?

I knew it was inevitable. He's right. I can't even walk around my place without feeling like an empty, sad fuck. How'd I live like this before her? More importantly, how do I fix this? Can I even fix it? My frustration built up too much. I shouldn't have let Aaron affect me like that. I'd let words affect me too much when I was younger; I thought I was past that. I thought I'd be stronger by now.

'You could never deserve Azalea. She's too good for you.' 'She'd never stay with you.'

It takes me back to a fucked up place in a fucked-up house during a fucked-up childhood. Never having *reassurance,* never being told something is wrong or right. Never being guided, no matter what. The only words being spoken were words about how life is unfair, the world is unfair, no one ever gets what they want, and expecting failure, expecting the worst because you'll never get the best.

And I took everything that I kept in, out on the one person who cares. Maybe she could've been my reassurance? The one single person who *loves* me and who cares not only about me but about how I feel and what I'm thinking. Those words flew out of my mouth before I could think or stop them. I regret every fucking thing. I regret telling her 'nothing' when she asked what was wrong, I regret telling her that it wasn't her business because it *is* her business. She's so close to my feelings that everything of mine is hers, even my business.

I regret bringing up her dad. That was the shittiest thing I could've done. I regret not stopping even when her eyes started watering. And even more when she actually started crying. It hurt me to see that so why the fuck didn't I stop? I regret not being happier for her when she told me she made a friend. She talks about making new friends and I was the fucker that ruined her excitement.

"Grey..." Jai drawls out, glancing at me almost confusedly.

"Are you okay?" Theo asks, walking closer, confused too. I run my hand through my hair and internally curse on a nonstop wave.

"I'm fucked."

"You're fucked?" Linc questions.

"Why're you fucked?" Jai questions, sitting in a barstool across from me.

"Is he on drugs?" Theo whispers to Linc. I might as well be. I can't think clearly. All I can think of is her. So beautiful. Why didn't I tell her that more often?

"She dumped me," for good reasons. She deserved better than I was talking to her. She deserves the world but instead, she got me talking down to her like she was a piece of trash. Just like he said, she deserves better than me. *Fuck.* I've literally proved everything he said. I feel the guys' gazes go wide and look all over at each other. They don't say anything. Just like I couldn't say anything after she said she was done.

My heart stopped when I watched her take off my clothes and throw them at my feet. I went from barely registering what was happening around me when I was being terrible to her, to being able to hear my own pounding heartbeat. She can't be in Kentucky. She can't go to Kentucky. I'd do whatever she wants me to do but she's not here to tell me what I need to do. Or at Aaron's.

"Why?" Jai questions quietly. I'm sure they think they're treading on thin ice, not knowing when I'm going to suddenly lose my shit, but no thoughts have crossed my mind except for Lilah and how to get her back. Why did I let her walk out? She should've stayed and I should've gone. I could stay anywhere, and she couldn't. And now where is she?

"Because I'm a fucking idiot," I answer truthfully.

"Well, I guess she's one less thing to worry about," Jonas shrugs and everyone goes almost silent. I pick up the sweet tea that sits in front of me and I throw it at him. Glass and all. In shock, he doesn't see my foot coming right at his face. He flies back in his chair, and I sit back down. I look up at the clock and find that it's two in the afternoon. *She should be at Terrip's.* I shoot up from my seat and in a usual ten-minute walk, it only takes me six to get there. I'm not the best at apologizing. I've only apologized a few other times in my life. And mostly they've all been to her. But for nothing this big. We broke up. *She* broke up with me. I *need* her back.

I spot her near the back, a cart of books by her side. My heart does that weird shit seeing her. Her hair is braided down her back and she wears a dress that makes her glow. She's always glowing. Even the first time I saw her she was glowing. Even now. Was that why I tripped her when I first saw her? Knowing I'd be there to catch her, there's no hiding the fact that I did it on purpose. What was I looking for when I did that? Thank God I did it though. But then I messed it up. That alone shows how much she doesn't need me. But I'm selfish and I need her.

My hands itch to wrap around her small waist and my fingers tense in a desperate need to always touch her. She turns to grab more books off the cart and her eyes fall on my figure. Her eyes don't go wide, and a smile doesn't reach her perfect lips like usual. She has no reaction except for the little jump which signals that I startled her. She turns back around like she never saw me.

"Lilah," I mumble to her, pressing my hand against the small of her back. She moves out of my reach, and it sends a bang through my chest. But I deserve to feel like shit because I made her feel like shit.

"What are you doing here, Grey?" she asks. No lightness to her voice there usually is when she talks to me.

"I'm sorry," I try to meet her eyes, but she doesn't look at me, even turning her body away, "I'm so sorry."

"Okay," she says, picking up a handful of books. Okay? What does that mean? Okay, we're still together? Okay, I don't give a fuck? Okay, shut up? Okay, go fuck yourself?

"Look at me," I nearly plead. She closes her eyes and takes a calming breath. She turns and looks up at me with those eyes.

"I don't even want to hear it," her voice breaks a small bit at the end, and she raises her hand to me.

"I'll never do that ever again," I promise. I can't go through this shit again. I got no sleep, even Bear's got an attitude with me. I place my hand on the side of her hip, taking a step closer to her. She grasps my hand and pulls it off.

"You won't," she agrees and my eyebrows furrow in the least bit.

"It's not even been a day Grey, I'm not forgiving you or taking you back," she shakes her head and I feel like I've been stabbed. *What?*

"L-Like," I stutter like a fucking idiot, "ever?"

My chest constricts in fear. Full-fledged fear.

"Fuck, I'm sorry Azalea. Please don't say you're not taking me back. I'm never doing that again, I promise, I'm sorry," I shake my head. I'll get on my knees and beg for her to take me back. *Beg.* I once had said that I'd never beg for anything. Not even my life if it came to it. But that shit's out the fucking window when it comes to her. I'd beg all day for her.

"I should never have even thought about talking to you the way I did, I'm sorry," I tell her.

"Not even twenty-four hours Grey. It can't be enough time for you to do what I said," she steps away.

"What do you mean, do what you said?" I've been thinking too much about what I could have done differently and not about everything that she said.

"Figure. Yourself. Out," she speaks slowly, "figure out ways to be able to talk to me. You're not alone anymore and you get that physically, but not mentally. I need you to open up to me, Grey, and I know it's hard, but I can't do this if you're not going to be there with me emotionally. I'm *here* for you. I don't judge you and I can listen to all of your problems, but you just don't tell me anything."

She might as well be speaking Latin. Some things make sense, some don't. I don't know how to do this. I've never had anyone I've been able to tell everything to. Never.

"You still love me?" I mumble admittedly vulnerably. *Please still love me.*

"I can't stop loving you overnight," she sighs. I don't know that.

"Where are you staying?" I question. Aaron's?

"Mr. Terrip's couch," she mumbles. I breathe out a breath of relief. But even that's not where she should be. She once told me how he's got a one-bedroom apartment and the most uncomfortable couch that was ever made.

"Come home with me," I grip her side, and pull her just a bit closer to me. She's too far.

"Grey," she starts, "we're not together, I can't live with you. And respect my space, no touching."

I pull my hand off her side and hold it behind my back. I think it has a mind of its own. How long is this going to last? How long does it take for someone to 'figure themselves out?' I don't even think I know what that means. I almost reach out to pull her closer and I grab for the scrunchie that usually sits on my hand but it's not there. *God-dammit.* I hate what I'm about to say.

"Come home. I'll take the couch," I tell her, looking down at the dark blue carpeted floor, "don't stay on his couch. I won't bother you. Just, please come home."

She visibly hesitates. I can't live without her, and I can't *live* without her.

"I don't think it's a good idea," she shakes her head.

"Please Azalea," I need to see her every day. Ideally right when I wake up and when I go to bed. And all the in-between.

"Friends only."

My heart falls to the floor. Friends? Just like nothing happened? Like she never told me she loved me, like we never made out in the back of this place, like we never stayed up together watching anything she'd want to, like we never touched each other in places only *we're* allowed to? I can't fucking go back to that. I don't think it's possible. But it's whatever she wants. It came from my doings.

"Azalea," I start but she holds her hand up.

"Deal or no deal."

I'd rather have her in my life than not at all.

~~~

I watch in on her as she walks back into our, more like *her*, room now. It was only a few minutes ago that the thought of me being actually *single* hit me. I wouldn't call myself single though. It's not like I'd fuck anyone else. I'm single but not single. The show she likes called it a 'break'. But on that break one of them slept with someone else, whichever one it was. I can't stand the thought of being with someone else romantically. Let alone letting another woman lay her hands on me. No matter what, no matter how long we're 'friends' I know it'll never feel right. It'll always feel wrong.

I've gone as far as looking up what 'figuring oneself out' meant. It's taken two days to understand that she doesn't want me to change, she wants the way I hold in my emotions and feelings, and ways I release them to be pushed in a different direction: towards something, not someone.

I've been alone my whole life. Mom died hardly any time after I was born and dad never had shit to do with me, making me fend for myself. I heard once from him though that he and mom ran away from their parents when they were eighteen. She was pregnant, they were kicked out, so they ran, not knowing where they'd end up. *And that no one deserves anything in life and that life equals hell.*

On a night he had unexpectedly come home drunk, the night of my fifteenth birthday, he talked to me more than he ever had. It wasn't about me. It was about mom. I never had anyone to talk to about *me*. No family. In high school, people tried talking to me but most of them were either scared of me or left me alone because they knew that that was how I liked it to be. I liked that they were scared of me. I liked that they saw my tattoos, the look on my face, and my height and were scared of me. I didn't have to worry about the dumb ass drama that went around.

This one girl got involved with this guy's dad. The girl was full-on fucking her boyfriend's dad. On top of that, her boyfriend was seen with her younger sister, who was a goddamn freshman. Then, the freshman sister was also seen getting too close with the older sister's boyfriend's best friend, who was dating this other girl that ended up fighting both the freshman girl *and* her sister. The whole thing was a fucking shit show.

But I sat back with metaphorical popcorn and watched it all unravel. I never *wanted* friends. I was content with myself. And then I was content with just me and Lilah. Now it's me again. And I'm *not* fucking content.

An idea pops into my head and It's something I've never even thought of doing before but something I know she'd love. She loves flowers. Like, *loves* them. I could do that. The ones we have already, she said, need to be moved somewhere to get more sunlight anyway. Who knew she was a botanist or whatever it's called?

I arrive at the closest store I know that has flowers and I make it to the aisle that smells like someone's grandma. I recall the time she and I came here for the flowers the first time. It took nearly fifteen minutes for her to pick out two sets of flowers. The ones she had really wanted weren't 'bloomed' enough or whatever she said.

I look at the lilies, as she called them, and see that they look different than the time we were here. The flowers now have more actual...flowers or whatever. Blooms or some shit. Half the time I was watching her and the other half I was wandering back and forth down the aisle waiting for her to finish. She wouldn't let me leave the aisle too afraid she 'lose' me. I pick up the lilies, pay, and go back home.

She sees me as I walk in and I silently thank God when I see those eyes of hers light up when she sees me. Or maybe it's just the flowers, I don't know.

"I'm still sorry," I remind her, watching her closely as she takes the flowers and bites her lip as she admires them. *I want that fucking lip.* I have zero self-control. Zero. I'm going insane. This is the worst punishment I could ever get. Living with her, seeing her looking so beautiful every second and not being able to touch her in ways I want to. In ways I know she loves. But she's right. I can't treat her like I did, and I need to figure it out. But I need to do it fucking fast because I can't stay away from her much longer.

"You got these for me?" her voice raises an octave. I only give her a nod, never taking my eyes off her. She returns her gaze to me and gives me a sweet smile, her straight, pearly whites showing themselves. Every time I look at her, I want to kiss her. Did I kiss her at least twice a minute before? I need to now. Or, not now, after she takes me back. God, I hope it's soon.

"Thank you," she bites that fucking lip again and I get a headache. I lean my forehead against the nearest wall and curse.

"What's wrong?" she questions softly. I pull my head back and look at her again. Even after hating the fuck out of me for being a shitty person to her, she's still concerned about me. Still. God, I fucking love her. *What?*

"Baby, I want you. I *want* you," I'm desperate, clingy, pitiful, everything but I don't give a single shit. Not only the physical touches we give each other but I want her talking to me too. She's hardly said much of anything to me. We were done cold turkey. I want her voice.

I don't understand how I used to be annoyed at how much she talked and how often she asked me questions about anything and everything. Now I don't want her to ever stop talking to me. *I think I'm an attention whore.* Always wanting her touch, always wanting her looking at me, always wanting

Lilah — K. Pope

her talking to me, I'm a full-on attention whore for her. Because I'm 100% madly in love with her.

Chapter Thirty

Herb

❀ Azalea ❀

Five days now that we've been 'not together' anymore. Six days of not having slept in the same bed. No kisses or anything and I'm proud of myself. He's tempting, he's *so* tempting. Especially when he's behaving himself. Which he has been doing. He's so kissable. And he just sits there waiting for me to make a move on him. He's got 'kiss me' eyes and I'm struggling to hold myself back. Just as he's doing right now.

"What?" he asks.

"You're the one looking at me," I shrug. Even though I'm looking at him too.

"So?" he scoots closer to me. His intoxicating smell makes me want to put my face in his chest.

"So don't," I lick my lips and his eyes trail down to them. They stay in that position, looking there and not moving.

"Stop looking at my lips," I warn.

"I can't kiss you so I'm imagining it, leave me alone," he dismisses my warning.

"And other things," he mumbles. I scoot away from him and turn my head before I give in.

"Are you harassing her?" Jai's voice questions as he shows up at our table.

"Yes, he is, call the po-po," I nod to Jai.

"I thought y'all broke up?" he questions.

"We did," I confirm, "but it's hard."

"So am I," Grey mutters under his breath and I feel my eyes widen just a tad bit. I peek over at him and he's not-so-subtly looking down my black v-neck silky tank top.

"If you're still sitting here by the time Abby gets here I'm gonna pitch a fit and you'll never hear the end of it," I assure Grey as two o'clock quickly approaches, the time we agreed to meet up at. He shrugs like it's not a big deal.

"Abby, huh?" Jai takes a seat across from us, "she cute?"

"She's very pretty," I nod, and he nods too, a smirk on his face.

"Shit, I'm single now too, might have to do something with this girl," Grey grumbles, and I turn my whole body toward him.

"Do *not* try me, Grey Alexander," I warn, "I will end you before you can even blink."

We're only haphazardly broken up. We can't get with another person. We just can't.

"I wouldn't do that, Lilah," he throws an arm around my neck, pulling me into him. He kisses the side of my head and I melt into him. *Oh wait, we're not together.*

"You better not," I grumble, looking up at him. He looks down at me, our faces close. His lips part a little bit as his eyes search my lips.

"Kiss her," Jai whispers across the table. I pull away and Grey's jaw tenses as he sends Jai a scary glare. He raises his hands in surrender before deciding it's best to just get up and leave. I check my phone and see that it's one fifty-seven.

"Why don't you go over there," I point to a table across the floor, "and think about things because she'll be here any minute."

"One kiss," he says. I shake my head. There's no point in being broken up if you're still going to kiss the person. He grips the front of my pants and slides me closer to him.

"Five days," he reminds me of how long it's been since I've let him kiss me.

"Then you should have never talked to me like I meant nothing," I raise an eyebrow.

"I know," he says defeatedly. In a flash, I place a swift kiss on his cheek.

"Now go," I shoo him away and he licks his lips before slowly getting up and moseying over to the table I pointed for him to sit at. Hardly two minutes after his nice booty sits in his seat, Abby joins me at our table. A guy Grey introduced to me as Roman now sits with him at his table, the two of them going through random files.

Roman's the gun guy. The one with the gun in his butt. Or his pants, whatever. Jai comes and takes our drink and food orders as we begin a conversation about different things ranging from how many pillows we need to sleep with during the night to the name of her goldfish she had when she was fifteen. We get our food and even while eating we chat.

"How's your boyfriend?" she questions, eating on her fries.

"We broke up," I smile and her eyes furrow. Oh, I smiled. She's going to think I'm having a psychotic episode.

"And you're happy about it?" she questions. I laugh and shake my head.

"It's only temporary," I assure her, but she still looks confused.

"Are you confident about getting back together or is there something I'm missing?" she asks.

"Oh, I broke up with him, and I tell him when we're going to get back together," now saying it, it makes me sound totally and completely controlling. But that wasn't the situation.

"That sounded terrible," I admit, "it's more complex than that, I promise. I'm not mean to him. Our situation was just, that was what we needed, and he understands that. I promise you I'm not mean to him."

Even though he won't stop bothering me and asking when I'll take him back and quote "kiss me on the lips again."

"Do you love him?" she questions before taking a sip of her drink.

"I do love him," I smile. It would be impossible to not be in love with him by now. I find it hard to believe that he's never been officially with someone before. Who would want to be strangers with him? Well, I could understand why someone would want to remain strangers with him. His facial expressions hardly ever range from appearing mad.

"That's sweet," she smiles happily, moving her shoulders up in excitement. I move my eyes over to Grey's form where he sits watching me like I'm a steak dinner. *So sweet.*

"This place is really nice," she looks around and I take a big sloppy bite of my cheeseburger. It hits the spot. A drop of ketchup falls off the end of my burger and onto my chest, rolling down in between my gosh darn chesticles. She laughs at me, and I look around for a napkin. I catch Grey's eyes though. He holds his head down, his hand gripping onto his hair as he mouths a curse word. Abby hands me a napkin and I take it gratefully, wiping the ketchup off my chest. We resume eating and only a little while goes by before Abby gets quieter.

"Do you know those guys over there?" she nods her head to where Grey and Roman sit, looking directly over at us. Roman's trying to be less obvious about it, but Grey has his freaking chair turned in the exact direction of me. Good Lord.

"I don't," I shake my head, furrowing my eyebrows like I don't know my Grey who sits over there. She turns back toward them and Roman looks away, turning his head the opposite way of us but Grey, of course, continues to look at me, his bottom lip rolled into his mouth.

"I think the guy with the tattoos has a thing for you," she lightly pushes my arm, "he's gorgeous."

"Oh yeah, but Roma-the other guy was looking right at *you*," I give her a smile and her eyes widen a bit.

"Really?" she questions, looking over at him shyly. I give her a nod.

'Stop it' I mouth to Grey, and he shakes his head. I narrow my eyes at him, and he tilts his head down, his eyes shining in amusement.

"He's the local crackhead, the one with tattoos," I tell Abby, turning back to her. Her eyes widen a bit.

"Really? I would've never thought. He looks well-put-together," she tells me, tucking a dark strand of hair behind her ear.

"He does crack at night, not during the day," I shrug.

"Is he known around here for that?"

"Yep. His name is...what is it?" I try to think hard for a perfect name.

"His name's Herb."

"Oh wow."

"He's also got eight kids," I nod, sipping on my sweet tea to hold back my smile.

"He looks young to have that many," she says, exasperated.

"Well, he had them all around the same time, but with different women," I make a yikes face.

"Does he want *you* to be his baby mama now?" She gasps, leaning forward to me.

"I think he does," I nod, "he's been looking at my goodies since I got here."

"Y'all would make beautiful babies though, on a serious note," she tells me honestly and my eyebrows raise on my forehead. My phone dings and I peek at it. '*Stop fuckin staring at me*' Grey's message reads. I ignore the message and bite my cheek to keep the dumb smile off my face.

"He's got a nice phone for a crackhead," Abby speaks curiously and I let out a bark of laughter.

"That's because he sells crack too."

"I might have to get me some," I gasp at her words and nearly tear up. I think we're meant to be friends. I catch Roman's eyes and he raises his phone to me. I get a text a second later. '*Give her my #*' it reads. I'm going to punch Grey in the clavicle for giving my number to him. '*No do it yourself loser*' I respond and watch from the corner of my eye as he reads it. Grey chuckles when he shows him my response.

I put my phone down and turn it off. It's rude to text when you're having lunch with someone. It's not lunch though because it's after two but it's before dinner. It's *dunch*. I laugh a little at my own joke. Jai comes back to take our empty plates after we've finished, and Abby takes out her wallet.

"Oh no," I shake my head, "I'm not allowed to pay so you don't have to either."

She looks at me like I just lied to her face.

"Where'd you hear that?" She tilts her head.

"A crackhead told me."

"That crackhead?" She nods to Grey.

"Yes."

"Ew," Jonas passes our table on the way to Grey's.

"Come again fella? Walk away donkey," I call after him.

"Little bitch," he rolls his eyes.

"Keep talking and I'm going to punch your nose off," I raise my fist just a tad. He saunters off, flicking me off behind his back.

"I'm confused," she laughs.

"He's a donkey," I explain to her.

"Hey, baby doll," Oaklee leans over into our booth and kisses the top of my head.

"Look at you sitting there all sexy and stuff," he leans over. He peeks over at Grey who sits glaring scarily at him.

"I'll go before mama bear punches me in the dick," he ruffles my hair and I scrunch my nose at him.

"Is that your boyfriend, or ex at the moment?" She questions

"No," I shake my head, "that's Oaklee, he's crazy."

"Um, Azalea," she whispers, "the crackhead and the other guy are coming over here."

"Oh Lord, here we go," I mumble as Grey slides right into the seat beside me and Roman leans against the side of the table.

"Hi, I'm Roman," he smiles down at her. She looks down shyly.

"I'm Abby," she answers.

"I miss you," Grey whispers and I look at his gorgeous face.

"I'm right here," I watch his lips as he runs his tongue over the corner of his mouth.

"We were just leaving," I add and Abby watches Grey and I's interaction. His hand comes to rest on my thigh.

"You're going to scare Abby away," I tell him quietly.

"Why?"

"I told her you're the town crackhead and that you have eight kids," I smile.

"Of course you did," he doesn't act the least bit surprised.

"Hands to yourself, Sugar," I pick up his hand and move it off my leg.

"Abby, this isn't Herb. His actual name is Grey," I roll my eyes, "my half-ex-boyfriend."

"Ex?" he grumbles unhappily, a small glare on his face.

"So, not a crackhead?" she smiles.

"Not technically," I shrug, turning to Roman, "and that's Roman, he has the hots for you. Sorry Roman, I didn't mean to say that."

Grey wraps his strong arm around my waist, and he nearly yanks me closer to him like we would always sit before we got on our break. I lay my head on his shoulder and his hand rides up my shirt slightly before he draws random shapes on my stomach with his thumb.

"Yeah, broken up my ass," Jai rolls his eyes, slightly eyeing Roman. I lean away from Grey and just slightly catch the sight of his jaw tensing unhappily.

"Want to go get milkshakes?" The last time I asked someone this, it turned out terrible and I ended up with my feelings hurt. Ahem, Grey.

"Sure," she smiles, beginning to get out of the booth. I don't blame her. If I didn't know the three guys around us, I'd feel crowded too. And nervous. And like a pimp. Grey gets up and lets me slide out of the booth. Abby and I begin walking out, but I'm pulled back by Grey's monstrous hand on my wrist. He slides his hand down and interlocks our fingers, pulling me close to him.

"I thought milkshakes were *our* thing?" He leans down to me, pressing a kiss under my ear. I wipe the spot he kissed and place my fingers on his lips.

"Take your kiss back," I advise him, and he looks unamused.

"And you never get milkshakes with me," I raise my eyebrow, "so it's not our thing."

"I want you back now," he grumbles and I pull away.

"I'll see you at home Grey," I fall back into step with Abby and we begin on the walk to Momma's Milkshakes.

"Do you call him a crackhead often?" she asks and I throw my head back in laughter.

~~~

"I can't believe you, Grey," I groan, turning on the bathtub and checking the water to make sure it's not too cold or too hot. Grey looks at me hornish eyes. This man, I swear.

"Bear, control him please," I look at Bear who is completely covered in mud. We went to take him out for a walk and to get him to poop and Grey let go of the leash for what reason? There's probably not one. It had just rained and there were mud puddles everywhere. Bear oh-so-smartly decided to roll in one. I kind of wanted to roll in one too but I refrained. And now he's got to have a bath.

"Good luck," Grey mumbles, before trying to walk out. Uh, I think not.

"You best get back here," I warn him, and he stops in the doorway, "we're both giving him a bath, not just me."

I should be making Grey give him a bath by himself but I kind of want to see how cute Bear looks with all his wet fur.

"He doesn't like baths," Grey turns around.

"Then we definitely need both of us," I step forward and grip his hand, pulling him back over to the bathtub. Once the tub fills up, Grey picks up Bear and places him in the bathtub. Bear looks over at me like 'I'm going to jump out in point two seconds.' And he does just that.

"Little shit," Grey rolls his eyes, looking at me. I smile.

"I can't run darling," I tilt my head happily. A minute later, Grey comes back with Bear up in his arms. He shuts the door behind him with his foot and he places Bear back in the tub.

"Stay," he tells him. I sit on the edge of the tub and pour water all over Bear's thick black fur. Grey just stands there.

"I swear Grey, you better get over here," I shake my head at him, and he grumbles under his breath, sitting on the side too. Bear shakes himself wildly and we're both soaked. My white shirt sticks to me and my light blue bra shows through my shirt. Well, gosh, Grey is getting quite the view at the moment. I pour the doggy shampoo on Grey's hands and my own and we get to scrubbing. Bear continuously tries to get away from us. He gives me the look again. He hops out the tub and with the door closed, there's really nowhere to go so he runs around the bathroom like a psychopath. Standing, I fall on the slippery floor and silently thank Jesus that my knee didn't become an even bigger annoyance. My butt bone is broken though.

"You okay, Lilah?" Grey lifts me to my feet and Bear walks to me, licking me once on the arm before trying to find his escape once more.

"My butt's broken," I groan, rubbing my buttcheek. Grey ignores the sentence only looking at me intently, his eyes darting between both of mine.

"Azalea, I'm sorry," he says suddenly, "I know I have to open up more to you and I promise I will. I get it now. I need you back."

I can't count how many times he's apologized but this time seems the most serious of all. And I think we've been apart for long enough. I miss it too.

"You have to promise to never, ever talk to me the way you did ever again," I tell him, and he nods undoubtedly.

"I promise," he says without a beat. I give him a small smile and I motion for him to come to me. He walks into my arms, leaning down into the hug.

"I love you, Grey."

"I love *you*."

"You said what?" I pull away, confused. Did I hear something else? Was that voice Bear? Was it God's voice?

"I love you Azalea," he grips my chin and kisses me softly. I don't respond much, in shock.

"Kiss me back," he mumbles against my lips.

"You *do* love me?" I ask.

"I *love you,*" he nods.

"How do you know?" I don't know why I can't just shut up and accept the fact.

"The way you make me feel. The fact that you're the only person I'd ever want to be with. The way I'm always thinking about you. I'd do anything for you."

"Would you eat moldy cheese?" I gasp.

"If it came down to it," he nods, and I almost get teary-eyed.

"Now I can say 'I love you' and you can say 'I love you too'," I grow really excited, slipping on the floor again but being caught by Grey.

My Grey loves me. And I love my Grey.

~~~

"What happened that night?" I ask him and he lets out a quiet sigh.

"It's-it's just complicated and it's not anything that you did. I was just listening to things I shouldn't have been listening to," he tucks my hair behind my ear. I crawl over on his lap for my world-famous hug. I wrap my arms around his neck and squeeze him firmly but gently.

"I understand," I whisper. It isn't the whole story but if that's all for now, then I'm okay with it.

"There's still no excuse for me treating you the way I did," he pulls away slightly, kissing me softly. I place my hand on his cheek, not buttcheek, and I turn my head just to deepen the kiss only a little bit. He pulls me closer to his body and slides his hand up the back of my shirt. He rocks me forward a bit and groans quietly into the kiss. He gently tugs my shirt up and off my body, leaving me in only my bra and underwear.

"Fuck," he grips onto my hips. I look down to where he's looking. I spot Tubs, my food baby.

"Oh my gosh! It's Tubs," I place my hand on my stomach, although that's not where he was looking originally, that hornish man.

"Fuck, I love you," he groans, placing his head into my neck.

"And Tubs?"

"And Tubs," he confirms.

"Why am I almost naked?" I question and he pulls away, looking down at me.

"I don't know how that happened," he answers.

"Are you with me just for my body?" even though it's not that great. Or very good.

"Yeah," he says seriously but I know that he's joking by the way his eyes narrow in the slightest bit.

"I'm only with you for that reason too," I nod, wrapping my arms back around him after pulling the covers up around us both.

"Want to do under-the-cover smex?" I blurt and his eyes fade dark, "I kid."

"You kid?"

"I'm a virgin Mary," I lean my head on his chest, puffing out my cheeks.

"I know," his deep voice rumbles under me, "kind of."

"Kind of?" I furrow my eyebrows.

"My tongue went in yo-" I cut him off there.

"Excuse me sir, that's hush-hush information."

"And my fingers," he smirks. I squeeze my legs together just a bit and he notices. He notices everything because the crack he does heightens his senses, I'm sure of it.

"You're thinking about it," he says lowly.

"You don't know anything," I grumble, and he hums. He pushes me down on my back and leans over me, propping himself up on his elbows.

"I feel like we're not equal. I'm half buck naked and you've got your clothes on," I chide. He sits up, taking his shirt off before lowering himself back down. His silver chain hangs down and I wrap my arm around his neck, pulling the chain back so it's not hanging between us. I look over at his bicep and the tattoos that wrap around it. He presses himself down onto me like how we sleep, and he kisses the side of my face. He pulls the covers over us and Bear scratches at the door. Grey lets out a groan.

"Are you kidding me?" he grumbles, getting up and opening the door, letting Bear in, and closing the door behind Bear. He returns to me.

"I still don't have a shirt on," I remind him.

"I like the feeling," I feel his smirk against my neck.

"But I'm wearing a bra," I scrunch my nose. It's not really comfortable to sleep in a bra.

"Take it off," he shrugs. I reach around my back and unclip it. He leans off of me, letting me get it off and watching me like a pervert. It's nothing he hasn't seen before.

"Fuck me," he mumbles before laying back on me.

"Woah, woah, woah," I stop him, "now isn't the time to be saying hornish things. We're trying to sleep."

"*You're* trying to sleep," he slides his hands down the front of me.

"*You're* trying to *sleep* with *me,*" I scrunch my nose at him, and he kisses my nose.

"You're *not* wrong," he flips us over.

"I love you," I kiss him softly, "you hornish man."

Chapter Thirty-One

Party

❀ Azalea ❀

This isn't a good thing for me. It's really not.

"Why are you not confident about kicking their butts?" Abby laughs as we walk into the laser tag place. It was Oaklee's idea and since I've never been, I made Grey come. I've never seen someone so unhappy to be somewhere *in my life*.

"Before I tell you the reason, do you have any drugs with you?"

She looks at me like I'm mental.

"No," she draws out.

"Okay good. They're feds. Not fed-ex workers, they're like FBI level feds," I explain, watching as Theo and Lincoln get out of Linc's black Tahoe.

"Are you kidding?" she asks, her eyes a bit widened. I know she probably doesn't believe me. I *did* make up the whole story about Grey being an actual crackhead with eight kids.

"No, I'm not kidding this time," I shake my head.

"All of them?" she whispers looking around at them.

"Yep," I put my hand on Grey's butt, which doesn't even shock him at all, "this one."

I point to Oaklee who is flexing his arms at Grey for some reason, "that one."

"All of them."

"Let's beat some ass," Oaklee seems really into it, opening the door to the place with his foot.

"C'mon," Grey grips a belt loop on the side of my shorts, pulling me with him. I grip onto Abby's arm, pulling her too.

"You ready to get *whooped* by me and Abby? You're going to get *beat,*" I bump my body into him threateningly, a scare tactic I learned from a CIA video made by someone who's never been in the CIA.

"There aren't teams," he answers. I guess we're playing the 'every-man-for-himself' way.

"Well, me and Abby are underdogs so we're a team."

"Sanfred's held a gun three times," he rolls his eyes.

"Then he can be on our team too," I shrug. After paying for everyone, a lady hands us the vest things we have to wear.

"Dumb as shit," Grey grumbles as he puts his vest on. Then she gives everyone a headband. Grey looks at it and hands it back to her.

"That's not fair, you need one too," Theo points at Grey.

"I'm fucking shooting you first if you don't shut up," Grey warns.

"Okay, rules," the lady claps her hands and Grey tilts his head at that.

"No physical contact with each other, no running unless in the open part of the arena, no climbing anything, and to reload your laser gun, you press this button," she holds up one of the guns and shows us a button on the side of it.

"Reloading takes approximately twenty to twenty-five seconds."

"Are you fucking me?" Grey grumbles, wrapping his arm around my shoulders.

"Am I? Yes," I blurt, "oh." Sort of. He looks down at me and a little smile turns the corners of his lips up.

Lilah   *K. Pope*

"Everyone here knows how to hold a gun, correct?" the lady asks, bored.

"God bless it, I forgot how to," Lincoln taps his head. She spends five minutes showing him something he already knows how to do before we're released into the actual arena.

"Five minutes to get ready, turn on your lasers and vests. An announcement will sound when it's time," she closes the door behind us, and the place is just hardly lit up with fluorescent-like lights. The guys run off and Grey turns to me.

"Don't target me," I warn.

"I'm not going easy on you," he raises an eyebrow.

"That's not what I said. I said don't target me," I poke his chest twice. He grips onto my hand and pulls me to him, kissing me slowly.

"It could've been me and you, Lilah. We could've been a team," he mumbles in between kisses.

"Then I would carry our team the whole time," I tease, and the corner of his lips rise. I reach around and pat his butt a couple of times.

"I'll see you on the flip side Sugar," I smile.

"I love you," he kisses me one last time and my heart flutters out of my chest. I hold back from squealing, but I feel my body shimmer in happiness.

"I love *you*," I reply and start to walk away.

"Grey, you know what? You better take it a little bit easy on me, I can't even walk fast," I raise my finger at him.

"Go fuckin' hide somewhere," he shoos me away and I scrunch my nose at him to which he mimics.

~~~

"Oh my gosh," Abby whispers frantically. I think we're in a real warzone. I peek from behind our small hiding space and the sounds of the guys' laser guns going off is a nonstop ringing in my ears. And some shouting.

"Why couldn't we have gone bowling or something?!" I whisper.

"We're going to get found soon," she winces. Our hiding spot isn't the greatest. Footsteps pound the floor near us and in less than a second, Oakee is throwing himself between Abby and me.

"They're like animals. I need protection" he lays his head on my shoulder.

"Pew pew motherfuckers," Theo suddenly appears in front of the three of us and we all try to scatter. He shoots Oaklee immediately and tries to get Abby but she's able to run away quickly.

"Oh, I'm sorry Azale-" he pauses when suddenly his vest turns red and then his gun shuts off. His mouth drops open.

"Did I kill you?!" I gasp, holding my heart. Why am I feeling bad? He was about to murder me cold-blooded. *I'm an actual bad-butt.* I don't even know how to use the gun and I killed him? Wasn't I just standing there?

"Only I can shoot her, fucker," Grey glares at Theo and my mouth drops open.

"You killed me?!"

"You killed him?!"

I thought I did. Gosh dang it. Theo stomps away unhappily. Then Grey sets his sights on me. I poke out my bottom lip.

"I'll flash you if you let me walk away," I smile.

"Ten-second head start," he decides. I lift up my shirt and he looks for a second.

"I'll count slow," he licks his lips and I lower my shirt and walk out of the hiding spot. I almost trip over Oaklee who lies on the floor like he's actually dead. I walk by Abby who's trying to talk Roman out of shooting her. Lincoln's using the bear-hug tactic against Maxon so that he can't shoot him. Which ends up failing. Then Maxon comes for me, but he's shot before he can get to me. *Grey.* His arms wrap around me from behind and I lean my head back against him in defeat. Roman shoots Abby and comes for us but Grey shoots him before he can even raise his gun again. I turn around to him and look up at him. I look behind us to the leaderboard and we're the only two left. Really?

"On the way back home, we need to stop by the store," I pause and shoot him, "and get more Fruity Pebbles."

He looks down at his now red vest and then back up at me. My mouth is wide open.

"I swear, I don't know who just shot you, but I didn't see them, I was watching just to make sure, and I never even saw anyone."

"Mhm," he kisses my temple.

"Mhm yeah, that's right! I killed you fella! You can't beat me! I wake up in the morning and I tinkle excellence," I quote Ricky Bobby. We have two more rounds of the laser tag game. The second time I actually went around trying to kill people. I got shot within ten seconds so that the game didn't really last long. Then the third and final game, Abby and I really teamed up and we were two of the last five left. So basically, we're the best there ever was.

"Oh Lord help me, it's raining cats and dogs," I look out the large windows in the lobby of the laser tag place. Grey pulls me further into his side, tracing my hip with his finger.

"You're beautiful," he says, and I let a smile grace my lips. He takes a step back and stands in front of me. He leans down and wraps his arms around me.

"I'm still sorry Azalea," he mumbles, "about the way I talked to you. I can't stop thinking about it."

"You can't stop thinking about it?"

He lets his hands travel along the surface of my back before they stop, wrapped tightly around me.

"I don't deserve you," he kisses the spot under my ear. I get that he's made mistakes and everything, but we've overcome those things.

"Why do you say that?" I ask him softly. He doesn't answer, never moving.

"Are you hungry? Let's go eat somewhere," I decide, pulling away and watching him reach forward for me again, not wanting to let go.

"Everything's okay now," I rub his lower back.

"I forgive you, you're okay," I reassure him.

"It's not okay," I feel him shake his head.

"Grey, you're making me jealous, hugging on her," Oaklee nudges

Grey.

"Don't touch me," he replies grumbly.

"Let's go eat," I pull away from him slightly, he gives me a slight nod and we proceed to the door. We walk out and just as raindrops hit my head, Grey drapes his arm over my shoulders and shields the sideways falling raindrops from me, pulling my head under his chin.

"Aw, Sugar," I place my hand on his back, "so sweet."

He opens the door for me like the gentleman he always is, and I give him a little nudge for him to open Abby's door too. He does as he was told.

"Where would you like to eat Abby?" I question her, pulling down the mirror in front of me to check if my hairdo got messed up due to Grey's monstrous arm throwing itself onto me. Multiple times. And since it's raining, I wouldn't want to look like a wet dog.

"It doesn't matter to me-"

"Don't make me come back there and beat it out of you," I warn. Just say a restaurant, it's not that hard. I'll eat anything. Grey will too. He picks off my plate anyway. Hooker.

"It really doesn't matter," she chuckles.

"Where do you want to eat Azalea?" she questions.

"I don't know," I'm a slight hypocrite.

"Grey?" she wonders. He looks over at me like I'll give him an answer. I shrug. He shrugs back. I scrunch my nose at him. He scrunches his nose at me. He picks up my hand from the center console and he interlaces our fingers, bringing my hand up to his lips. My heart does a jumping jack.

"Let's go to Texas Roadhouse!" I spot one, "Make a U-ey Grey!"

We arrive, and I nearly fall out of the car. Of course, I do. The rain has eased up and we walk right in.

"How many?" A waitress asks.

"Three," I smile brightly. She picks up three menus and tells us to follow. She leads us to a table and Grey makes me sit on the inside because he has this weird thing about always having to be on the outside. I don't know what it's about, but I don't mind.

"Your waitress will be right with you," she smiles before walking off.

"I should tell them it's my birthday. They let you ride a saddle I'm pretty sure," I look around for any sign of a random saddle.

"Ride me inste-" he paused midway through the sentence, flitting his eyes over to Abby. Ride *him?*

"Never mind," he mumbles.

"Extremely inappropriate Grey Alexander," I smile smugly, using his lovely middle name. Our waitress arrives at our table and Grey scoots his chair closer to me as she stands close to our table.

~~~

I walk out of that place with a humongous food baby. Tubs is really here.

"So, there's this party tonight," Abby starts, "you should come with me."

We get in the car and Grey drives us back to his restaurant where Abby's car is. I get out with her to say goodbye.

"What kind of party is it?" I question. Like a birthday party? I wouldn't want to go to someone's birthday party when they have no idea who I am.

"No, it's just a regular college party," she shrugs, "it's actually at a house near SHU's main campus."

I've heard of SHU before. Southern Heilsburg University, the closest four-year college around. It's not a very big school though. And when I was looking to go to college, Jake made sure I didn't look at that one too hard, I'm not sure why.

"Are you doing anything tonight?" She questions.

"No," I shake my head. So, we're talking about an actual party.

"You should come, it'll be really fun," she smiles, "do you want to?"

After hearing her talk about it and how fun she says it'll be, I agree to go with her. Once I'm there, the party will actually start anyway.

"Good! I'm so excited. Me and my friend Bekah will come pick you up around eight tonight," I give her Grey's address and everything and she gives me a tight, happy hug before getting into her car.

"What took so long?" Grey holds his arm open for me to walk into and I do so as soon as I walk in the restaurant.

"Abby invited me to a party," I smile, content. I breathe in and get a whiff of his scent, which just butters my biscuit nicely.

"Oh really?" he hums, lifting me up onto his lap as he sits sturdy on a barstool.

"I'm going to hurt your legs," I warn. If it's not the bones in my butt, then it's my weight.

"Hush Lilah," he places a kiss on my neck.

"I'm telling the truth. Especially since I just ate a lot," I lift my shirt a bit, "see, look, there's Tubs."

He places his hand on my stomach and feels its tenseness from all that food.

"Hungry still?" he questions softly.

"Are you even feeling it? It's so tense, it's not even funny," I assure him. I stick my hand up under his shirt, feeling his stomach. Goodness, it feels so nice.

"You're hungry?" I mock him, making my voice deeper and slower just like his. It's weird but I love the way he talks. It makes me happy. Even though his voice hardly ever sounds like anything close to being happy, hearing his voice just makes me smile. His deep tone, his slowed words, and his soft drawl, I can't help but love the way they work together to create the most velvety voice in the world.

I could listen to him talk all day long. But he would never talk that much. Maybe that's why I love his voice so much, or at least a reason. It's because he only speaks when it's needed. His eyes tell most of what he's feeling. At first, I thought he had no emotion whatsoever. Now I know he's full of them. I look up at his eyes. They rest softly looking at me, his eyebrows not a bit furrowed and his lips set relaxed, only turned up at the corners the tiniest bit. He's content and he's happy. I'm sure I'm completely readable by even a stranger.

"You know we're completely different?" he says suddenly, the happiness off his face. It's replaced with a look that takes on a certain unhappy gleam. A slightly mad one but also a slight upset or sad one.

"Of course, I know that. You know how boring we would be if I was the same as you?" he narrows his eyes playfully and I laugh.

"I'm kidding. But being as different as we are just makes every day more interesting," I tell him honestly.

"And I couldn't imagine myself being quiet and calm. I just can't," I hold onto my heart just thinking about it.

"I can't imagine being wilder than shit," he grumbles, and I smile, picturing him with the same energy as me.

"So that party huh?" he changes the subject.

"I kind of want to go. Y'know experience and everything," I shrug, "want to come with me?"

"I have to work tonight," he tucks my hair behind my ear, "and I'm not a partier Lilah."

"Well, me either," I straighten his silver chain.

"But in metaphorical terms, I *am* the party."

"Obviously," he rolls his eyes like it's the most obvious thing in the world. Which it is.

"I'm a little nervous," I admit.

"You know what not to do," he places two kisses on my cheek. My eyes widen a teeny bit. What do I not do? Was there some sort of rulebook I'm missing out on?

"Let's go home," he stands with me in his arms and sets me on my feet.

~~~

Grey lies on the bed, his shirt off, looking all wonderful and stuff, watching me walk around the room like a chicken with my head cut off.

"What do you wear to these things? Not like fancy dresses, I know that but...do you wear like club attire," not like I've ever been to one but whatever, "or like a nicer dress?"

I look over at him. He sits there, his eyebrows furrowed slightly in confusion with his tattooed hand slightly down the front of his pants. Why in the world? I text Abby because obviously this man has no idea what's going on. I love him to death.

"Why is your hand there?" I point to his hand.

"Because," he answers simply.

"So, name off these things that I should know not to do," I suggest and his eyebrows furrow a lot further than before.

"Are you saying you don't know what not to do?" he questions. I smile.

"I've never been to a party before, no one's told me the rules," I shrug. There can't be that many. Were my parents supposed to tell me these things? Grey sits up, his eyes flash more in a small fit of what I would call his version of slightly panicking.

"Are you fucking me, Azalea?" He questions. I smirk a little and shake my head at myself. This is serious.

"I'm not freaking you, Grey," I nod seriously. His jaw tenses harshly and he stands up. He grabs me by the waist and throws me onto the bed, standing in front of me.

"Stop smiling, this is serious," he points at me, and I stop smiling, not even realizing I was doing it in the first place.

"You shouldn't go," he shakes his head.

"But I want to."

"It's not safe for you anymore. I don't feel good about it," he tells me honestly.

"Then tell me the rules," I suggest, and he breathes out harshly.

"Don't wander off anywhere by yourself," he starts, "just because you see someone who looks nice, doesn't mean they actually are."

"Okay," I nod.

"Don't fucking compliment people. Just don't. Maybe you can to girls because I don't know they're weird drunks, but random people don't."

My eyes widen at that.

"And do *not*," he stresses, "compliment-, look at me Azalea," he

350

grips onto my chin, making sure I'm paying close attention to him.

"Do *not* compliment *any* guys in *any* way. Better yet, don't look at them. They're frat guys. They fuck any girl who looks at them."

"Frat guys?" This is going to be a frat party?

"It's at SHU, Lilah. That's the biggest party school in Tennessee," he stresses. Oh shoot.

"Okay, got it. Don't look at the guys because they're way too hornish," I give him a thumbs up and he looks down at me for a second before bending fast and kissing me, then returning to his teaching mode.

"Don't take drinks from anybody. Don't sit your drinks down anywhere. Keep it to yourself, never take your eyes off your drink," he says.

"Why?" I feel stupid.

"They'll drug you quicker than you can blink," he grumbles, and I wince.

"If you see food; do not eat it."

"What if it just smells really good? And I get hungry?" I question.

"What did I just say?" he gives me a look like 'don't be stupid.'

"Don't eat it. I won't eat it, I promise."

"If you see someone sitting by themselves, do not go and talk to them," he knows me a little bit too well, "leave them the fuck alone."

"Don't even go to the bathroom. Just don't. Don't go upstairs into random rooms, I don't care who you're with. Unless you want to see shit, don't go upstairs in those houses."

"What crap? I ask.

"People full-on fucking. Threesomes. Foursomes. Orgies. God knows what you would see up there, just don't go up there, okay?"

"Okay," I nod, and his lips curve up at the corners, his eyes softening.

"You're so beautiful," my heart melts.

"Thank you," I smile softly.

"If someone tells you that, they're trying to get in your pants," he deadpans and my mouth drops open.

"Are you trying to get in my pants?" I question.

"I'm allowed to do that. Anyone else isn't."

"Oaklee has told me I'm beautiful," I tell him.

"Who's Oaklee?"

"Sanfred," I roll my eyes.

"Sanfred likes to fuck with me and piss me off," he answers.

"These are a lot of rules," I grow worried. What if I accidentally forget the 'don't go to the bathroom' rule?

"Just stay with Abby, Lilah," he sits down next to me.

"And if she leaves you alone- I swear to God, you better beat her ass Azalea."

"I-okay," I decide as an answer.

"Are you sure you want to go?" he mumbles. I nod with a smile and my phone dings with a text from Abby. *'A cute little dress is perfect'* her message reads.

I walk to the closet and pull out a blush dress with an open back and strappy straps. I slide it on and look at myself in the mirror. It swoops down in more of a v-shaped neckline. It doesn't show off much of my boobies. It's more than I would typically wear out, so I think it's a good fit. I walk out of the closet and stand in front of Grey. He puts his phone down and sits up.

"Mm," he hums, looking up at me. He grips onto my hips and pulls me down to him. I sit on his thigh, and he never strays his eyes from me. He stands me up and turns me around.

"Bend over," he orders.

"For what?"

"Bend over," he says again. I bend over like I'm picking something up off the ground and then stand back up.

"Don't bend over in this dress," he tells me, throwing his arms around my waist and pulling me back onto his lap. His lips find the base of my neck and I lean my head back against his shoulder. On the other side of the bed, Bear rolls onto his back in his sleep; sleeping through this whole thing.

"Will you be back by the time I get back?" I swallow thickly.

"Mhm," he hums against the skin on my neck. He grips my chin and turns my head around to him. He places his lips on mine somewhat urgently as his left-hand trails up my neck before resting it right under my jaw.

"I'll be here to get this dress off you," he mumbles against my lips.

"Aw, that's sweet Sugar. I did have some trouble getting it over my head when I was putting it on," I place my hand on his cheek, kissing him softly. He barely moves his lips against mine.

"What?" I pull away, tilting my head. He looks at me like 'are you kidding?'

"Nothing," he shakes his head, "I love you."

Chapter Thirty Two

Apples

❀ Azalea ❀

I watch as Grey sends Abby certain looks. Not necessarily nice ones. More like little glares.

"Grey," I warn him. He crosses his arms over his chest. He grumbles under his breath and picks up his boots, walking over to the couch. He was supposed to leave before Abby came to pick me up, but he told Jai that whatever they're doing can wait a little while longer. I'm not sure if that is a good thing. Someone could be on the verge of death and he's just like 'that fella can wait'.

"Where's your friend that you said was coming?" I question her.

"She's waiting in the car. She didn't feel like coming in. I have to warn you, she's not in the best of moods. Her boyfriend just broke up with her," she winces, and I grip my heart. That makes my heart hurt for her.

"I like your dress," I look at her dark red dress. It's more revealing than anything I thought she would ever wear. The neckline swoops low and it is risen up to her upper thighs. I begin feeling slightly self-conscious looking down at my dress. It's not nearly as short as hers in the neckline or in full-length. Abby has really nice, tan, long legs too. *And* she's wearing high heels? I don't even own a pair of high heels.

"Stop it, Azalea Delilah," Grey's dark voice interrupts my train of thought. I look over at him to see his face set in a stern and serious look.

"You don't even know what I was thinking," I try, and he stands up, moseying over to me, his harshly set eyes never leaving mine.

"The fuck I don't. Now quit," he softens the closer he gets to me. I don't doubt the fact that he knows exactly what I'm thinking.

Bear rubs up against my legs, steering clear of Abby just like we told him too. He's such a good boy. Abby's allergic and I don't think I've ever felt so bad for someone. I couldn't imagine being allergic to Bear. Jake was allergic to dogs too, that's why we never had one. My father too. And what dad said, went. He controlled the house and made us all follow what he said.

"Can I use y'all's bathroom really quick before we go?" she questions, and I turn my attention back to her.

"Of course! Down the hall and it's the first door on the right," I point, and she nods, following my directions. I look over to Grey.

"But she's wearing, like, show-ey stuff. Look at me, Grey," I hold my arms out and his eyes trail down my body.

"I'm looking. You look perfect."

"But nothing like her. And if that's what *she's* wearing then I can't imagine what other people are wearing. I'm going to look like a saint," I look down at the neckline of my shirt.

"And you are, don't fuckin' forget it Lilah. A child of God," he throws an arm around my neck and pulls my face into his chest. I groan. I think about biting him, but I don't.

"You're cute," he tells me. So is he.

"That's the problem," I scrunch my nose.

"Shut up. I'm not done," he says.

"You're cute. You're beautiful, gorgeous, everything great," he leans down closer to me.

"And you're sexy," he throws out the word 'sexy' lazily, lowly, and all with a beautiful smirk on his face.

"That's funny," I snort.

"You make me hard."

"Excuse me, sir."

"Who cares what other people think?"

"I don't know."

"You know when we first met?" he questions and I nod, a small smile threatening to break out on my lips.

"When I fell over your foot," I giggle.

"I tripped you," he says and I stop laughing.

"Why in the world? I could have died!" I gasp.

"Dramatic ass," he grumbles.

"Why'd you trip me?"

"Because I thought you were sexy," he smirks. I furrow my eyebrows thinking back to that day.

"I feel slightly like you're fibbing to me. I was wearing cloth shorts, a sweatshirt, and-"

"Flip flops," he finishes, "I know."

"So uh, you're into the homeless-looking type, huh?"

"Kiss my ass," he chuckles, kissing my forehead, "you didn't look homeless."

"You know I had no idea what you looked like? I couldn't see your face or anything," I tell him.

"I could see you. There was a sliver of light that was shining right over you. Damn I wanted to fuck your brains out," he draws out and my eyebrows raise.

"Then you opened your mouth," he says, and I narrow my eyes at him.

"But now I love you, so it's worked out," he shrugs, "and I still want to fuck your brains out."

He leans down and places his lips on mine, his hands trailing down to my gluteus maximus. I pat both his cheeks, smiling into the kiss. He sticks his hand up under the back of my dress and he fiddles with the top of my underwear. Just as I'm about to pull away to tell him that he better quit, he grips it firmly and he pulls it up. A freaking Texas Wedgie. I shoot away from him, gasping.

"Grey!" I shout. Bear jumps up excitedly feeding off our high energy.

"C'mere," he chuckles.

"Uh uh," I shake my head, "you're not touching me. And forget helping me take my dress off after I get home!"

"Abby's going to think we're horny motherfuckers."

"What does that have to do with anything?!"

"Jesus help us," he shakes his, pinching the bridge of his nose and I fix my underwear. I walk to our room really quickly and put on a pair of spandexes under the dress, figuring it'd be a good idea. Who knows, maybe I'll need to attempt a cartwheel and I don't want my dress to fly up to reveal my underwear.

"-don't leave her alone. She'll die." I catch the last part of what Grey is saying to Abby as I walk back into the room.

"I will most certainly not die. Who's the dramatic one now?" I place my hands on my hips.

"I just can't be there for you if something does happen Lilah," he says, "I'll be three hours away tonight."

That makes my heart sink a bit. What if I do need him?

"Abby, you best stay with me."

"I will, I promise," she laughs, "We should get going."

"Be good Bear. Don't poop anywhere please and thank you," I bend down kissing the top of his head. Grey keeps his hand on the back of my dress, holding it down so it doesn't rise up when I bend over. Even though I put those spandexes on. When I stand back up, he lets go, patting Bear's head a few times before grabbing his keys off the table and handing me mine. He turns the lights off except for one. He used to turn them all off, but I convinced him that Bear shouldn't be in the dark. What if he's scared of the dark? So now he leaves one on for him. We walk out into the chilly night air, and I wrap my arms around myself.

Grey grips onto me and pulls me to his Jeep. He opens the door and hands me the jacket he keeps in it.

"Look at you being all sweet, Sugar," I smile up at him. He rolls his eyes, pulling his jacket closed, keeping me warm.

"I don't like this at all," he tells me seriously. I know he doesn't.

"But I'm not about to tell you that you're not allowed to go. You've had enough controlling motherfuckers in your life. I just want you safe," he tilts my chin up to him. *I love him.*

"When you get back, we can order food," he places his hand on my stomach, "you're hungry now but what was the rule I told you?"

"First of all, I'm not even hungry right now, and second, the rule was don't eat anything at that party, no matter how good it looks or smells."

"Good. Be careful for the love of God. And you're coming home straight after, right?"

"Lord willing and the creek don't rise," I nod.

"I'll be waiting for you. Text me every ten minutes, I'm not fuckin' playing, you better blow up my phone. I love you," he bends, kissing me.

"I love you too. And you better be careful too. Watch for those headbutts," I smack his booty, turning to leave. He grips my wrist and pulls me back to him, kissing me once more.

"I love your *sexy, godly* little self. Don't forget that's what you are," he smacks his hand down on my butt.

"You're such a male stripper. Where am I going with this? You're going to make me some good money someday," I slap his butt too.

"Okay, I feel like you're trying to get me to keep talking, I'm going now you sneaky," I walk to where Abby is waiting for me.

~~~

"Bekah," Abby starts as I get in the car, "this is my friend, Azalea."

"Hi Azalea," Bekah says monotonously. I can't blame the poor girl, her boyfriend just broke up with her.

"Hi Bekah," I smile even though she can't see me. We set out on the hour-long car ride. Bekah mostly just turns up the radio, not making room for much conversation. I'd hate to be ridiculous, and I know that it's Abby's car but their taste in music is nowhere near similar to mine. I don't think I know a single word to any of their Ariana Grande songs. But I don't complain. But when I get home though, I'm busting Grey's eardrums with Cherry Pie. And Def Leppard.

We finally pull up to a huge house. My heart falls to my stomach and my hands turn clammy upon seeing all the people here. Hundreds. People out in the large yard, people on the wrap around porch, there are people everywhere. I'm starting to regret this just a bit. The girls get out of the car, and I follow slowly, swallowing nervously.

"You look like you've seen a ghost," Abby chuckles, coming up beside me.

"I'm just a little nervous," I admit, laughing sheepishly.

"Nice dress," Bekah flits her eyes over to me, her tone less than sincere. I look down at my feet.

"Bekah? What's wrong with you?" Abby scoffs, "just because you're dealing with your own shit doesn't mean you can take it out on her."

Bekah ignores the comment said by Abby and takes out a small-sized bottle of Fireball, chugging it. I send a text to Grey. *'I didn't make it to the party. We're currently being held hostage at a gas station-whoop never mind I've just been killed.*' Hardly any time passes before he responds. *'RIP'*

Abby leads us to the front door, and I admire the confidence she has. We walk past two guys who act as guards to the sides of the front door. I keep my eyes downcast. Music blasts through speakers throughout the house playing all the types of music I hate. Bekah walks off and Abby shrugs it off, rolling her eyes at her friend. They don't really seem like friends. Or good ones at least. Abby grips onto my hand and pulls me past a hall filled with couples. My eyes nearly bulge when I see one girl's hand down a guy's pants, tickling his pickle fully in front of everyone, with not a care in the world.

We make it to the kitchen and Grey's rules flood my train of thought. I decide not to take any sort of chances, even when Abby offers me an unopened water bottle. She mixes herself a drink with all the different types

Lilah

of alcohol that sit on the counters. Seeing the Jack Daniels sends flashes of bad memories into my brain, but I push them to the side, forgetting about them. I almost choke on air when I feel someone grip my hips and rub up against me as they pass behind me to get to the kitchen counter beside me. *Um...Grey never told me how to react to that.*

  Abby looks at the guy from the corner of her eye, a bit unhappily. He turns to me suddenly and smiles, flashing his pearly whites. He's actually very cute and his skin is clearer than anyone I think I've ever seen. *Don't compliment him. Don't compliment him. Don't.*

  "You shouldn't be hiding those hips under that dress," he bites down on the corner of his bottom lip. My eyebrows furrow down. I look down at the light blue polo shirt that covers his upper half. Grey doesn't like the guys who wear those.

  "Okaight," I stammer. I furrow my eyebrows in confusion. What did I just say? Abby grips onto my hand once more and she tries to conceal her laughter at the word I just spoke. We walk past a table and what I see makes my heart fall to the floor. I really shouldn't be here. I know I constantly talk about drugs but actually seeing someone snort white powder just shocks me to the core. Oh, dear Jesus take me out of this place. Places like these are no way my forte. Sleep is more like my forte. I don't think I like college parties very much. I think I want to go home and watch Hercules the children's movie again.

  "This party is bigger than any other one I've ever been to," Abby shouts over the music, her eyes narrowing in worry. We pass by a beer pong table and suddenly my arm is gripped by someone who is not Abby. I almost poop myself in fear until I'm met with familiar blue eyes.

  "Azzy, what the hell are you doing here?" Aaron holds me close to him, speaking to me over the music.

  "Partying like a party animal, what does it look like?" I laugh sheepishly.

  "Aye bro," a random polo-wearing guy from across the beer pong table says, "that your girl? Sweet little thing, huh?"

  Aaron lets a smirk on his lips, and I narrow my eyes at that smirk.

"Where's that little boy of yours?" He asks and I smell some alcohol on his breath.

"He left-" he interrupts me. *He left for work.*

"I was wondering when you were going to come to me telling me he left you," he says and my heart falls, "especially after our conversation."

"What?" I whisper. What is he talking about? Why would Grey leave me? Is he? What conversation?

"I knew you'd never work, what'd I tell you?" he smiles smugly, and I grow angry at him. Why is he acting like this?

"I'm here for you Azzy," he smiles but unlike when he usually smiles, I don't admire his adorable dimples. He raises his hand and places it on my jaw. When he moves his face closer to mine, I pick up a cup from the table and throw the contents onto him, shocking myself. Before seeing his reaction, I grip onto Abby's hand and pull her away from the scene.

"Are you okay? Do you know him?" she asks, worriedly.

"I know him," my voice wiggles so I don't elaborate, just nodding. Why would he ever act like this? What is going on?

"We can leave Azalea; I'm not feeling this party. It's too wild honestly," she notices my upset mood.

"Are you sure you want to leave?" I ask her. I'd hate to ruin her night just because I'm dealing with my own crap.

"Yeah, we can do something else. This dress is uncomfortable too. Bekah kind of made me wear it," she shrugs. I silently thank God that she hasn't left me. I don't know what I would do if she were to leave me alone. I'd probably die, just like Grey said. We stand over by a wall while Abby texts Bekah about wanting to leave.

"Where'd Grey go tonight? He said somewhere three hours away," Abby questions while waiting for Bekah to text back.

"I'm not sure," I answer honestly. He could be anywhere in any direction. All I know is I miss my Sugar. *And we need to talk.* What was Aaron talking about? I need to know. *I'm really missing Grey's hugs right now.*

"She's staying here and catching a ride from someone else," Abby speaks up over the music, her eyes set unhappily. I sneak a small peak at her screen and just barely see the message sent by Bekah.

'You and Miss priss can go ahead. I'm catching a ride from someone else.' it reads. I avert my eyes from the screen and push away the little pang that connects with my heart. Do I really come off as prissy? I don't mean to.

~~~

Having left the party not long after arriving at it, we drive to the nearest movie theater. Obviously after stopping by a Dollar Tree to get candy to sneak into the theater. Following the ending of the movie, we make the hour-long trip back to our small town. Abby drops me off at home and I thank her for inviting me out. I unlock the door, pushing it open and Bear attacks me with love. His butt wiggles excitedly as his tail wags quickly. I fall onto the couch and pull the blanket off the top down onto me. Bear jumps up and lays at my head, occasionally licking and sniffing the top of my head. I take to watching Dumb and Dumber on the tv and I drift off to the view of Harry and Lloyd's snot freezing below their noses.

"Azalea," I wake to Grey's voice.

"Wake your ass up and kiss me," he squeezes my leg and I sit up, a smile on my face. I open my arms up to him and he lowers himself down to me.

"You didn't text me and tell me you were coming home," he grumbles, kissing the side of my neck.

"I'm sorry," I sit up further, and the blanket falls off me. His eyes fall on my dress that I'm *still* wearing.

"Did you leave it on just because I told you I was going to take it off you?" he mumbles against the skin of my neck, his nose tickling me.

"Well," I trail off, "the bedroom is so far and I've had a long, scarring night so I decided it's a win-win."

That sounded more hornish than I intended.

"You want an apple? I want one," I stand up, leaving him behind me.

"We have apples?" he questions. He literally goes grocery shopping with me every week. I can't send him by himself because he'll only come back with every type of meat they have in the store. I can't go by myself, for one, because I get sidetracked easily and I will end up in the toy aisle of Target picking out which JoJo Siwa slime kit I want to buy. Galaxy or neon pink? I don't even know who JoJo Siwa is. Technically, we keep each other in check. That doesn't mean he pays attention all the time though. I swear he stares at and levitates toward the meat sections. Jerky: he's grabbing at every time we pass. And we pass the jerky section at least three times a grocery trip.

"Sure," he shrugs. He looks confused for some reason.

"What kind?" I open the fridge and take out the bag. He looks over at me, pausing as he unties his boots.

"Um."

"Red, Granny Smith, or Pink Lady?"

"Um," he draws out like there's no difference between the flavors of each apple type.

"Sugar, do you want a sweet one, a sour one, or a little sweet and a little sour?" I tilt my head. Is he okay? He's quiet. I pick up all three and walk to him. He looks up at me from his sitting position.

"Pink Lady is sweet and a little sour," I hold it up, "Granny Smith is sour. Red is very sweet."

He looks between all three. Then he fiddles with the scrunchie on his wrist. I sit the apples down on the coffee table. I place my hand on his forehead.

"Are you okay, Sugar?" I feel his temperature. He leans into me.

"It's only apples," I whisper. His hand trails around me. He snatches the bottom of my dress in a flash and lifts it off me. A small pack of Sour Patch Kids fall to the floor with my dress. What the heck? I was looking for those. He pulls away and looks at me, his lips turned up in amusement. I look down at myself. Then at the Sour Patch Kids on the floor.

"Now look," I point to my stomach, "my belly has goosebumps because of you."

He pulls me closer to him and trails his lips along my stomach.

"Now I have even more goosebumps," I wiggle a little at the tickly feeling of his soft lips. He pulls me onto his lap and looks at me. I lean down and pick up the Sour Patch Kids. I begin taking them out the package and he gives me a look.

"What?" I mumble.

"Can't you eat those later?"

"...I guess," I draw out, placing the package on the coffee table. His dark eyelashes cast a shadow over his cheeks, and I feel my heart growing just by looking at him.

"I'm almost buck naked," I mumble out, casually placing my arms around his neck. I look down at his full lips. He stands suddenly, lifting me with him. I cling onto him, and Bear starts to follow us until Grey tells him to stay. He walks into our bedroom, shutting the door behind us with his foot. He throws me onto the bed and takes his shirt off. I bite my lip to hold my smile back as he tosses his shirt near the clothes hamper. Every time he takes his shirt off, I get all giddy inside. He climbs on top of me and bites my lip once I release it. He pulls at it and releases a second later. He lifts me back onto his lap and connects our lips.

"Fuck," he quietly groans when I move my hips down into his. Jesus, forgive me, I love you.

I reach down and touch him. He breathes in a deep breath as I look slightly up at him. He licks his lips, looking at me with lustful, hooded eyes. I grip onto his belt and take it off. He takes his pants off and I'm met with those large, toned thighs of his. Stripper. The perfect stripper.

"I'm a little nervous," I admit to him quietly and he kisses me once harshly. He tucks my hair behind my ear before leaning down and kissing me softly.

He takes his time preparing me for what's about to happen. His tongue works wonders while his fingers feel heavenly. He's sweet with me yet dominating in the way he stares at me as I can barely handle the incredible feeling. He does this until he believes I'm ready for him.

I look up at him almost nervously.

"You're hesitant," he says confidently just as he says 'you're hungry'. I know it's going to hurt. After all, I did take health in high school and even middle school. But how bad? I have no idea. He leans down and kisses me. I shiver as his chain falls across my neck. Why's that thing always too cold? A thought causes me to gasp.

"We're about to have sex!" I gasp. He shakes his head against my shoulder, and I smile. He sits up with a small square package in his large hands.

"Where on earth did you get that?"

"It's obvious we would do this at some point, Lilah," he rolls his eyes. He carefully unwraps it in his hands and he slides his black briefs off. He lowers himself onto me, his teeth biting down on the corner of his bottom lip. I breathe out softly, preparing myself. He reaches up and tilts my chin up until I'm looking at him.

"I love you," he tells me softly, pecking my lips gently.

"I love *you,*" I reply.

"You're sure you want me to go on?" he asks. I nod. We need to do this. Well, I need to do this. I want all of him. His peter included. Oh yeah.

He gently moves his hips forward and I'm met with a chainsaw in my lady region for a few seconds. I gasp deeply and slam my head back onto the bed. I clench his shoulder harshly and tell myself not to cry. My crying will make us not hornish because I'm not a cute crier.

"I'm sorry," his voice comes out strained, *"fuck.* I'm sorry."

We both remain still while I adjust to him. He places soft pecks on the side of my neck and my cheek, my face cheek. The pain fades to a dull ache and I reopen my eyes, looking up at him. He hovers over top of me, his jaw tensed and his eyes half-closed. He looks like he feels good. I don't really feel good.

"You look like you feel good," I whisper up painfully. He opens his eyes all the way and lowers his head to mine.

"You feel so *fucking* good," he buries his face in my neck, a small moan leaving his lips. A moan? Good Lord. We're going to do this more often just so I can hear that sound leave his lips again.

"You can move a little bit," I tell him, and I suck in a deep breath when he does. He leans up slightly and grabs the sides of my legs. He lifts my legs up around his waist and slowly drives his hips forward. The aching intensifies for a while before simmering down. He leans his head down into me kissing me and whispering sweet nothings in my ear.

He intertwines our fingers on one hand and he guides my arm around his shoulders with the other. At one point I get this feeling of pleasure that sends a gasp rolling out of my mouth. He pulls away, looking at me and sees the pleasure on my face. The ache may still be there but there's a pleasure too that's making its way through.

"Fuck you're so beautiful," he leans back down, capturing my lips with his, "all mine."

I hold onto him for dear life when a familiar feeling breaks out in my goody region. He's made me feel that feeling many times. This one feels amplified a bit and I swear I cannot keep my toes from curling.

Catching my breath, he pulls away. I open my eyes to see what's going on. As soon as they're open, he's yanking my body up. He flips me over suddenly and an excited smile reaches my lips. He grips my hips up to him and pushes my head down onto the pillow. Holy guacamole. He starts again and the feeling in the bottom of my stomach is too good. I find myself in the middle of the blissful feeling again. Hardly any time after I've come down from the feeling Grey is clenching onto me harder and tensing his jaw twice as much.

"Fuck Azalea," he groans a few seconds before pulling me close and letting go. He sits me back up.

"I love you."

"I love *you,*" I kiss him back. I wait a few seconds.

"We did the dirty," I whisper. I pick up those Sour Patch Kids and I open them, placing a few into my mouth. He leans up further on his elbows above me, looking at me confusedly.

"Where'd those come from?" He questions. I pause and think about it. I'm not positive but I think I picked them up again just before we came in here.

"I picked them up, you said I should eat them later," I drawl out. I place a red one in my mouth.

"Want one, sugar?" I hold out a blue one for him. He looks at me for a second. Then he leans down, and I place it in his mouth. I hum the words to *Cherry Pie,* and he leans down chuckling into my neck.

Chapter Thirty Three

Weird

❀ Azalea ❀

  I wake up alone. I punch the spot Grey lays, picturing it's his arm. I pick up my phone from the table beside the bed and a message from him shows once I turn it on. *'I had to work early this morning. I'll be at the restaurant by the time you wake up so come see me'* it reads and I bite back a smile. I sit up slowly and fix the large t-shirt that hides the rest of my bare body. I pet Bear who lays at the end of the bed and eventually decide that it's time to get up.

  When I do, my lower region aches. I sigh, laying back down. I try again a couple of minutes later. I walk semi-slowly to the bathroom and do everything I need to do. Shower, sing like the best singer in the world in the shower, brush my teeth, do my hair, and tinkle. I throw on a pair of leggings and a thin pullover over top of my light blue shirt. I cuddle with Bear for a couple of minutes while watching a short documentary on what it will be like when I go to prison. I pick myself up, give Bear a kiss on the head, lock the door on my way out, and head to my car.

  Getting in my car I have to take it a bit slower. My extreme goody region is just really slowing me down today. I go eighty in a twenty-five-speed limit zone and one hundred in a fifty zone on the way to the restaurant. What if I did that? I would never. I don't think my legs would let me do that.

Arriving in town square, I stop by the coffee shop that just so happens to be my favorite and I get Grey and me the same thing. Iced caramel coffee. I know it's his favorite. Every time I get it he ends up taking it. I end up slapping his butt. He ends up slapping mine. It's a repetitive cycle. But this time he's getting his own because I'm drained, and I need a full one for myself.

Is it because of the sexy time we had last night? No. Prison documentaries make me nervous. *And the sexy time had a big part.* I push open the door of the restaurant and I'm greeted by Jai.

"Y'all are closed today?" I ask, looking around the place and noticing that it's empty.

"Yeah, we had a busy morning and just haven't opened back up yet," he nods, "Grey's somewhere in the back."

"Thank you, Jai," I smile, "I would've got you something at the coffee place, but I don't know what you like."

"It's okay," he smiles back, his blue eyes brightening. Such a darling. I bust through the door to the back and see Jonas.

"That for me?" he nods to the coffee.

"You wish buddy," I scrunch my nose at him. He takes a threatening jump at me and I lightly kick his shins.

"Expect the police to be knocking on your door looking for you for committing assault and battery on me just now," he says as he pushes through the door. *Too bad I'm an experienced escape artist.* I take a long sip of the drink in my hand. Maxon walks out of the bathroom.

"Hey big booty Judy," I acknowledge him, and he sticks his booty out a little bit, giving me a wink. I open the door to Grey's office and he's not in there.

"Aren't you not allowed back here?" I pass by Jaqueline. She and I have literally seen each other back here on quite a few occasions. There's no need to be rude just because I get to slap Grey's butt and she doesn't. I ignore her and come to the door at the end of the hall. The meeting room or whatever it is, I don't even know. I bust that joint open and walk in there.

"You shot a tree," I hear Grey's grumbly voice and I see him, Theo, and Linc all sitting at a table together.

"Yeah, okay, well it's not like it was on purpose," Theo mumbles.

"That's the fucking problem. How do you miss a target and hit a tree? We weren't even close to a tree," Grey crosses his arms and I bite my lip to conceal a laugh. He's all business right now. *Such a cutie.* I sneak up behind him and the two in front of him see me. Theo smiles and Lincoln gives me a look that says, 'scare him.' I don't think they understand how many times I've tried to scare that man. A few times after he gets out of the shower, I've tried to scare him as he comes out of the bathroom. He doesn't flinch and he picks me up and tosses me onto the bed like 'aw, cute. Nice try.' He cannot be scared. He's superhuman. He's got superhuman hearing too. I'm pretty sure he already knows I'm here anyway.

"You know what? I think Lincoln nudged me and my aim just when," he raises his hand in a demonstration, showing how his aim went way high.

"I was beside Grey, nice try," Lincoln gives him a pointed look. I walk right up behind Grey, and he leans back in his chair, obviously knowing I'm here. I bend down and press my lips to his cheek, face not booty. He turns his head and kisses me on the lips.

"Kiss me Lincoln," Theo leans toward him.

"Piss off."

I hand him the coffee and when he raises his hand and places it on my gluteus maximus, I open my mouth up.

"Oh baby," I hear Oaklee's voice as he comes through the door, "can someone come and hold onto my ass?"

"What ass?" Lincoln questions.

"Wow, okay," Oaklee scoffs in a reply. I grip onto Grey's hand and move it up to my back.

"We need to have a discussion about the poor tree-"

"We already had one," Theo groans.

"Well, it's fuckin' funny so we're about to have it again," Lincoln smirks.

"Aw, look. You have a caramel frappe Greyson," Oaklee places his hand on Grey's shoulder, giving it a little squeeze before releasing him. I smile at the disregard coming from Oaklee at how much Grey hates to be touched. And I'm sure he really doesn't appreciate being called 'Greyson'.

"Touch me again," Grey stands, taking a hold of my hand, "touch me *again*. And call me Greyson."

Oaklee backs down a bit. But I can tell he wants to touch him again just because he's insinuating that he better not or he's going to get kicked in the head. All I see is cuteness. The way his eyes narrow in the slightest bit and how his nose scrunches up only a little. *Ugh, I love this fella.*

"Pick up your caramel frappuccino cappuccino latte and follow your woman out of here," Oaklee says, possibly the most confusing sentence I've ever heard.

"Yeah, I fuckin' will," Grey picks up his drink, "jealous motherfucker."

He grips onto my hand with his empty one and turns back around right as we're about to exit.

"At least I'm not chasing after Lincoln's mom," Grey slams the door behind us and suddenly there's shouting on the other side.

"Is he actually?" I gasp.

"No. But I know Lincoln will knock him out," he pulls me into his office and shuts the door behind us. I take a seat in his nice spinney chair, and he leans against the desk in front of me.

"I have quite a few things on the itinerary that need to be spoken about," I fold my hands together.

"Oh really?" he questions lowly.

"Number one: what on earth did you do to me?" I place my hand on my lower stomach and watch as his lips turn up.

"You know what I did to you," he runs his tongue along the corner of his mouth.

"I'm sore."

"I'm sorry," he bends down, placing a soft kiss on my temple.

"You should be sore too," I tell him.

"I'm not sure what you want me to do."

"Let me punch you," I stand up and he slightly narrows his eyes.

"Punch me where?" he questions.

"I'm not going to punch you in your goody! Who do you think I am? Put your arm out and let me have at it," I grip onto his arm and stretch it out. I punch him. He chuckles and pulls me into him. Are you freaking *kidding* me? He could've at least acted like it hurt him or something I mean, good Lord. Now for the bad news. I know I should tell him this but, I don't know what his reaction will be. *Aaron tried to kiss me.* Was it only because he was drunk? I don't know. But I feel like it's something that he should probably know. And I would like to know what Aaron was talking about when he said he and Grey had talked.

"Let's have a seat," I point to his chair, and he sits. I take a seat on his desk so that he won't flip it if he gets mad enough.

"First off, I saw someone doing hard drugs and I'm a little shaken up," I lay the first thing on him.

"What is it that you really want to tell me?" he tilts his head, "I can tell that's not it."

"You're right. There's an elephant in the room. An elephant besides me. So, there are two elephants in the room."

"Shut up."

"You know what? I can't tell you if you don't have a smile on your face, I really can't," I smile at his emotionless face. I wait for him to smile. I wait a little longer. I climb off his desk and onto his lap. He wraps his arms around me, and I look directly at him.

"Smile."

"Grey, smile."

"You better smile."

"You're a sweetheart."

"Smile before I *make* you."

"I love you so that means smile."

I grip his jaw and kiss him all over his face. His cheeks, his chin, his temple, his forehead, his jaw, his cheekbones, his nose, and his lips until he's smiling and holding onto me tighter than before.

"Okay yeah so here's the deal. At the party last night, I saw Aaron and we talked for a second and then, you're just going to love this part, he like, well he tried kissing me," I just say it flat out and lean back to see his reaction. His face becomes void of any recognizable emotion, and he leans fully back in his chair. He runs his hand down his jaw.

"...What're you thinking?" I question him softly.

"Where's he at right now?" he asks calmly. Does this mean he's not that mad?

"I'm not sure," I tell him honestly and he nods.

"Tell him to come here," he advises me and my eyebrows slightly.

"Why?"

"I just want to talk to him," he shrugs, and I nod slowly, picking up my phone and sending Aaron a test. He calls me instead of answering the text.

"Azzy-" he starts off the call desperately.

"Oh, dear Jesus," I mumble.

"I'm *so* sorry beautiful," he apologizes, and I look at Grey.

"I don't think it's a good idea to call me that anymor-"

"I'll be there in five minutes, I'm sorry," he hangs up and I feel my heart beating out of my chest nervously.

"I think I'm going to have a heart attack," I grip onto my heart and Grey furrows his eyebrows.

"He's not been a good guy Azalea," he tells me seriously and my palms get sweaty. I think I'm seeing that.

"A while back he came here solely to tell me that I'm no good for you and that he was better," he tells me, and I close my eyes.

"Better for me than you? What, he wants me like you have me?" I let my eyes widen a bit. Grey nods.

"And I believed him, and I shouldn't have," he adds.

"That was the day we broke up, wasn't it?" I question quietly and he nods. I lean forward and kiss his lips gently. I wrap my arms around him, and he lays his head in my neck.

"Love you," I smile, giving his cheek and nice ole smooch.
"Who loves me?" he tilts his head.
"I love you."
We stay silent for a moment. Then I open my big mouth.
"Your initials spell GAK," I chuckle. It's funny because the Nickelodeon slime they sell is called Gak. I think one time I bought it. Why did I used to like slime so much? It wasn't even that long ago that I liked it.
"Thank you for telling me," he grips onto my hand and brings it up to his lips. I spot his new computer that sits on his desk. After Aaron leaves, I'm fixing to ruin this new one too with my illegal movie sites.
"Some dude is out front asking for Azalea," Jai pokes his head in and my heart drops to my toes. Grey just wants to talk; everything should be fine. Jai, Oaklee, and Lincoln follow us. Nosy heifers. Walking to the main section of the restaurant, I see Aaron. He looks nervous. Grey lets go of my hand, his demeanor never changing from calm.
"What's going on?" Oaklee asks me as I stop, and Grey continues to walk toward Aaron. I don't think I want to be a part of the conversation if I'm being honest.
"Aaron tried to kiss these amazing lips," I tell him, and his eyes widen.
"Damn," Lincoln winces, standing behind me and twirling my hair. I think he really likes my hair. I watch as Grey gets closer and closer to Aaron who looks to be getting more and more nervous. Grey throws his fist into Aaron's face as soon as he's into reach of him. I gasp in shock. *He said he wanted to talk!*
"Oh shit!" Oaklee calls out, "he rocked his ass!"
The door to the back busts open and more guys file into where we are. None of which make any attempts to get Grey off the smaller, shorter, and skinnier, Aaron. *Shoot, I'm not going near them either.* Two punches in, Grey takes a seat at a random table waiting for Aaron to get back up. He still looks calm.
"You just can't get it through your fucked up head that she's with me and she doesn't want you," Grey's jaw tenses looking down at Aaron who's

struggling to get up.

"It's one thing to talk shit," Grey stands, leaning down to Aaron. He grabs him by the hair on his head, lifting his head up so he's looking directly at him.

"It's another thing when you try to fuck with my girl," Grey releases his hair, and Aaron's head hits the ground kind of hard.

"You don't know shit about her," Aaron sneers and Grey scoffs. Oaklee rolls his eyes beside me.

"That man knows everything about you Azalea. Trust me, I know. You're all he talks about. I know more about you than whoever the guy on the floor is," Oaklee narrows his eyes at Aaron.

"Last night you had to have done something to piss her off because she was at the party all up on me," Aaron claims and my eyes furrow. In the famous words of the man under the initials GAK, ex-freaking-scuse me?

"Good try," Grey grabs him by the shirt and lifts him up. His light blue polo is covered in blood from his nose and mouth and Grey smirks at the polo. He tosses him out the door and closes it, locking it. He really hates those polos.

"Look at you Grey," Oaklee whistles, "mama bear."

"Why're you touching her?" Grey looks at Lincoln and Linc slowly takes his hands off my hair.

"Her hair is like the softest clouds, it's hard to resist," he answers. Grey reaches out for my hand and pulls me back against his chest.

"My mom would never cheat on my dad," Oaklee smiles at the two of us, giving me a wink.

"I brought your coffee, your majesty knight in shining armor," Theo bows slightly, handing Grey his coffee.

"I hate every single one of you," he grumbles, pulling me closer to him.

"He just got got!" I smile up at Grey. He places a gentle kiss on my forehead.

"He got got for trying to kiss those amazing lips," he chuckles.

"Dad laughed."

"Get electrocuted you fuck," Grey mumbles as a response to Oaklee. I follow Grey into his office under the watching eyes of the guys still in the hallway. I close the door gently behind me and he's stopped in the middle of the room, faced away from me. I feel my heart constricting. I don't know what he thinks about this whole thing. Even worse, one of the only people who I trusted and still loved, lied and I don't know *why* he lied.

"Grey, I *promise* you that I never touched his dusty lips, and I was never all up on him," I take a deep breath, controlling myself for the time being.

"He was drunk at that party, and I did see him there and he tried talking to me about you and then he tried to kiss me and I threw a drink over his head. I wouldn't ever do anything like that to yo-"

He turns around and cuts me off. He grips onto my arm and pulls me into his chest.

"I know you didn't do anything, idiot," he leans down, kissing the side of my head. I let out a breath of relief and sink into him.

"I was sitting over there," barbeque sauce on my titties, "having a heart attack when he was talking about me cheating on you."

"You wouldn't cheat on me," he shakes his head.

"Duh."

"Because you love the fuck out of me," he says confidently.

"I do love the freak out of you. Do you love the freak out of me?" I give him a little chest bump that only knocks me back and not him.

"Yeah, I love the fuck outta you," he slaps my butt but not *that* hard, "showed you that last night."

My eyebrows rise. My phone rings.

"Didn't know I was famous," I laugh at myself and answer my phone.

"Guess motherfreaking what?" Abby's voice questions excitedly through the phone. I get excited too, feeding off her excitement.

"What?" I shimmy happily and Grey chuckles gripping onto my hips.

"Roman asked me out on a date!" she squeals, and I gasp excitedly.

"Oh my gosh, I'm so happy for you!" I smile so widely my cheeks hurt.

"It's tomorrow, and he hasn't told me where we're going. I'm nervous. Can I come to your place tomorrow? You can help me get ready," she says and I feel myself rising off my feet and into the air. This is what I've been waiting for. The true girl-friend things.

"Of course!"

"Okay, great. I'll be there around four. I've got to go but I'll see you tomorrow, Azalea!" she bids goodbye, and we hang up. I let out a squeal and throw myself at Grey. He catches me in the air, and I squeeze the life out of him. I think the coffee I have is making me a little wild. Or maybe I'm like this anyway.

"Roman asked Abby out on a date and I cannot contain myself," I kiss his cheek, face not booty, over and over.

"Aw, you're so cute," I tell him, and he pulls away from me.

"Stop it, let me love you," I hug him tighter.

"Cute my ass."

"Yes, your booty is cute," I laugh at him, and he pinches my gluteus maximus.

~~~

Grey, once again, appears unamused.

"Turn that little frown upside down Sugar," I give him a smile of my own. I sort of forgot Abby was coming today and I had told Grey that we had the whole day to ourselves. Now he's pouty. He's frowning and sitting his only-boxer-wearing self on our bed in protest. Abby will be here any second.

"Unless you want Abby to see your goodies, I'd put clothes on," I warn him. He only raises his eyebrow like 'see if I care.' Abby is a wonderful person and I trust her but she's not about to see all his goodies. I walk to the closet and grab him a pair of gray joggers and a shirt. I throw it at his head, and he still doesn't move.

"Grey, I'm going to throw you off a balcony."

377

I slap his thick thigh just because it was looking extra juicy. He grips onto my hand and pulls me onto his lap. The slap backfired. He starts kissing my neck.

"Put clothes on," I mumble. He bites my neck gently but with enough force to make me gasp. I reach behind him and grab the shirt I threw at him. I suddenly lean back and yank it onto his head. *Bam sucker, you can't beat me at this game.* He doesn't take the shirt off, but he does yank mine off.

"Excuse me sir," I sigh. I yank my shirt from his hand and putting it back on, he grasps onto the buttons of my pants.

"Grey Alexander, I swear," I warn and there's a knock on the front door. I roll off him and button my pants back.

"Put your clothes on!" I stomp my foot. He smirks.

"I'm going to open the door. When I see you next, you best have something else on your body," I point my finger at him and go to open the door. Abby and I hug excitedly once I've opened the door and I invite her in. She comes in carrying three bags of makeup and possible clothing that she's going to wear for tonight.

"Is Grey working today?" she questions, noticing how his presence isn't in the same room as me like it usually is.

"No, he's here. He's acting like a donkey at the moment," I roll my eyes, a smile threatening to break out on my face. From the corner of my eye, I see him moping down the hallway.

"Well hello darling, I'm happy you've decided to clothe yourself," I smile at him and Abby giggles. He looks at me slightly scrunching his nose and mimicking my words to himself. Abby and I make our way to me and Grey's room where we sit for a good hour and plan out what she should wear and do with her hair and makeup. Grey called me twice asking when I was going to be done talking about bull-poop and come into the living room to effing "love him."

After Abby puts on her amazingly planned out outfit, I curl her hair for her, and she does her own makeup. I'm not really one to know that much about makeup, not wearing that much myself. My younger self tried the whole makeup thing. All the YouTubers couldn't even help me, so I gave it up.

Especially after one incident where I looked like a clown by accident and scared Jake. *I miss him.* She finishes up and we both stare at her in the mirror.

"I think you look marvelous," I smile.

"And you think it's good for the occasion? Not knowing what it is?" she questions nervously. I look at her black off-the-shoulder shirt and her light jeans. It may not be much but with the shirt tucked the way it is and it being nicely form-fitting, she looks classy and appropriate for any setting. Heck, even a strippery. Or strip club whatever it is.

"I think it's perfect. I have an idea," I shout Grey's name and there's no response. *I'm going to kick him in the throat if he doesn't freaking answer me.* I call him on my phone, and he answers.

"Get your booty cheeks in here," I tell him once he picks up and then I hang up. I hear him mosey down the hallway.

"What?" he grumbles, coming to where we are.

"Look at this outfit. What do you think of it, as a guy, for a date," I draw the scenario and he looks at me like I've just told him to kiss a cactus.

"Don't be weird, it's a question," Abby adds.

"Exactly, don't be weird, it's not weird, answer it," I urge him, and he looks at her outfit then back at me. Yeah, Abby isn't me but it's just an outfit.

"I don't know how you want me to answer the questio-"

"I don't want you to answer it in any certain way, I want you to be honest," I place my hand on his back comfortingly.

"You're asking too much of me-" A crease forms between his eyebrows and I internally awe at him. He's just adorable.

"Okay. Calm down, look at me," I tell him, and he looks down at me, "you're single-"

He cuts me off.

"No, I'm not."

"This is a scenario, it's okay, you're not single really," I pat his booty.

"You're single and you see a girl. You're all like 'holy guacamole she looks like my next lady friend, let me ask her on a date,'" I make my voice deep like a man's.

"I don't think I would be like that at *all*," He dismisses it and I hush him.

"She says yes to the date and y'all set a time but you don't tell her where you're taking her," I explain and I can already see a question forming in his brain.

"Why don't I know where I'm taking her?"

"No, you do know but you didn't tell her," I tell him.

"Where am I taking her?" he asks, and I pinch the bridge of my nose.

"A flippin' meth lab Grey, I don't know."

"I'm confused," a small little smile grows on his lips.

"Y'know what? Does this outfit look good or not?" I point to Abby, and he looks at it.

"Uh-" he trails.

"Okay, that's enough good work, thank you for your help, you did amazing," I grab his hand and pull him out of the bathroom.

"I think I lost brain cells from that," he mumbles.

"That's what crack will do to you, okay? Go back to the living room and I'll be in there in a few minutes."

He leans down, and I give him a soft kiss.

"Try to rest your brain for the rest of the night, I think you worked it too hard back there," I tease.

"Shut up."

Chapter Thirty Four

Baby

* Grey *

I open my eyes groggily and stretch. I wrap my arms around her small waist and connect my hands together underneath her. I squeeze the shit out of her.

"Grey," she groans tiredly, and I chuckle leaning down to kiss her collarbone. I push my weight off her and stand from the bed. Cracking my back and my neck, I mosey into the bathroom. Lilah says I'm not allowed to say 'pee' or 'piss' and that the only acceptable word is 'tinkle.' So, I tinkle. I'm flushing when she waltzes into the room. It amazes me how a minute ago she was asleep and now she's up and looking like she's been up for hours. Bear follows her into the bathroom like she's mother goose. She turns and looks at my bare chest. Then she looks at my boxers.

"Want something this early?" I grab my toothbrush, sending her a single glance.

"Excuse me, that's inappropriate behavior," she points at me, grabbing her toothbrush. I start brushing my teeth as she's just getting hers ready. She wiggles her hips unknowingly and I roll my eyes at her obliviousness to how much of a tease she is. We both finish up and she turns to me. Just by the look on her face, I can tell some crazy shit is about to come out of her mouth.

"What would you do if suddenly, I became nocturnal like an owl?"

I stare down at her. How *the fuck* do I answer questions like these. I know better than to question where she came up with this scenario because there wouldn't be an answer. She's just *her,* she's weird and in her own little world. Her mind is constantly running a thousand miles a minute.

"I'd make sure you got back on track," I say my answer in a slight question form.

"Okay, thank you," she smiles and walks out of the bathroom. I shave the slight scruff on my face and putting the stuff away, I catch sight of her toes just outside the doorway to the left. *She's going to try to scare me. Again.* I wipe my face, turn the light off, and start walking out.

"Boo!" She jumps at me and clings to my side.

"Did I get you?" She questions.

"You got me," I lean down, kissing the top of her head.

"I knew I got you."

She climbs up on the bed and stands in front of me. She walks around on the bed.

"Wrestle me Grey," she says suddenly, and I chuckle. This woman, I swear.

"I'm not going to wrestle you Lilah," I shake my head. She's wild. Absolutely wild.

"Why? You scared?" she teases, popping out her hip, and raising an eyebrow.

"You're going to hurt yourself," I warn her.

"Nope. And I think you need to be worried about me hurting you, old man," she eggs me on.

"Azalea-" she cuts me off.

"You need to remember that I'm CIA trained for this combat right here," she cracks her knuckles. I climb up on the bed with her and stand right in front of her.

"I won't go easy on you," I warn but that's bullshit. Like hell I'd be too rough with her. She weighs nothing for fuck's sake. I weigh twice as much and the top of her head just barely reaches anything past my shoulders.

"Okay good," she rolls her neck, "ready, set, go!"

She charges at me and jumps up on my front. I catch her and we look at each other.

"That was your plan?"

"Nope," she goes completely limp and falls to the bed like a sack of potatoes. She hooks her feet around the backs of my knees and tries all her might to shove me down. I roll my eyes and give in, falling down for her.

"Ha sucker, what are you going to do now?" She sits on my back. I hook my arm around her and roll over, pinning her under me.

"Woah, I blinked, and this happened?" She asks, slightly out of breath.

"Oh, I should headbutt you," she draws out and I narrow my eyes at her beautiful face. My phone rings from the bedside table and I lean off her to answer it. She takes that *to her advantage,* slipping out from under me.

"What?" I grumble.

"Sounding nice and jolly as ever," Jai replies and Azalea comes around behind me and wraps her body around me like a spider monkey.

"I got you love," she chuckles.

"We have a thing to attend to a couple of hours away about a-"

She gasps when I lean back and crush her between me and the bed. She suddenly slaps me across my face. Then she kisses me nonstop in the spot she hit me. What the hell?

"Oh yeah, crossing that off my bucket list right now," she giggles.

"Grey, are you listening?" Jai asks.

"Fuck no I'm not listening," I tell him the truth as I roll off her and throw my arm around her, lifting her up on my shoulder. She squeals and catapults herself backwards onto the bed, landing on her back.

"Grey-" he starts.

"Shut up," I tell him. She leans up and puts me in a chokehold.

Lilah

What the fuck?

"Are you having sex right now?!" He shouts through the phone.

"No, you fuck. Azalea has me in a chokehold," I grumble.

"Tap out Sugar," she whispers in my ear. It turns me on a little bit. The whisper, not the choking. *I do the choking.* I don't think she knows that her arm isn't in the correct position and that it's just barely above my collarbone but I'm not saying anything.

"That's honestly not surprising at all. I would've been more surprised if you were actually having sex," he says, and I wait for a couple more seconds before giving in and tapping out for her.

"You did good darling," she kisses my cheek before waltzing out of our room, talking about making waffles.

"Anyway, there's a case a couple of hours away with this runaway mother and her little baby. She's originally from Ohio but after the courts wanted to take her baby because she's an addict, she ran. It should be quick and easy so you can get back to your wrestling match soon," he tells me, and I start getting dressed.

"Alright, I'll be there in a few," I hang up, putting the rest of my clothes on.

"Watch out Bear, here comes the ultimate loser," Azalea announces as I walk into the kitchen.

"C'mere, it's okay you lost, don't be sad," she opens her arms for me and I walk right into them. She rests her head on my chest.

"Got to go to work," I tell her, and she nods.

"When will you be back?"

"Before three," I assure her, "it's a short one."

"Okay," she looks up at me and I lift her onto the counter. She grips onto one side of my face, and she pesters kisses all over the other side. I can't help but smile a little in anticipation when she gets closer and closer to my lips. Finally, she lands one where I really want it and I don't let her pull away, deepening the kiss. Eventually, we pull away.

"I love you, sweet-cheeks," she squeezes the sides of my face and I scrunch my nose at her like she does to me all the time.

"I love you too."

~~~

I glare out the window.

"It's not our fault you got here later than everyone else," Theo's voice travels up to the front of the SUV. Usually, I ride in the same car as Roman. He mostly remains quiet, and he drives the 'calm car.' That car was filled.

What was left? A seat in the car that everyone calls the fucking 'crazy train.'

Theo, of course, Lincoln, Maxon, me, and Jai. Thank God Sanfred doesn't do field work because I honestly couldn't handle another one of them. And I get to sit in here all because I got here *late*. There was no time I had to be here by. If there was, it would have been set by me. Lincoln sticks his head up between me and Jai, who's driving. He looks over at me and I try my best to ignore the fuck. He leans closer to me, and I clench my jaw.

"Get the fuck away from me," I grumble.

"You smell like Azalea," he leans back, and I narrow my eyes.

"Why do you know what she smells like?" Why does he get that close to her?

"I play with her hair all the time, I know what she smells like, you smell like her," he smells me again and I lean away from him.

"No shit I smell like her, we live together," I roll my eyes.

"No," Theo drawls out and I already know that stupid shit is about to come out of his mouth.

"You smell like her because you were all over her before you left! That's why you were late wasn't it?" He questions.

"She's my girlfriend, of course I was all over her dumbass."

How the fuck did he graduate elementary school? For two hours I sit in the car and listen to the bullshit that constantly comes out of everyone's mouth. We pull up to the nearly falling apart motel that Sanfred found the woman living at for the moment and walking into the main office, the guys hand me the warrant. Every other guy thinks everything's a joke, so they always let me deal with the warrant shit. They say I have a good 'fuck with me I'll kill you' face. The older woman that sits at the front desk perks up when we walk in.

"Oh my God, Lincoln there's your mom," Theo gasps and Lincoln punches him in the back. This is exactly why they don't deal with showing the warrant. They cannot be taken seriously to save their lives.

"We need the room number of Dawn James," I tell her and she takes a drag from her cigarette before blowing it out slowly. Theo coughs behind me and pulls his inhaler out his jacket pocket taking two puffs of it.

"Okay, right this way," her voice comes out croaky and raspy like she's been smoking for thirty years. She stands and steps down off her stool, cigarette still in hand. She's supposed to ask if I have a warrant, but this works too. The top of her head reaches the middle of my chest, and she looks up at me, taking another draw of her cigarette.

"Handsome young man," she gives me a smile and I fidget away from her. She motions for us to follow her and Lincoln steps up beside me.

"I think Azalea has some competition," he chides.

"Get out of my face," I push him away from me and back into the group of giggling fucks behind me. We follow the lady until she stops in front of the door to Dawn's room. Jai knocks on the door, and we wait for her to open it. The old woman beside me continuously blows her smoke in my direction. Jai picks up his knocking pace, hitting the door harder and faster.

"Man quit, it's going to scare the baby that's in there," Theo pulls him away from the door. He's excited to see the baby.

"Do you have the key to get in?" Jai asks the woman, and she takes a ring of keys out of her pocket. She sticks a key in the door and opens it. The guys turn to me. They look at me expectantly, waiting for me to walk in first. I roll my eyes and push the door open. Dawn's baby sits on the floor next to the small bed in the center of the room, his clothes dirty and tears in his eyes. Theo goes to him as soon as he sees him. Dawn's nowhere to be found.

I walk to the closed bathroom door and pray to God she's not in there doing something I really don't want to see. I open the door and she lies on the ground. She's pale and unconscious and has her head propped up against the bathtub, facing the sink. A dark spoon sits on the sink counter and a brownish liquid has spilled from it. I look down and a syringe hangs out of a large vein in her arm. She's not just passed out.

"Fuck," I whisper.

~~~

"Hello sweet," Azalea answers on just the second ring and I relax at hearing her voice.

"Are you on your way back? Because I was thinking about having spaghetti for dinner, I know how much you like it," her voice comes out sweetly and happily and I frown.

"I'm not going to be home until later. Some things did not go according to plan and now I have a shit ton of paperwork to do," I tell her gently and she lets out a soft 'oh.'

"I'm sorry."

"No, no, hush your mouth. It's perfectly fine, I understand," she assures me aggressively. I look down at the baby attached to my leg, holding onto it for dear life.

"Go and get your work done and I love you," she says.

"I love you too," we hang up and I look down at the one-year-old. Why does he like me? Hell if I know. He looks up at me.

"Dada?"

"Jesus Christ," I mumble. We could've been gone almost an hour ago but the CPS worker who's supposed to come get the baby left on vacation. So, they had to call in another. The fucker is really taking his time.

"Do you think you might actually be the dad?" Lincoln questions from beside me. I swear to God I'm going to break his arms. I look down at the kid's curly bright red hair.

"You know what? I bet I am his dad- shut the fuck up," I send him a glare. I feel a rumble from the kid's ass on my foot. I close my eyes and take a deep breath.

"Theo, this kid just shit on my foot."

"Nuh-uh," he dismisses.

"I *felt* it."

He bends down and picks the kid up. The kid starts crying. My headache worsens. The kid screams. I feel like lying in the middle of the road. He looks down his diaper. Then he looks back at me, his nose scrunched.

"He sharted on you," Theo laughs.

"You have to change him," Jai nods to the small diaper bag that was in the hotel room.

"No thank you, that's not a job for me," Theo dismisses the suggestion. They look at me. What the fuck?

"Hey, you're the boss here. You get the hardest jobs, so here you go-"

"Don't give me that baby," he pushes the kid at me, and I hold him under his arms, the fuck away from me. *I'm quitting this job and getting another job at a gas station.* I look at the police cars and the ambulance that are closer to the motel and avoid eye contact with the child.

"Dada."

"Not your dad."

"Dada."

"No."

"Dada," he giggles.

"God, help me."

On the bright side, it only took twenty minutes from when the kid shit himself to the time the CPS worker was able to pick him up. It hurt just a bit seeing that kid cry and extend his arms out to me when the worker took him. The kid's only a year old and he's already been through too much shit.

"Shit," Theo draws out as we get back into the cars to go back home, "I think I've got baby fever."

"I need a baby mama," he adds.

~~~

Paperwork fills up my desk and I look up at the clock on the wall. I can't even calculate the fucking time before the door is busting open.

"I brought you spaghetti Sugar," Lilah rushes through the door and I feel the corners of my lips rise. God her spaghetti tastes like fucking heaven. I glance at her figure. *Glance.*

"What? You looking at my goodies?" she walks closer to me. Even though I glanced, that doesn't mean I wasn't looking at her 'goodies'.

"Yes."

She places the bowl of spaghetti in front of me and she leans down, kissing the side of my head. I peek down her shirt just a bit and pull her onto my lap. She fits perfectly. I go to take a bite, but she stops me. She leans in close to me and she smells my shirt.

"Excuse me sir," she leans away from me, "why do you smell like cigarettes?"

"Smoked a whole damn pack that's why," I shove that spaghetti in my mouth, and she slaps the fork out of my hand. *I had that coming.* She stares at me. More like glares at me. Then she softens.

"No, you didn't," she calms back down. She suddenly bounces on my lap. I grip onto her waist, gritting my teeth.

"Guess what?" She smiles excitedly.

"What?" I mumble.

"Abby asked if I wanted to spend the day with her tomorrow and I am! I'm excited," she leans forward, quickly kissing my cheek. I'm a little jealous. Just a bit. A bit. I live with her though and I always get to spend time with her. Still a little jealous though.

Chapter Thirty Five

Doctor

❀ Azalea ❀

I've never seen anyone milk something as much as Grey has been. I swear he's the definition of *pitiful*. On top of him milking everything, he won't even get his lazy booty up to go to the doctor. I've just about had it. He sniffles from beside me and I pass him a tissue and he takes it. I look over at his poor little pitiful self. *Bless his heart.* I place my hand gently on his forehead and it feels as hot as hades.

It's obvious his fever is making him hot too, considering he's only wearing his darn boxers. I mean, I'm not one to complain about that but I know he doesn't feel good. Bear knows it too. He lays his head on my legs, never taking his eyes off Grey. But for three days he's had this going on and it's only getting worse. At first, I noticed his nose getting a little bit stuffy and then he started getting tired and now it's a combination of all kinds of stuff. He sniffles again.

"That's it. Get your gluteus maximus up. We're going to the doctor," I stand up and he looks at me like something's funny.

"No, we're not."

"Yes, we are," I assure him, "get dressed."

"I don't want to," he argues.

"I don't care, you're pitiful, you're going."

"I'm not pitiful," he disagrees.

"You look like you've been dragged behind a horse," I push his wild dark hair back and he closes his eyes briefly.

"I don't like going there," he grumbles.

"But you know it'll make you feel better so get up and put clothes on. I'll even drive, you can sleep in the car," I persuade him. He stands slowly and I smile. I smile up until he mumbles something about throwing himself off a bridge, but I choose to ignore the comment. I follow him into the bedroom to monitor him. He doesn't even *look* at the closet as he lowers himself down onto the bed. I let out a groan.

"Grey, I'm going to tie a rope around your ankle and connect it to the back of my car and drag you to the doctor."

"I'm not going."

"You're not winning this."

"Yes, I am," he argues. Jokes on him because the longer he's sick, the longer I don't want his lips on me.

"You're being ridiculous," I sit on the bed next to him.

"No."

"We can do anything you want after, but you need to go," I try and convince him. There's plenty of stuff to do after. We could go eat, we could go get him all the jerky he wants, anything.

"We can't do what I want," he flits his eyes up at me.

"Why?"

"I want to fuck you but obviously you're not going to let that happen," he grumbles. Can he be any more of a horny man?

"You're darn right I'm not going to let you do that to me. Now if you go to the doctor," I trail off.

"It would still be a no," I finish, "but you can get better quicker if you go to the doctor and then we can talk about it."

"I'm going to get better anyway, I'm not going," he rolls over, his back now facing me. I think about kicking him in the back, but I refrain. Brat. I walk around to the other side of the bed. I run my hand down his arm and as his eyes clothes, I yank my arm down to the small amount of hair he has under his belly button and I pull it. He lets out a groan, pulling my hand off.

"You have no consideration for me and how I feel," he turns his head and buries his face and the pillow.

"We'll watch the scariest movie ever when we get home if you'll go to the doctor," I continue trying to convince him and he only grunts. I still don't understand why those types of movies are pretty much the only ones he actually likes. I find it weird that he doesn't even get scared. He can watch a terrifying movie and then go to bed with his feet hanging off the bed and everything. After movies like those, I have to be curled into a ball with the covers covering every part of my body. I walk to our closet and pick out some comfy clothes for him to wear. Because that mother trucker *is* going to the doctor.

"Grey get your buns up," I poke his lower back.

"Not going," he grumbles back.

"I will stand here and dress you myself," I warn, and he turns over to me.

"How 'bout *you undress* and then we'll go from there," he reaches his hand out, gripping onto my upper thigh.

"I'm going to roundhouse kick you in the pelvis," I narrow my eyes at him.

"Mhm."

When my violence tactics don't work, I tune in to my persuasive, guilt-tripping tactics.

"Grey," I start softly and quietly, seemingly upset. I even add in a small sniffle and he's turning around looking at me.

"I'm still not going."

~~~

"Are you allergic to anything?" I peer over at him. He sits beside me, his milkshake in hand, and a grumbly look on his face.

"Being here," he grumbles, "and stupid fuckers."

I look down at the paper and then the room sort of filled with people waiting to be called into the back. *Dang right he's at the doctor's office.*

"I'm not sure I'm allowed to write that on the paper," I tell him, and he rolls his head over to me.

"Is that milkshake making you feel better, sugar?" I smile innocently. He narrows his eyes at me. I take that as a yes and I continue doing the paperwork he's supposed to be doing but doesn't feel like it, of course. A middle-aged woman comes and sits in the seat right beside him and I feel him tense. I roll my eyes at him. He's truly pitiful. He shifts toward me, away from the poor woman who had no choice but to sit in the seat next to him because there were no other seats. I finish up the paperwork and hand it back to the desk lady. She gives me a smile and I feel my heart grow a bit at that smile, so I smile back happily. I return to my seat and Grey drapes his strong arm over the top of my chair.

"Still love me even though I made you come?"

"That's what she said," he and I both utter at the same time. I turn my head into his arm to conceal my laughter.

"I still love you," he kisses the top of my head.

"If I get your sickness, I'm suing you for all you're worth," I warn him and he nods, already knowing the consequences since I've already told him them multiple times this morning. The door to the back opens and a woman in light pink scrubs looks down at a clipboard.

"Grey?" She calls out and he doesn't move until I push his arm forward. He finally stands. He looks down at me.

"What are you doing?" He questions me.

"Do you want me to come with you?" I ask. I didn't know he wanted me to come with him. He looks at me giving me a look that says, 'that's a stupid question.'

"Yes, get up," he grabs my hand and pulls me up carefully. The woman gives the two of us a smile and she motions for us to follow her. Grey grumbles something about how he's not doing this poop by himself in certain choice words. We enter a room where a patient chair sits in the middle of it, and she tells Grey to take his shoes off and to get on a scale. He turns up his nose at that, but I nudge him, silently telling him to quit it. She tells him to sit on the patient table and I just barely see his jaw tense. *What a baby.* He sits and glares at me while she takes his blood pressure. All I can do is smile at him.

"Okay, your doctor will be in in a few minutes," the nurse smiles and exits the room. Grey immediately gets off the large seat.

"I'm not fuckin' sitting there," he grumbles.

"I'm not freaking sitting there," I mock him oh-so maturely. There's only one guest chair and I'm sitting in it so he's going to have to suck it up. Big baby. On the other hand, I *did* drag him here.

"C'mere you poor sweet soul," I stand from my seat and usher him to sit in it. He gets up and takes it happily. Then he pats his lap and widens his legs a bit more than he usually does when he sits.

"It's inviting, isn't it?" He hooks his finger in one of the belt loops of my pants and yanks me down onto him.

"You're hornish," I whisper, kissing his forehead and standing from his lap. I stand beside the chair, and he leans his head over to me. The door opens and a nicely dressed man walks in, a computer in his hands.

"Hello, I'm Dr. McKinus," the younger man smiles, showing off his pearly whites. I don't think Grey likes him very much by the way he flits his eyes up at me in a look like says 'why did you make me come here?' He also just looks way too unhappy. I wait and the doctor does too. Grey makes no movements and doesn't even acknowledge the doctor. I roll my eyes at him.

"This is Grey," I pat his shoulder. Then I spot the polo dress shirt the doctor is wearing. I sigh internally.

"It's nice to meet you Grey," he flits his eyes up at me, "and.."

"Azalea," I smile.

"Azalea," he says before looking down at his computer.

"So, tell me a little about what's been going on," Dr. McKinus looks at Grey. Grey only shifts in his chair. He's the biggest and most ridiculous dramatic drama queen I've ever met in my entire life.

"He's been really sniffly, y'know a runny nose, pressure in his sinuses and stuff like that," I explain, giving Grey's back a small pinch.

"And this has been going on for how long?"

"I'd say three days or so," I nod, and he types on his computer.

"Fever?" He asks.

"Yes," I nod once again, and he types some more. I lean down to Grey.

"You're being the ultimate baby right now sugar," I whisper in his ear and before I can pull away, he kisses me on the cheek and smirks. I scrunch my nose at him, and he returns it to me.

"Okay Grey," the doctor stands, "I'm going to need you to come sit up on the table so I can examine you."

Grey doesn't move. Can he be any more of a handful? He gets up slowly and moseys slowly over to the table. The doctor backs up a bit at seeing the size difference between Grey and him. Especially when Grey narrows his eyes at him, he backs up. I only pinch the bridge of my nose, shaking my head. The whole examination is just terrible. Not once does Grey stop glaring at the poor doctor. Dr. McKinus doesn't even want to touch Grey, and I don't blame him. Awkwardly the doctor tells us he's got a sinus infection and that he's sending a prescription to the pharmacy before leaving swiftly. Then that's where Grey has the *audacity* to turn to me with pity-me-eyes. What a loser.

~~~

"C'mon darling," I pull on his hand, "I know you can do it."

He grunts. I climb onto the bed and flatten myself on his bare back. I kiss his shoulder twice. It's been a day since going to the doctor. Grey continues to be difficult. He turns over suddenly and places me back down onto him. I land right on his goody.

"Fuck me," he trails his hands up my sides, and I gasp. He grips onto my thighs and spreads them further apart, pressing me down onto him further. I gasp at the feeling. He grasps the bottom of my shirt and yanks it off me leaving me only in my amazing light blue underwear and matching sports bra. I can't believe I'm actually matching.

"I said we can't do this until you're better," I warn him, starting to slide off.

"Yeah, well there are positions where I'm not face to face with you so," he grabs onto my leg and pulls my butt against the front of him.

"I can do this way just fine," he squeezes my hips.

"Against the wall is good too," he starts pulling my underwear down and I get hot.

"What did you eat?" I mumble breathlessly. Something made him extra hornish.

"Not you yet and that's the problem," he tosses my light blue underwear somewhere and pushes me down on my back.

"Wait!" I call out, gripping onto his hair.

"I promised Mr. Terrip I'd be at the store by twelve-thirty," I grumble and look over at the clock which says that it's already twelve-twenty. My words go right over his head as he lowers his mouth down onto me anyway. He pulls away after making me feel like I'm floating on a cloud, and he grips onto my hand. He sits me up and instead of kissing my lips, he kisses my neck. After kissing it, he wraps his huge hand around the base of it.

"Ride me," he grumbles out and my eyes widen. *Jesus forgive us.*

~~~

"I don't think I've seen you in about ten years," Mr. Terrip says unhappily.

"I know," I hug his skinny frame, "Grey's held me hostage."

"I have chronic back pain now," I grasp my back.

"Oh really? From what? What happened?" He wonders and my eyes widen. Why did I tell him that? What am I supposed to say? 'Oh yeah Grey *killed* my back this morning while we were having sexy time. Oh also, that's why I'm here late.' I think not.

"I fell off the bed last night. I just rolled off," I tuck my hair behind my ear.

"Did you hit your neck, too?" Mr. Terrip's eyebrows furrow in concern as he looks at my neck. My eyes widen.

"Yep," my voice raises an octave. I need to have a three-hour-long church session in my car. And Grey needs to be there too but nowhere near me. He can sit in the trunk, all the way in the back.

"I'm going to get to work," I give him a smile and rush to the bathroom. I enter and straight away see the hickeys on my neck. I swear he rarely ever gives me them but when he does, he might as well have been sucking my whole neck off. I go back out and grab a handful of books from the book cart to put away. Hardly ten minutes later the bell above the door rings and I'm almost tackled to the floor by Abby.

"I can't believe I'm about to say this," she jumps excitedly, and I feed off her energy. She grabs my hands and twirls me in her arms. I laugh at her energy.

"Roman asked me to be his girlfriend. *Girlfriend*. Not a friend that's a girl but an actual girlfriend!" She hugs me to her tightly.

"Aw, I'm so excited for you," I swing us back and forth. She deserves someone who's amazing and although I don't know Roman all that well, I know that he's a great guy. And if he doesn't treat her right, he'll have to answer to me and I am so talented in the combat and spying area, he's got no chance against me.

"I saw your car in the parking lot, and I just had to run in here and tell you," he calms down a bit.

"I can't wait to tell Grey," I smile. I would've said that he's going to be excited, but he doesn't get excited. He probably won't care but I'll *make* him care because I care.

"Okay, I have class in twenty minutes, so I have to go but I also have this for you," she reaches into her jacket pocket and takes out the information I asked her to get for me. I open them up and look at them.

"I printed it out for you just to make it easier instead of just taking a picture of it," she explains. I bring her into another hug.

"'This spring will be great, don't worry, I'll be there with you," she assures me, knowing I'm nervous.

"Thank you," I squeeze her tight.

"Of course," she says, "Grey went a little crazy on your neck, huh?"

"I told him he's not kissing me because he's sick and so he does this. I don't even have anything with me to cover it up and I'm not about to go see him and all those guys with it being as obvious as it is," we pull away.

She tells me not to worry about it and she drags me to her car where she proceeds to quickly cover my neck up with her makeup. We're pretty much the same skin tone so it all worked out perfectly. After Abby and I say our goodbyes, I take a couple of hours to wander around the store doing whatever Mr. Terrip needs me to do. Dust, arrange books, put away new books, clean the windows, and whatever else he needs to make up for all the time I wasn't able to come here.

By closing time, everything he needs to be done is done and I feel accomplished with myself. I even got a few minutes just to myself. Of course, I love Grey, and I love spending time with him. *But,* without a doubt, there are times where he can be quite the character, and everyone needs time to themselves. Now I'm fully ready to slap the daylights out of his booty. We close the store and I give Mr. Terrip an extra-long hug goodbye before he gets in his car and drives off. I decide to walk to the restaurant to breathe in the fresh air. I even see an older couple which makes my heart grow. To top it off, they said *hi* to me. I don't think I've ever felt so special in my life. Are they my grandparents? How much money does it take to hire grandparents?

I check the pockets of my jacket and the pockets of my jeans. In the end, I come up with thirteen cents, a squished piece of gum in its wrapper, and some foreign object that looks like it was placed in my possession without my knowledge. I narrow my eyes and look around me. The old couple is gone and the only people around me are one pregnant woman and a middle-aged man who looks like he's got a lot of money. I look closely at the object. I've had the jacket for years so lord knows what it actually is. I throw it away in a nearby trashcan and make it to the restaurant.

"Look who it is," Jonas' voice just brightens my day as soon as I hear it.

"Hey little boy," I give him a smile and his rolls his blue eyes.

"You still have no tits," he grumbles. *Not what Grey says.*

"You still have a small peepee," I chuckle.

"Witch," he narrows his eyes at me.

"This could've gone much better if you would've just told me where exactly Grey was as soon as you saw me," I shrug.

"In the very back, outside," he flicks a crumpled up straw wrapper at me, and I catch it in my hand before it hits me in the throat.

"You wish you could do what I just did," I fake throwing it at him and he flinches, closing his eyes. Right when he reopens them, I throw it at him, and it hits him in the cheek. The face not buttcheek. I start walking toward the back but not before turning to him once more to call him out on how much of a loser he looked like just now.

"How does it feel to be the biggest loser here?" I smile, and he only flicks me off. I walk all the way to the back of the 'meeting room' where the door to the outside leads and I bust that thing open. When I see Grey looking all bootylicious, I smile. A group of six of them play basketball on the hoop that I didn't even know they had out here. Shouldn't they be attempting to run a restaurant? Or even attempt to find crime-committing people? Sidetracked by Grey being shirtless and pure gorgeousness, I forget that he's *supposed to be sick. I'm going to give him a wet willy.*

I watch him for a minute because quite frankly I cannot help myself. Now I know I don't know a lot or even a little bit about basketball, but it seems to me that Grey is pretty darn good. He scores a few buckets or baskets- I don't even know the freaking terminology, and even a few things that are like a dunk or something, I'm done trying to figure it out though. Someone calls a timeout and I cross my arms across my chest.

"Hey, baby doll," Oaklee calls over to me, wiping his bare chest with Theo's shirt who is gaping at him with disgust. Grey looks over at me and his lips turn up at the corners as he starts walking toward me.

"I don't think it's a good idea to be out here without a shirt on when it's mid-fall and you're supposed to be *sick,"* I raise my eyebrows.|

"It's sixty degrees today and," he sniffles, "I *am* sick. But I was sicker earlier."

"I'm happy you breathed in air and got better, why doesn't that happen to every sick person I wonder?"

He leans forward and wraps an arm around my waist pulling me to him and leaning down to my ear.

"I think *you* cured me this morning," he bites my ear and pulls away. I look up into the sky and I close my eyes.

"What are you doing?" he questions.

"Praying which is something you need to do," I mumble, and he kisses my forehead. I finish my prayer and open my eyes. He still stands in front of me, a baby smile on his lips.

"Are you good at this basketball thing, or what?" I question and he shrugs.

"Look at him being all humble," Oaklee walks up to us, obviously hearing our conversation.

"He played in high school. Almost went to college for it too. Kentucky, was it?" Theo calls out. Grey only rolls his eyes.

"For real?" I question. He never even told me he used to play it.

"Just 'cause I did it and was good, doesn't mean I loved it," he dismisses it. I furrow my eyebrows. If he didn't love it, what was the point of putting his time into it?

"I'm confused then."

The guys wander off, picking the basketball up again.

"I started it because I never wanted to go home," he shrugs, "I just did it to do something. I was never looking to go somewhere because of it, I never wanted to. I like what I do now better."

"Oh," I mumble.

"That's enough, c'mon," he pulls me to the 'court'. Watch out guys, I'm the real competition. Theo throws me the ball.

"Shoot it, show us what you got," he encourages me.

"Absolutely not, I have no athletic bone in my body, not even the metal parts of me help in any way," I refer to the right side of my body. You would think having metal plates in your body would make you cool and indestructible but in reality, it does nothing for you.

"C'mon Azalea," Linc encourages me. Why do they all have their shirts off, good lord.

"I can't even walk properly and y'all want me to-" I pause, catching sight of Grey as he stretches his arms, causing his back muscles to tense. I snap out of it, forgetting what I was saying. You know what? Who cares? Maybe I'll shoot it and make it and I'll become the next Michael Jordan. Except the girl version of him. Why don't I know any girl basketball players? I do, actually. Her name is Azalea Delilah Carson. I shoot the ball and it hits the orange rim thing and as I sit there watching it with my mouth slightly open, I don't have time to react when it comes back and hits me in the face. *This feels like deja vu.*

"Why didn't you move out the way?" Oaklee throws his head back laughing like I can't punch him in the jugular. I grab onto my nose and groan quietly. Can you get burnt from that thing? Because I feel like my nose is on fire. Oh my gosh, my nose is gone, isn't it? It's on the floor somewhere.

"You watched it hit you," Theo stomps his foot, barely being able to breathe through his loud laughter all while he hangs himself around a laughing Lincoln.

"Y'all shut up," Grey pulls my head into his chest but I feel his stomach tensing as he tries to hold back from chuckling. I slap his stomach.

"Let me see it," he tilts my head up and looks at my nose.

"It's broken, isn't it?" I sigh.

"Without a doubt," he nods.

"You still love me even though it's crooked and falling off?" I question and he hesitates. I lightly kick his shin.

"I guess," he says, and I pat his booty once. I turn around and look at those three rude people who laughed at me in a weak moment.

"Y'all are going to H-e-double hockey sticks, I hope you know that," I point at them.

Bud

* Grey *

"Look what I got mother trucker!" Azalea waltzes into the room, a smile on her face. She lifts up my high school yearbook.

"Shit," I grumble under my breath, running my hand through my hair she was previously messing with. Bear trots after her and I feel attacked. She raises the blue and red yearbook like it's some sort of sacred shit. She plops down next to me.

"You're an old fart," she pats my thigh and I narrow my eyes at her. Then she wiggles beside me excitedly.

"I can't wait to see lil' baby Grey," she smiles, opening the book.

"Oh, who's this beautiful man?" she wonders aloud, and I scowl knowing it's not me that early in the book. I look over and spot the principal back when I was there. The seventy-four-year-old principle. I lean back and relax, watching her emerald, green eyes travel over each and every page. *I thought she just wanted to see me but whatever, I guess that's fine. Not jealous.*

"You were a senior in this, right?" she looks over at me and I give her a nod. Around a minute passes and then she lets out a gasp. She leans her head down on my shoulder looking at my picture.

"I can't get over how cute you were," her voice remains soft. I frown.

"*Were*? Still fucking am," I grumble. She tells me that shit every day. I guess I have to come to accept it. She laughs as I glance at the old picture. I was skinnier then. Not exactly like a stick but I needed a damn cheeseburger.

"Yes, you still are," she speaks softly. She leans into me and presses her soft lips against my cheek. On the damn cheek.

"Really?" I grumble and she huffs.

"On the cheek, really?" She makes her voice deeper, mocking me. She closes the book suddenly. *Am I about to get lucky?* I smirk watching her as she starts to get up. I widen my legs a bit for her to come sit right on me. She turns and looks at my suggestive face.

"We're going to do arts and crafts," she says happily and the smirk falls.

"You're giving me blue balls," I grumble up to her. The first time I used that phrase with her, it took me five minutes to explain what it meant.

"You're giving *me* a headache," she replies, and I narrow my eyes.

"You know what? We're not doing arts and crafts, I'm going to show you how to do something for me," she says brightly. I internally hope it's sexual but deep down I know it's not. She walks off and goes into our room. *I should escape.* She comes back with all kinds of fingernail polish products. *Goddammit.*

"Welcome to Azalea's beauty school," she introduces.

"I don't want to be in Azalea's beauty school," I mumble, and she hushes me. She makes me do a lot of things I don't want to do. You'd think it's easy to refuse a girl half my size but hell no. She's an angel but do something she doesn't like; you'll regret that shit. She's not a physical person, she's a mental person. She'll fuck with your brain. I know it all too well. She made me try sushi. I refused with all my power to try that shit. She doesn't even eat it herself; I don't know why she wanted me to try it. I continually said no. So, she pulled out all kinds of shit to bring up in an attempt to get me to eat it. *'Love, I'm scared to try it and I need you to make sure it'll be good.' 'Grey, you know*

I love you so much. I only want the best for you, and I think you'll like it.' 'You'll be telling me how sorry you are when it's your favorite food.'

"Paint my nails darling," she smiles innocently.

"No ma'am."

"Yes sir."

"No ma'am."

"*Yes* sir."

"No ma'am."

"Okay," she shrugs and gets up. My eyebrows furrow because I know it's not that easy. She grabs Bear's leash by the door.

"Where are you going?" I wonder.

"Me and Bear and going to the park to attract nail artists. Preferably men," she hooks the leash onto his collar. I sigh. Knowing her, she'd go around the fucking park asking these people to paint her nails. She'd get excited when some random old creepy dude says he'll do it and then she'll get kidnapped.

"Get over here and sit your ass down," I roll my eyes when she smiles victoriously. She trots back over to me, and she takes a seat next to me, throwing her arms around my neck.

"I knew you'd do it Sugar," she kisses my lips, "because you're just so sweet, aren't you?"

"Mhm," I hum, kissing her back deeply. She pulls away and I'm left following her lips with mine. She giggles backing away from me.

"So," she picks up the color and opens it. She takes a couple of minutes to show me how to do it. It can't be that hard. It's like painting. I'm no fucking painter but this is basics.

"So..?" I trail off, wondering what she was going to say before. It's not like her to not talk. At all. I slowly drag the brush along her ring finger, flitting my eyes up to hers.

"I was thinking of going to college," she gives me a hesitant smile. I pause for a minute before continuing. I know it's something she's wanted to do.

"Yeah?" I mumble. A slight fit of nervousness contracts my chest. If my hands weren't already occupied, I'd already been messing with the scrunchie on my wrist.

"Which one?" I keep my eyes focused on her hands.

"UTK," she says softly. It's a four-year college. In Knoxville. Knoxville isn't that far from here. About an hour depending on traffic. *Still far from me.*

"I looked into dorm room exemptions for freshmen and there really isn't any category I fit into," she explains.

"But that only means that we just need to wait a year and then I can come back here!" she adds quickly.

"Well, I mean, if I make it into the school," she rambles on.

"You'll make it," I give her a smirk that seems to fade within seconds. I remain quiet for the most part. I'm happy for her. She's happy, I'm happy. We're just going to have to be happy without seeing each other almost every second of the day. *If* she makes it. She may have zero common sense but she's smart, she'll make it. I'm glad she's finally able to do what she wants though. She spent her whole childhood being controlled by her father that she never got to do anything she wanted. Now she's got all the time in the world to do anything she wants to, and I'll never take that away from her.

"Are you okay?" she whispers softly, "I don't want to make you upset or anything. I'm sorry, maybe I shouldn't-"

"Shut up," I tell her.

"Excuse me sir-"

"You're going to make it into UTK and you're going to go and you're going to do whatever the fuck you want to do there, got it?" I assure her.

"Got it good babe," she scrunches her nose when she smiles, and my heart does a fluttery fucking thing.

"And you're going to punch guys who like you in the dicks and tell them you've got a man when they chase after your ass," I add, just to make myself feel better.

"And when I get arrested for that, you'll bail me out," she goes along with it.

"And I'm going to try drugs-"

"No, you're not," I shake my head at her.

"I was just kidding," she gives me a sly smile. She looks down at her hand.

"If the whole fed thing doesn't work out, take up being a nail artist," she smiles. I only roll my eyes. I gather my focus back on her hands and I feel her eyes on my face.

"I love you very much," she says suddenly, and my heart flips.

"Kiss me bud," she mumbles, leaning closer to me.

"Don't call me bud," I grumble, pecking her lips.

"I do what I want," she retorts. She's not fucking wrong and that's the bad thing.

"Right now, I want an apple," she starts to get up.

"I'm not done yet, Azalea," I keep my grip on her hand.

~~~

❀Azalea❀

Where's Grey? Oh, he's just laying on top of me with his hand down the back of my pants. Excuse me? What does he think he's doing? I squint down at him and notice his peacefully sleeping face. I laugh evilly internally. I grip onto his nose and hold it closed. When his mouth wakes a weird sound and he starts to wake up, I lean my head back and act asleep. He raises his head off me. I feel him move his body off me only to grab onto me and pull me on top of him. He pulls my head down gently onto his chest and he presses a kiss to the top of my head. *Aw, I love him.*

I feel a little bit bad now. I covered his nose so he couldn't breathe out of it and he went and acted like a sweetheart. *It would be funny if I farted.* Why do I think these things? I poke my finger in his belly button. Why do I *do* these things? He jerks and lifts his head up.

"Fuckin' evil ass," he grumbles, running his hand down his face.

Bear leans over from his lying position, and he gives Grey a nice lick on the side of his face.

"You're my sweet Cherry Pie," I quote my all-time favorite song, pointing my fingers at him. He has no reaction to my proclamation.

"Go back to sleep," his sleep-coated voice mumbles.

"Can I be the big spoon and you be the little spoon?" I start sliding off him. I'm always the little spoon.

"If it'll make you sleep again," he grumbles, turning onto his side. I get behind him and throw my arm over his side. I feel pitiful behind him. I feel like I don't even exist behind him. And it's cold back here. And if I fart, he won't even feel it and what's the point in that?

"I don't think I like being the big spoon," I sit up and he sighs. He turns over midway almost onto his back and raises his arm for me to climb over and be the little spoon. He gently guides me over the top of him and I lay down in my spot. I curl up and he wraps his warm arms around me.

"Better now?" He rumbles behind me, and I nod against him. Within a minute or two, the doorbell is ringing. Grey has nothing but boxers on. Now that I think about it, he's only in his boxers quite often. He's got no shame whatsoever and I'll *never* complain about what he chooses to wear around the house.

"Go open the door," I mumble to him.

"No," he grumbles, pressing his face deeper into my neck.

"Freaking heck yes bud," I argue back.

"Don't call me bud."

"Okay bud."

He pinches my side and I thrash. Then he moves to stick his hand down the front of my pants.

"No sir," I roll away from him and the doorbell rings once more. What if I go to open the door and a robber is standing there? Or a kidnapper and they kidnap me.

"Open the door," he tells me.

"No. What if I get kidnapped?"

"Someone fuckin' kidnaps you they won't even get down the street 'fore they're turning back around to put your annoying ass back," he mumbles in a reply and my mouth drops open.

"I hope I do get kidnapped now and I'll make sure to keep my mouth shut just so they won't bring me back," I exit the room.

"Put goddamn pants on," he calls out and I return to the room and pull on some pants. I enter the living room and pull open the door. A tall man stands on the other side of the door. He wears an expensive-looking suit, and his hair is done up nicer than anyone else's hair I've ever seen in my life. *He's a spitting image of Grey.* Oh gosh.

"Is Grey here?" He looks down at me, his deep voice ringing in my ears.

"Uh..." I trail off. I'm not sure what Grey would want me to say. Bear appears next to me suddenly and I feel a bit better about the situation. The older man clears his throat.

"Who are you?" He narrows his eyes ever so slightly and I hold back from wincing. I hear footsteps from behind me and I nearly let out a breath of relief. Grey shows up beside me, pants now covering his lower half.

"Son," the man nods and even though I thought originally, he was Grey's dad, it still surprises me. And I thought he said his dad was a deadbeat. This man looks the opposite. I watch as Grey's jaw tenses.

"I'm just going to...." I trail off pointing down the hallway. I turn quickly and with Bear following, I return to our room. *Yikes.* I close the door behind me and place my ear up against the door. I know it's terrible to eavesdrop, but I can't help it.

"What are you doing here?" I hear Grey ask him.

"Your grandfather passed away yesterday," the man replies, "his plane went down."

"It's not like I was close with him," Grey retorts.

"That shouldn't matter, it's family," his father disagrees.

"I don't want to get started with the 'family' bullshit," Grey's voice grows agitated.

"Fine. Who's the girl?" His father changes the subject.

"That's none of your business."

"I mean it kind of is. She opens the door and then looks up at me and stutters like an idiot"

"*Don't* fucking call her that," Grey turns even more agitated. *That's such a mean thing to say about me.*

"Well that just told me she's not just a one-night stand," the man chuckles. There's a small moment of silence.

"Does..." he trails off, "does she live here?"

I can imagine him looking around the living room and seeing the flowers and decorations.

"Get out," Grey warns him.

"Fine, fine. I guess I'll have to tell the family that you're not coming to the funeral."

I hear the door shut and then silence. I move away from the door. I wait for a minute trying to decide what I should do. I decide to go see him. He sits on the couch, doing nothing.

"I'm sorry about your grandfather," I slap my hand over my mouth. I've just gone and basically admitted I was eavesdropping.

"I'm sorry. I didn't mean to eavesdrop-"

"Yes, you did."

"Well, yeah, I did mean to but," I pause and try to think of an excuse.

"I'm not mad at you," he says quietly.

"I really am sorry about your grandfather," I repeat.

"It doesn't matter," he monotonously replies.

"So, that was your dad," I mumble mostly to myself.

"Azalea, I don't want to talk about him, just drop it," he sighs and now I'm the one growing agitated. I've waited so long for him to tell me more about him and when I see the perfect opportunity, he shuts it down.

"Why are you crying?" His voice reaches my ears in a softer tone than normal. I reach up and wipe the tear under my eye.

"Because I'm frustrated," I furrow my eyebrows.

"I don't get why you're so hellbent on knowing everything about me. It doesn't matter."

"That's what *you* think! I care so much because I love you and I want you to be happy," I try to explain.

"What makes you think I'm not happy? I'm with you, I'm happy Lilah," his voice remains soft.

"Because when I kept all my thoughts in my head and never told anyone about anything, I was so unhappy and I don't want you to feel like I did," I angrily wipe under my eyes. I didn't mean to start crying.

"I'm sorry I keep bugging you about talking to me, but I want to be as much of a crutch to you as you are to me and I feel like I'm not," I continue.

"Don't think that bullshit," he exclaims sternly.

"That's enough," he stands closer and wipes the stupid tears from under my eyes.

"You're everything to me," he says, and I get happy-emotional.

"You've done more for me than you can imagine."

"But-"

"Shut up," he hushes me.

"What do you want to know?" He pulls me down to the couch and I grow excited. I can finally know all the juicy deets.

Chapter Thirty-Seven

Suspicious

❀ Azalea ❀

"I want to know about your dad," I start off and he nods slowly. I plop my booty cheeks on the couch, turning toward him, and giving him my full attention. He tilts his head only slightly, never taking his eyes off me.

"He never had anything to do with me," he starts, and I grow sad, "I lived in the house 'till I was seventeen, you know that."

I give him a small nod.

"I had to raise myself. Never talked to him. Didn't eat with him. I hardly ever saw him. So, I spent most of my time doing other things like basketball. I think I was so good because all I did was practice and anything else I could to keep from going to that house," he explains. *I know what that's like.* I feel my bottom lip wiggle and I grab a couch pillow and shove it over my face.

"Azalea, stop," he wraps his arm around my waist and pulls me to him. He removes the pillow from my face, and he wipes my damp cheeks. He was all alone for so long. And he had to *raise* himself.

"It's over. It's nothing, okay? You went through way worse shit, I'm fine," he runs his hand down the surface of my back. I wrap my arms around his neck and hug onto him tightly.

"So, I moved out," he continues, still letting me cling onto him.

"That was the best decision I've ever made," he kisses the side of my neck.

"I got into this training program after I turned down going to Kentucky and that's what started this all. I already had a two-year college degree from high school, which was something I knew would keep me busy and not paying attention to things at that house. I needed that in the program, so I was lucky."

"I went right from the training facility, straight to D.C. In D.C they did all sorts of shit, training, physical evaluations, mental evaluations, and every type of background checking they could possibly do on me."

"They wanted someone young enough to grow with the start of the FAA so they offered to give me permission to start it and I did."

"And when it came to getting the guys, every two months I would get files of each of the people in training and then I had to report back to D.C to pick a single person out of a group of thirty to be a part of this with me."

"You *voluntarily* chose Theo?" I laugh into his arm. Poor Theo has such a hard time sometimes.

"Those thirty guys I had to choose from were a rotten batch, he was the best chance I had," he shakes his head.

"Plus, I knew him beforehand, and it just so happened to work out that way."

"So, what about the restaurant?" I question. What does he need the restaurant for if he could just as easily have some nice headquarter?

"Everyone knows where the FBI headquarters is. I wasn't about to be involved with people that often. If they know exactly where we are, they'll be bothering us. So, I settled for the restaurant," he shrugs.

"The only time I didn't get to choose who was coming here was when the new girl came, whatever her name was. They thought she'd be an okay fit. She was removed from another unit for being unfit for the job. I guess they thought we could train her better here. She's fine, not doing any fieldwork," he rolls his eyes.

"Her name is Jaqueline," I remind him of her name.

"Like I give a shit," he grumbles.

"What about Jake? He never went to any type of training place," I wonder.

"He was a friend of Theo's and he wanted to help. I let him because I could see he was a good kid. As soon as he turned the right age, he was going to go to the training facility but," he trails off and I nod, understanding.

"Why was your dad so dressed up? And he called me an idiot," I furrow my eyebrows and scrunch my nose slightly.

"Almost every time I've ever seen him, he's wearing a suit. And I know he called you that, that tells you what kind of person he is right there," he tucks a piece of hair behind my ear.

"Why does he know where you live?" I wonder aloud. Grey lets a bitter, fake smile onto his lips.

"A couple years ago, I figured that since we were now both adults, we could talk things out. Turns out he's still a motherfucker and I guess he hasn't forgotten the address," he explains, and I wince.

"I think you and I are just better off without our parents," I conclude, and he allows a little smile onto his lips.

"I think you're right," he agrees.

"Especially since we can fuck whenever we want-"

"You just had to say that didn't you? I knew something like that was going to come out of your mouth soon, you haven't said anything like it in like ten minutes," I pat his cheek, face not booty.

"C'mon," he stands and pulls me up with him. I furrow my eyebrows.

"Where are we going?"

"The kitchen," he answers. He drags me into the kitchen, and I head to the fridge. I'm kind of hungry. I'm sure he is too considering this is where we are. I bend down to the level of where the drawers are in the fridge, and I examine the food items. *I'm about to eat really good.* Grey's presence suddenly appears behind me.

Actually, it doesn't *appear* behind me, I *feel* him behind me. I stand straight back up immediately, and his wraps grip my hips, holding me against him. He spins me in his arms and lifts me, placing me on the counter. He connects our lips urgently and he pulls away, lifting off my shirt.

"Grey? What are you doing?" I question once he grips the waistband of his Nike joggers.

"I'm about to strip for you," he answers like it's no big deal, meanwhile, I'm getting hot and bothered.

"Here? We're in the kitchen!"

"I'm horny," he places his lips along my jaw, pulling my body closer to him. I breathe heavier upon hearing the words and feeling his lips on my skin. He suddenly tugs my pants off.

"Are we seriously going to do this here?" I question aloud.

"What? Would you rather do it on the dining room table?" He offers and my eyes widen.

"Our room is not even that far away," I explain to him, but it appears to have gone over his head.

"Yeah. But this is hot; if you could see yourself right now," his eyes trail down my frame, "fuck."

"Sex drive is at a ten right now," I mumble almost inaudibly. He yanks my underwear off and I gasp in surprise. He leans to me and kisses me fervently, gripping onto the hair at the base of my neck. His free hand travels below my waistline and I have trouble focusing. After a while he pulls away and grips onto the waistband of his boxers.

"Woah there hoss," I stop him. He narrows his eyes slightly at me.

"Don't call me hoss," he grumbles.

"Don't we need a..." I trail off nodding.

"I'll pull out."

"Heck no," I shake my head, "what happens when you forget?"

"Fuckin' Grey Jr."

"Stop it," I bite my lip, keeping a laugh in.

"It doesn't feel as good with one," he mumbles, and I raise a single eyebrow.

"Excuse me, why do you know that?"

I understand he's been with other girls. I'm fine with that, that was when he didn't know someone as great as me existed. I don't think I'm okay with him having non-protected sexy time with them though. He smirks. *I'm going to roundhouse kick him in the esophagus.*

"I don't *know* a hundred percent, but I do have a hand and that shit feels pretty fuckin' nice-"

"Stop," I cover my ears.

"And think about it," he trails his hands up my thighs, "nothing between us. Just you and me."

I place a soft kiss on his lips.

"Why don't we just use one this time and then later today or tomorrow I can go to the doctor, okay?" I tilt my head. I hate to admit it because I'm going to have to have a church session in my car later, but he's really got that sounding pretty nice.

"Birth control?"

I nod. Abby's on birth control, she tells me about it sometimes when we have our 'girl talk.' I still can't get over having our talks. I love it so much. It's amazing and it fills my heart to the brim knowing I have someone who I can tell anything to. Of course, I can tell Grey anything and everything. And I do. But there is also just a satisfaction factor when complaining about him to Abby. I complain about him *to* him too, but I like having Abby to agree with me.

"Then we'll still have to use some other protection until it fully starts working but the sooner, I get it then the sooner you can y'know, go without one," I explain. He rushes off and comes back quickly with a package in his hand.

"I'll take that as an okay," I whisper. He slips it on and thrusts into me. My head tilts up to the ceiling and I try to keep the sounds to a minimum. He grips my neck and tilts my head back down until I'm directly face to face with him.

"Eyes on me."

~~~

I wake up with a jolt. Grey slowly lifts his head from its position on my chesticles.

"What's wrong?" his sleepy voice questions. I look down at my feet.

"A demon is going to get me Grey, my feet are out in the open," I nod to them, and he looks down toward them.

"Are you serious?" He groans, rising off of me. He leans down and places the covers back over my cold feet. Then he lays back down in the spot he was.

"Better?" he questions, and I nod. I wiggle my toes just to make sure they weren't eaten.

"What time is it?" I mumble. I raise my arms up and stretch greatly. Grey gives me a look that says, 'do you really have to do that right now?'

"It's one," he mumbles. Crud. The sexy time that occurred earlier this morning wore us out. I'm sorry Jesus.

"I've got to get up," I sit up and he reluctantly removes himself from me.

"Why?"

"I promised Mr. Terrip I'd be at the store by lunchtime and it's past then, so I need to go," I stand under the closely watching eyes of Grey.

"Would you quit it? You already saw enough earlier," I point my finger in his face, eventually poking his cheek, face not booty.

"You're pretty," he replies, and I allow a smile onto my face.

"As a mule's butt or...?" I trail off and he scoffs.

"Shut up," he grumbles. Yeah, yeah, yeah, I'm starting to think that's his favorite phrase. Of course, other than the combinations of curse words he uses.

"You look like a lion, by the way," he tells me before rolling over and acting like he hasn't just offended my heart. I walk into the bathroom and peer into the mirror. *He's not wrong. Brat.* This is what I get for going to sleep with my hair wet. I tinkle and brush my teeth again, just for good measures. Then I take out the darn straightener and straighten my lion mane. Halfway through doing my hair, he waltzes in the bathroom fully still down to his skivvies.

"You should let me straighten your hair-" I cut myself off when I hear him freaking tinkling.

"Grey Alexander!" I shout.

"What? I'm human," he replies.

"Yes, a human who could have gone to the *other* bathroom to tinkle!" I throw my free hand up in the air.

"This one's closer," he answers, and I shake my head at him, focusing back on my hair. Eventually, he stops and flushes. Why does he pee for so long? Good heavens.

"See? Not so bad," he slaps my booty on the way out of the room.

"I could've burnt myself just now because of you!" I call out to him.

"Yeah okay," he replies haphazardly, "oh hey, want to go to Montana with us?"

I set the straightener down and dart back into the bedroom.

"What?"

"Montana, Lilah, are you listening?" He slightly teases. I sort of lose focus watching him pull on his pants.

"The state of Montana?" I grow excited. He pauses.

"Yes darling, the *state* of Montana," he teases, "why are you so amazed?"

"I've never even been out of the state before," I smile, and he frowns.

"What? Why?"

"Well, my parents went on a lot of trips, and they offered to take Jake, but they always said that I needed to stay at home to watch over everything. Jake didn't like that, and it always ended up being both me and him staying at home, so I never went anywhere," I explain. One time they went to the Bahamas. Jake and I were so excited about going but when dad told me I had to stay, I was devastated. I already had my bags packed and everything. And I felt terrible that Jake stayed home with me. I knew how excited he was to go, and I was the one that held him back.

"Well, I'm just going to have to take you everywhere then," he sends me a gorgeous little smile that makes my heart flutter. *He's so sweet.*

"Now get your ass over here and let me give you a hickey," he raises his arm, calling me over. The love-struck look falls off my face and it's replaced with an unamused one. I look to Bear and internally plead him to control Grey.

"Don't act like you don't want it," he leans down to the end of the bed, and he holds his hand out to me.

"I just know that it'll lead to something that's already happened once today," I reach my hand into his and he pulls me gently onto the bed with him. Why did I still give him my hand if I knew what would most likely happen? Because I'm a sexy time addict, just like him. He pulls me closer to him and he places my back against his chest. He rests his back against the headboard, and I lean my head back onto his shoulder.

"I won't give you a hickey," he mumbles, gripping gently on a strand of my hair and twirling it. I *just* straightened my hair. But I let him twirl my hair anyway. It feels nice.

"I'm fucking with you," he leans his head down and presses his lips onto my neck. His tattooed hand travels around to the front of me and before I can even apologize to Jesus beforehand, he grips on my boob. *My boob!* His other hand trails up my neck and tilts my head slightly backward and to the side, giving him better access to the spot where he wants to *show how much of a horny man he is.*

"Grey," I whisper to him quietly. He hums quietly against my neck.

"I love you," I tell him softly. He pauses a split second and I feel his lips turn up in a little smile. As a part of my bucket list, which I partly forgot about, it says that I need to tell Grey I love him many times during the day, every day. I'm not too bad at telling him and he's pretty darn good at telling me. But I've just found that I love catching him off guard when telling him I love him. For example, a couple days ago we were at the restaurant. Grey, Theo, Oaklee, and Lincoln were in Grey's office.

I busted up in there and interrupted their little conversation without a care in the world. Well, I didn't really have a care in the world because Grey sent me the world's loveliest text. The text was asking me to get him the coffee that I usually bring him. First of all, in the text he referred to the drink as a drink for (another word for cats). If I'm being honest, it was only making fun of himself because he loves that drink.

    The second part of the text was just the regular romantic and chivalrous Grey being himself and it basically said, 'hurry up, I want to (effing) feel you up when you get here too.' After arriving and busting up in his office, he was exceptionally unhappy. Just because those guys were in his office. So, I walked over to him, sat his coffee down on his desk, and gave his heavily frowning face a look. Then I leaned down and just ever so softly whispered in his ear that I loved him very much. When I pulled away, his lips were turned up in that smile of his and I felt very accomplished.

    Even the guys were making fun of him for actually smiling considering they had pretty much never seen that beautiful sight. Then Grey proceeded to whisper a reply in my ear. *Such a sweetheart.* He said something along the lines of 'that whisper turned me the (f-word) on. It's too bad they're here.' At that point he had grabbed the back of my upper thigh, a spot where the guys couldn't see because we were behind the large desk. He continued with 'I'd (f-word) you on this desk if no one was here.'

    Of course, I wouldn't let that happen because that's just very out there and way too dangerous for where we were. At that point I had pulled away because I had gotten a little too hot and bothered but he pulled me back down to him. '*But I love you.*' Other than the inappropriate things he said after his adorable little smile, the interaction made my heart happy.

    "I love you," he replies. He suddenly bites down on my neck. I pull away from him and slam my head onto the bed in front of me, groaning into the sheets.

    "That was hard," I mumble. *That's what she said. Stop.*

    "It wasn't," he grips onto the top of my pants in the very back. I rub my hand on the spot he bit. I raise my hand up and I punch his stomach. *Well,* I thought it was his stomach.

    "Fuck, Azalea," he groans in pain rolling over and placing his hand over the top of his pants. I think I may have gone a little bit lower than his stomach by accident. I sit back up all the way and hold my hand over my mouth. I feel genuinely bad.

"I'm sorry Sugar!" I recollect myself. He sits still, his face kind of scrunched up in pain.

"Want me to rub it-Oh no! Never mind!" I pinch the bridge of my nose and roll my eyes at myself. He rolls off the bed and he stands up. Bear follows him, making sure he's okay. He's such a good puppy. Grey walks around the room, his jaw clenched as he does what he needs to...get himself better. I can't imagine what getting hit there feels like. I feel like yeah, getting hit in the boob hurts but I feel like getting hit in the peter hurts way worse.

"I meant to hit your stomach," I bite my lower lip in concern for him. I know it shouldn't, but it actually makes me laugh a little bit. He always smacks the daylights out of my buttcheeks, he bites the crap out of my neck, and so I feel like I've finally gotten even for all the things he's done to me. But this is the first and hopefully the last time I mistake his lower region for his stomach. I stand and
come up behind him.

"Oh lord, what if it doesn't work anymore? Can you break that thing?" I begin to worry. I hold my hand onto my heart, and he turns around to me.

"It's not a *thing* it's my *dick.*"

"Oh, same thing."

~~~

* Grey *

The week coming, we're off to Montana. It's last minute and it pisses me off that I'm the one that has to set up the planes and everything else. Sure, we could fly in regular planes with regular people *if* we didn't have a whole shitload of guns that we have to bring with us. We have a guy that's set up with us through D.C and all we have to do is drive to Knoxville and we're able to take off from there. Even though it's pretty simple, I don't like last-minute things. I really like to know my fucking schedule for the *upcoming week*.

But Azalea is coming. If she would've said no, I probably would've dragged her ass along with us anyway. I'm not about to leave her all alone all week. I know for a fact she'd be perfectly fine by herself. But I won't be so she's coming. I feel like I'm clingier to her than she is to me, but I couldn't give a shit. I hear a knock on my door, and I perk up thinking it could be her. But Theo's face coming into view makes me slump back down and turn my attention back to my computer.

"Hey," he says awkwardly, and I narrow my eyes a bit at that. He's *never* awkward. He probably fucked something up.

"What'd you do?" I grumble.

"What? Nothing!" he relaxes a bit, his voice almost returning to normal. From the corner of my eye, I see him take a seat in one of the chairs in front of my desk. He leans forward, resting his elbows on his knees. That makes me suspicious. Very suspicious. I turn away from my computer and look at him. He looks oddly shaken up.

"I have to tell you something," he starts off quietly.

Chapter Thirty-Eight

Club

* Grey *

I stare at him as he fidgets. He doesn't say anything and I'm growing impatient.

"If you're here to waste my time then get out," I advise him, and he looks up toward me. He shakes his head.

"I'm not, I swear," he answers carefully.

"Then what, Theo?" I sigh heavily.

"So, we were all in the meeting room," he begins, interlocking his fingers, "and we were talking about going to Montana and stuff. Then Jai came in and told everyone that he was opening the store. So, most of them left."

"This is such a god-awful, boring story," I give him an unamused look.

"I'm not done yet," he tells me.

"So, then Jacqueline came in," he swallows, "and she came up to me and you know how she is. She's all flirty and stuff and so she was flirting. Well, I wasn't having it and she...she grabbed onto me."

He takes a deep breath and leans back in his chair.

"What do you mean 'grabbed onto you' Theo?"

"She grabbed my dick," he mumbles uncomfortably. I run my hand down the side of my jaw. There's no doubt that Jacqueline is flirty. She's flirtatious with me and apparently the other guys too. I never thought she would result in this though. Working here though, with well-trained people, I've never had to deal with an actual issue like this before. I knew she was no good from the time she got here. I wasn't able to pick her from the group and that itself gave me a bad feeling from her.

"Do you want her charged?" I question, and he shakes his head.

"No. I just want her gone," he answers, shaking his head. I nod. I *should* unleash Azalea on her ass. That'd be a fight I'd pay a lot of money to see happen.

"I'll take care of it," I assure him, "Now get the fuck out."

"Good. Just like nothing happened. I like how you're saying that just as always. Bye-bye," He stands and exits. I wait a couple of minutes to finish up what I was doing on the computer and then I step out of the office to find Jacqueline. *Bitch.* I find her in the meeting room with a couple of guys all watching tv.

"Jacqueline," I call out and her head snaps to me. A smile appears on her face. I feel like throwing up on the floor, but I refrain because I'm a *nice person.*

"Come with me," I tell her. That stupid ass smile on her face turns more seductive and she rises slowly. I swear to God if she touches *me*, I'm going to lose my shit, unleash Azalea, and personally train Bear to attack the living shit out of her. I lead her back to my office. She closes the door behind us, and I turn around to see her way too close to me. I take three steps back and she starts following me as I go back.

"You're out," I tell her.

"Hm?" she hums, not paying attention to shit.

"You're fired. You don't work here anymore. You're done. I hate the fuck out of you. Get your shit and leave," I tell her. Her smile drops.

"What? Why!?" she nearly shrieks.

"Because I said so."

"You can't just do that!" she stomps her foot.

"Really?" I wonder, "Does my boss prevent me from getting rid of people?"

"Yes, he does!"

"That's funny. I don't have a boss, so I think you're making shit up now," I furrow my eyebrows mockingly at her.

"I'm going to report you!" She grows even angrier.

"Really? To who? How would you like it if Theo wanted to press charges against you for sexual assault?"

Her eyes widen, and she takes a step back. She remains quiet for a couple of seconds.

"Leave," I glare, and she does. I spend an hour or two finishing up setting up everything we need for the Montana trip right as Lilah comes strutting in the room. She's got a plate full of cheese fries and a huge grin on her face. She feeds me two fries even though I told her I didn't want any and she goes on and on about how much she's excited about getting on a plane and going to Montana.

"I heard Jai talking about Jacqueline leaving out of here looking really mad," she says, and I turn my head toward her as she shoves five fries in her mouth at once. *I'm happy she's eating.*

"I fired her ass," I tell her, and her eyes widen. Then she hugs me.

"Aw, I'm proud of you for firing your first employee. I bet it felt good, didn't it?" she kisses my cheek twice. She's only proud of me because just like everyone else, she didn't like her. If it was anyone else that I fired, she'd be sad.

"What'd she do besides be rude?" she wonders innocently.

"She sexually assaulted Theo," I sigh, and she pauses all her movements. Then her bottom lip starts wiggling a bit.

"Don't cry, Lilah," I whisper softly, and her eyes tear up. I hate when she cries. It just does things to me that don't make me feel good.

"I'm crying," she nods, her voice wiggly.

"Don't, it's okay," I try to assure her but there's no stopping it now. She stands from my lap, and I follow her as she walks out the door. She walks until she finds Theo and when she does, she wraps her small arms around his torso.

"Azalea?" he questions, looking up at me confusedly, "What's wrong?"

"I'm sorry," she cries into his chest, and I feel my own chest constrict in pain. She's too sweet and she cares about anyone and everything way more than anyone I even thought existed.

"For what?" he mumbles softly down to her.

"Jacqueline was terrible and she touched you and I feel really sad," she hugs him tighter. He smiles softly.

"Azalea, it's okay. You don't need to feel sad. I'm okay. And Grey made everything better by getting rid of her ass. She can't touch anyone else, *and* she can't be mean to you anymore," he explains and her crying calms.

"Are you sure you're okay? I'll beat her up if you want me to," she assures him, and I smile a little at her.

"I promise I'm okay," he nods, and she pulls away.

"I'm here for you if you're ever not okay, okay?" she pats his arm. He smiles.

"Okay," he nods.

~~~

❀Azalea❀

"I'm freaking ready bud!" I tell Grey excitedly. The only thing we're missing is Bear who stays with Dr. Weiner when Grey goes on trips. Apparently, Bear doesn't like flying and tends to have poops when on planes.

"Don't call me bud," Grey grumbles. We get our own plane. It's crazy to think that little ole me is going to be on a plane full of only great people that I know. It's crazy to think I'm going on a plane in general. And with Grey. I reach down and I slap his butt. I do it so much now that he barely even notices I do it. He lifts all our luggage out of the car and sits it on the asphalt. I reach in to grab a bag and he slaps my hand away.

"Let me help you donkey," I scrunch my nose at him. He pauses and looks over at me. Then he steps away from the car and gives me a 'go ahead' head tilt. Feeling smug, I reach in and grab onto the handle of the large black suitcase. I pull and it moves maybe an inch. I pull away and look over to Grey who is leaning against the car, a smug look on his face. I crack my fingers in front of me, show him my crazy amount of arm muscles, and try again.

"You purposefully gave me the hardest one to get out, didn't you?" I narrow my eyes at him, giving up. He walks forward and yanks it out with one arm in a matter of two seconds.

"Maybe," he whispers, placing a short, sweet kiss on my lips. We meet up with all the guys coming and our luggage is put on the plane. Upon entering the plane, I get a little sad thinking about Jake. He hadn't been on a plane either and I know he always wanted to. Grey leads me to where the two of us are sitting, mostly away from the other guys because he doesn't like to be around them on planes.

We sit and wait for about thirty minutes and then we start taking off. Grey couldn't have a care in the world meanwhile I'm beside him freaking out. I thought I was going to be excited and happy but being on the plane as it's floating up into the air is freaking me out. He notices that. Of course, he does. He notices everything even though I tried to hide it. He places his hand on the side of my head and pulls me into his chest.

"It's okay, Lilah," he kisses the top of my head. I drift off on his shoulder only to wake up again four hours later.

"Nice nap?" Grey questions, and I sit up in my seat.

"Sleeping beauty has awoken," Oaklee leans his body against the seat across from ours. I peek out the window to the left of me and sure enough, we're up in the air. Duh.

"Grey look!" I point down at the mountains below us.

"Leave," Grey mumbles to Oaklee but I'm too distracted by the view out of the window to scold him for being rude. He places his hand on my thigh.

"We have about two hours left on here," he tells me. Plenty of time for more sight-seeing what's below us. I'm excited.

"Want to be a part of the mile-high club?" he leans into me and kisses my neck below my ear. That sounds like it's got something to do with drugs. But knowing everything and everyone on this plane, I can understand that it's not. But it's a club? I think it would be nice to be a part of a club. Why not?

"Yes," I nod, and he pulls away, looking at me with a gorgeous smirk on his face. He moves out of his seat and pulls my hand with him. He rushes to the very back of the plane. I look at the guys who are sitting only in the front. They pay no attention to Grey and me.

"Where on earth are you taking me?" I question him. He moves past the bathroom and down a short narrow hallway. At the end of the hall, there's a door. He opens the door and closes it behind us. I'm starting to think this club is nonexistent. In the room, there's luggage everywhere. But not normal luggage. Gun luggage. Oh, dear Jesus.

"Grey! Why the heck did you bring me here?" I place my hands on my hips. He locks the door and turns toward me.

"Because this is the only place that no one will come to," he leans down and places his lips against mine needily. I pull away out of breath. The room is dark, barely lit up by some sort of light. *What kind of club is this?* He lifts me suddenly and places me on top of a counter-type ledge. He pulls his shirt off and yanks mine off after.

"Grey!" I gasp, "we are *not* about to have sexy time!"

"No one will hear us. And no one ever comes in here. The door's locked too."

"Still!" I whisper-shout.

"You don't want me?"

"No, it's not that, I always want you-"

"You always want to have sex with me?" a smirk rises on his face, and I roll my eyes.

"That's not what I meant."

He grips the waistline of my pants.

"I'm not sitting my booty cheeks on this freaking ledge! This isn't our plane!" I tell him. He lifts me off the ledge and takes everything off the both of us. I can't believe I'm doing this. I can't.

  Dear God, I'm so sorry for doing this. I feel like a bad child, and I just pray that you and Jesus can forgive me for such acts. Also, I know what I'm doing is bad but if y'all could just maybe prevent anyone else from coming in here or hearing us, that would be very greatly appreciated. Don't worry, I'm going to pray right after doing this and also later tonight. I love y'all, amen.

  Although I've recently gotten birth control, I'm still nervous about it since it hasn't been a full week, so Grey takes that familiar square package out of his pocket. He does what he needs to do with it, and he lifts me back up. He kisses me one harsh time before he presses his hand against my mouth and pushes into me.

~~~

  "What were y'all doing in there?" Lincoln's voice questions as Grey closes the door behind us. Lincoln hooks his belt from just coming out of the bathroom.

  "Nothing," Grey says nonchalantly and if I was Lincoln, I would've believed it. I keep my head down and I close my eyes harshly. *Keep your mouth shut Azalea. It's ridiculous. Don't say it.* Oh gosh.

  "Sex."

  "Goddammit," Grey sighs and Lincoln's eyes widen. I place my hand on my forehead and internally punch myself in the face. I say that all the time, for a reason I don't even know. And the one time that I should definitely not say it, I say it.

  "Did y'all really just have sex in there?!" Lincoln whisper-shouts.

  "I told him we shouldn't!" I defend myself even though it takes two to tango. I groan into my hands, my face probably tinged pink. Grey sneaks off into the bathroom to dispose of the condom. He flushes it and Lincoln hears it and it's just all worse.

  "You horny motherfuckers!" Lincoln laughs, "in the gun room? My God."

  "We didn't touch anything! I promise! He held me up-"

"I don't want to hear details!" Lincoln covers his ears and I wince. Grey returns to where we are and when he sees Lincoln holding his ears, he looks toward me and sighs, shaking his head.

"What did y'all just want to be in the mile-high club or what?" he questions, and my mouth drops open.

"*That's* what that is?" I gape at Grey who only smirks to himself. I can't believe myself. I need to go to some sort of school that teaches these sexual phrases because I can't keep driving the struggle bus like this.

"Tell anyone and I'll kill you," Grey shoves past him. Lincoln gives me a look.

"Actually, try not to tell anyone because I'm already dying of embarrassment just because you know. Unless you want me to have a stroke, please don't tell anyone," I give him a quick smile and follow Grey. I sit down in my seat, and I put my face in my hands. I really can't believe myself. I send Grey's arm a little punch.

"You did this," I tell him.

"How was I supposed to know he'd be coming out the bathroom the same time we'd be sneaking out of the room I just fucked you in?" He questions back. Good Lord the way he says that is so vulgar. Why not something sweet like...making love. Or even better, making music or something, I don't know. Heck, saying sexy time is great.

"You're a terrible influence on me."

"Yeah well, not all rules should be followed" he kisses my temple. I quite like following the rules. Thank you very much. Rule 342,941 I like to follow: *Don't have sexy time on a plane.* But that obviously went right out the window. I grip onto both of Grey's large hands, and he already knows what's about to happen, so he turns toward me and he closes his eyes.

"Dear heavenly father, we are so terribly sorry for doing what we just did. I'm ashamed to say I'm a part of the mile-high club, forgive me. And father forgive Grey because he's just a chronic rule-breaker. Also forgive him for dragging me into-"

Grey interrupts me during *prayer.*

"Excuse me father, forgive Azalea and help her understand that she knew what we were doing after a certain point, and she could've stopped it at any time."

If he curses, we're going to have to start this prayer all over and make it longer by having to apologize for that too.

"And yes, forgive us for all the times we did things we probably shouldn't have in places where it's probably not appropriate but that's love for you," he continues and a little smile reaches my lips at the last part. He gives my hand a little squeeze which means I can continue.

"Father, we'll try to behave better. More like heavenly children. Please help this plane land safely, in the Jesus name, amen," I end and Grey and I both lean down and kiss each other's hands once.

~~~

We got off the plane pretty late. We got to the house we're staying at really late, and it was so late that no one explored. It was late and we all went straight to bed. Especially me. I was basically a zombie and Grey was making fun of me but whatever. I can't even remember anything about the house. I think I slept walked into a random room and from there it was just claimed to be mine and Greys. I raise my head from the pillow groggily. I look around the room and it's completely pitch black. Is it still dark outside or is there just no windows?

Oh gosh, what if I sleep-walked into some random closet and just brought a pillow with me?

Grey's not even on me. Oh Lord. Why am I totally bunched up in all the covers? Am I even in Montana? My eyes adjust to the darkness, and I just barely see the outline of the window and the outside world. It's just still dark outside. I reach over gently, and I search the other side of the bed for any sign of Grey. I softly poke a foreign part of the body. Oh, help me, what if this isn't even Grey? I lay my hand flat, and I identify the part I'm touching as the back of someone. The person lays on his side. Grey doesn't even sleep on his side. He sleeps on his stomach or on top of me. I swear if this is someone else, I'm going to have a fit.

I reach around to the person's stomach. It is definitely not Grey. This guy is too skinny. I shoot out of the bed. Is sleeping in the same bed as someone cheating? *I just felt up a random person?!*

I crawl on my hands and knees, feeling around for a door or anything. I find a door and feel my way up to the handle. I open it and a sliver of light comes from the clock on the stove in the kitchen. I stand up and close the door softly behind me. I hold my head in my hands feeling horrible. Who even was that?! I rush all the way into the kitchen and turn on the light over the oven just to give me some light. I immediately go to the coffee maker and begin on some coffee to distract myself. Where is Grey and I's room? Am I even in the right house?

It's seven in the morning. But already nine in Tennessee. I let the coffee finish and then I make a cup for Grey. Maybe giving him coffee will make me feel better about *sleeping with someone else*. I fix the coffee just the way he likes it with extra love, and I go on the search for him. I open the doors to two more rooms and conclude that nope, none of those other two are Grey. It's embarrassing but I got close enough to smell each of them to determine if they were Grey or not.

I don't even have my phone so I can't use a flashlight or anything. And I'm not about to just flip on a light, no sir. I'd hate to wake anyone up. I decide to carefully go up the stairs. Of course, being in hallways I can turn lights on if I can find them but not room lights. The first room I come across is a closet so that does nothing. But then I open to door to a bedroom. The guy is on his phone, and I see him turn to the door where I am.

"Azalea?" Oaklee's voice questions out and I breathe out a breath of relief. I flick the light on, and he sits up.

"Oaklee, I'm dying," I groan, shutting the door behind me.

"Tell me all about it baby doll, I'm all ears," he pats the bed beside him. I sit down carefully.

"I feel like a terrible person," I admit and his eyebrows furrow.

"Why?"

"I slept with someone else," I deadpan, and I don't think I've ever seen someone's eyes get so wide.

"What?!" He whisper-shouts.

"Exactly! I woke up and was right next to a stranger," I defend.

"Who?" he gapes. I throw my hands in the air.

"I have no clue!"

"How do you know it wasn't Grey?" he questions. I look down sheepishly at the coffee in my hands.

"I touched him."

"Oh my God, did you touch his dick?!" he whisper-shouts again.

"No! I touched his back and stomach, and he was too skinny to be Grey!" I defend again.

"Help me find Grey," I plead.

Chapter Thirty-One

Flowers

❀ Azalea ❀

"His room isn't far from this one, I'll help you," he nods, standing up. The comforter falls off him and I cover my eyes.

"Put clothes on, Lord help me," I whisper. He laughs at me, muttering sorry for only sleeping in his boxers. I've already been through so much this morning I don't know how much more I can handle. The only boxer-wearing man I like to look at is Grey. Mostly because he's nice and juicy. And because I love him and whatever.

"Okay, I'm good now," he tells me, and I remove my hands from my eyes to see him with a pair of pajama pants on his lower half now. We leave his room and go out on the search. After searching two rooms and determining that the guys in them weren't Grey, we walk to the door at the very end of the hallway. I walk to the bed and place my hand down on a butt accidentally. I almost pull away, but it feels familiar. And nice, of course. I lean down and catch his scent. It's Grey.

"I found him, Oaklee!" I whisper excitedly. I walk back toward Oaklee and flick on the light. I don't care about waking Grey up. He'll get over it or I'll *make* him get over it. Because he's my b-word. I look around our room and it's safe to say we got the master bedroom. The room is pretty huge. And at the end of the room, there's a balcony.

I look at Grey who's still fast asleep on his stomach, facing away from us. I grip onto the coffee Oaklee was holding for me and I walk to Grey. I sit the cup down on the table beside the bed and I climb onto Grey's back. Oaklee laughs from the doorway. Little does he know; I do this to Grey almost every morning.

"Wake up *darling*," I stick my finger in his neck, wiggling it. I know it tickles him. I laugh evilly internally. He scrunches his shoulders up.

"I brought you a coffee, Sugar," I tell him.

"Alright, y'all have fun," Oaklee tells us goodbye, closing the door on the way out.

"Get your gluteus maximus up. I want to watch the sunrise with you," I pat his shoulder. He tilts over and I fall off his back. He pulls me closer to him and lays his head on my chest.

"Oh, and I slept with someone else," I tell him. He jerks away from me and sits up quicker than I've ever seen him move in my life. I'm not saying he's a lazy person because he's not. He's just never in a rush to do anything. I'm always go-go-go and he's always like stop-wait-a-effing-minute-god-darn-it.

"What?" he says lowly. His eyebrows furrow down almost into those stupid old glares he used to give me. I'll kiss him on the lips right now.

"I know right!" I sigh, shaking my head. I pick up his coffee.

"Here, c'mon, drink it so you will be happy," I hand it to him. He's never happy in the mornings. He looks at the coffee in my hand like I've poisoned it.

"Are you fucking serious?" he questions almost angrily. My eyebrows raise.

"Yes, I'm freaking serious," I reply. What the heck? Does he think he's *not* grumpy in the mornings? He *needs* coffee. I roll my eyes and sit the coffee back down. If coffee won't make him happy then I guess a little hug/snuggle will have to do. I scoot closer to him, and he leans away from me.

"Get away from me," he glares. I lean back, tilt my head, and hold my heart.

"I swear if you're sleep talking again, don't be surprised if I slap you to get you out of it, okay?" I warn him.

"Azalea, I'm really about to cry," he says quietly. My heart falls. Why on earth?

"What?" I say softly, "Why?"

"You just said you slept with someone else," he replies.

"I did sleep with someone else. I don't even know which guy here it was yet," I shake my head, still not being able to believe myself.

"You cheated on me?" he says in the most hurt tone I've ever heard. My mouth drops open slightly.

"Of course not! Why would you think that? I'd never do that to you," I explain.

"You said you slept with someone else."

"Like sleeping, like closing your eyes and sleeping. I said I *slept* with someone else. Oh wait," I realize that I probably should've explained that first thing.

"Azalea," he groans and places a pillow over his face.

"Oh yeah, that's my bad right there," I wince. He removes the pillow from his face.

"You can't say things like that. You need to think about what you say before you say it, oh my God," he grips his hair, running his hands through it.

"I'm sorry," I say sadly. I lean to him, and he leans to me. He lays his head on my shoulder and I hug him to me.

"Were you really going to cry?" I ask softly. He doesn't respond. Only about ten seconds later does he just slightly nod his head.

~~~

Freshly showered and feeling great, Grey and I walk out onto the balcony. I convinced him to watch the sunrise with me. He's still sad about earlier. And I feel absolutely terrible. Now he's very clingy and touchy since I accidentally made it sound like I cheated. I made sure to apologize twenty times, but I still ca tell he's upset even thinking about getting cheated on.

"Holy guacamole! It's freezing cold out here! My nipples could cut diamonds Grey, don't look," I tell him, and he looks. I rush back inside and grab the comforter off the bed. I wrap it around Grey, and he sits down in the chair we brought out from inside. He opens it up and I take a seat on his lap. He wraps his arms and the comforter around me and sits his chin on my shoulder.

"Sunrise is very soon," I tell Grey. I found my phone. Apparently Grey had it since I left it in the car last night and he plugged it up for me. We also figured out how we got separated. I walked into the house first once it was unlocked and I laid down in the first room I could find. Or I might've chosen that room because it is closest to the kitchen, I don't know. Well, Grey came in with our bags and he got the master bedroom. We were all really tired, so Grey went straight to bed, on top of the covers, waiting for me to finish exploring like he thought I was doing. I feel like the guy I slept in the same bed with did the same thing because when I felt his back and stomach, he was still wearing a flannel shirt. At least it felt like flannel.

But I can't remember who was wearing flannel so it's still a mystery as to who it was. Grey and I sit back and watch as the sky changes colors and the sun rise over the mountain range.

"It's so pretty, isn't it?" I question aloud, not expecting any sort of reply from Grey. He's not really one to sit back and enjoy nature's beauty. He's more the type that does what I tell him to because he's my b-word. I told him to come out here and watch the sunrise with me and he did.

"Love me?" he mumbles quietly. I smile softly, turning my head to look back at him.

"Always," I nod, "I love you."

"Lilah?" he questions. I hum in response.

"When do I ask you to marry me?" he questions softly, and my whole heart stops beating. Is he serious?

"...Why?"

I can't fathom the reason why he would want to marry me. If that's why he asked that question. I still can't believe I'm dating him and now this?

"Why do you think?" he responds, amusement in his voice. *I might as well be honest in response to his first question.*

"At least a year from now. Let us be together for a while just to make sure that this is what we really want, okay? And I need to stop being a teenager before you ask me. And when you ask, make sure I don't know you're going to ask," I tell him truthfully. I look back to him to gauge his reaction to my words. A small smile, his own little smile, sits on his lips as he looks back at me. Then he slowly nods.

"Okay," he says softly.

"You're crazy, I swear," I shake my head at him.

"Yeah, *I'm* crazy."

"You're the one who wants to marry me," I defend myself. It's crazy to want to marry me, in my opinion.

"You're the one who wants to marry me too," he replies. I pause. I bite back a smile. I do want to. But I'm not going to admit that to him. Not yet at least.

"What do you think about me getting a tattoo?" he questions and my eyebrows furrow. I open the comforter and take a look at his tattooed-up arm that hangs loosely around me.

"Hm, Grey. I don't know. Are you sure you want a tattoo? I mean, you don't really have any so you might be scared to get one," I respond sarcastically, and he rolls his eyes at me.

"Shut up."

He lifts his arm out of the comforter and he turns it over showing the narrow almost empty space beside the large dead tree on his forearm.

"Flowers," he mumbles.

"Flowers?" I question. That's surprising. Something alive on his death-themed arm sleeve.

"Alive flowers?" I question just to make sure he's not going to put dead looking flowers on his arm.

"Fully alive ones," he nods, "Azaleas."

"Say what?"

"Azaleas," he repeats. The flower I was named after. Oh my gosh,

Lilah   *K. Pope*

he actually loves me or something. *Don't cry. There's no reason to cry so don't.*

"Why are you about to cry?" he questions, and I smile. I turn around on his lap and wrap my arms around him in one of my famous hugs.

"You make me happy," I explain, and his arms tighten ever so slightly.

"You make *me* happy."

With the sun now fully up, I lead him back into the bedroom where we lay down and just hold each other for a bit. Neither of us falls back asleep, we just stay in each other's embrace. Me in his embrace for a while then we switch and he's in my embrace. It goes on for probably an hour and a half. I don't even worry about exploring the house or the fact that I could eat a horse at the moment. Our door suddenly is thrown open. At this point, Grey is laying with his head on my chest, so we are both able to look at who came in. Theo and Oaklee.

"There's an indoor pool in this fuckin' house. Let's put that bitch to use," Oaklee calls out to us. Theo nods beside him enthusiastically. Oh yeah, I forgot Grey told us that a few days ago. *Too bad I can't mothertrucking swim.*

"Oh, and the food's cooked downstairs so eat," Theo mentions. They shut the door with smiles on their faces and I sit up. I roll off the bed and bend down to get my bathing suit out of my suitcase. Then I get Grey's black colored swim trunks out of his suitcase.

"Come on, put them on," I throw them at him. He sighs and gets up slowly.

"I got to piss-"

"Excuse me?" I raise my eyebrow at him, and he pauses at the doorway to the bathroom.

"My bad, Lilah. I got to *tinkle* babe," he shoots me a look before going in, not even closing the door or anything. I strip and put on my light blue two-piece bathing suit. It's tied in the front even though you can't untie it and the rest is normal. I stand up on the bed and look in the large mirror that's directly across from it. The scar on my ribs immediately catches my attention. Then my eyes fall to the scars on my leg. They're horrid. And all around are smaller but still noticeable scars from the glass and the impact of the crash.

I sigh and plop down on the bed, slipping under the covers to hide myself from the mirror. Grey comes out of the bathroom looking as gorgeous and as confident as ever with his juicy thighs and toned muscles.

"What're you doing?" He questions me.

"Wallowing in self-pity," I mumble as he comes closer. Gosh he just looks so good. He rips the covers off me and tosses them to the other side of the bed.

"Why?" He asks. I look down at myself. Then I point to the huge scar on my rib that is exceptionally visible. His eyes travel slowly to where I'm pointing.

"What about it?"

Then I point to every other one, which is a lot, and his eyes never stray from mine.

"*What* about them?" He questions almost *daring* me to say I think they look horrid. I turn my head away from him, looking out the balcony at the mountains. He grips my jaw with his whole gargantuan hand and turns it back to him. He leans down and kisses me harshly.

"Beautiful," he pulls away, "you're so beautiful."

"Now come on before I decide to fuck you instead of going swimming," he grips onto my hand and helps me up. Vulgar man. He picks up one of his t-shirts and he throws it at my face.

"Put that on 'cause you turn me on too easily," he mumbles. I pull the oversized shirt over my hand, and he grips my hand as soon as I'm done.

"Where is the pool?" I question. I know it's indoors because hello this is Montana but I'm not sure where since I never got to explore.

"Over yonder," he shrugs. Great answer.

"Oh okay, now I know exactly where it is, thanks so much love," I say sarcastically, patting his booty. He decides to ignore my comment as we make it down to the kitchen. He slaps my butt as hard as ever and the sound just resounds throughout the house, I'm sure.

"Goddamn, I heard that," Jonas says as he exits the room I came out of earlier this morning. You're *actually* kidding. I melt down to the floor and mourn over the loss of my buttcheek. When I start getting feeling back in it, I rise back up and take a seat at one of the tall stools at the kitchen island.

Lincoln stands at the kitchen counter fixing himself some coffee.

"See what I have to deal with?" I question Lincoln and he nods.

"I feel bad for you," he gives me a smile.

"You *should* feel bad for *me,*" Grey grumbles in disagreement.

"You don't know what you're talking about," I tilt my head over at him.

"You make my hair gray," he sets his chin on his hand, his dark eyes focused on me.

"I do not! You make *my* hair gray because you make me want to strangle you sometimes," I flick his hand.

"*You're* the one who talks my ears off."

"Oh yeah? Well, *you're* the one who just apparently *needs* to be babied when you're sick," I scrunch my nose at him. Gosh he's the biggest baby in the world.

"*You're* the one who leaves your damn hair all over the place."

"Listen here, *boss*. I can't even help that! And *you* love to leave the stupid toilet seat up in the middle of the night. I've almost fallen in because of you!" I point at him.

"*You* don't know how to keep your fuckin' frozen feet off me during the night."

"You're always warm you donkey! At least I don't snore!" I raise my eyebrow at his gorgeous face.

"Oh, bullshit. Your ass snores every now and then. And unlike you, I don't find it fun to watch the *comedy* movies you *make* me watch."

I scoot my stool closer to him and he watches me come closer.

"At least I don't watch the world's scariest freaking movies and find amusement in them like *you,*" I narrow my eyes at him.

"*You* love your flowers more than you love me," he turns his head away from me, hiding his sulky expression.

"Not true! You're just saying that because I always make you get up off me in the morning so I can go water them. And *you* don't like fixing yourself coffee so you always get me to do it by saying you don't know what to do, even though you *do."*

"That's 'cause you make it better than me," he turns his head back to me, "you don't like making it for me?"

His eyes flit between both of mine. I tilt my head low and give him a soft smile.

"I'm just teasing, I don't mind it."

~~~

"I'm scared," I admit, looking down at the heated pool in front of me. The past hour, I've sat with my feet in the water, watching all the guys have fun in the pool. Now just recently, they've all gotten out to get lunch and do other things. They all tried to coax me into the pool, but I'd rather just sit and watch everyone have fun. But now that they're all gone, I have no excuse to keep me from getting in other than 'I don't want to.'

"You think I'm going to sit here and let you drown or some shit?" he rolls his eyes.

"Come on," his voice turns softer, "I've got you Lilah."

"What if you accidentally forget I can't swim, and you let me go and I sink like a rock?" I come up with probably the most realistic question in the world.

"I won't let anything bad ever happen to you, okay?" he gives me one of his baby smiles. I sigh softly and pull off the t-shirt I have on. I sit it on one of the chairs by the pool and I walk to the stairs. Grey grips onto my hand firmly and doesn't let go as I walk into the pool.

"Not so bad," he tucks my hair behind my ear as I still cling to him even though we're in the three-foot part of the pool. We walk a little deeper and I cling tighter.

"What would happen if I peed in the pool?" I question aloud. He sighs softly.

"I'd feel the water turn warmer beside my *fucking* legs."

"It's not like I'd actually do it," I tell him.

"I wouldn't put it past you," he grumbles.

"Lean back," he tells me, and I shake my head rapidly.

"No ma'am."

"Shit ass," he grumbles under his breath. He bends quickly and hooks his arms under my legs. I close my eyes like the scaredy cat I am. He lays me flat on the way, holding his hands under me. I'm stiff as a board.

"Relax," he touches his hand to the top of my chest, and I get a little turned on. I peep open one eye and give him a little smirk to which he rolls his eyes at.

"I can't relax, I feel like I'm going to sink like the Titanic," I breathe out slowly.

"Worst case scenario, you sink but you'll only stay under for a bit 'cause I'll get you," he shrugs like what he said isn't a big deal.

"That's exactly what I'm scared of! You're helping my situation zero percent!" I squint my eyes tighter closed. He places his hand under my shoulder blades and pushes it up slightly. He raises my legs up to the surface of the water and before I can even start to say anything, he lets go of me. I almost pee in this pool. I remain calm but, on the inside, I'm having a heart attack.

"Look at you," his amused voice sounds muffled since there's water in my stupid ears.

"So brave, aren't you?" He continues and I internally give him the middle finger. I'm too scared to move. And I'm not sure if I've taken a breath since he's let go of me.

"You want me to grab you?" He questions and I still don't move. I feel like if I move a muscle, I'll sink.

"Lilah? You know you can stand up here, right?" He questions quietly and my eyes open. From the corner of my eye, I see we're not very far from the ladder in the three-foot part of the pool. I must've floated back here. I let my leg sink down and I stand up. Grey looks down at me like he's silently making fun of me.

"Don't make fun of me you boob."

Chapter Forty

❀ Azalea ❀

December twenty-fifth. It's motherfreaking Christmas. And I'm ashamed of myself for still being in bed at the moment. The shower in the bathroom turns off. I rub on Bear's belly who sits next to me, rolled over onto his back. I'd been up for hours. Since about six. I already showered and did everything I needed to. Then I had laid back down with Grey because I needed a cuddle buddy. I didn't even want to let him go this morning when he woke up. The little smile he had on his face when I wouldn't let him go was a sign that he liked that. He seems happy today and that makes me happy. What also makes me happy is how juicy he looks. Oh yeah.

The bathroom door opens, and I hear Grey's footsteps as he walks out. I sit up slowly and admire him. His arms are raised as he dries his hair with a towel roughly. His joggers hang low on his hips, and I narrow my eyes at the defined top of a 'v' just above the waist of his pants. His long sleeve shirt covers the rest of what I want to see. He lowers the towel and tosses it into the hamper near the door. He raises his dark eyes to me, and a slow smile pulls at his lips. He begins walking over to me and I raise my arms for him. He leans into me, and I hug him tightly. Sitting on the bed, he pulls me onto his lap gently. Bear lets out a soft whine.

"I know you're lookin' hard at my goodies," he uses the same term I use and my heart flutters. I nod softly against him. I pull away from the hug and place a long kiss on his lips.

"Merry Christmas," he pulls away, pecking my lips one more time. I smile.

"Merry Christmas, you filthy animal."

"You got to always be so mean to me?" he shakes his head, but I know he's teasing.

"I'm never mean to you."

His eyes suddenly take on a certain look. I know that look. I've seen it too many times by now. His hands trail lower on my waist, and he pulls my body closer to his.

"You hornish little buttnugge-" he cuts me off.

"Are you going to give me my present now or later?" he leans down to me, uttering lowly.

"Right now," I whisper. His eyes flash excitedly. I raise my hands up to his booty and I slap his butt quite hard.

"Merry Christmas, that was it," I smile, and he looks more unamused than I've seen him look in quite a while.

"You're a little shit, you know that?" he squeezes my waist and I squirm a bit.

"Want to know something?" I ask him and before he can answer, I continue anyway, "I don't give a fart."

"I got you something," he says, and I perk up. He made me not get anything for him. Like, fully kept me from getting anything. He also said he'd be mad if I got anything which made me mad, and I didn't talk to him for three minutes. So, then I said if I'm not allowed to get him anything, then he's not allowed to get me anything because that's not how this works.

"You did?"

"Fuck no, kiss my ass," he pulls away, smirking to himself and my mouth drops open. Then he comes back closer.

"I'm kidding," he shakes his head, rolling his eyes. So, he did get me something? I swear he doesn't like to listen to me. He reaches into the pocket of his joggers and when his hand comes back out, it's tightly closed. He brings his hand up, level to my face and I furrow my eyebrows. He extends out his pointer finger, all while still keeping the hand clenched shut. He pushes his hand closer, and his eyebrows furrow down at the neckline of my shirt, and he points to it. I look down at what he's looking at and he opens his hand, running his monstrous hand up my face. I give him an unamused look.

"Really, I did get you something," he nods, putting his hand into his other pocket. He brings his hand up and shows me his middle finger. *Someone has jokes today.*

"I'm sorry," he pulls my head into his chest, and he kisses the top of it. He reaches down and interlaces his hand with mine, pulling away.

"C'mon," he begins walking somewhere.

"I trust you as far as I can throw you. And you know what that means? That means I trust you zero percent," I explain.

"I'll pick your ass up so you ain't got a choice, Lilah," he gives my hand a tug. I wish I was a freaking bodybuilder. One good time I just want to outpower him so bad. If I contact The Rock, I wonder what the chances are of him responding. He brings me to the dresser.

"If you're about to open your underwear drawer and shove one over my head like you did that one time, I'm going to run away," I warn him.

"Like hell your lazy ass would run anywhere," he glances at me, a smile tugging at his lips.

"What is this? Make-fun-of-Azalea Day?" I place my hands on my hips. I mean, even if my knee would allow me to run, he's right, I wouldn't but whatever.

"It's make-fun-of-Grey Day every day for you, I think you can deal with this today," he nods.

"You're fixing to get got, you know that?" I roll up my invisible sleeves.

"Yeah?" he teases, rolling up his actual sleeves. I catch sight of a patch on his arm that looks like it's covered in saran wrap.

"What's that?" I question, looking up at him. He gives me one of his baby smiles. He removes the patch and I look at the new edition to his sleeve.

My heart beats wildly and my eyes automatically get watery. A single beautifully detailed azalea sits in the previously blank space. Around the flower lies the leaves that go up and begin to wrap around the dead tree beside it. Where the leaves have wrapped around the dead tree, there have been lighter highlights added. Where the leaves of the azalea touch the dead tree, the tree seems to come back to life.

"What're you crying for?" his voice questions softly.

"It's like you actually love me or something," I joke, wiping under my eyes.

"Well, you like it?" he asks, "I mean, that shit's permanent so even if you don't, you're still going to have to look at it, but do you like it?"

I love it. I love him. I love those Colby Jack cheese squares too- stop.

"I mean it's a commitment," he shrugs, looking down at his arm. His eyes remain happy. He loves the tattoo too.

"But shit, an even bigger commitment is dealing with your ass every day and guess what? I do that," he adds. I throw my head back and laugh at his ridiculousness.

"I love it," I smile at him happily, "I really do."

"Good. I have another thing for you," he winces back because he knows I'm about to slap his boob.

"Grey Alexander Kingston. This isn't fair," I cross my arms.

"I already have everything I want, I don't need anything," he shakes his head.

"Does it look like I care?" I raise my eyebrows. I grab his wallet off the top of the dresser. I bring it in front of me.

"Merry Christmas you butt," I hand his wallet to him. I'm such a great last-minute gift giver. He opens the drawer that he keeps his freaking guns in.

"Your nosy ass. This is the only damn place that you wouldn't stumble upon it," he rolls his eyes and I watch him pull out a large flat box. I recognize the brand name on the box to be one I cannot pronounce because it's foreign and obviously expensive.

"No," I deadpan.

"Yes sir," he tells me. He's stealing my phrases, but it tickles my pickle.

"That's too much. Thank you, Sugar, but I can't take it-"

"You don't even know what the hell is in the box," he interrupts me.

"I can't even pronounce the name on the front of that *velvet* box. That's too expensive," I hold my heart.

"It cost me two bucks," he lies straight to my face. He opens it and a gorgeous necklace lay inside it perfectly. I gasp softly. The chain of the necklace is the cleanest platinum silver I'll probably ever see. The part that makes my eyes water again is the solitaire diamond pendant that rests against the dark blue velvet padding of the case. It's perfect. It's simple and absolutely gorgeous.

"Grey this is too much," I keep my hand on my heart. He sits the case on the top of the dresser, and he picks the necklace up gently.

"Turn around," he tells me. I point my finger at him.

"I cannot."

"You don't like it?" he asks.

"I love it. Oh my gosh, I love it but-"

"Then turn your ass around," he tells me again. I give him the I'm-about-to-make-a-run-for-it look, and he narrows his eyes. He picks up on that look. I'm tackled by my third step onto the bed. He leans me up against the backboard and straddles me, but keeps his weight off me. He unclasps the necklace and there's no point in me struggling.

"It's too expensive, Grey," I whisper, and he only flits his eyes up to mine for a quick enough second to give me a little smile.

"Your ass deserves the world; this isn't anything," he reaches around my neck. It takes him a few seconds, but he finally gets it clasped back. I love how his compliments are always so *him*.

"If I can't put a diamond on your finger yet, then one's going to be one around your neck," he tells me sternly before leaning down and giving my lips a soft kiss.

"I love you, Sugar."

"I love *you,* Lilah."

"Oh!" I suddenly remember, "We have to wake up Bear to give him his toys!"

"He can wait," he grumbles.

"Nuh-uh, he's a Santa Claus enthusiast, he needs his presents asap," I nod, and Grey only rolls his eyes, moving off me.

~~~

* Grey *

Bear lays on the floor, all the toys and bones Azalea says Santa Claus got for him surrounding him. From beside me, Azalea sits with her eyes trained on Bear. She loves that damn dog more than she loves me. Her hand fiddles with the necklace that sits around her neck. Abby was half behind the necklace. I wanted to get her something. I've been wanting to get her something, but I didn't know what. She deserves more than just a few thousand-dollar necklace. But I know if I got her anything bigger, she'd not talk to me for at least ten minutes.

I don't think I can go that long without hearing her voice. Ever since she's moved in, the longest I've gone without hearing her voice with her beside me had to have been at least five minutes. Goddamn, she's talkative.

"Guess what?" she rolls her head over to me and I'm placed in a trance upon seeing her looking over at me like she loves me. I don't think I'll ever get used to that look she gives me.

"What?"

"Bear totally just farted," she snorts.

"You sure it wasn't you?" I question.

"Nope. If it was me, you'd know it," she explains and that's true. She's brutally honest and she doesn't hold anything back. If she's got to do something, she's going to do it and she's going to make sure you know it's *her* that did it. She leans into me and grips onto the side of my face. She places her lips on my cheek before trailing them down to my jaw. She knows I like it when she does that. The kisses are innocent but when she does it, it makes me think thoughts that are far from innocent. Then she blows a damn raspberry on my cheek and pulls away, laughing at her own actions. She stands up and grabs onto my hand, motioning for me to get up too.

"Want to help me make cookies for tonight?" she asks me excitedly, a smile on her face. *I can't say no to that.* I know shit about baking but it's obvious she wants me to help her. I only give her a little nod and her smile widens as she starts to pull me into the kitchen. I stand in the middle of the kitchen watching her as she skitters around grabbing ingredients from everywhere. I don't really know what to do with myself. She washes her hands then instructs me to do the same and I do. She passes me the carton of eggs and a metal bowl.

"Crack two eggs in the bowl for me, okay?" she tells me, keeping her eyes focused on whatever she's mixing together. I look at the eggs in front of me. My egg-cracking skills are very shit. I can cook them, that's easy. But I can't crack them open without getting the shell everywhere.

"Um," I mumble, and she pauses, looking over at me. Her eyebrows furrow in sweet concern.

"You need a little bit of help?" she questions, scooting over closer to me. She grips onto one of the eggs, cracks it on the side of the bowl and shows me slowly how to open it without getting shells anywhere. Then she stands back a bit and watches me as I successfully crack my own egg without getting any shells anywhere.

"Look at that!" I hear the smile in her voice, "such a good helper."

My chest fills with pride for *cracking a fucking egg properly*. She gives me a few other ingredients to mix in with the eggs and before she can tell me to mix it in with the 'dry ingredients' as she called them, my phone rings. The name Sanfred appears on the screen and the call better not be what I think it is. It's nine in the morning on Christmas.

"Yeah?" I grumble.

"I know you said we won't work today but this is really important," Sanfred explains on the other end of the phone. I wanted today to be completely work-free. The guys need a break and I do too. I wanted to spend all day with Azalea before we go to Jai's house tonight for the annual 'gathering' he has.

"What is it?" I sigh. He explains all the details he's got access to and the whereabouts of the case. It's only about an hour away so it's not terrible. A kid has been taken from his family into this state from Georgia. All we have to do is retrieve the kid and turn the guy in. I place my phone down on the counter and she looks at me, a smile on her lips.

"You have to work?" she questions softly. I nod hesitantly.

"Okay," she nods, "I'll just finish these up and then I'll go see Mr. Terrip for a while."

"I'm sorry," I tell her honestly. She shakes her head immediately.

"No, no, I understand that you have to do this and it's perfectly okay," she smiles. She leans to me and wraps her small arms around my torso. I place a kiss on her head.

"I love you," I tell her. Her hands trail down to my ass.

"I love *you*."

~~~

🌸Azalea🌸

I am very pleased with today's events. I feel like I've gotten a lot done. Not only did I make cookies for Mr. Terrip and for Jai's house tonight, but I also went to see Mr. Terrip. When I came home, I curled my hair too which is something I haven't done in forever. Not that I'm complaining, but Grey's been away for a while longer than I thought so I've had some extra free time. I also had a mini runway show for Bear. He loved it, I'm sure. I'm more of a Spring/Summer type of person so I have a lot of clothes that I wear when it's warm, and not a ton of clothes to wear while it's cold. So, since I haven't worn my warm-season clothes in a while, I decided to show them to Bear.

Once I was done with that, I did laundry then sat down to watch *Incredibles 2* because I love baby Jack-Jack. Halfway through the movie, Grey walks in the door and a smile automatically lights up my face. He's not smiling. I pause the movie and stand, walking to him. He keeps his eyes on the ground and my smile falters. Without a word, he tugs me to him. He bends, wrapping his arms tightly around my waist. In only a second, he lifts me up so he's not bending. I grow worried.

"What's wrong?" I ask softly. He remains quiet. He doesn't move.

"There was a kid," he starts quietly, and I squeeze him tighter.

"Some psycho took him from his parents, and we had to go get him," he continues, still holding onto me for dear life. I don't say anything, I just let him talk. I let him tell me what's wrong.

"When we got there, I walked in first like I always do and the guy was there waiting for us," he trails off.

"He shot the kid in the head right in front of me," he presses his face into my shoulder after finishing and my eyes widen but I don't say anything. I'm usually a person of many words. But now, I have no idea what to say to him. So, I just hug him as tight as possible, figuring it's what he needs.

"What do you need me to do?" I keep my voice strong but soft.

"Just let me hold you."

"Okay," I nod, kissing his temple. I hear Bear's collar below me, and I peek down to see him, rubbing his head against Grey's leg. He walks over to the couch and sits down, situating me on his lap, never taking his hands off me.

"That's never happened to me before," he says quietly, removing his face from my shoulder and looking at me. His clenches and my heart breaks when it makes me think he blames it on himself. He runs his fingers through the hair at the back of my head.

"You look beautiful," he leans forward, placing a sweet kiss on my lips.

"Thank you, Sugar," I smile, and his face lightens.

"I'm always here for you, just like now, okay? Whenever you need me," I place a kiss on his cheek, and he nods.

"Thank you."

~~~

Grey understood when I told him we didn't have to go to Jai's house tonight, but he insisted on going. I think it's because he wanted to get his mind off things. But he's still shaken up by what he saw, I can tell that much. I think anyone would be. He's being quieter and he's not let go of me since he got home. Even in the car on the way to Jai's, he's got his hand over in my lap, interlaced with my own. I'm happy to know that he recognizes that I'm here for him, but I just want to take his thoughts and pain away. It hurts me to see him hurt.

"We can leave whenever you want to, Sugar," I remind him, "just tell me when okay?" He turns his head over to me as we pull into the driveway of Jai's craftsman style house.

"Okay."

We get out and Grey's automatically by my side. On one hand, is the plate of cookies I made and in the other is his hand. He opens the door for us and walks right in.

"Look who it is," Oaklee calls out as Jai gets up to greet us.

"Merry Christmas," he smiles before he sees the cookies.

"Oh my God, she brought cookies," he notices them, taking the plate from my hands and giving them to the grabby hands of Oaklee. Jai brings me in for a hug and Grey never releases my hand.

"Hey man," Jai gives him a slightly sad smile, "you good?"

Grey only nods at him, tugging me closer to his large frame.

"Azalea!" Abby's voice calls my name and I gasp. I don't let go of Grey's hand; I wait until she reaches us.

"Are you here with Roman?" I wiggle my eyebrows at her and her face turns only a little pink. She gives me a nod and my smile widens. Then she looks up at Grey.

"Hey, Grey," she throws up a friendly smile and he gives her a nod.

"Y'all come in here," Maxon calls out, the plate of cookies in his hand, "we're about to start watching The Grinch."

"Aka, Grey," Oaklee coughs and the guys laugh. Grey rolls his eyes, shaking his head as he holds back a little smirk. We take a seat on the couch, and he leans his whole body into me. I place my hand on the top of his back and run my fingernails along the surface. He relaxes and sets his sights on the movie in front of us. A quarter of the way into the movie, most of the guys get up and follow Jai into the kitchen. Grey looks down at me.

"Do you care if I go have some drinks?" he questions, and I give him a soft smile.

"I don't mind," I shake my head. He gives me a soft kiss and follows a few others into the kitchen. Abby scoots over to me.

"Is Grey okay?" she questions, "I mean he's usually pretty quiet but tonight just seems a little more than usual."

"He had a tough day today," I explain without giving too much detail. She nods in understanding. Abby and I talk and watch the rest of the movie for another forty-five minutes before the guys start filing back in. Some stumbling already. Grey comes out walking smoothly but by the way his eyes look tired, I know he's drunk. *He's about to get real sweet.*

"Watch this," I giggle a little, nodding to Grey.

"Oh gosh, is he a horny drunk?" she laughs. Not even.

"He's very, *very* sweet," I smile as he gets closer. Actually, depending on what he drank, it may not have set in all the way yet, but he still looks pretty drunk even right now. Once he's close enough to touch me, he does. He plops onto the couch.

"I *need* a kiss. *Need* it," he points to his lips, drawing closer to me. I give him a kiss and he pulls away satisfied.

"Pretty girl," he leans his forehead against mine. At least he doesn't have a chicken leg this time. He looks down at the necklace he got me that lays against my chest.

"Thank God for you," he lays his head down on my lap, and Abby moves out of the way of his legs, laughing a little bit.

Lilah *K. Pope*

"I love you and Tubs," he places a kiss on my stomach, and I laugh. Running my hands through his hair, I thank God for him too.

Chapter Forty-One

Scared

❀ Azalea ❀

I rub my eyes with the back of my hand as I take out the keys to get into the mailbox of the complex. *Good Lord, Grey kept me up all night last night.* I pull open the box and go through the mail. Mostly they're all in Grey's name but there are a few magazines in my name. I do a double take when I see the University of Tennessee letter. I rush back to the apartment, walking as fast as my legs will let me. I bust open the door like I'm in the S.W.A.T and Grey jumps, spilling some of his coffee on the counter in front of me.

"Oh my gosh! Did I scare you?!" I smile happily. I can't believe I actually scared the unscareable.

"Ain't scared me," he grumbles unhappily, wiping the coffee from the counter. I place the mail on the counter beside him and then hold up the letter. His dark brown eyes trail over the envelope.

"I'm scared to open it," I tell him honestly. What if I don't get in? And if I do get in, I start so soon, a couple of weeks actually. That's terrifying to think about.

"Yeah, well I'm scared to see your reaction once you realize you got in so let's get this over with," he motions for me to hurry the heck up. I open it carefully and slowly lower my eyes to the words. *Congratulations!* I fall to the ground, and I start to cry. Since I was little, I always wanted to go to UTK and now I finally can. Now no one is stopping me, not dad. I feel Grey's body slide down onto the floor next to mine. He pulls me up onto his lap and hugs me tightly.

"I'm proud of you, Azalea," he wipes the tears from my cheeks, "you deserve this."

I sit up, wrapping my arms around his neck. I can't believe I've gotten so lucky. I have Grey and I'm going to college. This is everything I've ever wanted.

"Oh my gosh!" I pull away from him, "I need to tell Mr. Terrip! He's going to be excited!"

I throw my jacket off, hot from all the celebrating I've done in the past two minutes.

"Okay, I've got to go to work and do paperwork from the past two days," he kisses the top of my head.

"I'll come see you after talking to Mr. Terrip," we bid goodbye and I decide on taking a nice, calming bath to hopefully calm myself down from my hyper episode. Before the bath though, I have a concert in the bathroom mirror. Then I stare at the letter while in the bathtub, effectively making the bath almost an hour long. Once I'm out, I dress myself and decide on braiding my hair. Once I'm finished, I start the drive to the bookstore.

I get giddier and giddier just thinking about what his reaction is going to be. He's known for years that I've wanted to go to college. I hold the letter tightly to my chest as I open the door. The bell rings over my head and a smile lights up my face. He's not sitting at his desk, so I figure he's somewhere hiding from me as he does sometimes. *Crazy old man.*

"Mr. Terrip, come out of your hiding!" I call out, biting back a laugh when I picture him hiding behind a bookshelf. I start walking around in search of him.

"Mr. Terrip, you sneaky old man, I have some exciting n-" I pause mid-sentence. My heart drops to my stomach. His frail figure lays on the ground in the back of the store, unmoving. The letter in my hand drops to the floor and tears flood my eyes. *This can't be happening.* With shaky hands, I call 911. During the call, I struggle to maintain a calm voice. Once the call is over, I immediately call Grey. He answers within a second like always and I feel myself freaking out. *I don't know what to do. He's not breathing.*

"Hey, Lilah," he answers softly, "are you on your way here?"

"Grey," I let a sob break my voice.

"Azalea? What's wrong?" I hear him start to freak out.

"It's Mr. Terrip," I hold the phone away from me as another sob shakes my chest.

"At the store? I'm coming baby," he speaks softly, "I'll be there in just a minute."

He hangs up and I'm left completely alone with my thoughts and just him.

"Mr. Terrip?" I bend down to his unmoving body, "please wake up."

I wipe the tears from my face, seeing that he has no reaction. I place my hand under his nose and he's still not breathing.

"Please, Mr. Terrip, you can't leave me too. You can't," I shake my head. The only thing on Earth I want right now is for him so sit up and get mad at me for talking so much. I want him to talk to me about the new books that have just arrived, and I want him to tease me for always going to get 'go-go juice' from the store down the street.

"God, please, don't take him away from me too, please," I close my eyes, praying as hard as I've ever done, hoping that it will work in the end. *I should've gotten here earlier.* The bell above the door rings loudly and multiple footsteps come running towards where I am. Strong hands grip onto my arms and I cry silently, not being able to take my eyes off Mr. Terrip. Jai and Roman lean down to Mr. Terrip, one of them pressing their fingers under his neck and the other checking for a head injury, I guess from when he fell.

Roman's face falls when he pulls his fingers away. That's when Jai moves to the side of Mr. Terrip, pressing his hands into his chest and pushing down in rhythmic moves. I turn away from the sight, into Grey's chest and sob harder than I thought possible.

"We got him back," Jai rushes out as sirens begin to come closer. Relief floods my chest and I begin to calm even though I know this whole thing isn't over yet. *He was dead.*

"It's okay, Lilah," Grey's hands rub up and down my back as he tries his best to comfort me.

~~~

I pace back and forth in the waiting room. Two hours and twelve minutes we've been here, and we haven't heard a single thing. Grey leans up against the white wall beside me, watching as I pace back and forth.

"I'm *scared,* Sugar, I'm *so* scared," I feel my voice start to crack near the end. The guys went down to the Subway across the street to get food because the food here is just not okay. Abby's at work but she's coming as soon as she gets off.

"Come here," he opens his arms and I walk into them. He tilts my chin up to him and with his thumbs, he wipes away the two little tears under my eyes.

"It's going to be okay," he tucks my hair behind my ears, pressing a kiss to my forehead. I take a deep breath to calm myself.

"Want to kiss mine too?" he questions, and a little smile grows on my lips. I give him a nod and he bends down letting me kiss his forehead too.

"You're the best thing that's ever happened to me," I tell him honestly, laying my head onto his chest. I feel him intake a breath and his heart speeds up a bit.

"*You* just made my heart speed up and made my dick tingle all at once."

I shake my head at his brutal honesty.

"Miss Carson?" A woman dressed in scrubs calls out and Grey and I both turn to her.

"If y'all would follow me," she offers a smile, and we follow her. She leads us into an isolated waiting room that looks like it's only made for a couple of people, not a big one like we were just in.

"A doctor will be with you in just a minute," she closes the door behind her, and Grey and I are left alone with each other. I grow even more worried but also more anxious. The last news I heard was good news, he was alive. I hope this news is good. We wait for a while. Why is there so much waiting?

"Let's play a game," I speak up, turning my body more towards Grey. He turns off his phone and looks at me.

"we say anything that comes to mind. But we can't repeat what the other person said, and it has to be a real thing," I explain, and he nods.

"Dingleberries," I start off.

"Azalea," he smirks.

"Mustaches," I continue.

"Azaleas," he tilts his head.

"Tennis shoes."

"Your ass."

"Ribbon."

"Your boobs."

"Perfume."

"Your legs," he places his hand on my thigh.

"Blankets."

"Your lips." Can he think of anything else?

"Umbrellas."

"Your eyes."

"Bear."

"Your *other* lips-"

"You better stop that!" I gasp and he smirks wider than ever. I can't do anything with him, I really can't. I lay my head down on his shoulder, figuring it's probably best to refrain from playing these types of games with him. A knock sounds on the door and I sit up, watching a middle-aged man in a white coat with a dress shirt and tie underneath enter the room. Grey and I stand to greet him.

"Hello, I'm Dr. David Adams," he gives us a nod.

"I'm Azalea," I shake his hand and Grey introduces himself, shaking his hand too. He takes a seat in the chair next to the couch Grey and I were sitting on, and we sit back down.

"I'm the senior clinician here, and John Terrip's case was assigned to me," he explains, and we nod, listening carefully.

"I'm afraid the news I'm here to tell you isn't good news," he begins gently. What does that mean? What kind of bad?

"John arrived here in cardiac arrest and we successfully resuscitated him. After testing, we determined he had a brain aneurysm which is what caused the initial stroke," he explains, and I just feel my heart falling deeper and deeper into a pit.

"We took him to surgery as quickly as possible and did everything we could but unfortunately, he suffered bleeding to the brain from the ruptured aneurysm which led to the second stroke. I'm terribly sorry, but John died on the operating table."

I snap my head to Grey, wondering if he had heard the same thing I just had. I had to be hearing things. Grey's eyes close and I watch as his jaw clenches harshly. He heard the same thing. *This can't be happening.* This is my fault too. If I wouldn't have thought about myself and my own excitement, I would've gotten to him sooner. None of this would have happened if I would have just stopped thinking about myself. I rise from my seat and dart out of the door in front of us.

I can't be in that room. It's too small. It's too filled with bad things, bad thoughts. I run. I sort of run. I half jog out into the lobby of the hospital and I know I shouldn't run but I just want away from everything. I hear Grey's deep voice shouting after me and I know he's going to end up following me. Maybe I'm hoping to run away from the thoughts in my head or maybe I'm trying to run away from the man who tried to save Mr. Terrip, I don't know.

"Azalea?" I whiz past the guys who have bags of food in their hands, and I don't turn back to apologize even though I know I should. I try to push open doors that lead to a small outside balcony and the door is so heavy, it takes a lot of force for me to open it.

"Baby, please," Grey's voice speaks from behind me, "you're going to hurt yourself doing this."

I finally get the door open, and I walk out to be met with the view of the small city in front of the hospital. Tears run down my cheeks at an almost unnatural speed and I'm breathing heavily. I feel Grey's presence behind me.

"I can't do this Grey," I breathe out and it's true. I *can't* do this. I went through Jake, and it almost ruined me. Now Mr. Terrip is gone too. *What did I do wrong?*

"He's gone," I whisper out, still not believing my own words. He's gone because I was so selfish.

"I should've been there sooner-"

He grips onto my arm and yanks me into his chest.

"I'm not letting you beat yourself up thinking that this is on you. It's not. Do you understand me?" I can tell he's not happy. He grips onto my chin and forces my eyes up to his.

"This was a health thing Azalea, not something you can blame yourself about. There was nothing anyone could have done."

"I know this hurts you so bad love, I know what he means to you, and it's unfair, so *fucking* unfair that things like this happen to you but you can't do this to yourself," he shakes his head.

"I can't sit here and watch the one person on earth I love beat themselves up over something that they couldn't control. It fucking *kills* me, Azalea," his eyes begin to well up.

"I'm sorry," I whisper, my bottom lip wiggling like it usually does when I'm crying.

"Lilah, you just can't do this to yourself, okay? You don't deserve it. You did nothing wrong, you never did," he pulls me farther into his chest and I cry into him.

~~~

Dear Azalea,
Unfortunately, this letter means something not too great. It means this old man

Lilah   *K. Pope*

is no longer there with you. I made a will not too long ago, because I'm getting old and all and I thought it would be a good idea since only the Lord knows what will happen in the future. Hopefully, this letter was delivered on time. I set the send-date to be exactly a week after I passed and if it didn't arrive on time, I'll raise hell (up here).

      I want to start by saying I'm sorry. (When the time comes and I'm no longer here), I'm sorry for leaving you honey, and I can assume that you're upset at me for doing so. Just know that once I'm gone, I'll be up in the sky with Mrs. Terrip, living out the years with her that she was gone too soon for. So don't feel sad. The last thing I want you to feel is sad darling and I'm sorry if this letter is making you feel as such. I'm sorry that I'd have left you after Jake and that you're probably torn up about my going.

      You were the granddaughter I never had but needed. You meant everything to me, just know that. With your help at the store, it made me a happier man. You brightened up the store even though you didn't know it. That's another thing. You're oblivious to your powers. The power you have over people and the power your mind has over your heart. You think too much. Don't let your overthinking lead you somewhere you don't need to be.

      Recently, little miss Azalea, you've met a man (not a boy, as you've told me). His name is Grey if I'm correct. You look at him like my wife used to look at me. I can see he doesn't quite look at you the way I looked at my wife though. I'm hoping that will change, which hopefully it will (I think y'all are just new in the "relationship"). I'm not sure what's going to happen as of the date I'm writing this letter on, but in case his look toward you never changes, never settle for less. You deserve the world darling, not some fool who treats you wrong.

      I can understand your confusion while reading this letter. Why would I write this? There were things I needed to say that I've never really been able to. Like how much I love you. You first met me when you were just a little girl. Almost every day since then you've come to help me, and I can never thank you enough for everything you've done for me. I've never been able to tell you how strong you are either. You, dear, are the strongest person I've ever met. And the happiest. And the kindest. Don't ever let any of that change, it's what makes you, you.

      I know throughout the years I was always a "listener" for you to talk to. I did actually listen to you (I know right, can you believe it?). I always listened to every word you ever said, even though sometimes I act like I didn't. No matter what I was there for you and even though I'm gone, that still doesn't change anything. You need a listener, I'm here honey.

Lilah   *K. Pope*

Thank you for taking care of me all these years. Don't forget, I love you.

Love,

Mr. Terrip

P. S, I'll make sure to say hi to Jake, darling.

Chapter Forty Two

College

* Grey *

"You're beautiful," I smile over at her. She turns her head over to me and a soft smile breaks out on her lips. Stopping at a red light, I lean over to her and kiss her. Pulling away, I still can't keep my eyes off of her. *She's been through too much.* Fate hasn't been good to her; it's never been good to her. She's been through more shit than anybody I know, and she still manages to smile and be happy. She's Wonder Woman.

When Mr. Terrip died, it killed her. It absolutely broke her to pieces, and she didn't stop crying for a couple of days after. I was there with her every second. I watched as she pieced herself back together in amazement. She's so unbelievably strong. So fucking indestructible. She's stronger than I'll ever be, tenfold. And driving on the way to UTK, I don't know how I'm going to be able to go almost a year without being with her every single day.

I don't like the thought of her constantly being surrounded by horny college fuckboys. I wanted a damn ring on her finger before she went but she wouldn't let me. Still. She wouldn't even let me get a damn "promise ring". She says her necklace is enough, but I say they don't know who gave her the fucking necklace.

"I'm going to miss Bear," she sticks her bottom lip out slightly. Well, fuck me, I guess.

"Aw, baby, I'm going to miss you so damn much too," I grumble, and she giggles. The frown fades off my face.

"You big baby," she grips onto my hand, pulling it up to her like she's hugging it.

"You know how much I'm going to miss you," she says softly, and I smirk.

"You showed me how much last night," I recall the greatest sex of my life.

"I'm going to pretend I didn't hear that," she pinches my hand gently. She taps her fingers rhythmically on my hand.

"I'm nervous," she admits. There's nothing for her to be nervous about. Her roommate is Abby and I'll always be only a call away.

"What if I accidentally lock myself out of my room and Abby isn't there? What if I get offered drugs?" she gasps at the last one.

"You're thinking too much, Lilah," I give her hand a reassuring squeeze. The only thing I'm worried about is her realizing how much she doesn't need me. Because she really doesn't. She's so fine on her own, I'm astonished by how much she doesn't need me. *But fuck I need her.*

"I don't know what I'm going to do without you with me," she tells me and my heart flutters.

"Talk to Abby," I offer.

"You're not the same as Abby. Plus, I can only kiss *you* and love *you*," I can hear the smile in her voice.

"I can only fuck you," I just throw the truth out there.

"You know what? You're so vulgar," she shakes her head, but I can see her legs clenching together. She'd die at the sexual things I think about her on a day-to-day basis. I tell her 1/5 of what I think.

"We should get a cat-"

"Fuck no," I dismiss that thought *right* away.

"Not now, obviously," she shrugs.

"Not ever," I shake my head. Cats aren't my thing. All the cats I've ever been around have been little shits. Spawns of fucking Satan.

"Mm, I don't think you're correct," she hums, and I close my eyes, sighing internally. Within the next year, we're probably getting a cat. She's spoiled.

~~~

"What the fuck," I watch as a college male walks through the halls of Azalea's coed dorm. With nothing but a towel around his waist. He smirks at the new coming freshmen girls as he walks past them. I almost laugh. I almost giggle at the fuck.

"What in God's name?" Roman stops beside me, carrying some of Abby's luggage just like I'm carrying Azalea's. He snorts from beside me.

"Dude," he throws his head back, "this motherfucker."

"It'd be funny if the towel fell and everyone saw how small the fucker's dick is," I nudge Roman. He laughs harder as the guy gets closer to passing us.

"Man? Did you forget your clothes?" Roman blurts out to the guy who stops in front of us. *I bet he wears fucking polo shirts.*

"Nah," he chuckles, and I almost have to gag, "got to show off a little bit."

"Show off what?" I blurt. What the fuck? I guess I'm Azalea 2.0 now. He halts his steps and turns to me, the cocky grin off his face now.

"Look, sorry you're jealous that I'm more fit than you, big guy," he gives me a shrug and I can't help but smile a little. Pretty sure he just contradicted himself.

"And plus, I've got a girl waiting for me in her room, I bet you don't," he shrugs. Just because I'm juicy, according to Lilah, doesn't mean I'm not "fit." *"I'm a confident, strong, and independent woman."* -Azalea Carson (soon hopefully Kingston) talking about things I should say to myself. Even though I'm not a woman. And I'm glad I'm not fucking some college stranger. I'm fucking a college girl who just so happens to love the shit out of me. And I'd rather be doing that. Or her.

"Okay, buddy," Roman rolls his eyes, "run along now."

"No, I think I'll stay and talk for a bit," he says, acting like a child that doesn't want to be told what to do. God this guy's boring to look at. The elevator dings behind us and opens.

"Good heavens," Azalea exclaims, obviously seeing the guy in front of us. I narrow my eyes as the guy's lips curl up into a flirty smirk. Yeah, he better fucking *not*.

"Do you need clothes?" her sweet voice questions him. She probably thinks he's homeless. That makes me smile. God, I love that woman.

"Yeah, the fucker needs clothes," I nod to her, and he clears his throat.

"This is a conversation between me and her, so why don't you go find your sister that you're helping move in or whatever," he tries shooing me away with his hand.

"It'd be funny if your towel fell," Azalea blurts.

"Or would you like it?" he smirks. Yeah, that's enough.

"Try something," I glare at him.

"Oh," he draws out the word, "I see what this is."

"*She's* your sister," he nods like it's obvious. First of all, the guy knows we're not related, we look absolutely *nothing* alike. Lilah laughs. She thinks he's joking. Her common sense is shit but at least she's school smart.

"Yeah, you think that," Abby speaks up sarcastically, "'til they fuck each other like rabbits."

My eyes widen a bit. I don't think I've ever heard Abby talk like that. Azalea's mouth opens a bit but she's still smiling. The guy's face in front of us falls. It makes me wonder what all Lilah has told Abby. About the things we do. Together. In bed. And how often we do those things. Apparently, we fuck like rabbits though. *We've got good stamina.*

"Is that all?" Abby questions him. He opens his mouth then closes it again before sauntering away. The two girls lead the way to their room in front of Roman and I.

"They really talk about that stuff?" Roman asks. I can't even begin to imagine what all Azalea has told Abby.

"I guess since Abby knows we fuck like rabbits," I sigh.

"Darling!" Lilah calls from in front of me, "Walk a little faster please."

"Yes, ma'am," I pick up my pace.

"Yes, ma'am," Roman mocks me quietly and I shoot him a glare to which he chuckles.

"Rome, step on the back of my shoe one more time and see what happens," Abby warns him.

"Sorry, hon'," he mumbles.

"Sorry, hon'," I mock him. Lilah opens the door to their room, and she places the few things she's able to carry on her bed. I sit down the things I was carrying. Over the next couple of hours, Azalea fixes up her bed. I do everything else in the damn room. She lays on the bed watching me as I finish up putting her clothes in drawers. Roman and Abby have *been* done because they worked *together*. I pull out my wallet and hold up the platinum bank card for her to see.

"On this is however much you need. It's linked with my bank account, okay? So, whatever you need, you use this to get it," I pick up her purse and place the card in a space in her wallet, then I show her where I put it.

"You don't have to do that," she tells me softly, "I have the money that Mr. Terrip left me."

"You don't want it, I'll take it," Abby says from the other side of the room.

"That fucker beside you makes 750,000 dollars a year, he can get you whatever the hell you want," I point at Roman.

"You make 750k a year?" Azalea gasps.

"Don't look at me, ask Grey how much he makes," he nods to me. I'm well off, I guess.

"Well, he told me one time. He said he made 24k year," she mumbles. Her common sense, seriously, nearly zero percent.

"Wow. He was joking, by the way," Roman chuckles, leaning his head back against the pillows on Abby's bed.

"You dingleberry," she scrunches her nose at me, and I lean forward to her, placing my forehead against hers. I lean away and place a kiss under her ear.

"A couple million," I mumble, and she shoots away, a gasp leaving her lips. There's a lot that goes into the job. There are bonuses we get from doing jobs handed to us by the FBI, there are percentages each person in the FAA gets from each property we clear, and there are annual earnings, of course.

"Woah, hoss," she mumbles.

"Don't call me hoss," I place one more kiss on her lips.

"Well, I won't spend all your money, I promise," she grips onto my arm and pulls me onto the bed. It turns me on a little bit but obviously there are other people in the room, unfortunately.

"It's *our* money."

~~~

❀Azalea❀

Grey's sad. I can tell that much. Sitting at the end of my bed, fixing my hairdo, he still lays underneath my covers looking down at me. Abby and Roman are already saying their goodbyes as our orientation time comes closer and closer.

"I'll walk you to the car," I hear Abby tell Roman and soon I hear the door opening and closing. I scoot closer to him and eventually, I just wriggle my way on top of him. I feel powerful above him. I feel like he really *is* my b-word. Even though he already is. I lay my body flat on top of him, not worrying about crushing him like he tries not to do to me. I lean down under his closely watching eyes and I place a kiss on his jaw because I know he likes it when I do that. Sure enough, when I pull away his eyes are closed. He slowly opens them back up and I smile at him. He reaches his arms around me, and he just hugs me tightly to him. Then he trails his hands up the sides of my legs, but I ignore that.

"I can come home on the weekends, and you can drive up here whenever you want, okay?" I assure him. He just nods, never taking his head out of my neck. He sits up and I pull away slightly.

"And I'll call you all the time," I smile.

"Promise?"

"I promise," I nod, "I can't go very long without talking to my very best friend."

"Aka the love of your fuckin' life," he grumbles.

"Yeah, yeah, yeah, the love of my life," I admit. Of course, he's the love of my life.

"Don't leave Bear out, hear me? Let him sleep with you and you best water my flowers," I point my finger at his face. If I come home this weekend and my flowers are dead, Grey is going to be dead.

"Okay," he nods, and I'm pleased with his seemingly convincing answer.

"And I promise that I will behave myself, I won't do drugs, I'll stay away from polo-wearing frat boys, and I'll remember to feed myself," I assure him. Walking down to the car with him, I'm also a little sad. We won't be sleeping together anymore. *That's what she said.* At the car, I slap his butt a nice, good time. He kisses me for a good thirty seconds and then he leaves. Then Abby and I head off to orientation, scared for our lives.

In the building where the presentations are supposed to take place, there are a lot of people there. Thankfully, Abby and I have each other because if we didn't, I don't even know what I'd do. We sit for quite a while going over presentation after presentation about everything anyone would need to know that has to do with college. I have a hard time sitting still so eventually Abby resorts to letting me tie and retie her shoes. I just can't stay still for long at all.

Once the presentations finally finish, they release us to walk around through a big hall filled with a lot of people trying to recruit frat boys, sorority girls, and people who might want to be in clubs. Having our schedules already planned through earlier meetings, we pretty much just get to walk around and scope out the cute guys. *Sorry, Sugar.* We can both look at the menu, we just can't order. I wouldn't want to anyway. Grey has my entire heart, the big brat. There are many different fraternities that have taken on the act of making huge signs of recruitment and it's obvious that some of the new freshmen will definitely be joining them.

"Hey!" a voice calls out from one of the stands and I feel like running away. Abby and I turn to the source of the voice. The towel guy smiles at us. I sigh.

"Why don't y'all join our sister sorority? You're free to party with us," he smirks and the guys behind him turn toward us. I thought he lived in a dorm?

"No thanks," Abby clears her throat and his eyes dart over to her for a second. They narrow before flitting back over to me.

"Where's your big fuckbuddy?" he questions me, and I narrow my eyes. This guy just isn't worth my great insults, he's really not. It's a shame his attitude is so crappy. He's actually very attractive but his attitude makes him ugly. I want to compliment his cheekbones, but I refrain myself very well.

"Don't be mean to me, honey," he smirks at me and my face falls. Mr. Terrip used to call me honey a lot.

"C'mon, Azalea," Abby grips my arm and starts pulling me away.

"Pretty name for a pretty girl," he calls out as we walk away. I roll my eyes and shake my thoughts away. I really want a Grey hug right now.

~~~

Within a few days, classes have started, and my routine has been set. I'm pretty good at my routine and I've been keeping busy. The past four days, Grey has visited twice, one time bringing the guys with him. I missed them all. They said they were going to try to sneak Bear in but he's a little hard to hide a dog that weighs 145 pounds.

Grey says he's sex-deprived, being away from me so much. I say he'll be fine but I'm also quite deprived. The first few days of classes were very, very stressful. I felt so out of place and so anxious, it was horrible. I was

Lilah

mixed in with the freshmen that had started back in the fall and were just now taking my classes and I was also mixed in with some other people who looked to be older. After a while though, it got better. Sitting in class, I would still get really fidgety and have a hard time keeping focus, so I ended up getting a little stress ball toy from Abby and that helped a little bit.

By Friday, I'm excited to go home for the weekend. I've missed Bear a lot. And Grey. *I've been missing Mr. Terrip a lot too.* Abby and I decided to drive separately due to the fact that we're going to two separate places, but we still leave and eat breakfast together. When I get home, I bust up in the front door like the SWAT. I go straight for our bedroom where I find Grey and Bear peacefully sleeping. *My two boys.* I lower myself onto Grey and start sticking my fingers in his neck which wakes him up quickly. Bear wakes up too, attacking me with love. When Bear calms down a bit, Grey hugs me to him tightly.

"Fuck," he grumbles against my neck.

"You get me for the whole weekend," I smile, and he tightens his arms around me.

"But first," I pick up my bag and take out my computer, "let me just do my homework really quick so I won't have to do it all on Sunday night."

"Or you could do that a little later," his hand travels up my thigh.

"Why wouldn't I just get it done and over with now?" I question him and he gives me a smirk. His hand moves up and he cups my most sensitive part.

"Because you and I both need a little stress reliever right now," he picks up my computer and places it on the bedside table, shutting it. He pushes me back onto the bed and he begins taking all my clothes off.

"It's been like a week and you're already this hornish?" I giggle a little bit when he starts kissing my bare stomach. He looks up at me, still traveling downward.

"You have no idea how addicting you are, Lilah."

Chapter Forty Three

Jessica

❀ Azalea ❀

"I can't believe you dragged me in here," I mumble. He doesn't respond, only continuing his trail of kisses all around the sides of my neck.

"You missed me a lot?" I hum. Last night we were *busy*. Getting down and dirty, oh yeah. This morning he's constantly touching me, and I can just tell me not being home all the time has an effect on him. Especially since he dragged me into the shower with him. Like what on earth? Not going to lie to myself though, it kind of ruffles my truffles.

"I missed you a lot," he mumbles against my neck. I lean my head back into the stream of water coming from the showerhead. He steps closer to me to do the same. As soon as the water hits him though, he steps almost all the way back.

"Why the hell is that so hot? Burn my damn skin off," he rubs his shoulder where the water touched him. He's such a drama queen. I turn it down a little bit for him and he eases his way forward. He stands close to me letting the water rain down on his head before shaking his head roughly and sending water droplets right at my face. Butt nugget. I rest my forehead against his chest thinking about how much I love this man. He's truly the best thing to ever happen to me. And to think he used to hate me. That only makes me laugh now because he's such a sweetheart now.

We've had bumps in the road, him and I. Those bumps only ever make us stronger. And I've had bumps in my own road too. Aaron, Mr. Terrip's passing, Jake's passing, my dad, a lot more. Those things, at least I hope, have made me a stronger person too. I don't know, I'd like to think I'm decently strong. But I'm happy, I do know that. And most of the happiness all leads back to Grey. Where would I be without him? Probably still in that house getting whipped by dad's belt. That thought alone sends shivers down my spine.

"Do you know how much I love you?" I lean my head off his chest, looking up at him. I don't wait for him to guess.

"More than anything in the world," I tell him honestly and his lips raise up in the corners. He was probably expecting me to say, 'just a little bit,' jokingly.

"More than your flowers?" He questions and I smile.

"More than my flowers," I nod. His smile widens into one of his rare, big, genuine smiles and I'm left in awe like every time. I lay my forehead back onto him and start tracing the large lion head tattoo on his chest.

"What do you think about getting a house?" He questions suddenly. My eyebrows lift a bit.

"I want something that's just for us, something that's private and not an apartment. And Bear needs a yard," he traces my shoulder blades with his finger.

"You want a house with me?" I raise my head back up, looking at him.

"You already know I want to spend the rest of my life with you, let alone just get a house," he presses a kiss against my forehead, and I think about crying. *He's too good for me.*

"Only if that's what *you* want though. If you don't want a house then we can stay here," he adds. He could say he wanted to move into a shack, and

I'd follow him happily. It doesn't matter where we are, as long as I get to see his juicy self.

"I want that," I tell him honestly.

"You know what I want?" He leans down and his lips brush my ear. I hum in response, figuring he's about to say something sweet.

"I want to fuck you against the wall right now."

"I can't deal with you anymore."

I'm sore. We did things multiple times last night and my body hurts. And I'm tired. Sure, I'm a little bit turned on at the moment but that's unfair because it's *him*.

"We can just have a nice little sweet shower, we don't need to do the dirty," I poke his chest twice.

"Think about it," I can hear the smirk in his voice. *Yeah, my hoo-ha is thinking about it. 'I'm tired' is what it is thinking.*

"Can't you just hug me and be sweet?"

"I'll be extra sweet to you," he grips my booty cheek and I gasp a bit.

~~~

He's been staring at me for a good thirty minutes. I think he's staring because he's waiting for me to pay attention to him. Usually, I'm completely focused on him and not on schoolwork. Now, I'm focused on schoolwork and he's protesting with his eyes. I scoot my body closer to his and press a kiss to his lips.

"You should just hide me in your dorm," he sits his forehead against mine.

"I don't think Abby would appreciate that," I tell him honestly.

"You know if we got married you would be able to live somewhere other than the dorms."

"I do know that. I also know that I'm nineteen," I scratch the top of his back like I know he likes me to.

"I know that. But I know I love you a lot and I don't want anyone but you."

He's probably the most unromantic person but he has a way with words. Sometimes.

"Well listen here Buck, I don't want anyone but you either."

"Don't call me Buck," he grumbles.

"I do what I want."

He takes the skinny hair tie off my wrist and he twists it onto my ring finger.

"Imagine that as a diamond," he adjusts it on my finger the way he thinks is right. His phone rings and he takes a peek at the caller. He shoves his face into my shoulder.

"I'm not answering it," he deadpans. I answer it.

"Hello, this is Jessica," I greet, making my voice higher than it usually is.

"Jessica? Yo, what the fuck?" Oaklee's confused voice questions.

"What are you calling my man for?" I purposefully say things that I would *never* say. Grey only shakes his head at me, a small smile on his lips.

"Your man?" his voice grows even more confused.

"Yes, my baby, Grey," I bite my lip to keep myself from giggling. My phone dings with a text. I pick it up and see it is from Theo. *'Some girl answered Grey's phone calling him her baby, you better get him straight right now before we do.'* My heart grows at his concern.

"Listen, *Jessica*, Grey has a girl, and you aren't her."

"Baby, come back to bed," Grey speaks closely to the phone, playing along. I hear a gasp on the other end.

"I swear to God. I swear to him. Theo, get the fucking car, bro! I swear to everything-" he hangs up mid-sentence and I laugh into Grey's chest.

"They're definitely on their way," he nods, kissing the top of my head. Bear jumps up onto the bed, situating his big body on my feet. I wrap my arms around Grey's neck.

"Chokehold, what're you going to do?"

He only lays back down acting like I'm only cuddling him. So, I just cuddle him.

"I tried calling mom yesterday," I begin. I was genuinely excited to hear from her. I had texted her before but our conversations through text never really went very deep. I missed her voice.

"She didn't answer me," I clear my throat. I had told her before about Mr. Terrip and his funeral date, but she didn't show up to the funeral. That made me sad because I know he cared about her and would have probably wanted her there. I know *I* wanted her there. But I'm sure she was just busy with her new job and all.

"I know you love her Lilah. But she loves you nowhere near as much as you love her," he grips my face, tilting it up so I can see how serious he is.

"But-" he shuts me up by placing a gentle kiss on my lips. He sits me up, making sure I'm paying close attention to him.

"*You* have been the only one to call. Not once has she called you. You don't deserve to be treated like that, okay?"

"Distance yourself, or you're going to get hurt. I don't want to see you upset," he tucks my hair behind my ear.

"I just want one parent," I tell him truthfully. One normal parent. Has mine ever been normal or is it just me?

"C'mere Bear," Grey pats the bed beside me and Bear follows his direction. Grey points to my cheek.

"Kisses," he tells him, and Bear's big tongue licks the side of my face. Grey stretches out his legs and pats his thigh. His juicy thigh. His huge foot lands on my computer, sending it nearly off the bed. I shoot forward, grabbing it. Closing the lid, I catch sight of the words on the screen. '*Your essay has been submitted!*' Oh Lord Jesus help me.

"I'm going to start flipping my crap in three seconds," I tell Grey honestly. The essay was not even half done.

"Oh shit," he winces, "can you unsubmit?"

"The professor has to return it, I can't unsubmit," I faceplant into my pillow. I can't even email the man on Saturdays. I pull the covers completely over me and curl into a ball thinking of terrible possibilities. What if my professor gets mad at me and says he's not returning it? What if when I email him tomorrow, he doesn't answer anyways? What if he starts hating me?

"Your freaking monster-feet," I grumble aloud.

"I was just tryin' to love on you," he says softly and my heart beats quicker.

"I know," I mumble into the bed. Suddenly, we can hear the front door burst open.

"You didn't lock it," Grey groans. Footsteps come running into our room.

"Grey, step away from her," Oaklee's voice says.

"Jessica, do you have clothes on?" Theo's voice asks me. He sounds a little sad. He's too sweet.

"She does-"

"Shut up you cheating asshole!" Lincoln shouts. Grey doesn't respond and I'm quite surprised. The covers are ripped off of me and the guys stare back at me.

"Who's Jessica?" I question innocently.

"Where is she hiding?!" Oaklee rushes to our closet pulling the door open and walking inside.

"Come here," Theo pulls me off the bed. I bite my lip to keep from laughing. It's really terrible we're doing this to them. But it's funny they kind of believe it. Grey wouldn't cheat on me. 'Cause if he did, he'd be a dead man and I'd make *sure* of it.

"C'mere," Grey holds his arms open for me to walk into. I start shuffling away from Theo, but he grips onto my shirt and pulls me back to his side.

"No, he's evil, don't listen to him," he tells me.

"Y'all think so terribly about him," I shake my head teasingly.

"You really think I would cheat on that?" Grey points at me, his eyes running down my body. I give him a little look of appreciation.

"Who the hell is Jessica?"

"My alter-ego," I smile, walking over to Grey. He throws his arm around my shoulders.

"We were going to invite y'all to the movie we were about to go see but now I don't think I want to," Oaklee crosses his arms across his chest, "how could you do this to me, baby doll?"

"What movie are we watching?" I get excited, forgetting about apologizing to them. If it's not scary then Grey won't really want to watch it. He's really the weirdest person I've ever met.

"A movie about this guy who gets sent to a foreign planet," Lincoln announces, seemingly excited about it.

"You want to go?" Grey leans down to me, kissing my temple, asking me quietly. I nod at him happily. I like hanging out with the guys, they're good friends.

"Abby and Roman are coming too," Theo says and I smile wider. Look at me having all these friends, I really can't believe it. The three guys stand there looking at Grey and I, no one saying anything.

"Well get the fuck out, she's got to get ready," Grey points to the door, his voice annoyed. The guys follow his directions quickly. He already knows my routine. I walk in and out of the closet showing him different clothing options every day. And this past week I've been facetiming him so he can help me pick my outfits. The second option is the one he likes best. So, I wear the skirt and shirt he likes, and I brush through my hair. Grey and I do what we need to do in the bathroom, that includes him tinkling at the same time I'm trying to change my earrings. It also includes him trying to stick his hands up my skirt when I'm bent over the sink brushing my teeth.

When I'm finally done, I stand straight up, looking in the mirror. He stands behind me looking at me in the mirror as well. I pull my sleeves back down from where I had rolled them up and his hands find their way around my waist. He gently pulls at the tight fabric that rests against my stomach.

"You hungry?" he questions softly. I roll my eyes, a smile pulling at my lips.

"I'm not hungry," I shake my head. He leans down to me, kissing my neck one soft time.

"I'm hungry," he bites my ear, and my eyebrows raise a bit.

"That doesn't mean you can eat my ear," I bite my lip, keeping my smile small. He places his large hand under my chin, turning my head to look back at him. I can't even blink before he's kissing the daylights out of me.

"Get ready for tonight," he pulls away from my lips only slightly, "you're not leaving the bed."

~ ~ ~

"I'm fuckin' bored," Grey grumbles next to me. I mostly ignore him, munching on my popcorn. He sighs and all the candy he got me that sits on his lap rustles a bit. Abby chuckles at Grey from her position beside me. He places his hand on my thigh and begins tracing things I guess in an attempt to become less bored.

"You want to know what I just spelled out on your leg?" he leans in close to me. Barely paying attention to him, I only nod.

"I said 'will you marry me?'" He says nonchalantly. I raise my eyebrow at him. I didn't feel him trace a question mark.

"Technically I said, 'I love you' but what I really mean is I'm going to fuck you 'til your legs won't stop shaking," he leans in close, and my eyes widen. What did he eat? He places a short trail of kisses from my jaw to my cheek.

"Can you not make out while I'm trying to watch the movie?" Lincoln nudges Grey.

"Don't touch me and don't tell me what to do," Grey shoots him a glare.

"You know what? Everyone just needs to calm down, okay? Lincoln, he'll stop and Grey," I lean in close to him, "stop being the most hornish person on earth."

"Then let's fucking leave early and we can take care of that," he suggests. I pull the food off his lap and hand the stuff to Lincoln, grabbing Grey's hand and pulling him up. I lead him out of the theater room and out into the lobby where it's desolate. He gives me an innocent little smile. I look around for anyone and tug on his shirt, motioning for him to lean down.

"I like you taking control," he smirks, his eyes trained on my lips. He connects our lips softly at first, but the kiss soon turns more urgent.

"Fuck, I love you," he mumbles against my lips. I trail a couple kisses along his jaw, and he quietly groans in the back of his throat.

"God, you're the best thing that's ever happened to me," he squeezes my sides and I pull away at his words. Is he serious?

"What?" I question softly.

"You're the best thing that's ever happened to me," he repeats. I can't help but get a little teary-eyed. No one has ever come close to saying anything that sweet to me. It's honestly the biggest blessing to be loved by him. I wrap my arms around his torso, placing my face into his chest.

"You're the best thing that has ever happened to me too," I reply. And it's the truth.

Chapter Forty-Four

Birthday

❀ Azalea ❀

After cheating my way through two tests on this lovely evening, I return to the humble abode. More like the dumpster-dorm. That's a little dramatic. It isn't really dumpster-esque. It's actually quite nice. But it's just not home.

"We meet again," a male voice says as I make it to the elevator of my building. I turn to the guy. Towel guy. I only sigh. I enter the elevator and he follows in after me. I click my floor and he only stands beside me, not clicking any other floor. I think about letting loose an air-biscuit just to suffocate him in here but unfortunately, I don't have any brewing at the moment.

"I think you and I got started off on the wrong foot, the times we have seen each other," he begins, turning toward me. I will laugh in his face if he tells me his name is Brad.

"I'm Jake," he says, and I close my eyes. Jake. His name seriously has to be Jake? Nope, his name's not Jake, it's James. I'm calling him James.

"Nice to meet you, James," I watch the floor number as it stops at my floor.

"W-Well, it's Jake, but yeah, you can call me whatever beautiful," I feel his smile on the side of my face, but I don't look at him.

"What is it? *Jade?*" I turn toward him, scrunching my eyebrows.

"James," he says, then his eyebrows scrunch together, and he shakes his head, "wait, no. My name is Jake."

"Oh," I draw out, "sorry Jack."

I laugh evilly internally. Grey would be proud of me at this moment. I walk out of the elevator and toward my room. He follows.

"Like I said, name doesn't matter. What are you doing later?" he keeps up with my pace, walking beside me.

"Probably spending the rest of the night on Facetime with my b-word while he sits in his office doing nothing," I tell him honestly.

"Your bitch?"

"Yep," I nod.

"So, is he your boyfriend or what?" he asks. Duh, what else would I be talking about? I only give him a nod.

"Yes ma'am," I add when I realize he might not have been looking at me. He chuckles at my answer.

"Just so I know, is there any chance you and your bitch would ever break up?" he stops as I stop at my room.

"Yeah, no," I give him a smile and he nods understandingly.

"Okay well, I obviously don't have a chance. Want my number though? Solely for friendly conversations," he says honestly. Oh my gosh. A friend.

"You promise? Don't flirt with me or I'll jack you up," I warn him. We exchange numbers. We definitely got off on the wrong foot but maybe, just maybe he won't turn out too bad.

~~~

'Happy birthday, love'
I smile at the text from Grey.
'Wrong number' I sent back to him. He responds almost instantly.
'I love you baby'
My heart flutters and I just stare at the text for a good minute.
'Marry me' he sends after I didn't respond for a while. My heart flutters even more than before.
'Hush. I love you too' I reply.

"Happy birthday, Azalea!" Abby catapults herself up onto my bed, bouncing like a crazy person. She hugs me tightly to her.

"Come on now let's get you up, get you dressed, and let's get this school day over with so we can go home for the weekend!" She pulls me up excitedly.

"It's supposed to be sundress weather today," she opens my drawer and looks through the selection. She tosses me a light pink sundress that ties on each shoulder. I change quickly then do what I need to do in the bathroom, including tinkle. I send Grey a little mirror picture of the outfit too just because he likes to see them. He says he likes to see me, but I think he secretly likes to see my cute dresses.

'You're making me horny.' he replies, and I just sigh at the insane amount of romanticness the man has. I go through the rest of the birthday texts I've gotten, mostly just from the guys. Duh, I don't really have any other friends. By the end of the messages, I'm left wondering why mom hasn't sent me anything. I look at the digital clock on the counter. It's still morning time, maybe she's just not awake yet.

'You need a jacket, it's chilly this morning' Grey sends and I smile. I send him an okay and finish getting my stuff together for my first class. Nearly done with my second class of the day, I'm more fidgety than ever. Usually, I have a fidgeting and sitting-still problem but today I'm just out of control. My mind is all over the place, my legs and feet are constantly moving, and my hands are continuously messing with something. I cannot believe I'm twenty today. I'm an old fart.

"Miss Carson?"

I can't imagine how Grey feels. He's basically fifty.

"Miss. Carson."

Then again, when I woke up this morning, I felt no difference. I feel the same today as I felt yesterday.

"Miss Carson!" the professor yanks the pen out of my hand, and I jump in fright. I wince. I guess I was clicking it. On my first day in this class, I may or may not have gotten here late. The only seats left available were near the very front. Everyone kind of has unassigned assigned seats. So, on either side of me sit two people who type down every single thing our professor does and says. I feel dumb beside the two, but I don't really have anywhere else I could sit.

"I'm really sorry. I'm extra fidgety today. I think it's because it's Friday and I want to go home. It's also my birthday so-"

"Well, isn't that fun?" She smiles at me like she doesn't care at all.

"...Yes sir-I mean ma'am," I close my eyes tightly. I think I'm going to have to drop this class.

"Quiet, Miss Talkative," she looks down her nose at me. I crack my fingers just to fidget with something. The cracks of my knuckles can be heard throughout the room pretty much.

"S-Sorry," I wince, "I didn't know the cracking would be...that loud."

This is almost comedic by now. I knock my knuckles together anxiously. But hearing the sound that makes too, I stop. Why is she still just staring at me? Oh, I don't know, maybe because I keep making noises. Oh, my Lord, what if I fart? I just end up tapping the pads of my fingers together, noticing how it thankfully doesn't make any noise.

"Stop moving and fidgeting!" she exclaims, startling me again.

"Well, I can't really," I laugh nervously, "I have ADHD."

"Well, get medicine," she tosses the pen back on the table in front of me just before she releases the class. I try not to let her words affect me even though they do a little bit.

~~~

* Grey *

"You look perfect," I lift her up and she wraps those legs of hers around my waist. I grip the back of her dress, making sure it doesn't ride up. She plants three kisses on my cheek as I rub her back with my free hand. She pulls away slightly and those green eyes stare back at me.

"What kind of ring do you want?" I ask with no hesitation. She slams her head down on my shoulder.

"You know what?" She raises her head back up, "How about I get you a ring?"

"That's not how it works," I shake my head.

"Why not? Beyonce once said, 'if you like it then you should have put a ring on it' and I like it," she wiggles her eyebrows at me. I set her on the counter and place my hands on either side of her. She bites that lip. Fuck. She clenches her legs together and I smirk. I love seeing what I do to her. I look over at the clock. We've got ten minutes. I trail my hands up the smooth skin of her thighs. It's cute how the only time she's ever quiet is when she's aroused. I slide my hand under her thin fabric, and she gasps, gripping onto my bicep. For such a small thing, she's got a damn good grip. It's the pleasure.

I tease her for a moment, watching the way she quietly moans and the way she pushes herself closer to my touch. She breathes deeply and reaches forward, grabbing my shirt and pulling my neck onto her mouth. I close my eyes at the feeling, letting her continue for the time being. I'm too caught up in the feeling of her lips on my neck to remember that this isn't about me feeling good, it's all about her. Going against my conscience, I pull away from her lips. My fingers enter her, and she lets out a moan that has my pants growing tighter. She bites her lip which only fuels my arousal. With my free hand, I pull her bottom lip from her teeth, leaning down to bite it myself. Only *I* can bite that lip.

"You're mine," I bite her ear and she whimpers, pulling me impossibly closer to her.

"Yours," she replies breathlessly, and I smile against her neck. I feel her closing around my fingers. Gripping the top of her throat, I make sure she's looking right at me as she comes undone. She leans her head against my chest as I take my fingers away. Placing the fingers in my mouth, I know that just what's on my fingers isn't enough for me. With her legs already shaking, I pull her underwear all the way off. She watches me as I lean down.

It took a little longer than ten minutes to do everything I wanted to do to her. But neither of us complained.

"Sugar," she leans down, whispering in my ear. Sanfred, sitting in the chair across from me, wiggles his eyebrows.

"Yes, ma'am?"

"A pear-shaped ring," she tells me, and a smile takes onto my lips.

"Yeah?" I wrap my arm around her, pulling her from my side to my front, sitting her down on my lap. She nods a smile on her lips too. I lean up and place a gentle kiss on her lips. Pulling away, she smiles excitedly before hopping off and going back over to Abby.

"What was that about?" Sanfred questions. I don't see how that's any of his fucking business. But I'm in a good mood today.

"Engagement ring," I take a swig of my beer. His eyebrows raise up in surprise.

"Did I hear you say engagement ring?" Theo plops down in the chair to my right. I scoot away from him when his elbow brushes my arm.

"Don't touch me," I grumble. The two call Jai, Linc, Roman, and Maxon over. I glare a little at Maxon when he sits his *fat ass* in one of the chairs.

"This guy is going to ask Azalea to marry him," Sanfred tells the rest and faces of surprise is all I see.

"He's the last one I would think to be engaged," Lincoln blurts. I narrow my eyes at him.

"I was surprised as hell when he and Azalea actually started dating!" Jai exclaims and I turn my look over to him.

"And when I heard him tell her he loved her for the first time! I tell you, I was shocked," Theo laughs. Fuck them all. *Just y'all wait.*

"Where'd she go anyway?" Roman looks around, "Abby too?"

"Probably tinkling," I mumble, taking another swig of my almost empty beer. Girls go together for some reason. When I put the bottle down, they're all looking at me crazily. Some with their mouths open and some on the verge of bursting into laughter.

"Tinkling?" Sanfred nearly fucking giggles. I roll my eyes.

"Yeah, tinkling. That's what I fucking said."

They laugh. Yeah, they won't be laughing if Azalea hears them say anything but 'tinkle' when they're talking about piss.

"Y'all should hear some of the other shit that happens when those two are together," Roman laughs and I send him a glare.

"He's like a big ball of goo when it comes to her. I swear if she told him to climb the Eiffel Tower, he would without even thinking about it," he says honestly. Shit, I would think about it. I'd think about what time she'd want me home after I did it. She's fucking everything to me. They don't understand how much she actually means to me. It means a lot to be the only person on Earth that I love. So, if she tells me she wants something or that she wants me to do something, I'm going to fucking do it. Why the fuck else would I have gotten a cat that's supposed to be picked up tomorrow and brought home to her? Damnit.

A pair of hands come to rest on my tense shoulders. Automatically under her soft touch, they loosen. The bell above the door rings and Jonas walks in. Azalea gasps as he walks closer and closer to the table. They look at each other emotionlessly.

"I missed you, brat," Azalea grumbles. They hadn't seen each other since she left for college.

"Yeah, you would," he says as an insult before simmering back down, "I missed you too."

He holds his hand out for her to shake but she's a hugger. She opens her arms. They awkwardly hug. She sends his stomach a light punch and he jerks away from her constantly. It's the most pitiful fucking thing I've ever seen. Eventually, they get in a regular three-second hug. Barely though.

"Happy birthday," he tells her once they pull away.

"Yeah, you better tell me happy birthday."

~~~

"Marry me," I tell her first thing in the morning. I already got the ring. Last night when she fell asleep, I was right on it. I looked at the ring sizes of the rings in her jewelry box and I went from there. I found the perfect one and I got it before I could start to overthink it.

"I will later," she mumbles tiredly. She suddenly sits up like she wasn't just dead asleep two minutes ago.

"Am I too hyper and fidgety?" she questions out of nowhere. I don't even know where that came from.

"What? No," I lie slightly. Not really though. She's really not too hyper. Actually, she is but I'm just used to it by now. And she's always been fidgety, it's not really a big deal.

"My professor said I am," she looks slightly upset, "she said I needed medicine."

"Yeah, and tell *her* to go fuck herself," I nod. Who does that lady think she is? She has no right telling her she needs medicine. Sure, she's wild as hell but that's what makes her who she is. And I wouldn't want her any other way.

"You're perfect the way you are, you hear me?" I grip her chin, making sure she's looking right at me.

"I was clicking the pen a lot and she just flipped out," she explains.

"Next time, don't let her talk to you that way, okay? Better yet, if she does, call me in the middle of your damn class and pass her the phone," I tell her. Oh, the shit I'd tell that professor. The doorbell rings. The damn cat's here.

"Stay here," I place a kiss on her forehead, "I'll be right back."

Opening the door, Lincoln looks right back at me unamused. He hands me the small cage with the baby cat in it.

"You know, when you said you wanted me to go on a top-secret mission, I wasn't expecting to drive four fucking hours just to pick up a damn kitten," he grumbles.

"It *was* top-secret, and it was four hours away. I'd call that a mission," I give him a sarcastic smile.

"It's a ridiculous mission," he groans.

"Quit being a bitch. You'll get a bonus for it, now leave," I shut the door in his face. I place the cage on the counter. I open the front and a cat as big as my hand comes walking out confidently. How the fuck do you even pick up these things? Bear shows up by my side and sniffs the air curiously.

"I don't like it either, Bear," I grumble to him. Eventually, I just pick the thing up. It may be small now, but this thing is supposed to get pretty damn big. I found a little cheat to getting the cat. I got the most doggish cat that there is. A Maine Coon. It's going to get big. It's kind of doggish. It's as best as I could get. I wasn't getting a damn pussy ass cat. It's going to be the manliest cat and I hope I've succeeded. I hate to admit the baby is a little cute. And the thing better like me too. I've got two months before Lilah gets out of school for summer. If it hates me, I'm sneaking it into her dorm and not dealing with it.

"This thing isn't a toy, Bear," I explain to him. He eats meals three times as big as this thing.

"And you can't eat it, or momma will be very upset with you," I tell him sternly before giving his side a good pat. I mosey my way back into the bedroom where I find that Lilah is in the bathroom. I sit on the bed with my back to the door and I look at the thing. It's a furry little shit but it is cute, I'll give it that. *Is it a boy or a girl? I can't remember.* The door suddenly opens. I stand up and start walking to her. She doesn't notice the little thing until I'm right in front of her. And when she does. She falls to the ground, crying. I sigh, shaking my head. I kneel down to the ground with her and sit the thing in her lap. She picks it up and holds it like it's pure gold.

"Oh, my goodness!" she sniffs, "It's the cutest thing in the world!"

"Mhm."

"Do we get to keep it?" she looks at me, hope filling her eyes. I give her a smile.

"Of course," I nod. With the cat in hand, she crawls onto my lap kissing every inch of my face. Yeah, getting that thing was definitely fucking worth it.

"Boy or girl?"

"I don't fuckin' know," I shrug. An hour of googling later, it's a girl. She fucking named it Princess Eleonora Caroline Kingston. Callie for short.

She already loves the damn cat more than me.

Epilogue

❀ Azalea ❀

  The moments leading up to this very day have been a roller coaster. The craziest roller coaster that has had many loops and twists and curves. I have a feeling nothing in my life will ever be normal and if I'm being honest, I'm not too upset about that. If my life would have ever been normal, I would not have met Grey. More importantly, he wouldn't have met me. I help him keep his crap together, there's no denying that. But he also helps me keep my crap together.

  Right after freshman year, we moved out of the apartment and got a nice welcoming house together. During that summer, I did summer classes to finish the year early. It took him two weeks after my birthday to propose. It took me to the old lookout we used to go to a lot, he got down on one knee, and he said those words I'll never forget.

  'Marry me or I'll pitch a fuckin' fit.'

  So now in the spring break of my sophomore year, I sit in the bridal room of our suite in Hawaii. *We're getting married.*

"You look stunning, you really do," Abby smiles at me as we both look into the mirror. The wedding, we both agreed, should be small. It should be quick and only the closest friends should come. No family. Frankly, because neither of us actually has any family. Mom couldn't make it. Even though I offered to pay for her plane tickets. She said she was busy. I didn't try to convince her, and I just left it alone. We also wanted the wedding to be casual. No fanciness. Plus, Grey doesn't really do fancy and I agreed, no fanciness.

We also wouldn't have any groomsmen or bridesmaids. I would pretty much have one bridesmaid and he would have all the guys as groomsmen so to make it fair, we just took out that part. Oaklee did offer to be a bridesmaid though. I straighten my pretty but simple white sundress. My blonde hair falls down my back in pretty beach waves and pinned in my hair lays a simple but gorgeous flower crown that matches the flowers in my bouquet.

"It's almost showtime," Abby turns me toward her, touching up the light pink lipstick on my lips. As a kid, I had always wanted a beach wedding. They just seemed so peaceful. I also imagined Jake being there and maybe even my dad walking me down the aisle. Then later, Mr. Terrip walking me down the aisle. But I'm not sad that won't be able to happen anymore. I know the two of them will be watching. And I just hope they're both proud of who I have become and who I've chosen to spend the rest of my life with.

My love.

Abby adjusts her light blue dress in the mirror and then turns to me. She pulls me in for a hug.

"I'm so happy for you and Grey. You two have such a deep and amazing love," she holds onto me tightly. I nearly get emotional at how lucky I am to have her as my friend. Or any friend, honestly. She pulls away, straightens the flower crown on my head, and then places her hands on my shoulders.

"Okay, I have to go sit with Roman now. You have five minutes before you need to be out here," she tells me, and I give her a smile and a nod. She exits the room and I take a deep breath. Oddly enough, I'm not really nervous. I'm confident in us, I really am. Plus, if Grey were to leave me on this day, he would be seeing the light of day for the last time. Because he's my b-word. So, what do I do with five minutes left to spare? I grab my phone and blare "Cherry Pie".

I finish my very last cherry pie session as an unmarried woman before grabbing onto my bouquet and closing the door behind me. *Gosh, I hope I don't cry. I'm an ugly crier.* Right as my feet touch the soft white sand of the beach, I hear the music softly playing. All our friends sit in chairs in front of the priest and Grey. They stand as I walk toward the decorated altar. Abby is already crying when I pass her, and I give her a soft smile. The waves crash gently behind the altar, and I feel like I'm in heaven.

I finally make it to Grey. He stands there looking all juicy and gorgeous as always. The top few buttons of his white button-up are unbuttoned and he's just breathtaking. Before I can look at his face, his hands grip my waist, pulling me to him. He wraps his arms around my body, and he hugs the daylights out of me. It shocks me. I wasn't expecting him to do that. With my free hand, I wrap it around him too, rubbing against his back gently.

"You okay?" I question him softly. He only nods against me. After a few more seconds he pulls away. When he pulls away, I'm met with a sight I wasn't sure I'd ever see. A tear rolls down his cheek. That causes a wave of emotion to roll over me. With tears now starting to blur my eyes, I reach up and wipe the tear on his face. He returns the favor when a tear of my own falls.

"We're gathered here today for Grey and Azalea to join in holy matrimony," our priest begins but I hardly pay any attention to what he's saying. *'You're beautiful'* Grey mouths and I smile.

"Okay, now your vows," the priest says, and I suddenly remember that I totally forgot about vows. Like totally. I keep my calm though. I look at Grey. His eyes are slightly widened. Looks like somebody else forgot too.

'Go first' he mouths. I shake my head.

"Yes," he mumbles.

"No."

"Yes."

"No."

"Goddammit," he says, knowing he's not winning the argument.

"Go," I encourage, and he clears his throat.

"Uh, I love you a lot and you're very beautiful," he ends, and I laugh, leaning my head against his chest.

"That was pitiful," I tell him.

"I know. Shut up," he grumbles.

"Azalea, your vows," the priest nods to me. I take a deep breath.

"You're my cherry pie. A cool drink of water, such a sweet surprise," I rake my brain, trying to recall the next lyrics of the song. Because this is all I've got.

"Tastes-no," I realize how inappropriate the next line sounds. Grey leans his head back ever so slightly and lets out a breathtaking laugh.

"You're just my sweet cherry pie. And I'll love you always," I smile.

"That was...one of a kind," the priest chuckles. I'm just glad everyone else can't hear us.

"Now Grey, do you take Azalea Delilah Carson to be your lawfully wedded wife?"

Grey takes my wedding band out of his pocket, already gripping my hand before the priest can even finish the sentence.

"I do," he slips the band on my finger. Before the priest can ask me the same question, Grey is holding out his hand for me. I take the ring out of my bra, because where else would I put it? Our friends chuckle. Grey smirks.

"Do you Azalea, take Grey Alexander Kingston to be your lawfully wedded husband?" I'm already slipping the dark silver wedding band on his finger.

"I do."

"By the power-" Grey reaches forward and pulls me to him, kissing me deeply.

"Okay, well, Mr. and Mrs. Kingston everybody!" The priest announces as we pull away.

I'm Mrs. Kingston.

Lilah   *K. Pope*

Thank you all for reading <3

FOLLOW ME ON INSTA: @KARRIE_ASHLYN